Praise for *T*

If David Borofka were, say, a studio guitarist, he would be equally adept at jazz, rock, hip hop, country, reggae, fado—you name it. In *The End of Good Intentions*, his first novel in more than twenty-five years, he proves himself a master of tone and mood, perfectly capable of making you laugh and cry on the same page, or even sometimes in the same paragraph. He writes with unfailing sympathy of people so radically different from each other than one wonders if he couldn't also be a superb actor if he chose. Thank goodness that he has elected to reserve his formidable skills for those of us lucky enough to be his readers. *The End of Good Intentions* is a treasure. So is its author.

—Steve Yarbrough, author of *Stay Gone Days* and *The Unmade World*

The End of Good Intentions is an uncommonly well-written collage of a novel whose ironies, humanity, and insights will urge you to piece it together. Borofka's fearlessness and top-flight voice are not to be missed.

—Mark Wish, Founding Editor of *Coolest American Stories* and author of *Watch Me Go* and *Necessary Deeds*

Past Praise for David Borofka

Grace, a persistent element in [*Hints of His Mortality*], is twice described as having a tangible presence, even to the point of caroming "around the room with the velocity of hockey pucks" in the aftermath of a near-fatal choking episode. Such moments of giddy redemption leaven the woes of Mr. Borofka's characters, but the real miracle is the deftness, subtlety and humor with which he makes their many bedeviled lives cohere in a single vision of well-earned affirmation.
—Elizabeth Gaffney, "Men without a Clue," *The New York Times Book Review*

Where else but in fiction—both reading and writing it—can one try on so many different kinds of salvation? The comedy of seeking is rarely so sympathetically portrayed as in Borofka's hands; he captures perfectly the poignancy of dopey mortals dreaming and scheming to reach the divine. Making sense of the universe and one's place within it is of course a deadly serious business—theologian Paul Tillich called it "a matter of ultimate concern"—but we are so often so far off the mark that the search cannot help but seem ludicrous too.
—Paul Manseau, "Comedies of Seeking: New Fiction at the Borderlands of Belief," *Image*

Also by David Borofka

Hints of His Mortality (stories)
The Island (novel)
A Longing for Impossible Things (stories)

The End of Good Intentions

David Borofka

Fomite
Burlington, VT

ISBN-13: 978-1-953236-91-3
Library of Congress Control Number: 2023941326
Fomite
58 Peru Street
Burlington VT 05401
www.fomitepress.com
08-02-2023

For Deb, as always

My thanks to the editors of the journals in which two of these chapters first appeared in somewhat different form: "You've Arrived at Your Destination" (winner of the *Prism Review* Fiction Award, under the title "Flight") and "Holiday for One" (*Carolina Quarterly*).

Contents

My intentions were good, really. Really, they were. I'm telling you: they were meant to be good. But maybe you couldn't see it. I'm a better person in theory than I am in practice.

—Overheard just before midnight in The Early Terrible, Woodstock, NY

"Isn't it pretty to think so."

—Jake Barnes in Ernest Hemingway's *The Sun Also Rises*

[i]

You've Arrived at Your Destination

(Eivar Mortenson, 1974)

THE MORNING FLIGHT FROM PORTLAND was delayed. According to the pilot, a forward hatch on their 727 wouldn't close. He said this in a hill country drawl, suggesting that the aircraft was no more than a temperamental dog that had gone off its training. Eventually, an orange jumpsuit with a wrench emerged from the bowels of the terminal. This was followed by a chill-inducing metallic screech and three hollow booms, and then the plane was backing away. Ninety minutes later, the pilot announced that, due to their earlier delay, they now needed to circle above Fresno in order for the fog to dissipate.

"It comes, it goes," he said over the PA system. "If it doesn't go, we'll land in Bakersfield and bus you to your destination."

In seat 12D, Eivar Mortenson signaled a flight attendant. "Would it be possible to get some orange juice?" He licked his lips. "My stomach," he said and made a face indicating pain. In the seat to his right, the burly insurance adjuster from Boise muttered, "My god," and pulled a sleep mask over his eyes. Through the porthole window, there was nothing but the flat gray expanse of cloud.

The flight attendant was at least as old as Eivar, fifty if she was a day, wearing the navy polyester uniform of the airline. It was an outfit meant to suggest a life of kicky, carefree fun—vacations, sunny skies, and warm blue waters—but, although the hour was early, there was a brown indeterminate stain on her right sleeve, and her lipstick had disappeared into the lines above her lips. "Don't worry," she said. "We'll be on the ground before you know it."

"Yes?" he said. "But the orange juice?"

They circled. Banked and turned, banked and turned.

Six hours earlier, in the small kitchen of their small house in Estacada, Eivar's young wife had set a plate of fried eggs and biscuits in front of him. The yolks had glistened; the whites curled brown under the harsh blue of the fluorescent light fixture. Elisa's biscuits had been as heavy as ever, and they turned over now in what he imagined to be the viscous yellow froth in his stomach.

Lord. Lord. Lord.

How embarrassing would it be to reach for the paper bag in the pocket of the seatback in front of him? How embarrassing would it be not to have it, should it be needed? He accepted the orange juice and drank before acknowledging that it was not likely to improve his condition.

Half an hour later, they descended through a hole in the fog that only the pilot could see and landed on a runway all but invisible but for a row of dull blue lights on either side. The effect was disorienting. As though they had landed in a cloud. Heaven. And that was when it happened. Eivar's stomach turned over without warning, and its orange contents spilled out into his lap. His seat mate removed his sleep mask, stood, and craned around to get his carry-on from the overhead compartment.

"Really?" he said, before stepping over Eivar. "My god."

"I'm sorry," Eivar said. "I thought I was going to be okay."

"No D.B. Cooper, he," his former seat mate said to those passengers, now bunched up in the aisle behind them and averting their noses and eyes.

"I'm sorry," Eivar said a moment later to his flight attendant, who had walked down the aisle to wait for this last passenger and then stood with her arms folded across her dull navy chest while Eivar attempted to stand.

"I'm sorry," Eivar said to the cleaning crew who came in response to her summons. "I don't handle it well. Traveling. I don't do it often enough." The crew leader, who evidently spoke no English, handed him a rag and motioned to the bucket of sanitizing fluid.

"*Apesta*," the cleaning man said and wrinkled his nose.

Eivar wiped the front of his shirt and his brown pants. "Really. I'm so sorry."

Elisa's brother had brought him the tickets the night before in a folder containing an itinerary and confirmations for a rental car and hotel. "Meet Gilbert, get him squared away, and then have some dinner. Get a good night's sleep," Carl said. "You'll be back here before you know it."

Carl had just come from church, from a meeting with the rest of the Christian Soldiers executive committee. He wore his one church suit, taking off his suit coat the moment he came through the door, draping it over the back of one of the kitchen chairs as though it belonged to him, as though the kitchen and the house, the bedrooms and bathrooms, belonged to him rather than his brother-in-law. His short-sleeved dress shirt was open at the neck and his tie was an opened noose.

He was one of those men, Eivar realized, who look better in a ball cap and more appropriately dressed, better when their foreheads are hidden, their eyes shaded. More intelligent, perhaps. And for the hundredth time, no, the thousandth time, he wondered how he had gotten into this…

"I don't know why you need me to do this," Eivar said, not for the first time.

And not for the first time, Carl encircled the older man's neck with a bare arm that, no matter how long he had scrubbed, smelled of grease and undercarriages, of the off-road Jeeps he rebuilt after their owners buried them in mud or sand or high-centered them on treefalls. "Oh, my brother, my brother," Carl said. "I need someone to be my eyes and ears. They're watching everything we do, and I need someone to be His sheep among the wolves. You know I wouldn't ask if there were any other way."

And Eivar was struck once again with how easily brotherhood could be invoked and how easily it affected him.

"How much we love the Lord," Carl said. "How much we would do for Him."

"Yes, of course," Eivar said. "Without a doubt."

THE YOUNG MAN waiting in the hotel parking lot could not have been more than twenty-five years old. Thirty at most. He was leaning against a battered olive-green pickup, his dark arms crossed against his chest and the Hawaiian shirt he wore despite the chill of the dank, gray air. His shirt was gaudy, festooned with parrots; his hair had evidently once been shaved but had now grown out to a marionette's dark cap, the dark green and orange lines of a tattoo faintly visible through the stubble above his left ear.

"Gilbert, I presume," Eivar said. He had hoped to adopt a jaunty, light tone, his mock Stanley once again discovering Livingstone, but given his recent distress, it sounded as awkward as it felt.

"Yes." The younger man extended a limp, moist hand. "Welcome, Brother Mortenson." He sniffed.

"I'm a mess," Eivar said. The odor of his shirt still sharp, bitter in his nose, his trousers yet damp in the crotch. "It was a bumpy flight. My stomach is not as strong as it could be."

They stood in the parking lot behind their respective vehicles while the morning fog drifted, rising and falling, and a husband and wife yelled at four children who were jumping up and down to get into a station wagon with peeling laminate sides. Four suitcases and a small Christmas tree had been roped to the roof rack, the asphalt parking lot was damp in the mist, and a sheen of gasoline and oil made rainbows on the pavement.

"Shut the fuck up," the father said. He shouted, but he shouted the words so slowly that each made its own sentence. Shut. The. Fuck. Up.

"It's okay." Gilbert motioned to the back of his pickup. "We told your brother we needed gas, he told you that, right?"

Eivar opened the trunk of the rental, a Malibu still redolent of the factory in spite of its recent occupant. Four five-gallon gas cans, filled at the Chevron next to the airport, waited to be tied together inside the pickup's bed.

"I didn't know if they'd fit," Eivar said, pulling out his overnight bag and setting it on the asphalt. "These new cars."

Gilbert shrugged. "They did."

"Brother-in-law," Eivar said. "Carl is my brother-in-law."

Gilbert shrugged again while transferring the containers from trunk to truck bed.

"I married his sister after my wife died. I've known Carl for a long time, but he's only been my brother-in-law for two years."

"Okay."

"What I'm saying is that we're not family by birth."

"Okay," Gilbert said."

"I like Carl, I'm here because he asked me to be here, we have similar beliefs, but we're not brothers in the biological sense."

"Okay."

"It doesn't matter, really."

"No, not really." The younger man fished out a sheet of paper from the cab of the pickup. "Directions to my apartment. You can rest. You can clean up and change. And then, you can pick me up at six o'clock. I know a place to eat, and then we'll go to the campus where the service will be. Okay?"

"Yes, of course. That will be fine."

"If you're hungry, that is."

"Maybe," Eivar said. "We'll see."

Gilbert backed his pickup out of the parking stall and then lurched forward out of the lot and onto the street. The gas cans rattled together in back. The air was damp, clammy, and Eivar held the sides of his sports coat together. This morning, on the second day of his Winter Break, in his chilly bedroom in Oregon, he had dressed as though for the tropics.

7

Who knew that California could be so cold, that his clothes would be so damp, or that he'd be met by a man decorated with red and green and yellow parrots? He picked up his travel bag, slung it over his shoulder, and opened the door to the lobby of the hotel.

"I have a reservation," Eivar told the young, slender woman at the reservation desk. Rosie. Her nametag said Rosie. "Actually, I have many reservations," he said then realized she wouldn't understand the joke. "I've had a bad morning and a rough flight, and I really need to take a nap."

Rosie nodded gravely. As she hammered away at her type-writer and his registration card, he couldn't help but notice the contrast between her crisp white blouse and blue suit with his own rumpled and sour and orange-stained self.

"It's chilly," he said, exaggerating the chatter of his teeth. Why did he feel the need to perform for her?

"Yes, sir," she said. She slid his room key across the counter to him, using the tips of her fingers, as though afraid to make contact. "Welcome to the Other California."

ONE SUMMER, EIVAR'S WIFE took to her bed for two weeks with a case of what her doctor diagnosed as the flu. They had planned to travel to the Grand Canyon and take mules down the steep trail to the river at the bottom during his first week of vacation after the end of the school year. Eivar had made the reservations more than a year in advance as he did every year, booking their trips to places drier and warmer than the rain forests of the Pacific Northwest. To their friends, Helen made jokes about how Paris couldn't touch a pile of rocks. The French just wanted your money while the desert took your breath away. They went to Death Valley, one year, Joshua Tree, the next. They hiked with bandanas around their necks and took pictures of each other dwarfed by the landscape. But, when Helen became ill and then could not shake the virus, Eivar canceled their Grand Canyon plans. She was tired after feeling so lousy for so long. Didn't feel up to the trip. Even with a week's notice, the tour company held firm on its refund policies, and he was left regretting the loss of the trip and the hundred-dollar deposit. "It's not the money I mind so much but the waste. Our plans. All the things we had looked forward to doing." Eivar said this more than once to those who asked about his summer. But then summer lingered and turned to fall, and Eivar went back to his middle school social studies classroom without having seen the red rocks of the desert southwest or the spectacular vistas from the top of the canyon. He spoke of Manifest Destiny, aware of it only as an abstraction. He had not had his backside chafed by the grudging motion of a recalcitrant mule. Helen repeated how sorry she was. She knew how much he looked forward to their trip. One morning in early October, as rain splashed against the windows and pelted the trees, Eivar woke up, went to the kitchen, drank coffee while he read the newspaper, and then poured a cup for Helen. But she didn't respond—not when he said her name nor when he shook her shoulder. Her head fell to one side of the pillow. The reality of death rather than the dim counterfeit of sleep. The house had been quiet, but in that moment when he knew beyond certainty, the rain drummed in his ears. He called the fire department, and the paramedics conducted their business, but Helen had stopped breathing hours before. *Dear Jesus.*

A heart attack in the middle of the night. Snap your fingers. Just like that.

Their daughter drove from Seattle, grumpy and sullen and blaming her father. For nothing in particular and everything. For her mother's death. For her own unhappiness. A litany of fault, ticked off point by point.

Point 1: "She was depressed, but you never saw it."

Point 2: "It had been years since she knew what to do with herself."

Point 3: "You never listened to her."

Point 4: "She didn't give a shit about the Grand Canyon, you know."

Point 5: "And she never knew how to talk to you. About your vacation plans or anything else."

A difficult and defiant teenager throughout her adolescence, Jody had left home for college and never returned. When she was in high school, he had come home early one afternoon only to interrupt her and a boyfriend having sex on the family room couch. He had yelled. Had called the boy's parents. Taken her to the hospital for testing and antibiotics. And nothing Helen had said to him—*patience, forgiveness, forbearance*—had made the slightest bit of difference. In hindsight, he might have overreacted, and Jody had hated him silently—*oh, where was that silence now?*—and their phone calls for the past ten years had been brief and reserved. Her absence had taken something from Helen, but he managed not to say this to his daughter.

"I was not a perfect husband," he said, adopting what he hoped was a tone of humility and contrition. "Or father. Obviously."

"That's easy to say now."

"Not so easy."

"You're an asshole."

"So you've said."

They suffered through the week together. Notifying Helen's extended family. Making the funeral arrangements. Calling their lawyer. The funeral itself. Silence in the aftermath, interrupted by periodic recriminations. During the funeral, Jody sat in the pew, stoic, self-contained, a mere delay of those accusations Eivar knew would be his private portion once they were alone together in the house of her childhood. Helen's prayer group offered their sympathies, condolences, and labeled casserole dishes. Their Presbyterian minister offered quiet assurances of Helen's place within the heart of God.

Eivar took three days for bereavement leave, and then he took two more weeks of accumulated sick leave. Jody went home at the end of the first week. Over the course of seven days, she called her father an asshole sixteen more times. Eivar offered no defense.

Jody left on a Saturday, and he went to church the next day hoping for consolation, but he couldn't concentrate on the service or the sermon, only that the lay reader, a woman he'd known for more than twenty years had worn a dress unaccountably red, unattractively tight, but provocative nonetheless. A secretary in the school district's billing office, she had been married for twelve years, divorced for eight, and subject to periodic rumors and innuendo. No matter her church attendance and participation, it was known that she drank and liked a good time. She was not above dancing until the honky-tonks shut their doors. *Shame*, he thought. *How can you?* Eleven days after the death of his wife of twenty-seven years, and already he was fantasizing about bedding another. All while a woman in a red dress was reading the passage from Philippians about purity and thought. How ironic was that?

But, what turned out to be ironic was that, a year later, rather than becoming entangled in a relationship with another woman Helen's age, he had married Elisa, one of his former students, the sister of the aforementioned Carl and three years younger than Jody, the daughter who hated him, hated him for the humiliation he had caused her, and who, after she received the wedding invitation, sent it back with the following note scrawled across it: "I will never see or speak to you again."

His sleep was not restful, a collage of nonsensical and chaotic dreams. In contrast to the chill of the day, his room was warm and humid, and the dreams had pulled at him the way a cook makes a crust for pizza. His undershirt was soaked when he woke, a little before five, to the jangle of the room phone on the end table next to the bed.

"Yes," he said.

"You said you'd call." Elisa's voice, petulant and yet bored. "When I didn't hear from you, I worried."

"I'm fine," Eivar said. "That is, I had a bit of problem on the plane, but I got here. And then I was so tired, I had to take a nap."

There was noise in the background, and then he heard Carl's voice distinctly: "Ask him if he's met Gilbert."

"Carl wants to know—"

"Yes, he met me at the hotel. We're all set."

"Okay," she said, and then he heard her voice as an indistinct mumble. Evidently she had put her hand over the phone. "Carl wants to talk to you."

"Fine." He rubbed his forehead and eyes.

"Eivar, aren't you supposed to be meeting Gilbert?" Carl's voice was unaccountably nervous, tense.

"In an hour. I'll pick him up, we'll go to dinner, and then we'll head to Golgotha."

"Okay. Then I guess you'd better get a move on." The recitation of Eivar's itinerary seemed to have calmed him, his good humor magically restored. "I won't keep you, brother."

"Sure."

Carl hung up before Eivar could ask to speak with Elisa again.

GILBERT'S APARTMENT WAS TUCKED AWAY in the corner, on the second floor of a two-story u-shaped complex, overlooking a drained and bereft-looking pool. A shopping cart lay on its side at the bottom of the deep end. The sort of place that Eivar had escaped thirty years before. Resentment boiled like fog. A chaise longue with broken straps had been folded up underneath the stairs leading to Gilbert's metal door. Eivar knocked, and after the sound of multiple locks and dead bolts, the door swung open revealing Gilbert's double: the same height, weight, and bulldog tattoo. The only differences were the freshly shaved head and a Hawaiian shirt with parrots of more virulent hues.

"Hold on," this Other Gilbert rasped, "he's coming."

Gilbert emerged from the darkness of a hallway, rubbing a towel over his likewise newly shaved head.

"Brother Mortenson," he said, "my cousin Victor."

"Good to meet you," Eivar said. "Did you know you guys could be twins?"

"We've heard that," Victor said. "Once or twice before."

"Victor will join us a little later," Gilbert said. "After dinner. He'll drive my truck and meet us."

"I can't get over it," Eivar said.

In the empty pool, two nine-year-old boys had righted the shopping cart and were now taking turns pushing each other down the incline and shrieking when they hit bottom and were thrown onto the cement.

"I CAN'T GET OVER IT," he said again while they waited for their dinners to appear. Gilbert had guided Eivar to a road-house in the foothills perched next to the highway heading into the mountains. There were three men on stools, drinking beer, knocking back shots, and teasing the bartender while a black-and-white television blared *Jeopardy*. Gilbert and Eivar had slipped into an empty booth. They were the only ones eating, and the man behind the bar, who wore an apron that said, "Call me Big Dick," didn't seem all that happy that he now had to walk food and drink from behind the bar to their table.

Gilbert nodded. "When we were kids, even our mothers had to look close."

"That could have been problematic."

Whereupon Gilbert launched into a story about his history as a "double," how he and Victor had used their likeness to one another to fool teachers and girlfriends, and more

15

seriously, their fellow gang members and then later their parole officers.

"When one of us was drunk or asleep or had something else going, the other would cover," Gilbert finished. "Kid stuff."

Kid stuff included prison terms for assault and possession and a miscellany of bad behavior, but it all ended when Gilbert had attended church at the urging of a girl he'd liked. Something happened. He had been hollowed out, cored like an apple. Slain in the spirit. The minister had been speaking about sacrifice, about soldiers throwing themselves on grenades to save the lives of their friends, about women covering the bodies of their children. About the savior climbing onto a cross for sins he did not commit. "And then I was speaking with words I never heard before. You know what I mean? I didn't know what I was saying. It was like nothing I ever felt before. Like there was somebody, something else inside my body. One of the women in church said I was speaking Hungarian. Or Danish. I was all busted up, but I was happy. So happy. Jesus loves me, this I know. It's all I want to know."

On the television behind the bar, Art Fleming read, "Home of the Johnson Space Center," and when one of the contestants blurted out, "What is Florida?" the men threw popcorn at the screen from their stools and yelled expletives.

"A week later," Gilbert said, "I brought Victor, and now look at us. We're the same all over again."

Gilbert's eyes took on a faraway look, focused somewhere beyond Eivar's left shoulder.

"And all that," Gilbert said, "because of a girl. A girl who dumped me three weeks later."

"What a fuck whistle," Big Dick laughed.

"It's a familiar story," Eivar said. "I mean really. You're not the first."

"She has six kids and they have four different daddies," Gilbert said, "but I've been faithful to the Lord."

EIVAR WENT TO THE GRAND CANYON the summer after Helen's death, hoping the trip would relieve the lingering sense of anxiety he had tried to ignore. But as often as he told himself how majestic God's creation was, he couldn't get over the fact that he was marveling over a hole in the ground. When he came home, he found that he couldn't bear to sit down. He made coffee in the kitchen and then forgot to drink it. He circled the dining room, den, and living room. He prayed for forgiveness, hoping the telephone would ring. He opened the doors of the bedroom closet and rifled through the last of Helen's dresses. He brushed his teeth in the downstairs bathroom, rinsed his mouth out upstairs, and wondered how he had gotten there. He kept moving. At night he fell onto the couch in the basement to sleep for three or four hours before light began streaming through the egress windows at four-thirty in the morning. In the fall, he went to school in the disorientation of fatigue, and during the second week of September, when the school year was yet young, and optimism had not begun to fade, he fell asleep while driving to work and ran his two-year-old LTD into an irrigation ditch. Only the trunk and back axle were visible from the road. The deputy who came to pull him out and insist on a breathalyzer was a C student from fifteen years earlier, and the emergency room doctor, who taped his ribs and stitched the gash in his forehead, only a shade better, at a B-minus. Neither seemed particularly fond of or eager to recall their time in Mr. Mortenson's class. His battered car was towed to the auto body shop owned by Carl Burkhardt, a D-plus if ever there was one. Carl, who had sat in the back and propped a *Popular Mechanics* inside his copy of *On the Oregon Trail*, had had a miraculous conversion experience in his twenties, the result of a rollover accident involving country roads and excess speed, alcohol, a buddy, and two girls from Pendleton. He and his three passengers all had blood alcohol levels above 1.4, none wore a seat belt, and all were ejected. Only he had survived. *Why?* Jesus had come to him in his hospital room during the hours he had been unconscious. Declared him anointed for the struggle ahead, gave him a purpose and a mission, and ever since, Carl had been true to the conviction of his experience: he established The Immaculate Warrior of Truth Tabernacle, located in a barn five miles from town; he kept boxes of tracts in his tool box; and after he smeared blood across the windows of a downtown Portland clinic as a protest of abortions, he had landed on the FBI's watch list as an extremist, a member of a radical organization. When his younger sister came back from San Francisco with tattoos on her back, shoulders, and behind her ears, exotic lingerie in her suitcase, and vague stories of her past year of employment, he took matters into his own hands. "Brother Eivar," he said, standing in front of Eivar's crumpled LTD. "Brother Eivar," he said again, placing one thick arm around Eivar's shoulders, "we've both lost someone precious to us, but this can't go on. Not when we can save each other. You see that, don't you? This can't go on." He showed Eivar a picture of his sister and wept. A month later, he was married to a girl less than half his age, a woman with more than twice his experience, more knowledgeable than he would ever be.

THE CAMPUS WAS TUCKED AWAY in the foothills of the Sierra. At one time, Gilbert said, it had been a monastery and then a convent, one order replacing another. During Prohibition, an entrepreneur with a sharp eye for possibility made informal arrangements with the few remaining elderly nuns for the use of the convent's cellars and underground passageways. But, with passage of the Twenty-First Amendment, secrecy and storage were no longer necessary, and the buildings and grounds went into a precipitous decline. Near the end of World War II, a group of Presbyterians from Los Angeles purchased the property and established a seminary and a college; they had looked into the future and saw waves of GIs returning home, and those whose experiences hadn't blasted them into cynics and nihilists had clearly been set aside for the Lord. The campus would be a haven for the strait-laced and polite, the blessed and the chosen. Or so the story went. And then in the turbulence of the nineteen-sixties, the school had slipped away from its roots and became as secular and as god-forsaken as any public college or university. A little Berkeley in the boondocks with just as much hair and beer and cannabis, while in the administration building the square black-and-white photographs of past seminarians were referred to as the Ice Cubes, as in the Frozen Chosen. The picket fence of their faces—white and male, beatified by a Sunday School Jesus—were growing dimmer and more faded by the year. A reminder was necessary, Gilbert said. A statement. "They knew the truth, and then they didn't," he said. Sadness tolled in his voice. "They chose to ignore it."

Seventeen miles into the mountains, following Gilbert's directions, Eivar turned onto a graveled service road. A mile in, Gilbert's truck blocked the road going any farther, and Eivar made a five-point u-turn, careful to avoid the mud on the shoulder and parked the rental heading back toward the highway.

"Your getaway car," Gilbert laughed.

They had stopped at a promontory just above the campus. Surrounded by grassy rectangles was the cone-shaped roof of the chapel. Colored lights twinkled on and off around the eaves, making haloes in the misty air. White lights traced the outline of the cross. The pines swayed above their heads, and when the wind shifted, they heard bits and pieces of "O Come, O Come, Emmanuel." Voices here, pipe organ there, and then gusts of damp, chilly air.

"I'm not sure I understand," Eivar said, as he had been saying for these past weeks to Carl. "Listen. Can't you hear it? They have a church, they hold services, they sing hymns. What's to get upset about?"

"Only the form of godliness," Gilbert said, "while denying its power. They desecrate the holy with their casual disregard."

"Oh."

Gilbert put a meaty hand on each of Eivar's shoulders. "Soldiers for the Lord must believe. Wholly and purely, nothing halfway, nothing lukewarm, no room for uncertainty. A sacrifice of the self."

In that moment, he sounded like Carl, and Eivar smelled grease.

"Yes," Eivar said, recognizing the sour wash of nausea at the top of his stomach, "of course. Of course I believe."

"You've had a loss. Victor and I have had losses, but Jesus has given us everything back. And more. We can't possibly repay Him, but we can serve him."

It sounded cute, even before he said it, but Eivar couldn't help himself: "Even we who only stand and wait?"

"We," Gilbert gripped Eivar's shoulders even more tightly, "we will burn with his righteousness."

Holding a covered flashlight, Victor motioned to them from the darkness of the trees while Gilbert and Eivar carried the gas cans from the bed of Gilbert's truck through a light drizzle.

"Everything else is set up," Victor whispered. He led them to an outcropping on the hill above the campus. Eivar recognized Golgotha from the pictures Carl had shown him. Three eight-foot high crosses made from rough-cut six-by-sixes, and at their feet lay a tangle of rockets and fuses on a scrum of tarps and beach towels. "We just need to empty the cans."

Three ladders had been propped up against the crosses.

"Come on," Victor hefted one of the gas cans and began to climb the first of the ladders.

"You're a little close to the fireworks," Eivar said, "don't you think?"

"In this weather? Don't worry," Gilbert said, also ascending. "He knows what he's doing."

Eivar climbed the middle ladder, and like Gilbert and Victor, unscrewed the cap and began pouring gas down the center pole and along each arm of the cross piece.

The fumes were enough to make Eivar feel a bit wobbly, as though he had been deposited back in time, back to his crumpled LTD and the irrigation ditch and the sleep deprivation of grief and guilt.

The sounds from the chapel had ended, and the large double-doors were opening to columns of worshippers carrying lit candles and singing "Silent Night" *a cappella*: "… all is calm, all is bright…"

"Okay," Gilbert said. "Here we go."

They were students mostly, with an adult here and there, professors, maybe. They were all scruffy, in the fashion of the past decade, as though soap and water and a pair of scissors were to be avoided. At least half of the women wore caftan-like dresses and boots with puffy down parkas over the top. One of the young men wore a hat reminiscent of the Mad Hatter in the Disney *Alice*. Their Sunday best. This is what our best intentions had become, this infantilization of our best and brightest. Day care for those in hormonal turmoil. He could hear Carl now. The mist turned to rain and began to fall more insistently. "Round yon virgin…"

"Let's go," Gilbert said. "Brother Eivar, maybe you could get the car started, warm up the engine, and I'll be with you in a minute."

"Here," Victor said, handing him the flashlight. "We'll be able to see just fine."

He was halfway back to the rental when the first of the rockets went up, spraying red and green fire in its aftermath. He was turning the key when the explosion rocked the car, the road, and the forest, and an orange glow took over his rear-view mirror.

ONCE, NOT LONG AFTER HE AND ELISA WERE MARRIED, Eivar woke in the middle of the night. His bedside clock read 2:46, the bedroom was dark, but his child bride was not in bed beside him. In such moments of sleeplessness, Helen had been in the habit of boiling water for tea and reading a book in the basement den, where her light was not liable to bother him. She read books about Edgar Cayce or Jeanne Dixon or by those who claimed to have had mystical experiences. Elisa, on the other hand, had shown no interest in books or reading, not even the Bible, nothing beyond magazines like *People* or the tabloids in the grocery store.

Eivar paced the house, upstairs and down, but Elisa was nowhere to be found. Not reading, watching television, or sleeping on the foldout sofa bed.

Elisa?

She had made it clear that their marriage would not be a marriage in anything but name. She would sleep with him, but she wouldn't *sleep* with him. Not even in summer when the nights were warm and she wore nothing but her tattoos under the top sheet. She was done with all that. He accepted this as only just, the penance of a fifty-plus-year-old husband deigning to have a twenty-something wife, a woman with a diverse history to boot. God's joke of redemption for them both. Penance comes in many forms. He thought of writing to Jody: *your father is the fool you believed him to be.* And, *you couldn't punish him any more harshly than the sentence he has already received.* Maybe Elisa had decided that enough was enough, brother Carl and her sullied reputation notwithstanding. She left me, he thought, and we never got to know each other.

Her suitcase still stood in their closet, though, and the repaired LTD sat silently in the garage. If she had left, she had done so on foot with the clothes on her back.

Out the back window of their second-floor bedroom, a light blinked near the toolshed, and then the motion-activated light on the side of the shed carved a cone of white on the ground: Elisa. She hadn't left him, after all. Smoking one of the cigarettes she had sworn to Carl she had quit, and wearing nothing but one of Helen's old robes, untied. Her lack of summer sleepwear evident beneath, she was moving in some sort of pattern or ritual, an incantation or dance. A ceremony for one. And, then, Eivar understood: high school and a routine from when she had been a cheerleader not so many years earlier. *Chukka, chukka, Rangers. Chukka, chukka, yeah!* Just a girl, after all. And, he, so near death...

THE SOOT AND CHAR refused to come off his face. Scrubbing only seemed to result in further smearing, and the black that was on his forehead only now extended to his cheeks, his chin, and the bridge of his nose. *Oh, dear Jesus. Dear, dear, sweet Jesus.* He was still wearing such war paint when the room phone began to ring. *Carl, no doubt. Let him wait.*

The phone rang and rang and then mercifully went silent, and then five minutes later began to ring once again. *No.*

Not to mention the smell of gasoline which he would never be able to remove. *No, and no.*

But he answered the phone the third time because enough was enough, and he needed to shout: "What? What do you want now?"

"It's me," Elisa said, "not Carl. What happened? He's been shouting in tongues and slamming cupboards."

"It was a mess. An unholy mess."

He told her about the explosion that felt like an earthquake underneath the car and the orange light behind him. How tempted he had been to leave right then and there, the engine had been running, after all, and he felt like running, too. But, no, he had turned off the ignition and ran back toward the fire, only to find that the fireworks that had been intended to call attention to the burning crosses, had exploded all at once and not in the controlled way that Victor had planned. And, not only had the rockets and peonies and chrysanthemums exploded but so, too, had the gasoline on the crosses and the extra can as well. And, as if that weren't enough, Gilbert and Victor had been caught up in it, somehow. They had climbed the ladders on the two outside crosses, each embracing post and crossbeam as though in a lover's hug, until wood and body were conjoined in carbon's crust.

"I don't know, I don't know," Eivar said sobbing into the

phone. "Why did they do it? That's what I don't understand."

"You just don't get it, do you brother?" Carl. At some point apparently, while Eivar had told his story, Carl had wrested the phone away from his sister—*when had that happened?*—and now he was going to set matters straight, for in faith there was no room, no need for doubt.

"They loved the Lord, brother, that's all, with their whole hearts, minds, and souls. What they did, they did out of joy and love and commitment. They were the thieves on either side of our Lord, and they died as a sign to others, they died as evidence of their faith. You helped them do it."

There was more, and Carl's voice continued to rumble forward and back, "an accessory to their lives and a participant in their gladly-given deaths," but in Eivar's hand, the receiver had become a foreign thing, the black artifact of an alien civilization.

By the time he had returned to the crosses—*two minutes, five minutes?*—he realized that there was nothing he could do. Flames shot above Gilbert's and Victor's heads, and he imagined the parrots of their shirts flying through the sparks. He guessed what they had done with the fourth can of gasoline. They had waited for the inevitable spark and accepted the outcome that they had chosen. "Silent Night" was no more. Instead, he heard gasps from below, the sound of tears, and moans insufficient to undo the reality in front of their eyes.

He ran back to the car, and then drove through the winding darkness, blindly, through blinking, unseeing eyes, back to a life that was unknown and unrecognizable.

[ii]

Wild Life

(Elisa, 1994)

THE BIG CATS FROM THE ANIMAL SANCTUARY roar each evening at dusk. Deep guttural chuffs bell into the gathering darkness and then rebound against the wall of mountains. To hear them for the first time is to feel surrounded. Elisa Mortenson Rabinek hears them, though without much notice, while tending bar at O'Malley's. The effect no longer registers, and she doesn't think much of them. Not anymore. They're cats, she has decided. Size matters, but in a way that doesn't. Big cats roar while domestic tabbies purr. This much she knows—she's taken the tour after all—but not enough to care. What she cares about is the fact that Joe Dwyer and Abel Ramirez have been sitting at her bar for the past two hours, pouring a third pitcher of Budweiser Light between them and eyeing her ass collectively, while she keeps an eye on them so they don't forget to settle up before stumbling out the door, pretending a trip to the privy outside. It's a routine that has become their favorite form of vaudeville *schtick*. Otherwise, she tries to ignore them, her thoughts elsewhere.

"You could be a little nicer," Joe says, "and pay attention to your customers."

"I pay attention to paying customers." The response is automatic and perfunctory, and just like that she has been incorporated into the act. She knows without having to think about it that if she failed to respond, their little lives would experience a loss, no matter how bored she might be, no matter how much she'd rather be anywhere else. "Paying customers are one thing. Skipping customers are another. Tipping customers are nearly extinct."

"Morty, I'm shocked." Joes uses the nickname he and Abel devised during her first day behind bar, back when they were in the habit of sifting through all the documents sitting next to the register while Michael, who owns O'Malley's, was outside in the walk-in fridge. She stopped that practice, but not before they had scanned her job application and W-9 and not before they had glommed onto her first husband's last name. "I'm shocked and I'm hurt. One time a fellow has to use the gents, and he's doubted the rest of his days."

"Don't you two have anywhere else to be? Maybe you could feed the tigers up the hill? I hear they need some fresh meat, and you two might just be the ticket."

"It's so sad," Joe says to Abel, as though she weren't

standing in front of them both, "to watch a young woman turn so old."

THERE'S SOME TRUTH TO THAT, Elisa has to admit. She's become increasingly aware of time's passage. The pain in her hips after hours of standing behind the bar. The lines at the corners of her eyes and mouth. The roll of flesh at the waistband of her jeans that never used to be there, that even the loosest tops don't entirely disguise.

The moment she starts seeing streaks of gray will be the moment that she heads for the drugstore and the haircare aisle.

It doesn't help to go home, go to bed after two in the morning, her head and lungs still thick from the fouled air of "prohibited" cigarettes and cigars, and then wake up at seven in the morning to find her son sitting at the kitchen table in his boxers, eating cereal like a six-year-old. Gil should be on campus—his room and board are part of his scholarship—but instead he's here, at home with his mother, in his mother's crappy three-room shack, and while she's not unhappy to see him, her long-limbed boy, she suspects that he comes around to check on her as much as he does to raid her pantry.

He has slipped through the side door at some pre-dawn hour, without waking her, and now puddles of milk dot the Formica top of her thrift-shop table, her *Fresno Bee* propped up on the cereal box in front of him.

"No practice?" she says, by way of greeting.

"Nah." He drops his spoon into the ceramic bowl. "We're a lame ass team for a lame ass college."

"That lame ass team is paying your lame ass to stay at your lame ass college and swim in your lame ass lane," she says, "and go back and forth in the stupidest, boringest sport known to man."

"Don't I know it." He raises his eyes from the paper and smiles, chunks of half-masticated Cheerios and milk dripping from his teeth and lips in a way that he knows she hates.

"You're impossible."

"And you're my mother."

She sighs. "I remember. I was there."

Nineteen years ago, her water broke at midnight, and this was what emerged: the product of one moment of sympathy for husband number one.

"Are you here long?"

"No. I have class in a couple of hours."

"Goddamn right you do." Stats, at eleven. The Reformation and Evangelicalism at one. Monday, Wednesday, and Friday. She has his fall schedule memorized by heart. He has once again ditched morning practice at five; Coach Watkins will be livid at three, and he'll be swimming an hour after everyone else has left the water.

"Don't you get tired of being a pain in the ass?"

"Not really." He pushes back from her table, kisses the top of her head. "Potty mouth."

"You know I love seeing you," she says, "but you should be in the pool."

"You'd miss me."

"I miss my cereal," she says shaking the now empty box. "And my youth."

When she was Gil's age, her parents had long since surrendered any thought of parenthood. Her mother was born tired, and her father's notion of fatherhood consisted of yelling louder. By the age of sixteen, her brother Carl—older than she by four years—had turned feral, staying out all night, drinking with the men from the lumber mill, goosing fast cars down the gravel and potholes of one-lane logging roads, and picking up god-knows-what from the women who likewise frequented The Saw Break. And by the time she was eighteen, she had launched her own rebellion, hitchhiking from Estacada to San Francisco and Berkeley in a journey that was as much of a cliché as it was profound self-discovery. She got an all-back tattoo in the Haight, she dropped acid in People's Park, she lived in a Victorian where Janis Joplin had once partied regularly, and yet she never could rid herself of the sense that she was traveling a path that was already obsolete, a role that she couldn't make her own because she couldn't make herself believe it. Been there, done that, yes, but—*yawn*—without much enthusiasm. A summary of her late teens and early twenties gave her a kind of reputation among those who know her history, but she knows that it is a reputation built on false pretenses. Or at least a lack of originality. Or true wildness. As though her actions, following her brother's, were only one more instance of following others' expectations. Like brother, like sister. That's what others thought. She watched, she learned, but she never gave herself over entirely. She had sketched the outline, but she'd never inhabited the scene. Given her own sense of imposture, how does her son manage such self-possession?

THE COLLEGE THAT GIL ATTENDS is only seventeen miles away but two thousand feet higher than O'Malley's and the Cat Haven next door. Like Einstein's concept of time, the distance is relative. The college sits at an Olympian remove; while the residents of Fresno suffer from the air of the San Joaquin Valley and the inversion layers of every season, the college looks down upon the fug at a stately, indifferent remove. Nice if you can afford the view. Elisa has visited twice, and both times she felt as though she were trespassing. Lock the doors, count the silver.

Now and again, professors from the college will come halfway down the hill to O'Malley's for an afternoon of slumming. They sit in their impeccably laundered jeans and those corduroy jackets with ridiculous elbows and pretend that they share the same kind of useful knowledge as the CalTrans workers and farmers, Cal Fire and US Forest rangers and retirees of various blue-collar stripes, who drink here regularly. Now and again, a conversation will take place, usually of a political nature, and Elisa will have to call Michael to intervene. He'll offer the corduroy jacket a drink, tell the offending regular to behave, but he'll do so in such a way that the professor will know that he is not the one who belongs. This, Elisa thinks, is a gift beyond all others, a skill she does not possess. He speaks the language like a native whereas all she hears is Blah, blah, blah. She'd rather break a bottle over somebody's head. At least she thinks so, but truth be told, she's happy enough making a phone call and letting Michael deal with it.

Today, just after the last of the lunch-time boozers have left, one of the jackets comes in by himself, but he's not standard issue. So not standard. No corduroy for one thing. He's a forty-something nightmare, overweight and rumpled, his belly folding over his waistband, adorned in a pink silk shirt and a purple bow tie. A white panama on his round head. She knows instantly and intuitively that what he sees in the mirror is an image that no one else has the eyes to see: a cosmopolitan, a suave man of the world with an eager and ready vocabulary when, really, he's just a *schmuck* with a sensibility his body does not share.

"What?" she says, all the welcome she's willing to give.

"Elisa Rabinek?" Professor Fatty asks. "Gilbert's mother?"

"Why?" she looks at her watch. Two-thirty. "What's the problem? He's probably in the locker room getting ready for practice. He'll be in the pool by three."

"That's fine, but you're the one I wanted to talk to."

"You'll have to wait. I have to get a pitcher to Statler and Waldorf over there." She points to Joe Dwyer and Abel Ramirez, who, ten minutes after sitting at their reserved spots, are already beginning to make mooing sounds, their best attempt at humor.

"Fine." He looks pained, but he manages to hoist himself onto a stool at the bar. "I'll wait. When you're done."

She takes a pitcher and their free bowl of chips and salsa to the two reprobates in the corner, while Joe does his level-best to appear innocent and naive: "Receiving visitors, are we?"

"Drink your beer and keep your money on the table."

Outside the plate glass windows, the wind has kicked up, and pollen from the pines has begun to blow in thick green swirls. Rays of afternoon sunshine pour through the prisms hung like Christmas ornaments from the window frames and break into pieces. Reds and blues and greens dance like fairies on the wall. At a moment like this, her life is sweet, still. In repose. Then, she remembers what the facts of that life truly are—she carries beer from one side of a room to another, a room decorated with bras hanging from the rafters—and her stomach feels hollow, and it's all she can do not to pull her own vaudeville act and walk out the door.

She takes a breath and confronts the man at the bar. "Okay. Let's have it. What's up with Gil?"

"I'm sorry," he says, "I haven't been clear. I'm not here about Gilbert, *per se*. Rather, you see, I once knew your husband."

He speaks in tones overly precise. Fussy.

"Are you gay?"

"What? No, I'm married." The accusation has made him stammer. M-m-married. "Does that matter? I need to tell you about your husband."

Oh, God, so here's the other shoe. Ric "Ricky Boy" Rabinek, her second husband and the most unlucky and godawful crook she had ever known, meaning that he was terrible at being a crook—name the game and he found a way to get around the rules, without ever figuring out how to get away with his crimes. Charming but clueless, good fun until it wasn't. How many times had she lived through a fist pounding on her door at three in the morning?

"Okay, he owed you money, he cheated you, I get it, but he's dead, and I can't pay everyone he might have owed."

"What?"

"Ric was a shitfaced liar. Everyone knew that."

"What? Who's Ric? No, I'm talking about Eivar. Eivar Mortenson. You were married to him, weren't you?"

She hasn't had a conversation about Eivar in years. Not even Gil asks about him anymore.

"He was my first husband, Gil's father. But Gil never knew him."

She reconsiders, looks again at the pine pollen blowing in waves outside the windows. "*I* never really knew him."

SHE HAD COME HOME TO ESTACADA, suddenly aware that she had missed the gloom and the dripping silence of the mist in the trees. She had changed this much, unaware that more changes were in store. Somewhere along the way, her brother, that aforementioned wild man, had undergone his own, much more radical, revolution: after rolling his car along one of the many logging roads near town, he and his three passengers had been ejected, and only he had survived. He had met Jesus then, and when Elisa returned—with her tattoo and her suggestion of carnal habits—she had been subjected to the totality of Carl's newfound obsessions. The force of his beliefs was wearying, and she found it easier to acquiesce than to resist. She was that tired, and her character was that suspect. It wouldn't do, he said, for the leader of The Immaculate Warrior of Truth Tabernacle to have a whore for a sister. Changes would have to be made, starting with her appearance and a renunciation of her former life and ending with her marital status. Yes, Carl. No, Carl. Yes, Carl. Like her brother, she would belong to Jesus. He (Carl, not Jesus) presented her with an ultimatum: marry Eivar Mortenson—thirty years her senior, their former social studies teacher, no less—or hit the road again, never to be welcomed back. She chose the former, for reasons that not even she could or can explain—other than fatigue. But she did impose her own conditions upon her new old husband: he was not to touch her, thank you very much. Physical proximity without intimacy was the best she could offer, and although nothing could have been further from the truth, she intimated that this had to do with her former life. She expected him to say no, but he surprised her, and she had the sense that their marriage had been precipitated by some sense of her husband's guilt as much as it was her desire for her brother to shut up.

Meanwhile, her brother seemed incapable of not stirring up trouble in the name of his newfound virtue. There was the abortion clinic in downtown Portland and the red paint that he and his followers had lobbed at the mayor's office, for reasons that were obscure at best, but which Elisa believed were rooted in Mayor Goldschmidt's Jewish heritage. After the FBI started coming by the church and the house and the garage that Carl used for his auto repair business, Carl had enlisted Eivar in one of his schemes. Then, wasn't she surprised when Eivar had come home in a much more fragile state than when he had left—nervous and jumpy, prone to weeping for no apparent reason, saying only "They burned. I saw them burn." A response to something he had seen, something that he had done, something about which she refused to ask questions since the last thing she wanted was an answer. It was during one such episode while they lay together, without touching, in bed that she let her sympathies get the better of her and not touching became touching and touching became something else. That worked out well, didn't it? Eivar wept when he was through, and in that moment, she had glimpsed the future. Nine months and a week later, Gilbert had been born, his name one of her husband's last requests before he died in September of 1975. Proving the point that no good deed goes unpunished.

THE TELEVISION RARELY STRAYS from *Jeopardy* in the morning or *Donahue* in midafternoon, but now that the soap opera of Tonya Harding is front page news, knocking Whitewater below the fold of the *Bee*, it seems to be the only story on the thirteen-inch set above the bar. Wouldn't you know it? Another girl from Clackamas County known only for her missteps, misdeeds, and misadventures. She is seven hundred miles away and twenty years older than Tonya, but Elisa still feels the shame as if it's her own. So, when Professor Fatty next comes in, a week after his first appearance, she's not feeling particularly self-possessed. No joy in Mudville, none for her, thank you very much. If anything, she feels undone, as though the entire world is now seeing the life she knows as normal: the grubby little upstart, looking up at the bottom of the middle-class rung. During her marriage to Eivar, she had been granted the palest experience of another life, and when Professor Fatty mentioned Eivar—to whom she had been given in marriage, as though arranged in some Third World family bargain, and with whom she was no better acquainted—she had been flooded with that briefest of moments when the silverware and the plates and the towels matched, when the floors and the windows were clean, when the mail did not include collection notices. And in that flood of past experience, she had lost it entirely: she had cried, no, she had wailed—*with abandon*—running out of O'Malley's and into the outhouse out back. Closed the door, bolted the latch, alone with the heat and the stench and the flies, until Michael knocked an hour later.

"I'm not going to ask anything," he said. "I don't need to know, but we have old men in there, and sooner or later, they're going to start pissing in the parking lot, you stay in there much longer."

Fine. She pulled herself together, she came out, and she went about her business, pouring beer, listening to the geezers and their empty, know-nothing, bull-shitting excuse for conversation, pretending that all was fine, just fine, thank you very much and *shut your ass, Abel* and *fuck you, Joe.*

This reminder of Eivar was so unexpected, so unlooked for, that she could not help but replay the entirety of her brief marriage and the years following his death. How Eivar, when she realized she was pregnant from their one desperate coupling, had told her about his wife, how she had died in her sleep, how their adult daughter blamed him for her mother's death, blamed him for being controlling and overbearing, blamed him for being male. How he asked Elisa to forgive him from whatever crimes he might have committed against the female of the species because he had not a clue what his daughter was talking about, because his daughter had been describing a man he did not recognize, certainly not himself. He told Elisa that he would take care of her, he would take care of the baby, she was not to worry, and then, as if on cue, he had slipped on a sidewalk covered in wet leaves from an early fall rain shower, lasted in a coma for a week, and then died, leaving her alone with said baby, in a house free of a mortgage, and his retirement benefits entirely in her name, with no mention of the daughter in his amended will or any further instructions to her therein, only that Gil be christened Gilbert Victor Mortenson and that she bring him up in their shared faith.

She had tried, hadn't she? She had taken him to church now and again, not to her brother's barn with its army of the crazy and the brainwashed, but to one of those standard, organ-playing, pew-organized auditoriums, with its razor-cut, blow-dried pastors, who might as well have been selling cars, bonds, or insurance. Was it her fault that each time she attended one of those services, she returned feeling as though she needed to take another shower, to wash off the oily coat of smug certainty and self-satisfaction? She had played that game before: acting out roles that were not her own. She had done it once in response to current events and once for her brother's sake, and both times she had doubted whether she had a personality of her own. Why go through that again for the sake of a dead husband?

So, in spite of the house that she owned outright, she had come to live in ways that grew increasingly haphazard, and the unraveling began to show everywhere. She got a job pulling the beer taps at The Saw Break, leaving Gil in a car seat behind the bar. She got involved with that hapless sack of sad excuses, Ric Rabinek. And then, with Ricky Boy in hock to every low life in Clackamas County, her life nearly went off the rails for good, and only a letter addressed to Gil, then a high school junior, woke her up and saved them both. A full scholarship to a school neither one of them knew and for which he had not applied. The Helen Jody Endowment from Sierra Presbyterian College. Who knew? She had called at once; she determined that the offer was genuine, and began to take steps: divorced the loser husband, repainted and reroofed Eivar's house and then sold it quick at below market value, and moved from the dripping forests of the Willamette to the hellish heat of the San Joaquin Valley and the parched foothills just above the dust. She and Gil drove seven hundred miles in her corroded piece of shit Corvair, dropped his bags off in a bare dorm room, and then because Michael never saw what was coming, she talked her way into this job at O'Malley's and the broom closet cottage fifty yards away. It was like reading three books and finishing the last chapters simultaneously. Who says you can't change your life?

BUT NOW, A WEEK AFTER SURPRISING HER the first time, like a bad penny, here is Professor Fatty entering O'Malley's once again, this time wearing a blue silk shirt and a bluer bow tie while carrying a vase with yellow roses past her cadre of personal hecklers. And what is that under his arm? Good Lord—chocolates. Too much. Too much, too much. He has come, he says, to tender an apology, but he seems to have mistaken an apology for a flamboyantly attention-getting Valentines' Day.

"I didn't mean to surprise you the other day."

"And flowers aren't a surprise?"

And chocolates hyperbole. Yes, she knows some language beyond the obscene.

"Well," he says, "they're an offering of sorts. I could have handled things differently. I could have written a personal note."

"A personal note." She snickers. "A personal note would have been nice."

"You know. Something like, 'Dear Mrs. Rabinek, it has come to my attention that I once knew your first husband, Eivar Mortenson, and so on and so on.' That wouldn't have been so hard. I could have invited you to dinner rather than springing myself upon you."

"I was working," she says, "and I'm no Mrs."

"After, I mean. After work."

That begged the question of whether or not she would have said yes, which isn't entirely a sure thing. She doesn't think so. "So, you knew him. Eivar. That's what you came to tell me. You told me. What else is there to know?"

44

Professor Fatty's face grows red, as though he's about to confess something shameful: "He was my teacher."

"What's new? He was *my* teacher, too. And my *husband*. At least briefly. But I didn't know him. Not very well. And, I don't know *you*."

"No," he says, "you don't. You never did."

THIS IS THE SMALL-WORLD STORY he tells her: he was a grade behind her at the middle school, and everyone in Estacada knew Carl and Elisa and the Burkhardt family saga: how Carl had gone from wild adolescent to the reincarnation of an Old Testament prophet calling down fire and brimstone upon an unrepentant and ungrateful world, and how she had gone from quiet mouse to Janis Joplin acolyte to a character out of an Atwood novel.

On the other hand, there was no reason why either Carl or Elisa would have known little Walter Book since he was younger and without any remarkable characteristics, either intellectually or physically. His father, Aldus Book, was an Estacada newcomer, relatively speaking, an assistant manager for Portland General Electric and the hydroelectric engineer responsible for the dams on the upper Clackamas River. Although he held a responsible position, no one seemed particularly inclined to respect or admire a man who wore rimless glasses and carried a slide rule and a phalanx of mechanical pencils in the pocket protector of his polyester dress shirts.

He did not cut his own firewood. He hired others to perform routine maintenance on the family's 1963 Belair station wagon. And, then he died during the spring of 1968 in that year of so many more important deaths, as though he had chosen to die at the precise moment when his death would cause hardly a notice. Walter had been in middle school then, and Eivar had been his teacher, and something about the lost and grieving fourteen-year-old caught the attention of his grouchy social studies instructor. Eivar didn't exactly talk with Walter, it wasn't as though, in a burst of sympathy for the recently bereaved, Eivar took Walter to ball games or movies; no, instead, Eivar's great contribution to Walter's welfare was to allow him to sit quietly in the classroom during the lunch period, without a barrage of questions or conversation.

"We didn't talk. I don't think he said two words to me that whole time," Walter tells Elisa now. "He just let me be."

Years later, when he was in college in Portland, Walter heard about the death of Eivar's first wife and then his subsequent marriage to Elisa, and while this second marriage seemed odd and out of character, he understood what strange mutations grief could engender. He had, after all, in the wake of his father's death, borrowed an axe and chopped down sixteen trees in the back half of his parents' property, trees for which he had no plan or purpose in mind other than destruction. The newly opened gaps in their woods opened the backside of the house to whatever sunshine was available, and the felled trees lay there for ten or more years collecting moss and decomposing until his mother had them hauled off to a woodlot on the northside of town.

"So, I heard you got married," Walter says and then adds apologetically, "to Eivar, but I had—I have—no idea why. It's none of my business, but it was a surprise."

"You're right, it's not your business. But, if you really must know, I was just as surprised."

He doesn't need to know that the marriage was an arrangement worthy of a third-world culture. Nor that she was complicit by virtue of weariness and indifference.

"Do you think," he says, his face glowing red again, his voice halting as though speaking of something tragic, "I could invite you to dinner, after all? I would like to invite you to dinner. Not like a date or anything. This is not a romantic invitation. It's just that there are things I need to tell you, things you need to know, more things, and I can't do that here."

Which makes her conscious, again, in a way that she has only in glimpses, of the dust motes in the sunlight, and the bras hanging from the rafters, and the glassy eyes of the deer hanging above the bar. That schmuck Donohue is burbling on about what a friend he is to women, what a champion he is of their rights, while Abel and Joe keep her squarely within their view.

"Sure," she says, staring down the geezers by the back windows. "Fine. I could do with another venue."

I WENT TO COLLEGE, Walter Book says, and then, like every other unemployable with a degree, graduate school. I didn't know what I was going to do. I applied for teaching jobs after college, but no one wanted to hire me. *I* wouldn't have wanted to hire me. I don't think I really wanted any of the jobs for which I interviewed. I probably realized subconsciously how hard those high school teachers worked, the belligerence from students they had to put up with, the expectations of their parents, the edicts from administration. God knew what He was doing when my prayers went unanswered or rather were answered with a resounding No.

They are sitting in a booth in a fern bar in Fresno, a place so anonymous, it could be used for planning a bank job, and Elisa thinks about what a bad idea this was. Yes, it is nice to be away from the mountains for the evening, but to listen to this crap? She is a captive. He's the one driving, he's the one buying dinner, and she's the one stuck with nodding her head and drinking gin-and-tonics as fast as she can wave her empty glass at their server. *My name is Tiffany, and I'll be taking care of you this evening.* Meanwhile, little Walter Book is talking talking talking as if she cares.

So, I went to graduate school, Walter Book continues, and I fell in love with Virginia Woolf and the Bloomsbury set, and I finally found my feet. And then, just before I defended my dissertation and got my degree, I received a call from a lawyer. Eivar's lawyer, as it turned out. He had an unusual request. I was to be the executor of a scholarship that Eivar had endowed.

He has finally said something interesting, and she stops tearing at a dinner roll and pushes her latest and deadest G&T to the edge of the table.

The scholarship, Walter Book says, was to be extended to one Gilbert Victor Mortenson at the moment he turned sixteen, and every effort was to be made that Gilbert come to Sierra Presbyterian in memory of what Eivar had witnessed there.

"Although," Walter says, "he—or rather I should say, the two of you—didn't require much convincing."

Is he being smug when he says this? Yes, but then maybe he has a right to be because no, they hadn't needed the slightest bit of convincing; the identity of the donor and the circumstances of the scholarship had remained a year-long mystery that hadn't mattered to either of them. That scholarship letter—from the grave as it turned out—had been their impetus to move, their literal salvation. Did knowing or not-knowing change that whatsoever?

And would you believe it? Walter Book exclaims. How ironic was it that I got hired at the very college where Eivar's scholarship for Gilbert was housed?

Like everything associated with Walter Book, Elisa thinks: too much is too much. And this is definitely too much: too much coincidence, too much easy interpretation of divine will. And as a result, all that too-muchness ends up totaling nothing.

THIS IS WHAT EIVAR SAW: two men, cousins Gilbert and Victor Martinez, burning themselves to death while hanging from crosses on a knoll above the college chapel. There were three crosses, the two on the outside burning with two men aboard while the center cross burned alone, as if Jesus Himself were present in spirit if not in the flesh. There was some question as to whether the cousins had intended their self-immolation or if their deaths were the result of an accident and a plan gone horribly, horribly wrong.

So, this was the gist of Eivar's babbling and the outcome of her brother's demented demagoguery. Not to mention the source of her son's name.

She imagines the cousins burning in the December darkness, at a moment when students were exiting the chapel from an evening service, full of themselves and an imminent Christmas, their egos and their desires on full display in the misty air. The very sound of their voices would have betrayed the triviality of their concerns by contrast with the fires on the hill. This, Walter Book says, was the commitment to the Savior that they needed to see. One that went beyond the students and their own appetites.

"And the end of that was what exactly?" Elisa says, knowing she can't disguise her disgust. "Two human corn dogs?"

It is Walter Book's turn to look offended. His face becomes a dictionary picture of rictus; he goes into what she thinks of as high dudgeon mode and the insufferable pomposity of her brother. "They were willing to sacrifice themselves in order to change the culture of the college and the culture of this area. A call to righteousness."

What is it with these lemmings, these true believers?

"Pretty small potatoes," Elisa says. She can feel her anger rise from some place within herself that she can't locate. But, why is it that, at such a time, her wits and words desert her? Small potatoes, as if that might be some sort of final condemnation. "Light yourself on fire in order to scare a bunch of college kids? Sounds like the sort of thing my brother would convince someone else to do while he's a million miles away. He might have smelled like gasoline given his auto repair business, but I never saw him with a match." One more strike against Carl, that sanctimonious bastard.

ANOTHER MORNING SOME WEEKS LATER and another sighting of Gil in her kitchen. This time he's scrambling eggs in a skillet while bread crisps in the toaster. Coffee is dripping into the carafe. Her newspaper is unfolded at her place at the table, which has already been set with knife and fork, plate and coffee mug. The butter dish has been paired with a jar of marmalade.

"What gives?" Elisa says, yawning. It's six-thirty in the morning, and she's been asleep for maybe five hours. It's a

Thursday morning, and it's October, nowhere close on the calendar to Mother's Day. "You're not swimming."

"Nope," he says. "I'm not. And never again."

"Fine," she says. "No swimming."

Since her dinner with Walter Book, she has been assured that the conditions of Gil's scholarship have nothing to do with his participation with the swim team, only that he must maintain a grade-point average so ridiculously low he'd have to stop breathing to miss it, and as a result, she's grown less and less rigid in her insistence that he go to practice or to every one of his classes. Now, it seems that her permissiveness has become his license.

He uses a spatula to scrape eggs onto her plate, brings her the toast when it pops up. Here it comes:

"You're right. It's the most boring sport known to mankind. Back and forth, back and forth. You might as well be a hamster. So, I quit. I told Coach Hammacker yesterday."

She refrains from saying that hamsters don't appreciate getting wet, but she understands the analogy well enough: a wheel becomes a lane hemmed in by ropes, and a journey becomes unending. Especially when said journey is accompanied by a raving maniac in board shorts and a straw hat, whose yelling penetrates under water.

"Well," she sighs, "you'll have more time for your classes."

He sets the skillet gently into the sink, so his back is turned to her when he says, "That's the thing."

"Just don't go overboard on the religion stuff," she says before processing what he's said and what he's about to say, and now she's wary and alert to her greatest fears: "What? What's the thing?"

"Don't get mad."

No wonder he's appeared out of nowhere and made her breakfast. She runs through her private catalogue of his possible offenses that might result in him leaving school: he's flunked sociology because he didn't care; he flunked biology because he did; he's been caught drinking in his dorm room; he's gotten a girl pregnant. It's this last possibility, she thinks, that's the most likely. Maybe it's all of them. Nature and nurture, after all, will out, and she can no longer help either.

He sits down across from her, slouching in his chair, staring off into the nothingness behind her left shoulder. "These people are nuts," he says. "Do you realize that?"

Once again, she thinks of doughy Walter Book and his wide-eyed, bow-tied insistence that the college ought to be a breeding ground of Christian goodness and virtue. Walter Book and his certitude, in spite of the fact that she suspects that all is not quite as he would like it to appear.

"They're lunatics, without question."

After her dinner with Walter Book, he had insisted on taking her for a tour of campus. She had mentioned her previous visits and her sense of discomfort, of not being welcomed, of being viewed unfavorably, as though she were inferior goods.

"That's terrible," he said. "That's not the image that the college would like to project. We are making some substantive changes in that regard."

The first step, he said, was that the college was changing its name. In another year, Sierra Presbyterian College would become Liberty Christian College, and the Prospectors would become the Patriots, marking the evolution of the college from its historical origins, that moribund mainline denomination catering to the wealthy and well-placed, to an Evangelical powerhouse in which all who believed were welcome. Times were changing, and the college, like the church at large, would need to change as well, or die of indifference and neglect. The students had changed, the faculty and curriculum had changed. The college was merely catching up.

They drove through the hills and vales of the darkened campus, the infrequent blue emergency lights making ghostly shadows of the pine trees and oleanders. The chapel, the shape of a sixth grader's volcano project, loomed.

"It's a lovely, lovely place," Walter Book said, "by daylight or night. I will always be grateful to the good Lord that He brought me here. Jesus and Eivar directed my path."

"Okay," she said. "If you say so."

"Don't you see that as well for yourself and Gilbert? Think of all the choices you've made and the circumstances you've endured, the way they've been orchestrated for you to be here, for Gilbert to be enrolled here. Think about what it means."

"That's just it," she said. "To be honest, I'm not sure what any of it means. Maybe it doesn't mean anything, other than the fact that this is where we are now. Who knows what tomorrow might bring?"

"Well," he said, as if her comments were irrelevant, as if that was an issue now settled.

He drove on a series of access roads, pointing out the various buildings: Sciences, Humanities, the Student Union, the dormitories named for alumni of the distant past.

"That one is Gilbert's," he said, and she remembered that first day when they had dropped his two duffle bags into a bare room with its institutional extra-long mattress, dirty window, and an asphalt tile floor. She could just make out the window on the second floor that she thought might be his.

They turned one final time and parked at a dead end in front of one of the campus gatehouses. "This is me," Walter Book said. "I've lived here ever since I was hired, and it's so convenient, I've never thought to leave." He shut off the ignition, and when he opened his door, the dome light turned on, illuminating the white baby flesh of his cheeks and forehead. "I was hoping you would come inside and meet my wife. She would have come to dinner, you see, but she had another commitment."

What was she to say? That she had no desire to meet this fussy man's wife when she hadn't believed that a wife even existed? Curiosity, however, beckoned. Inside, the gatehouse was dark, and Walter Book began turning on lamps with elaborately decorated shades.

"I don't—" he began, stopping for a sound at the back of the house.

They stood in a small, impossibly low-ceilinged living room with exposed beams. Tchotchkes and clocks and ceramic figurines of girls with dogs filled every flat surface.

"She was meant to be here," he apologized.

"Maybe something came up," she said before the sound of someone snoring became impossible to ignore.

"This might not be the best time," Elisa said.

"No, no, it's fine, believe me," Walter Book said. "Just give us a minute or two. She'd never forgive me."

He followed the snore to one of the back bedrooms while Elisa took advantage of the bathroom. She ran the water and dried her hands but when she emerged despite delaying as long as she thought appropriate, she could still hear two voices talking high and low, indistinct but with varying levels of insistence behind the closed door. On the other side of the bathroom was a second bedroom, and Elisa caught a glimpse of an unmade twin bed, adjacent to a file cabinet and a trestle desk stacked with papers and books.

"I sleep there some nights," Walter Book said startling her from behind, "when I'm working late."

"Oh."

Behind him was a woman of indeterminant age in a housecoat decorated with the dancing tomatoes and cucumbers of Veggie Tales characters, along with little Bibles and crosses. Her face was pale, her eyes were so dark as to appear bruised, and her hair was thin and drawn up into a small, tight knot on the back of her head.

"Dr. Book," she said, extending her hand to Elisa, "didn't tell me we were expecting guests. I would have prepared something. Snacks. What can I get for all of us?"

"Susan," Walter Book said, "this is Elisa Rabinek, Eivar Mortenson's wife. You've heard me speak of them."

"I'm so sorry to bother you," Elisa said, taking a small, moist hand, feeling in that handshake that she was a pillar steadying the smaller woman. "I feel terrible. Please don't trouble yourself."

"No trouble, no trouble at all," Susan Book trilled. "We have an open bottle right here. Just the other night, I was just saying to Dr. Book that we really don't entertain as often as we ought."

She had pulled a bottle of Moscato out of the refrigerator and glasses from the cupboard with more efficiency than Elisa thought the woman capable.

"Really, I'm—" Elisa said, hoping to deflect the offer of this too-sweet wine and whatever revelations it might bring, hoping that Gil might possibly be back in his room and available to drive her home. *Save me.*

"Nonsense, in this house we are the hands and feet of the Lord," Susan said while Walter Book pointed to a seat on one of the couches in the tiny living room. "Any time of the day or night. You make yourself comfortable, and I'll tell you everything Dr. Book neglected to mention."

"You think I don't know they're nuts?" she says. "They're mad as hatters, but this is where we landed and the school you've got."

She says this to her son, recognizing with a pang that for the last two decades he has been the one constant in her life. The one good thing. And all she has ever done for him is to follow the next fork in the road without any plan or discussion when she needs to be, as the magazines suggest, more deliberate and more approachable. More thoughtful. "So, tell me. Spit it out."

"I'm withdrawing. I lasted a year, I gave it a shot, but I can't face another minute of these people and the way they talk. It's like they're reading from a script that someone else wrote. I haven't talked to a real person since we left Oregon."

She counts to herself as she exhales: one, two, three, four. "Okay," she says.

"Okay? Really?"

"Okay," she says. She's thinking now. Really thinking. Turbo mode thinking. Fully deliberate and engaged in this problem that will only be solved by giving it her most inspired thought. The one thing she will not do is lay his father's guilt at her son's feet. "Really. It's not like everyone in California is a Goody-Two-Shoes-zombie. You know that. School in this state is dirt cheap. Community college for a couple of years, then we'll see what you can get for financial aid. Don't worry. It won't be as easy as the free ride here, but we'll figure it out."

"But, that's the thing, Mom."

Another but, another thing. Goddammit to hell.

"I don't want to stay in school. I've been trying to tell you." There it is, but it's going to get worse. "I've enlisted in the Marines. I passed the test and the physical, and now I have a month before I go to San Diego."

It turns out that he's been up to no end of mischief. She had worried that he had knocked up some poor unsuspecting virgin when, instead, he has signed his name to another kind of wild life, one that could, in the near future, see him dead. She wants to stand up, in order to take him by the shoulders and shake some sense into him, but simultaneously it seems very important that she stay in her chair, the only guarantee that she won't fall over on her face, she feels that disoriented. How embarrassing would that be? Although she can't discount the fact that a good faint might buy her some time.

"I knew you'd be pissed."

"You can't finish school first?"

"No," he says. "I'm done. Maybe I'll come back to it, but right now, the only thing I want to do with a book is burn it."

"I hate you," she says as she stands finally to hug this man, her son. "I hate you for so many reasons. Don't ever make me breakfast again."

"Morty, you need a better attitude." This from Abel Ramirez.

Fuck you, Abel.

"Smile, and the world smiles with you," Joe says.

Fuck you, Joe.

The refrain that never ends.

What does she have to smile about, anyway? she wonders. It's not as though the weather is about to improve her mood; they are in the middle of a January funk, and the Valley fog, tule fog, is so thick and so pervasive that at moments of the morning, it extends even to their elevation. A gray blanket that is as glum as her mood. Just that much higher, the college is not affected by such climatic concerns, and as if to rub it in, a letter arrived yesterday marked Second Notice, detailing the fees that were due as a result of Gil's midterm withdrawal last fall. At the lonely remove of O'Malley's, midway between mountain top and valley floor, she seems to be experiencing the worst of both worlds: the fog from below, the sense of inferiority from above, while next door, the tigers begin their evening chant. In the meantime, the Demented Twins of Senile Stupidity continue their tone-deaf baiting.

60

Today is Tuesday. Gil has been conscientious—freakishly so—mailing his mother a letter every Thursday afternoon, so she is expecting to see an envelope in her mailbox with his APO in the upper left-hand corner. *Everything is great, Mom. This is exactly what I needed.* On and on, his assurances, although her mother's sense tells her—no matter how dull that sense might be—that he's telling her nothing like the truth. All summary and spin, no fact, no detail.

But maybe, just maybe, she's better off not knowing. There is such a thing as too much information, a cliché perhaps, but a truism of which she became uncomfortably aware while meeting Susan Book.

What Dr. Book had failed to mention according to his wife was the entire history of their relationship from the beginning to the present, the minute granular details only interesting to those involved. How she had been the department secretary for the Humanities division when he had been a brand-new hire with his slicked-down hair and flushed baby face. He was so cutely apologetic and uncertain of himself, then, so hesitant. In her eyes, he was not fat, particularly, but pinchable, like a plush stuffed animal. Cute, if prone to moments of nervous sweat and anxiety. She called him Honey Bear and he called her Peaseblossom for one of the fairies in *Midsummer Night's Dream*.

"And now," she wailed, "seven years after our wedding, he doesn't need me anymore. Look at his silk shirt. Does he look like Gatsby to you? He has his shirts and his place in the world, he's tenured, and I quit my job. I stay at home and read romance novels and magazines that tell me how to keep my skin looking younger, and we don't sleep together. And now you're here, I suppose, to replace me."

"What?" Elisa raised her hands. "No. Please, I'm nobody's replacement."

"You're right." The other woman staggered in front of her. "I'm nobody, that's for sure. And you're welcome to all this. This palace." She spun around in the small room, throwing her wine-glass against the back of the front door. "Take it, take it, take it."

"Susan," Walter Book said. He held his wife's face between his hands, even as the rest of her body struggled against him. "Look at me. I brought Mrs. Rabinek home to meet you because she was Eivar Mortenson's wife, and Eivar was my mentor. I've told you this and I've told you this. And Gilbert Mortenson is Eivar and Elisa's son." Susan struggled, then sagged into his embrace.

"I should go," Elisa said. "Maybe Gil is home. He's got the car, he can drive me."

"Please don't," Walter Book said. "Give me just a minute, please."

He ushered his wife back to her bedroom, supporting her the way one might an obstreperous child. Elisa heard the hic-cupping of tears and the murmur of low voices. In a small pantry off the small kitchen, she found a broom and dust pan and swept glass shards as best she could and used a towel to wipe wine from door and floor.

"You don't need to do that," Walter Book said.

"It's no problem," she said. "It's not like I'm not used to it. Working in a bar, cleaning up alcoholic messes comes with the territory."

"That's just it," Walter Book said, "alcoholic messes."

Susan had been meant to go to an AA meeting that very evening, she had insisted she could be trusted to do so on her own, but instead she'd drunk one bottle of Moscato and was starting in on a second when she had passed out in her room.

"And it's not just alcoholism or depression," Walter Book said. "It's not just me, what she thinks of me." He was no expert, not in this, but he suspected something else was wrong as well, some sort of mental health issue that had revealed itself both suddenly and slowly. Could a woman in her mid-forties become as irrational and unmoored from reality as someone thirty or forty years older?

"I didn't mean for you to see this," Walter Book said. "I was hoping that Susan and I could welcome a guest to our home and have a nice evening like a normal couple with a friend, but that was clearly not to be. All we got was ugly, and ugly breeds more of the same."

Ugliness, it seems, is catching in both the past and present tense, and present unpleasantness will always claim the greater attention.

"Morty, Morty, Morty." Joe and Abel are chanting her nickname in unison.

"Boys," she says, "you are fatheads of the highest order, but today is your lucky day. I am buying you each a pitcher of your favorite water-as-lager, straight from our tap to your table. I am doing this in order to ask you a favor, that you would please please please shut the fuck up. Do not ask why, do not say a word, do not pass Go. Just please leave me be for once." She sets two pitchers on their table when Joe flips the switch that she has resisted for so long.

"Now, Morty," he says, "this is more like the girl we thought we were going to see."

"Girl?" she says, "when have I acted the juvenile?" And she gives in to the anger she knows has been there all along. She takes the pitchers in each hand and pours them over the men's heads, bald spots awash with the finest products of Milwaukee and elsewhere, shirts, laps, and trousers drenched, the beer pooling below each chair, while the two old men sputter and fume.

This will do it, she thinks, this is the end, and as if on cue, Michael walks in, hands each of the men a towel, and says, "You don't think you didn't have this coming?"

64

[iii]

Onward, Pigskin Soldiers!
(Michael, 2001 / 1975)

L ET ME SAY THIS FIRST before you get the wrong idea:
after the program was resurrected the first time, the qual-
ity of football at Liberty Christian College was only slightly
better than that of the high school teams that played two
thousand feet lower in the heat and the smog of the Central
Valley of California. The players were just that much older—
some were several years older due to commitments to mission
work between their high school and college years—but they
were no more athletically intelligent and a lot less talented on
the whole. None of them were in danger of being recruited by
a Division II or III school much less Alabama, SC, or Notre
Dame. If they were stronger and faster than their high school
counterparts, that was only due to their age and their off-sea-
son conditioning program.

And the coaches—my god, what a sad collection of has-beens

and never-wases they were. Several had never coached at the high school level, much less college. The linebackers' coach had once been a prison chaplain, and that was his lone credential: a man who knew how to interact with aggressive personalities. The Board of Trustees had hired Woody Bonaventura as head coach, a man who had once coached the wide receivers for UNLV during the Randall Cunningham years, but UNLV, never a football powerhouse, had slid to an afterthought, and by the time Coach B had been hired, he'd been selling insurance for ten years or more and drinking for at least twice that long. He drove onto campus in the summer of 1998 in a Mercury Monarch with Nevada plates, peeling paint, and a magnetic insurance logo on the side, advertising his former office. The Board was committed to reviving the football team because, in their collective wisdom, a college without a football team was only a soccer club with textbooks, but they weren't willing to pay for much beyond uniforms and ice packs.

To make matters more difficult, the team practiced and played on a field that was little better than rocks and dirt and half an inch of topsoil topped with a stressed and spiny Bermuda grass. A mountain field, in other words. They were lucky it was mostly level. A few years later, that field and the practice facilities, the players who played and the coaches who coached there would undergo a dramatic transformation, courtesy of the Chairman of the Board of Trustees, that fat, lying fuck, Bobby Thornton, and the foundation he'd established from the profits of Chronos Athletic, but as I said, that would come later. Much later. When the trustees, in the person of Bobby Thornton, decided that what was needed was a return to a muscular Christianity, to trumpet to the world that God indeed blessed the righteous and the faithful, and winning belonged to the favored while losing was the province of chumps. No, what I'm talking about happened in the fall of 2001, that season that straddled 9/11, when before the World Trade Center was targeted, all was innocent; afterwards, no one could be more than ambivalent. Was a game, any kind of game, especially one so violent and so able to stoke the fuel of mass hysteria, appropriate anymore? Given that the world had gotten just that much closer to hell. I was going to say "closer to hell than it was in the best of circumstances," but there were no best circumstances that September. You remember it, don't you? Three thousand miles away, and even we were afraid of what might come from above. Before 9/11, the LCC football games had been prefaced by a team of amateur skydivers bringing in the game balls. Sometimes the winds were not cooperative and game time was delayed as the balls and their carriers, intended for the fifty-yard line, ended up in Dunlap or the tiger enclosure at the animal sanctuary. One sudden gust produced a tangle of lines and a broken leg before the game could even begin. But after 9/11, the airspace over large events was restricted, and although attendance at our games was never more than a couple thousand, we were all willing to comply. There were no more game balls from the sky, pregame fractures, or errant parachutes, all such joy sacrificed for the sake of patriotism and security.

"MICHAEL," COACH B SAID, "Would you mind?"

This was early August of 2001, and while there was an entire wall of bottles behind me and I had just tapped a new keg of Bud Light, Coach B was pointing to the glass in front of him, a glass now empty of a red wine that was so foul, it might as well have been labeled government surplus. Sediment sludged the bottom. He was cutting back, he told me, and the best way to do that was to drink the worst thing possible. His contract stipulated that he not drink at all, but neither of us was likely to tell.

"Of course," I said, pouring his glass to the rim. Breathing, that wine would not.

"We are a bad team this year," Coach B said.

"We're used to that," I said. "Why rock the boat with something different?"

"No, we are truly, fully, fuckingly bad this year."

It was the second week of August and the first week of two-a-days. Coach B was sitting at the bar between the morning and late afternoon practice with his wine and a plate of nachos with its processed microwaved cheese forming an orange slick in front of him. While his players were supposed to be resting or stretching or working in the weight room, he was sitting at the bar, drinking bad wine, eating unhealthy snacks, and keeping an eye on the windows in case the president of the college or a trustee happened to show up. If that were to happen, we had a plan: I'd lower his wineglass behind the bar and set a cup of lukewarm coffee in front of him. Not much of a plan, but we figured there was not much chance of Dr. Newland or one of the new members of the Board appearing in a dive bar seventeen miles from campus.

"Weaker, slower, smaller, and," he said, smacking his lips, "much, much less talented."

"Now, now."

"I have a running back who squeals when he's tackled, a quarterback who can't throw a spiral, and—"

"And a linebacker who refuses to tackle with his head," I said. "You said the same thing last year."

"And that worked out well, didn't it?"

They finished the year with two wins and eight losses. Not a banner year.

"No one got seriously injured," I said. "You didn't have to make hospital visits."

The year before that, he'd had two ACLs, a broken collarbone, and a ruptured spleen.

"Small favors," he said.

Elisa Rabinek, who worked afternoons and evenings and tended the social security regulars and their watered-down light beer, sat at the bar, flipping through an old issue of *People* and yawning. "Be grateful," she said. "No spinal cord injuries or head trauma, no broken legs, arms, or necks. Just sprains and strains. What's a fumble by comparison?"

"A turnover," Coach B grumbled.

"And turnovers are another form of death," the three of us said in unison.

We had the routine down.

Okay, so what you need to know is that I played once upon a time. That's right: I played for LCC, back when it was known as Sierra Presbyterian College, back in the '70s when we were known as the Prospectors rather than the Patriots, when the locker room reeked of the pot and beer that came out our pores along with the salt and grease and anxiety of everyday sweat. I roomed with a Samoan nose tackle named Telofa, and my best friend, Derrick Williams, was a wide receiver, who admitted to me that he didn't like the game very much, he didn't like contact, and he didn't like all the coach-speak that we had to endure, but he didn't know how to do anything else so far as creating an identity for himself.

"Look," he said, "I need something to tell girls. And, Accounting and Finance isn't the sexiest thing."

On the other hand, when Telofa was tired of the reading he had to do for his pre-med major, he was fond of breaking down a twelve-pack of Coors and then hanging from our second-story window like a trapeze artist with chunky, tree-stump legs, and chanting the Manu upside down.

Since I played center, Telofa and I were often lined up against one another in practice on that crappy dirt field, and I had grown used to seeing his eyes glaze over in that fanatical way, and it didn't surprise or scare me anymore.

"Telofa," I said, "give it a rest. We're just running plays. It's theater."

To which he would shake himself like a dog and then smile beatifically.

I knew that I would get another three or four repetitions of gentle-Telofa before the maniac would show himself again. An open hand to my earhole, a forearm to my cage, a knee to my groin. An average afternoon.

Derrick once asked me why I put up with it.

"I don't know," I said. "He's my roommate. He doesn't mean anything by it."

Derrick looked at me in that way he had, that are-you-kidding-me, don't-let-them-get-your-mind way.

"Everything," he said, "means something. Even when it's nothing."

I knew what he meant, but I couldn't paraphrase it any more than I could have spoken Farsi. Any more than I could have told you all the variant meanings of the word "mean."

I don't know that I liked the game any more than Derrick did, but I was too insecure to say so. In high school, I hated practice, which was boring and repetitious and the province of our coaches—in other words, the small-minded and the sadistic—but I enjoyed the games, the colors of the uniforms and the grass under lights, the sounds of the bands, the buzz from three or four thousand people who had some vested interest in the outcome as a validation of one's community; I loved it all except the last fifteen minutes before kickoff when I was throwing up in the locker room and rehearsing my "I quit" speech for the coaches. In college, though, something changed: I took pleasure in the two hours of activity each afternoon, Telofa's abuse notwithstanding; if I could have skipped the games, I would have. There was the travel, of course, which grew old by the third six-hour bus trip, but much worse was the lack of interest by anyone other than ourselves. We played in front of mostly empty bleachers masquerading as spectators. Even our fellow students didn't show. Not in those Vietnam-colored days, and not for a game with its authoritarian tone and militaristic language; we could all recite the George Carlin bit by heart. There was no home to go to à la baseball, and we had no bands and no cheerleaders to make up the difference. It wasn't like we were getting anything for it; we still had to pay for our tuition and books, our room and board, all for the privilege of being ignored—with the additional gifts of potential injury and inevitable pain. For the level of viciousness on the field during game time was much higher than anything I had ever experienced in high school. Telofa-at-practice was but a good-natured imitation by comparison. Biting in pile-ups, punching at the line of scrimmage. Eye-gouging. We were fighting over nothing as if it were something. Who was it—Hamlet maybe—who talked about soldiers fighting for land not large enough to bury the dead? That was who we were, god help us. We were just that stupid, as if the outcome of a game no one else cared about was going to determine the course of our pathetic, sorry little lives. Although, come to think of it, maybe it did.

If coach B was adamant about his team's shortcomings, he was equally sure that this year was going to be different, an opinion he shared only with a select few. Myself. Elisa, when she could be bothered to look up from her out-of-date magazine *du jour*. Those recent additions to the Board, Bobby Thornton especially, had been promising increased funding and support, and Coach B couldn't wait for the day to come. But more importantly in the short term, he had a secret weapon, imported from Avenal State Prison, one Dalvin-Demarius Philipi Jenkins. DDP for short. Sentenced to thirty months for car theft and assault, he was so recently paroled that he was still looking all around him in something like a state of wonder.

"But he never finished high school," I said. "I've heard horror stories. He can't read. He can barely talk."

"Where'd you hear that?" Coach B took a gulp of his plonk. "He's a smart kid. If he's got learning problems, we'll figure something out. We'll get a tutor. We'll get a proctor. We'll get a proctologist. Horror stories, my ass. You think this is a real college?"

"I don't know. What do you think? Should I call Dr. Newland to find out?"

"No. No need to ask Cheryl."

"First name basis," I said. "Good for you. That's special."

"Don't be a shit."

"Well," I said, "he'll definitely stand out."

"Is that a racist thing to say? I'm shocked," Coach B said, throwing up his hands. "Shocked, I say. I never pegged you for a racist."

"I'm not," I said. "I just think he'll be noticed. He's not—"

"White?" Elisa said.

"No, damn it," I said. "He's not *socialized*. He hasn't had the benefit of any nurture whatsoever. Everyone will know why he's here, and it won't be for his scholarship. He has neck tattoos."

At which point, Elisa left her stool at the bar and hitched up her tee shirt just enough to remind me of her own all-back illustration and the ink that she knew I loved. Hypocrite that she knew I am.

DDP's story had made the local news stations the week before. Orphaned at six, in juvenile hall at seven, a junior member of the Crips and arrested three times before the age of fourteen, he had played football at Edison his freshman and sophomore years, bowling over other players like ten pins, before he was arrested again and his schooling administered by the prison system. But now, newly paroled and the possessor of a GED, DDP had been free to go back to the streets before Liberty Christian had intervened. He had been offered an alternative, and DDP had accepted.

"How long do you think this is going to last?" I said. "Have you heard the word 'recidivism'?"

"He's a believer," Coach B said. "A reader and a literalist, by all accounts."

"What?"

"You heard me. He's a Freak, a Bible Thumper, one of your people."

"There you go," Elisa said, coming back with yet another three-week-old magazine. "Crime, check. Prison, check. Conversion story, check. Lily white, middle-class college. What could go wrong?"

And that was the other shoe.

JESUS CAME TO DDP's CELL in the middle of a hot night in July, not long after he was transferred to Avenal from the county jail. His cellmate was snoring and farting that evening's mac-and-cheese. DDP woke with a start and listened to the ever-present tensions of the prison, which to his ear sounded like the high pitch of a mosquito, the squeal of air escaping from a punctured tire.

"What the fuck are you doing?" Jesus asked him.

DDP was impressed that the savior would use the word *fuck* in a discussion about his life. His grandmother had never hinted that Jesus would talk in any way other than the King James English of 1611. Thee, Thy, Thine. Thou art. Although Jesus was not visible, DDP was convinced that he was in fact talking with the Lord of Lords, that the experience was real and not some shitty lame ass dream, even though the encounter was much more judgmental and accusatory than DDP would have expected, not that he'd ever been churched-up all that much.

"I said, What the fuck are you doing?" Jesus asked him again.

"Doing the best I can," DDP thought or thought he said. "We don't got a lot of options."

"Sitting there feeling sorry for your sorry ass, I bet," Jesus said. Jesus had a mouth on Him. "You need to get right, boy."

"What I need—" DDP began.

"Is a new fucking life," Jesus finished. "But you're not getting a new fucking life while you sit around on your sorry fucking ass feeling fucking sorry for your old fucking self. Use some manners. Clock in. Read a book. Think a little."

"Yes, sir," DDP said, feeling entirely cowed by this invisible, profane specter of a savior.

"Hell's bells," Jesus said. "Like I believe anything you have to say, you little ass-wipe."

Two hours later, a guard found DDP on the floor of his cell, a white foam ringing his lips.

"Saved," DDP kept saying apropos of nothing. "Lost and found. I been lost and found. Lost again and found again."

IF YOU HAD ASKED ME in 1975 where I thought I'd be in fifteen years, I probably would have said a small church in the wilds of northern California, maybe southern Oregon, and a congregation of no more than a hundred and fifty, a wife, two kids, and a dog. I'd develop a community in which the members would come to depend on one another deeply. We'd be a family dedicated to intimacy and kindness and forbearance. How that would happen, I didn't know, but I figured seminary would give me some clues. My wife would be beautiful, of course, fully committed to and actively engaged with the goals of our faith family, the dog would be large and mostly asleep, obedient and devoted in moments of wakefulness, but the children were outlines, lines on a door jamb, because I didn't really know what having children meant except that they grew.

I went to Sierra Presbyterian because it was a religious school but not stridently so, unlike the reeducation camp Liberty Christian would come to be years later. We had a chapel and regular services on Sunday, but no one was obliged to attend, much less take it seriously. We had a chaplain, who played darts and drank beer with the students in the name of relatability. We had our future seminarians, but we also had our hippies and stoners, as well as our politicians and activists, scientists and artists. I had been brought up in the

Episcopalian church by parents who believed that everything had its place, order was prized, and moderation was the rule in all things including, and especially, spirituality. Church on Sunday morning. Communion once a month. I served as an acolyte each Sunday, wearing ministerial drag, a uniform without the harshness of military discipline. These were the habits I knew and practiced without thought. More extreme expressions of faith such as altar calls, speaking in tongues, and testifying about one's relationship with Jesus were embarrassing social tics, such as digging in one's ears at the dinner table or bragging about one's salary, which were behaviors to avoid at all costs. Faith was personal but, more importantly, it was private and conducted in private, with respect for the complexity of the world.

I was brought up with these beliefs and this world view, but when I graduated from college in the year of the bicentennial, I did not proceed to seminary as planned; I got a bank loan instead to buy a foothill bar with a dozen stools, six tables, two booths, four taps, a mini-fridge, and a toaster oven. Big Dick's grandchildren threw in the moose head and the bras in the rafters for free. Deal, I thought. Not knowing that what looks like a momentary detour can become a lifetime of entrapment.

"He's not your classic dive-bar, pickled eggs racist," Elisa told Coach B. "I see him as more of a full meal: he's an *entrée* of classism with *sides* of oblivious racism and narcissism, along with *notes* of obsession and substance abuse. Hence the addictive use of tonic water and/or Diet Pepsi."

"Since when did you become my therapist?" I said. Now and again Elisa took pity on me, but she had a son who was USMC fodder in the Balkans, so she could be tough and cynical as only military families can, and this was not one of those times when pity was on offer or display.

"He's got his middle-class pretensions, his secrets, and he hates to share."

"Huh," Coach B said. "Makes sense."

"You were going to be a priest, right?" Elisa said.

"Never a priest." I shrugged. "I'm no Catholic."

"Okay, Mr. Martin Luther Protestant. Minister, then."

I shrugged again. "I thought about it."

"And, you still think you're a kind of minister. With a bar instead of an altar."

"Now you're being ridiculous," I said.

"Then you really shouldn't be a racist," Coach B said, "being an almost-priest and all."

Christ almighty, I thought but let it go.

"You gotta meet this kid," Coach B said. "You really do. He's enough to make Muhammad a Christian."

ALL OF WHICH MAKES ME WONDER: how did I get from point A to point P to point Z, from Religious Studies major, a nominal

79

member of a mainline denomination, even one intending to become part of its pastoral hierarchy, to bar owner and indifferent agnostic? The easy answer would be to say a girl, and it would be factually correct, but it wouldn't be entirely true. Emily was one of those ethereal young women, who seemed to move in an alternative reality; she didn't seem conscious of where she walked, for instance, or of what obstacles might be in her path, and many was the time that I guided her away from parked cars, trash cans, or pathway benches. If you had watched her from a distance, you might have been forgiven for thinking her blind, so engrossed was she in the internal drama developing on the other side of her eyes. She wasn't conventionally pretty—her mouth and chin were rabbit-like and she was so slim in the bust and hips that at twilight and from a distance you wouldn't have been the first to mistake her for a twelve-year-old boy—but her other-worldliness made such caveats petty and beside the point. Here's something else: she was a music major and she played the harp, so how could I see her as anything other than an angel? She had come to Sierra Presbyterian from a dot in North Dakota surrounded by corporate farms, and everyone in her family was a rural savant of many skills. Her brother spoke seven languages and repaired tractors as though they were violins. She worked fourteen-hour days driving a combine for her father before practicing another couple of hours with the regional symphony. She accompanied the church choir in her spare time and made lunches for the migrant laborers on the neighboring farms. So much a product of suburban ease and my own lack of ambition, I couldn't picture it. She was so lost inside her own head, but she produced tangible things at every turn: a crop, an etude, a ham sandwich.

And I was so lost from the moment I met her that fall that I immediately revised my fantasies of who my wife would be and what she would be like. I chased her down the moment I saw her, and I pushed next to her in the dining hall and pestered her until she couldn't ignore me any longer. I might have been a bit overbearing, but I was a football player and older, and she didn't stand a chance and didn't seem to mind. I took her to movies and to restaurants, to parties in Fresno, mini-golf and bowling in Clovis, and hiking in Kings Canyon. I told my parents that finally, after three years of little to no social life in college, I had a girlfriend.

"I'm going to marry her," I said, despite the fact that I was a senior and she a freshman. I knew some waiting would be involved. And nothing my parents said, none of their usual Episcopalian caution and moderation, could stop me from believing our marriage to be imminent. Nothing could stop me, not even the biggest warning sign of all: the fact that our time together was spent mostly in a vacuum of conversation. That's right, we never spoke about marriage or faith, our classes or mutual friends. It sounds unbelievable, I know, but it's true; I assumed that she believed as I believed and she thought as I thought, and any discussion we might have had was subsumed by activity instead: when we weren't going to a party or a movie, when she wasn't practicing in a rehearsal room or when I wasn't at practice on our dirt field, we were generally in bed in my dorm, two innocents enjoying what our bodies were able to do, healthy young animals with the freedom to play. Telofa was rarely there that year, he had two or three girlfriends of his own, boyfriends, too, for that matter because he wasn't picky or so blinkered as our denomination's doctrinal stance might indicate, and he took his pleasure as it presented itself. Each of his liaisons had single rooms or accommodating roommates, and he never said a mean word about finding a tie on the door knob. He welcomed the confirmation that his roommate wasn't opposed to sex out of some misbegotten principle. Which is what he said when he joked about me robbing the cradle.

The inevitable surprise happened on the weekend of an away game, and nothing went right, even from the start. On Friday night, our bus broke down on the Grapevine while cement trucks and semis thundered past us. The coaches, who were driving school vans, arrived in Pomona at four in the afternoon, but the rest of us—players and trainers and our equipment manager—didn't arrive until one the next morning, seven hours late. Our game that next afternoon at Merritt Field was a disaster. On an end sweep, our quarterback was kicked in the head and wobbled away to the wrong side of the field, looking for all the world like a soldier about to surrender. Telofa and another defensive lineman were thrown out for fighting, and the Sagehens gashed us through the middle, taking advantage of our undersized, inexperienced, and frightened back-ups. By the end of the third quarter, we were down 31-7, and although our coaches were raging along the sidelines, the point of continuing was unclear. In the huddle, I told our freshman second-string quarterback, "Don't you dare throw an incompletion. Keep the clock running, damn it."

When it was all over, we had lost 45-7, and we were all grateful for the final whistle. We showered our misery and then boarded our less than reliable bus with the dew still clinging to our backs and foreheads; in the meantime, our coaches zoomed away in their air-conditioned vans without the benefit of a word, nothing encouraging, consoling, or corrosive.

Campus was quiet upon our return, dark as a mountain night in November could be, not long after the time change. The lights in Fresno made a dull glow to the west, the moon a thin sliver. Only a single light shone from the portico to the library. I hiked from my dorm room, past the chapel and the site where two true believers had torched themselves a year earlier, and then on to Emily's, sore and tired but horny and expectant nonetheless. But when I knocked there was no response, and the door was locked. I walked to the music building only to find the rehearsal rooms dark and the building shut tight.

Oh, Emily, I thought. Tonight, of all nights. I could use a little tenderness. Yes, I could.

But I went back to my room without.

Telofa kept his minifridge stocked with cans of Coors, but I also knew that under his bed, he kept a bottle of generic bourbon, which was caramel brown and nearly full and could be used for lighting a fire in a Weber as well as one's heart and head. I drank, and sometime, maybe two in the morning, after realizing that I would need to buy Telofa a new bottle, I started singing off-color frat songs and hymns of the more martial variety, and I did so for at least an hour before campus security showed up. An overweight man in Kevlar shoved me into the showers in my clothes while a student in an orange reflective vest turned on the jets. I didn't resist.

"Sober up," Kevlar said, "and then let your fellow residents get their beauty sleep. You could use a little yourself."

Because by that time I wasn't looking beautiful at all, just wet and sloppy and blood shot. I'd also begun to cry, which disgusted the two authority figures in front of me.

"Good lord," Kevlar said, "get a grip."

"'Suicide is painless,' Mr. Reflector sang, doing his best karaoke of the *M*A*S*H* anthem while taking advantage of the acoustics in the showers. "'It brings on many changes.' Or so I've heard."

"Go to bed, goddammit," Kevlar said, "and don't listen to a thing he says."

Good advice. I went to bed but was up again in an hour, unable to sleep and unable to lie down without the bed and room spinning in opposite directions. I went back to Emily's room, which was still locked, and then because nothing else would be open, I went to the chapel, and that's where I found her.

I met DDP in Coach B's basement office the next day before their evening practice. Did I want to? I admit that my curiosity was piqued, given all I'd heard, but if I'd had anything else to do, I would have taken a pass. Elisa told me to take advantage of an afternoon off.

"See some other sights," she said. She pointed to Joe Dwyer and Abel Ramirez, who came every afternoon at 1:00 before leaving at 5:00 so they could make dinner at the appropriate time. They were that far under their wives' thumbs, and we would know how far their leashes extended by whether or not they returned at 7:00. "The old farts in the corner will still be here."

"You won't abuse them too badly?" I said, because she could be cruel with them in ways she didn't realize, especially now that Gil was gone. "You know they love you."

"Pissants," she said.

And I knew they'd be taking their chances with their pitchers of Bud Light and their flawed sense of wit and repartee. *Caveat emptor.* She would eat them alive. But they would always come back for more.

Coach B's office was cut into the hillside above the bowl of the football field. I would have said stadium, but that would have been much too grand for what it was. Even so, the office was in the basement of the athletic building, below the basketball, volleyball, and racquetball courts, and the rhythm of the building had much to do with the season and the bouncing of the particular balls that were in play. At the moment, it was quiet except for two elderly faculty members playing crippled-men's racquetball, negotiating each rally like a debate tournament. The echo of the ball hitting the front wall was slack, and I could imagine them needling one another about their lack of prowess, sexual as well as physical.

"So, you didn't chicken out," Coach B said. "I had my doubts."

"I'm here," I said. "Where's the kid?"

"Getting taped."

They were prepping for a full scrimmage that evening, and DDP was expected to play a major role.

"I'm not saying he's indispensable," Coach B said, "but we can't do without him."

But it was so hard to know what was fact and what fiction since the stories had been swirling nonstop since the first announcement of his enrollment. He bench-pressed two-hundred-and-twenty-five pounds thirty-six times. He ran a 4.8 forty. If that weren't enough, he had called the professors of the three classes in which he was enrolled, and they were uniformly impressed by the questions he had asked and the issues he had raised. He wanted to know the first reading assignments so he could be ahead when the term started.

So, when DDP came in, nothing registered with me at first. He was not tall, and while he entered the room with a dancer's stillness, he was as solid as a concrete barrier. He wore gym shorts and a cropped tee shirt, and it was clear that, along with his GED, prison had been good for his strength, if not his conditioning. If his chest was a barrel, his stomach was a washboard, and his undershirt was overmatched. His calves bulged over the white athletic tape that girdled his feet and ankles. He wore glasses, steel-framed as though they'd come from a prison warehouse, lending a vulnerable contrast to his physical presence otherwise.

"Coach?" he said.

"Dee, I want you to meet someone," Coach B said. "An alum and former player. Michael Wayte."

I stuck out my hand, and he took it, but his grip was strangely slack and tentative.

"Welcome to the college and the team," I said.

"Yes, sir," he said. "I'm blessed to be here. Very, very blessed."

"I'm sure the blessing is more on Coach B's end," I said.

"Amen." Coach B put his hands together as if in prayer. "Preach it, brother."

"He saved me," Dee said. "Jesus, not Coach B. Coach is good, but you know."

"He's not that good at all," I said, "He might think he is, but really he's just an insurance salesman."

"Yeah, he's the insurance man," Dee said.

"Thanks," Coach B said. "Thanks for the vote of confidence."

"I don't mean nothing by it," Dee said. "I'm getting an opportunity, and I need to take advantage." Which was when he testified regarding his road-to-Damascus experience, feeling it necessary to apologize for the profanity. Apparently, the Savior was welcome to throw F-bombs around because it was His right, but His servants needed to be a bit more circumspect.

"Jesus loves me," Dee said, "no matter how He do. Or he do," he said, pointing at Coach B.

"Or what you do. Or did. That's what the Bible says," I offered.

"He loves everybody," Dee said, "including me and you. Whether we deserve it or not, know what I mean?"

"That's why they call it grace," I said, but I couldn't help but feel a bit sick to my stomach.

He would play, he said, to bring glory to Him who had saved him. And to the school and the coach that were nurturing him. Then, Dee offered up a prayer for his coach and his team, his new life and his new friends, such as myself, and when he thanked Jesus for choosing *him*—DDP, of all people, convicted car thief and goon—to be His servant, I couldn't help myself from drifting toward a certain bitterness and resentment.

THE CHAPEL AT SIERRA PRESBYTERIAN was distinct in several ways: it was round and conical and minimally lit, its ceiling extending forty feet up into the darkness, and there was no altar *per se*, no front or rear, only a raised dais in the center, which given the darkness had a certain dystopian, apocalyptic end-of-the-world feel, which given the story about Golgotha and our two self-immolating martyrs became all the more dire. I never entered that space without feeling that someone was about to be condemned. Curved pews surrounded the dais while above the pews on the north side, an enormous pipe organ lurked on a balcony, the bequest of some long-forgotten alum. Pipes lined the wall behind the organ, and more pipes were suspended from the center of the conical roof. On the north side a cross had been hung, seemingly an afterthought, so dwarfed was it by the organ that it faced. When I wandered in, still lost and hungover, Emily was kneeling on one of the steps leading to the dais, surrounded by four or five other young women who were nearly indistinguishable from one another and whose hands were on Emily's shoulders and the crown of her head. They were praying *Lord, Lord, oh, bless her, Lord, be gracious to her, Jesus,* and there were tears and snuffles and hiccups, from Emily as well as the cohort surrounding her. *Grant her Thy peace, dear Jesus, bring her into the sanctuary of Your arms, yes, Lord, yes, Lord, oh, yes.* Etc., etc., etc. After several minutes of this,

Emily raised her arms into the air, shrugging off her supporters' hands and began to babble something out of Lewis Carroll. Nonsense of a davening kind.

The better part of wisdom should have encouraged discretion and a quiet backing away, but what did I know, drunkard that I was in that moment?

"Emily," I called. "What do you call that noise? Poetry, prose, or pun?"

The young women turned as one, with Emily at the eye of their reproach.

"An ecstatic moment," one of the young women said. I recognized her as someone who worked the breakfast line each morning, scooping hash browns with a slotted spoon while wearing cellophane gloves, a hairnet, and an accusation of service. "She was meeting God, and then you interrupted."

"Broke the spell, did I?"

"Michael," Emily said, understated as ever, "this is not a good time."

"This whole weekend has been a disaster," I said, "so why should now be any different?"

"I think you should go."

I could have stood there and argued, but I could see that it would do me no good. Instead, I stumbled away into the Sunday darkness, still two hours before dawn. What did it mean, I wondered, that the love of my life was sending me away in favor of the murmuring of others and the unintelligible gibberish coming from her own lips? And, how could she do that when I was still so sore and hungover? I was that self-centered and needy.

For a week she refused to see me; I was going to say she refused to talk to me, but we were so unused to talking that I'm not sure that a refusal of serious conversation would have sounded any different in practice or the abstract. And then, when she consented to see me it was with the condition that we meet in the chapel Saturday night at eleven. Fine, I said, although since we would have our last game of the year that afternoon, I knew I might not be much good for anything that late in the day.

"I'm not trying to be difficult," Emily said. "I just have some difficult things to say."

What could be so hard, I thought, other than the fact you've lost your mind?

The week passed in a blur. I went to classes, but I remember thinking that it was a waste of time, given my own preoccupation. Professors talked, students raised objections, but nothing really registered. And the game that Saturday—our last game of the season and my last game to play, ever—likewise passed without much to remember. We lost, I do remember that, but I couldn't tell you the score or even who we played, so irrelevant had it become. Sleepwalking, going through the motions, dead in my shoes, that's all it was.

And then, that night, back once again in the dim darkness

of the chapel, I woke up when she hit me with it: "I'm going away," she said, "after this term is over."

"Back to the farm? Back to the snow and the wheat stubble?" I said. "No one sticks around this place at Christmas, anyway. I got here three days early one January, and it was like a ghost town with a dining hall." I was babbling, but I couldn't help myself because she was shaking her head and I had no interest in hearing what came next.

"I'm not coming back. I'm withdrawing from school."

"What about Berklee?" I said. "What about your harp?"

"Jesus," she said, with an inward smile, "has other plans for me. I wanted to have fun like everyone else, I wanted to feel my body and enjoy the pleasures that the flesh can provide, but I was playing Jonah all this time, running away from what I knew in my heart to be right. That's what I realized the other night. Here in the chapel. When you came in, remember?"

"When did all this happen?" I said. "I had no idea."

"No, you didn't."

"So, if you're Jonah," I said, beginning to realize my position, and that my position was precarious, "if you're Jonah, I must be the whale. And here I thought I was just football-sized."

"I wouldn't say that," she said, and she touched my cheek with her fingers. "But you have been a bigger distraction than necessary."

THE SCRIMMAGE THAT EVENING was revelatory. Coach B had Dee playing both running back and linebacker, the only two-way player on the team, and the scrimmage was entirely dependent on which side of the ball, he happened to be assigned. When he ran with the ball, he didn't need a hole; he made one, or he carried other players with him. When he tackled the ball carrier from his linebacker position, we heard his backup squeal, as Coach B had promised. Dee sacked the quarterback twice on blitzes, the last time causing a fumble, before Coach B blew the final whistle of the evening. They were not a good team, that much was true, but they had at least one good player, and he would cover a multitude of shortcomings.

"As advertised," I told Coach B later. "You've got something to look forward to. So long as you can keep him healthy. He'll be every other team's target."

And during their first game that fall, such optimism seemed warranted. The skydivers were on target, the weather was hot but clear. A moderate crowd came to the mountains to watch the game on a field that seemed almost like a stadium.

On defense, DDP was credited with fourteen tackles, three for a loss, all of which was impressive in itself, but on offense, he had had quite a day: three hundred and thirty-two yards rushing and five touchdowns. The Patriots won 42-24, and the excitement was guarded but palpable. Dr. Newland shook Coach B's hand, and they made plans to contact all the local sports anchors. "We can sell this," the President said, "and the Board will love it."

Three days later, the planes flew, the towers fell, and nothing was the same and nothing else mattered.

EMILY LEFT IMMEDIATELY after her last final was over. I told her I didn't understand it; she was leaving at the end of the term anyway, why bother sticking around for finals? Did grades matter that much at this late date? But, she said, she was committed to finishing what she started: the term, if not the degree. And, who knew? She might change her mind at some later date, and then, she would have some classes on her transcript.

I waited outside her last final with a cone of roses, hoping one last gesture might affect her decision, but no dice. Her way was clear: she was leaving for San Diego after the new year in order to work with Central American refugees who hoped for asylum while she plotted their salvation. She and her cohort had been meeting together for the past month, supporting one another in their effort to hear God's command for their futures. If I had no clue what she and they were up to, she said, that was because I couldn't see past myself and my own concerns and because I'd never thought to ask.

"This is what Jesus has called me to do," she said. "It's so good to know, finally. You have your football," she said.

She inhaled the fragrance of the flowers, not realizing that the football part of my life was over. Done and done. "You can go on to seminary and debate three-point sermon structure or the best way to enhance the weekly offering. That's just church. I don't need that or a degree or a career, music is everywhere, and boyfriends," she said, looking only a little apologetic amongst the roses, "are a dime a dozen."

That was our last conversation.

She died seven years later in Tegucigalpa, the victim of stray gunfire. I didn't hear about her passing until ten years after the fact, when a note in the alumni bulletin mentioned her by chance, in a thumbnail about another classmate. She was left as an asterisk. Not an alum, after all.

GAMES WERE CANCELED or postponed the weekend after the towers fell, and no one felt their absence in any particular way, with the possible exception of Coach B, who saw the momentum of his game one win slipping away.

"I get it," he said. "We'd look like peckerwoods to play a game this week. All I'm saying is—"

"If you had lost that game, you wouldn't have minded the one-week vacation."

"I'm not saying I wouldn't have, for Christ's sake. And, I'm not saying I would have. Quit putting words in my mouth."

"You think those planes hit the towers and killed all those people just to ruin your life?"

"I'm not saying that," Coach B said. "Goddammit." He sat with his usual glass of terrible wine and watched as Elisa topped him off. "But that's what it feels like."

There was more, he said. DDP had started a weekly prayer group for the football team during two-a-days, but now, ever since the tragedy, that prayer group had been meeting for a couple of hours each day in the room that Dee shared with one of the defensive backs. Players and friends and then more friends and more players came and went, from seven to nine each morning, Dee sat cross-legged on the rug in the center of the small room, saying little out loud, but murmuring throughout. He went to his classes, he dressed out for practice, but at a moment when everyone was preoccupied with the events in New York, Washington, and Pennsylvania, he seemed even more distracted than the rest. He told Coach B that he was waiting for a sign as to what would come next.

"He's skipping breakfast to pray," Coach B grumbled, "he's skipping lunch because he's fasting, and he's skipping dinner because he's abstaining. I mean, it's not that hard to turn down what the dining hall is offering, but I think he's lost ten pounds already. Another week of this, and I'll have a wide receiver, who won't know a damn thing about his position."

"If only he could be transformed into a quarterback who did," I said.

"If only."

I drove to campus the next morning and knocked on his dormitory door at six-forty-five.

He opened the door, wearing gym shorts, his washboard stomach, and his glasses. He looked tired and worn and his mouth was set in the approximation of a scowl, though I suspected the latter was more contrived than real.

"Do you mind?" I said. "It's earlier in the AM than I'm accustomed to."

"Mr. Michael," he said. "What's got you here?"

"The wings of angels, Dee," I said. "We could all use a little intercession here and there."

"God's truth, that is."

I sat down with him on his rug. He folded down on top of his legs, and I imagined that with that body, he was something of a god in study halls and philosophy classes, as well as the football field, but I don't think I was imagining that his chest was already smaller than it was two weeks before.

"It's not my business, but I've heard some concerns," I said. "People are worried about you."

"Sure," he said, "I bet Coach has been talking to you. 'He's not eating, he's not paying attention,' but I'll be ready to go come game day. That's all he cares to know."

"I'll admit it: he's had better moments. Last week, for instance, when you were carrying everyone's water. But that's not to say he doesn't care about what's happening to you."

"Uh, huh. If you say so."

"You're praying every morning?" I said, and when he didn't respond to what was obviously a rhetorical question, I soldiered on. "I mean, it's commendable, of course, especially now when everyone and everything is so unsettled. Having a little comfort in the midst of global uncertainty is no small thing."

"He told me to kneel," Dee said, "so I got down, and I'll stay down until He tells me to get up. And I'll eat when He tells me to eat."

"But you have other things to do," I said. "After all, you're only praying two hours a day, which is quite a lot, I know, don't get me wrong, but that leaves you time for other things as well. And that's smart since we all have to compartmentalize our lives one way or another. 'Render unto Caesar,' he said. Those are his words, not mine. Like you have classes and football, your faith and your friends, your team and your convictions. One thing doesn't necessarily have to intrude on the others, if you know what I mean."

"No?"

"Just because you see the world turning to shit doesn't mean you have to live like a prisoner in an outhouse. You only have to visit every now and again."

"Mr. Michael," Dee said, and he put his hand on my leg and spoke slowly, as though to settle someone off his meds and fading fast, "God bless you, but I'm thinking that's the dumbest thing I ever did hear."

THE GAME ON THE FOLLOWING SATURDAY attracted a larger than normal crowd, in spite of the somber and watchful mood. A color guard brought in the flags, and a troop of Boy Scouts carried the game balls. Our linebackers coach/prison chaplain offered an invocation followed by a moment of silence for the victims of the attacks and those first responders who lost their lives. Bob Pettis, the public address announcer, let the silence linger: a minute, ninety seconds, two minutes. Silence turned into a metallic rumble as spectators nervously began to shuffle their feet on the aluminum bleachers, and then finally, Bob said Thank you and released the crowd from the constraints of their best behavior, and we all applauded. Still, it seemed awful, sacrilegious even, to play such a game at such a time when such horrors had been so recently unleashed. What were we clapping for? No one quite knew the proper tone to adopt, but everyone was willing to try, so eager were we to forget for a moment the planes and smoke and catastrophe that we had witnessed in replay after replay, the worst injury highlights any of us had ever seen.

But the game was still a game, and DDP was still the best player on the field, regardless of his regimen of prayer and fasting. He scored from thirty-six yards on a trap play up the middle, punctuated with an exclamation point when he hurdled a safety at the twelve-yard line. He made eleven tackles before halftime and recovered a fumble after stripping the ball from a wide receiver, who had dared cross his territory between the hashmarks. If the Patriots were trailing the Red Raiders 17-7 at halftime, that was through no lack of Dee's efforts or talent, and if he was a step slower here or weaker there, I'm not sure how many would have known enough to notice. There was a palpable sense among the spectators that somehow, given DDP's presence, fortune would be turned in our favor.

When the teams came out to stretch and warm up before the second half, I wandered back to the locker rooms. Coach B was smoking a cigarette over the trash can in his office while an oscillating fan blew the smoke away.

"I could kill for a real drink," he said. He rubbed his eyes and stared at me hard. "A good bourbon. Or one of those fancy tequilas. They're going to kill us this half, and it would be easier with anesthetic."

"You never know," I said. "Stranger twists and turns have undermined many an expectation."

"Dee's done," he said. "His tank's dry. If we had an honest-to-god medical staff and IV fluids and oxygen, maybe. But we can barely get Gatorade on the fucking sidelines."

"Maybe you need to give him a series off, here and there," I said. "Give him a chance to recover."

"Wouldn't that be nice?"

"What's the worst that could happen?" I said. "Lose the game? That's happening already."

"Thanks for the pep talk," he said and crushed out his

cigarette in the bottom of the trash can. "Maybe you should go visit some hospitals or rest homes. Read obituaries to the elderly and the infirm. Gather some orphans and tell them sad stories."

"It's an option," I said.

Coach B was right: Dee was gassed, but he didn't take him out for a single play. The Patriots stayed within reach—the score was 24-14 at the start of the fourth quarter—but it was becoming increasingly clear, even to the most casual observer, that Dee was wearing down. Red Raider runs up the middle turned into eighteen-yard gains, and Dee's own carries were gaining fewer and fewer yards as the entire Red Raider defense keyed on the one player who mattered. On a third-and-five play early in the fourth quarter, Dee turned the right corner on a sweep. A linebacker hit him high from the left side while a defensive back slammed into his knee on the right, and the devastation was audible at the top of the bleachers. So, too, were Dee's gasps of pain. The trainers and Coach B hustled onto the field, both teams knelt in respect, and the spectators grew as silent as they had for that awkward moment two hours earlier. No one could miss the connection of silence.

"Oh, my god," Dee gasped. "Oh, my Lord, oh, my good Lord."

"There, there," I heard Coach B say while the trainers unfolded their stretcher and a grounds man drove a golf cart onto the grass. "Grit your teeth, son." He patted Dee's shoulder pads the way one might pat the back of a baby.

"Jesus," Dee yelled. "Jesus."

Some halfwit in the stands at the ten-yard line said, loud enough for all to hear in the unnatural quiet: "They shoot horses, don't they?" To which there was a titter of uneasy laughter and nervous disapproval. "I mean, Lord, have mercy, suck it up."

I moved from my seat near the PA announcer's box to where the wiseacre was holding forth. Wearing a Liberty Christian Patriot tee shirt with its Christian flag emblem and the school's cheesy eagle mascot, Mr. Opinion was the stereotype of an all-too familiar cliché: fat, in his fifties, a balding sunburned head, ballooning Bermuda shorts and a flask cradled between his pasty knees.

"You'd think he was dying," he was saying. "Is this a game for sissies, or what?"

The friends sitting next to him laughed politely but then gasped when I said "What?" and punched him hard enough on the side of his mouth that his head turned, and it was only then that I recognized him for who he was, Bobby Thornton, CEO of Chronos Athletic, newly elected Chairman of the Board of Trustees.

So, HERE'S THE LAST THING YOU NEED TO KNOW: money talks. But you knew that already, didn't you? DDP's knee was dislocated and an artery was torn, and while he was lucky that he was able to keep the leg—there was some doubt, initially,

102

that blood flow could be restored—his football-playing days were over. And, because his football-playing days were over, the Patriots' season was effectively over as well. They didn't win another game, and some felt that the season should have been canceled at once for both pragmatic and sentimental reasons. For Dee. For 9/11. For the fact that Dee was the only reason the team was viable. Coach B was fired the moment the final whistle of the final game blew, and the program was put on hiatus once again, not to return until seven years later, not until Bobby Thornton had consolidated his allies within the Board. He had the money, and he had the leverage of his position, no matter if the rest of the world was teetering on financial collapse. He could tempt players and buy coaches, fund facilities and dictate the overall direction of the program, and he said it was the duty of the college to present itself to the world as a model of excellence. He would show the unwashed that the football team of a Christian college was not manned by pussies or losers, crybabies or those with a bad investment strategy.

Given Bobby Thornton's upper incisor that had to be replaced with an implant, I was banned from attending the final games of the program's second incarnation, and I was certainly not invited to attend the games of the third.

I couldn't have cared less. It reminded me of nothing more than that spring twenty-five years earlier when I graduated. Emily was gone, my last classes seemed stupid and beside the point, and when I thought about applying for seminary, my mouth went dry and my throat scratchy. Emily's life among the poor and downtrodden seemed much more real than any church fantasy I could conjure. God didn't have a thing to say to me. One Friday afternoon I drove from campus, intending to visit my parents in Fresno, and although I'd driven past O'Malley's many, many times before, this was the first time I had really seen it. Maybe that was due to the For-Sale sign in the ditch grass by the highway. Maybe that was due to self-hatred. You decide. The long and the short of it was that I intended to stand in front of an altar, but I ended up standing behind a bar.

Which is where Coach B came to see me on his drive out of town. It was early December, and a chilly mist was drifting in the air. The Mercury was packed to its sagging headliner, and the magnetic insurance placard had once again found its place on his door.

I had pulled out the bottle of my cheapest red when I saw his car crunching into our gravel lot, but he shook his head when he saw it. "Give me a double of that Wild Turkey."

"I've got better."

He shook his head again. "That'll do. Make it a triple, and an argument won't be our last conversation."

He was heading back to Nevada: whole life and disability policies and how many cold calls he could stomach on a slow morning before the lure of the casinos beckoned. He never wanted to see a football or shoulder pads again. Or church people, for that matter. Like that lying sack of shit, Bobby Thornton, who had promised him the world but gave him his termination notice instead. The sooner he could get away from those fuckers, the better he'd like it. Lying sons of bitches. Give me your honest huckster, he said. At least you know what to expect.

He had visited Dee in the hospital for the month that he was there, and at least once a week he dropped by Dee's grandmother's house in Fresno to check on the progress of his rehab. He was still in a cast and on crutches and would be for some time to come, so there wasn't much to report.

"He is such a good kid, no matter what he did once upon a time," Coach B said. "I don't know how he's not depressed. I'm depressed every time I look at his leg. It's still twice the size of his other one. Do you know," he said, "that the college's insurance tried to get out of paying the kid's medical bills? They'll never let him come back to school, that much is sure."

In addition to being a lying sack of shit, Bobby Thornton was doing everything he could to distance the college from DDP's past, his brief tenure at the college, and the possibility of any future he might have had there since you don't build a reputation on a foundation of hoodlums or insurance claims.

From the animal sanctuary half-a-mile up the highway came the evening noises of the tigers in their enclosure.

"Fuckers," Coach B repeated. "Grade-A, sanctimonious fuckers. I have half a mind to open the tiger pens and point them in the right direction."

I had gone to see Dee in the hospital once or twice myself, but unlike Coach B, I had not come away quite so inspired.

"Jesus has stopped cursing. When I hear Him now," Dee said, "He is much kinder and gentler. He is a cooing dove."

I refrained from providing some possible explanations and let him talk. I know I can be something of a know-it-all and a smart-aleck. After all, he was the one in a hospital bed with his leg in traction and still in doubt and lines running in and out of his arms and legs. If his Jesus now wanted to play nice, that seemed only fair, given what Dee had gone through. But then he said something that surprised me:

"He says I will be of use to Him, and I don't have to play football no more."

Once again, Jesus had chosen someone else, and it hurt to be overlooked, but maybe it didn't hurt as much as the first time. Then I realized what he had said as opposed to what I had heard.

"You didn't like playing?" I asked. I was genuinely surprised since, of anyone I'd ever known, he seemed born to run and collide with others. And given the mediocre stage that was Patriot football, he would have been a superstar if he could have lasted.

He closed his eyes. "In moments," he said. "I liked it in moments. But they were over so fast."

That is true enough, I thought, about so many things.

"So, Mr. Michael, I heard that you were going to be a preacher man before you bought the bar. Am I right?"

"For a moment, I was," I said, "A moment at the end of a long story, but maybe now you've got time to hear it."

[iv]

Holiday for One

(Susan Book, 1992)

Two tour buses from a retirement village in Redding had arrived the night before, and the dining room of the hotel was crowded to the doors. Senior citizens—most of them wearing the Festival's purple *WILL POWER!* tee shirts—filled the available tables, and a ragged line of the aged and infirm spilled into the hotel lobby.

Susan sighed, then quickly took a place in line before another geriatric foursome could hijack the spot in front of her.

"Two," she said to the hostess half an hour later. Jesus had rewarded her patience. Sure. "My husband's upstairs. Dr. Walter Book," she added. "Sierra Presbyterian College," as though that might mean something, although clearly it didn't.

She was seated at a small table near the waitress's station, inspected by a booth full of slack-armed women wearing muumuus. They were dying, she could tell, to engage her, a younger person, in conversation. She opened her menu for cover and waited for Walter, the exalted one, to appear.

The dining room buzzed with the clatter and crockery of breakfast: the phone on the hostess's stand rang constantly; every time the door to the kitchen opened, Susan heard cooks swearing at the busboys and dishwashers. The waitresses, high school girls wearing ill-fitting Elizabethan costumes which were intended to make them look like buxom British barmaids, unloaded trays of eggs and bacon and English muffins on every table, and Susan watched jealously as the senior citizens at the booth across the aisle wolfed down their food. Walter could be such an infant sometimes. He was four years younger, but so many more years less mature. She knew so much more, and she suffered twice as much. She'd probably have her breakfast ordered and eaten by the time he'd be through pouting, and then he'd whine about how she hadn't waited. Though really, it would be more like him to let her wait in line for half an hour, letting her suffer the dining room alone, so that he could slip in just as the waitress was ready to take their order. When you were married, you learned to make accommodations, and when you'd been married for five years, Susan thought, you learned to overlook certain inequities, and it would be up to *her* to placate *him*. There was the Seven-Year Itch. But, five? Like last night. They had driven eight hours north to Oregon and the Shakespeare Festival, seen a disagreeable performance of *The Merchant of Venice*, and now Walter was upstairs, the morning after their anniversary, petulant, complaining of migraine, sulking, while Susan, after a horrid night without sleep, was holding down a spot for him at breakfast. You learned to make sacrifices; it was a career decision. More than kin, as the saying went, and less than kind.

"Whattya have?"

One of the high school waitresses, a wasted little cretin with purple hair and a dirndl top, stood in front of her. Out of the corner of her eye, Susan saw The Couple again.

"Who are they?" Susan asked, pointing at their table in the center of the room.

The waitress shrugged, impatiently popping her gum, and her costume, which bagged both in the front and the back, seemed to move of its own volition. "You want the hotel breakfast or not?"

"Yes, fine," Susan said, "and a Bloody Mary." Oh, what was the matter with her? She had wanted to have French toast and strawberries and Canadian bacon instead, and she shouldn't be drinking, not so soon in the day, not so Walter could see and give her that look of disappointment, but she didn't remember that until after she had spoken and the girl had stumped away to the kitchen.

The man and the woman, her Couple, were sitting at the table directly underneath the dining room's huge chandelier, the one element of décor that dated back to the hotel's heyday in the twenties. They seemed aware of the fact that all heads had turned when they entered the room, but they weren't uncomfortable with the attention. Amused, rather. Susan thought that the man looked quite a bit like a certain rock star, and the woman like the model whom the rock star had recently married. The man was fiddling with a camera, trying to hold it steady beneath the center of the chandelier for a shot which Susan would have called artsyfartsy if Walter had tried it; for a rock star, it seemed rather touching and innocent. Naïve.

The rock star had taken three pictures. Now, he was actually lying on the table, and the model was holding his head in her hands, curling his too-long hair around the index finger of her right hand. Then, a wall of green, widewale corduroy blocked her view, as Walter stood between herself and The Couple.

"Quit staring."

"I wasn't." She shook her head, as if trying to clear from her eyes some vision.

"You were. You're doing it again, as a matter of fact."

She closed her eyes, attempting by force of will to alter her expression. Without looking further, she knew, simply by that swathe of green and the tone of his voice, what Walter was wearing: his homeless-teacher-on-holiday costume—the red cotton turtleneck that highlighted the flaccid tire around his middle; the green corduroy trousers that showed wear only in the seat; the Birkenstock sandals which made him talk with the pretensions of a liberal intellectual, albeit a fussy Christian type of the subset, though she knew for a fact that he'd voted for Reagan twice, Bush once, and would do so again in the fall, and he listened to Limbaugh on the sly any chance he got. The flush of the hypocrisy made her cross her own pair of Birkenstocks underneath her chair, making her wish that this morning of all mornings she had worn her one good pair of pumps and a nice dress instead of bolting downstairs with a scarf over her unwashed hair and her own set of falsely advertised feet.

"Sit down," she whispered. The four witnesses across the aisle were taking in the whole encounter. "Please. Don't make a scene."

She smoothed her napkin on her lap, busying herself by examining texture and weave, anything to keep from staring at other people.

"I already ordered," she murmured, "I had no way of knowing when or even if you were coming down."

Walter's green trousers moved to the other side of the table, revealing the rock star at work on a steak; the model toyed with a softboiled egg and read a newspaper. Susan's high school cretin smiled as she poured The Couple's coffee, and Susan wondered how they'd gotten their food so quickly.

"It's an invasion of privacy," Walter was saying in an aggrieved, injured tone—he'd been talking all this time, not letting up, lecturing, "as bad as eavesdropping."

"I wanted French toast, but I ordered the usual breakfast," she said, hoping to stop the tirade. "One Bloody Mary," she said in response to his look. "Only one. I was worried about you," she added, a guilty postscript.

WHEN SHE WAS THIRTY-FOUR YEARS OLD, her only worry had been that she would be alone forever. She had grown up in the flat farmland south of Fresno, the youngest of eight children and her father's favorite object of sarcasm and verbal abuse. She was stupid and airheaded because she was so often alone with her thoughts, and the sight of her staring into space or with her nose in a book infuriated him. They lived in a sprawling six-bedroom house in the middle of eighty acres, but her father was no farmer. He sold tractor parts and diesel equipment out of a shop in Hanford, and the house had once belonged to the farmer, Dale Davison, who had owned the land. Each time his wife had another child, he had added another bedroom, and the house extended in all directions with crazy ells and doorways hidden within closets. But when Mr. Davison turned seventy, he had sold the acreage to an international conglomerate and the house to Susan's father since none of his children had any interest in farming. All day long in the long hot summers, machinery worked through the cotton fields that surrounded the house, and cotton dust and defoliant rose into the air; in the winters, they were locked within the white nothingness of fog, more cotton, and Susan had hated every minute of it. Hated the crop, hated her father, hated the feeling she had of being trapped inside a field of negative space. She had vowed that nothing would keep her there once she was finished with high school, and at the age of twelve she had written this bargain between herself and God in her confirmation Bible: if I get out, and I make something of myself, please, dear Jesus, help me be important and famous and loved.

And she seemed to be making good on her part of the bargain: her high school grades and SAT scores were good enough to earn a patchwork quilt of scholarships, enough to get her from the floor of the San Joaquin Valley to the mountains of Sierra Presbyterian College. She studied Business because it seemed practical and useful, and graduated *magna cum laude*, but in 1973, few businesses were hiring women, no matter how proficient they might be, and she had no time to waste, waiting on God to fulfill His end of the bargain. Her fallback position, in order not to move back to the house in Hanford, was to become the interim secretary of the Humanities Department while that beautiful dumb bunny, Julie Horst, was away on maternity leave. But then, Julie—a dim bulb if ever there was one—couldn't stand the thought of leaving her baby in the care of others, and Susan's temporary position became permanent, even as she vowed to keep looking for jobs that were more in keeping with her talents and skills.

That was so long ago. When she was in her early-twenties. By the time she was in her mid-thirties, her original dreams seemed like fantasies, unreachable and unrealistic, the province of others. She was alone, working at her isolated college in the mountains, and although God was constantly in the air, He was evidently not interested in Susan Morrison's plight. She was toying with the idea of getting a cat, except that she was afraid of the message that would send to herself and others. She sat behind a typewriter and a three-line telephone, feeling her rear end broadening by the minute, her skin growing sallow under the fluorescent lights, while students and faculty members bustled in and out to see her boss, the Dean, each with a sense of his or her own importance. *What did they know? She had once been one of them, and now look...*

And then, in the fall of 1986, a new faculty hire came into the office, Dr. Walter Book, a bit affected but sure of himself: him with his silk shirts and hand-tied bow ties and his dashing little British racing cap. A little pudgy and soft around the middle, but with a Puckish sense of humor and a twisted little smile that Susan could not quite categorize. Sweet, sardonic, superior—what was it? He was four years younger than Susan, a fact that she did not bring to his attention, and soon enough and all too quickly, he was asking her to coffee, then to dinner, and then to a shared life as husband-and-wife. Oh, how happy she was! And how important she felt as Mrs. Dr. Walter Book. Jesus had finally relented. They were married in the Sierra Presbyterian chapel, officiated by the college chaplain, Reverend Dr. Felton Richards, whom Susan did not altogether trust for reasons she didn't entirely understand but whose homily was better than she could have hoped. "Equality," Dr. Richards had intoned, "is the bedrock of any relationship and the most important ingredient for two people to live together companionably. Without it, there is only resentment."

Hear, hear.

If only she could say that now. For while her initial joy lasted through the first year of their marriage, she was growing increasingly disenchanted and distraught. Her husband, she realized, was a soft man running to fat in expensive clothes and affectation, a flawed scholar, and an over-inflated ego, one who seemed not to need any sort of physical affection, at least not from her, and while he ascended in rank and self-importance at the college, she had quit her low-level and worse-paying job, only to find that there was little if anything for her to do, and nothing to look forward to except a drink before dinner, wine with the meal, and a brandy before bed. After their wedding, she had moved her few things from her studio apartment into the tiny little gatehouse on the college grounds that Walter had snared upon his first arrival, and she seemed to exist only as a guest in someone else's house. And she watched the unending parade of younger and younger students, especially the women, who went past the gatehouse, becoming fairer and fresher with each passing year while her hair grew limp, her body sagged, and she grew tired. Tired and unappreciated. The years were a signal of what she should be worried about: abandonment by her bilious caricature of a husband in favor of the newer model. How fair, how equitable was that? And, what kind of joke was Jesus playing? Worries upon worries upon worries. *Dear Jesus.*

AND YET LAST NIGHT she had worried only whether she would be able to get through dinner without slapping her fat fraud of a husband. First there had been the wine, which he had declared to be vinegar. He had sent it back in a voice loud enough for the manager to come scurrying. Then it had been the soup.

"How good it is," she had exclaimed—as much to make up for the embarrassment about the wine as for the pleasure of the soup itself. She was always willing to be agreeable, more than willing to make an effort, to get along. She wondered aloud what could be in it to make such a taste.

"Allspice, turmeric, fresh scallions, a half clove—no more—of garlic," he had said, the spoon hardly pausing in its movement from bowl to mouth to bowl again. It wasn't the items he had mentioned, which were so obviously wrong, but the tone of his reply, the pompous, authoritative instructor of the ignorant, a tone which could only be excused on the grounds of too many classrooms, the constant delivery of easily digested "truths" when there was, in fact, no truth, no certainty.

Next had come the play itself. Walter had long loved *The Merchant of Venice*; it confirmed his professor's faith in literature to transcend traditional, ingrained prejudice: Shylock a model of flawed moral humanity rather than Jewish villainy. But last night, Shylock had struck his bargains in tones more suited to a Brooklyn fruit peddler who did a little loan sharking on the side rather than a figure of tragic determinism.

"Three thousand ducats," Shylock had mused through a nose worthy of Cyrano. He fingered his beard, jingled his purse, played with every caricature and cliché of the Jewish Moneybags. Walter sat beside her, his affected liberalism and his Christian humanism turned to stone, while she stared at the stage with a sudden, unpleasant distrust of everything Walter had told her over the years. The play was an ethnic joke after all. Bassanio, Antonio, and Portia had the last laugh while the Jew, losing both money and daughter, suffered the pleasure of coerced salvation. Susan felt betrayed. By Shakespeare. By Walter and his deluded, professorial insistence that tried to force the world into a moral order. By God, goddammit, once again. This was the best His creation could do?

In the hotel bar afterwards, Walter had gotten into an argument with the stage manager who sullenly kept repeating, "Shakespeare is Shakespeare. He's a product of his time and place, you know." Walter, his bow-tie threatening to come undone, had kept saying that the performance had been a "theatrical perversion" even as he kept placing his hand on the other man's forearm in a gesture that seemed more intimate than argumentative.

It was also at the hotel bar that Susan had first seen The Couple. Sitting in a corner, halfhidden behind a potted palm tree, the man and woman were talking to each other, their heads inclined toward one another on graceful necks. At first, she thought they were people she had once known. Such familiar faces. But they were too young to be acquaintances from school. Then, Susan thought of the rock star and the rock star's new wife, their faces having recently appeared on the covers of national news magazines and the fan magazines at the grocery check-out counter The magazines she bought surreptitiously and hid from her husband. The articles and photographs that gave her a glimpse into another, more sexualized, more brightly imagined life. She devoured the rock star's curling hair, sunglasses, the black tee shirt with the too-short sleeves. His model wife's slim arms, a thin gold chain that she turned and turned and turned around one wrist. In the flesh, their appearance seemed oddly unreal without the border of a television screen or a page as a frame and yet so hyper-actual—confirming their youth, their promise, their romantic heat, their status as representatives of a society's lusts—that they had a greater claim to existence than anyone else in the room. The light of the divine shone about them.

She had never been a follower of popular fashions or trends, even less so of popular music, noise that devoted itself to teenage angst and hormones, and yet she found herself strangely stirred by this...this boy and girl. As if touching them would be a translation of herself. An entrance into a world more rarefied, where one could see the object that casts the shadow.

The Couple looked up at her as she approached so that she heard part of what the model was telling her husband, "...I could have killed the little...."

"I know," Susan started to say, thrilling to the fear that she couldn't possibly be right. *What could she possibly know about rock stars or models?* She was making an utter ass of herself, but she pressed on regardless.

The rock star was about to offer her a drink and a chair. She was sure of it. Yes.

"You're," Susan blurted out. If she could just say it, then it would be true. "You're—"

"Lord God Almighty," Walter had shout-whispered into her ear, spinning her around and away. The stage manager had gone, the bar was nearly empty, and Walter's bow-tie now lay flat atop his man boobs. *Where had the time gone?* "Quit bothering those poor kids, you look like you're in a trance or something."

"Shakespeare sucks," Susan said. Searching, searching. "He's not god. You fat, effeminate tub of goo," she finished lamely.

Pressing one hand to his forehead as if he'd been shot, he had turned on one heel, walked to the elevator and gone to bed in his clothes. Susan spent their anniversary night alone. First in the bar, where she downed three shots of Glenfiddich in quick succession, and then in the bathtub of their room, waking with muscle cramps in both shoulders to go along with the vise that gripped her temples and the feeling that she would be hunchbacked and blind for the rest of her days. Walter had talked gibberish in his sleep all night, and she had fled the room without taking a bath though she had spent hours there.

"I DIDN'T MEAN TO WORRY YOU," Walter now said, and though he was just across the table from her, his voice was truly jumbled, indistinct: blue sound. "I went to bed with one headache and I woke up with another one."

"Are you any better?" For an instant she had considered telling him that it was over, *finito*, they were history. It didn't have to be this way. No more. But he looked so miserable, the circles underneath his eyes were so bruised, that all she had the heart to say was, "are you any better?" and to pat his hand gently as if she were his mother.

"I never heard you come in," he said sheepishly. He was holding his head at a funny angle and she could see what kind of effort this was causing him.

"Oh," she kept patting his hand, "it's all right."

Walter nodded, still with his head tilted in that funny way. Just to the right of Walter's left shoulder the four women in the booth watched them with the studied indifference of spies; to the left the rock star held up one breakfast sausage then stuffed it into one nostril so that the model nearly choked on her coffee, and Susan also started to laugh.

"What's so funny?" Walter said.

"Nothing," Susan had to remember not to look in The Couple's direction, "I was just thinking about how silly the whole thing was. Shakespeare. It was a bad night."

"Well," Walter said. "I think I better go upstairs, lie down."

"Yes." *Pat, pat, pat.* Still with that smile tacked to her face. "You'll feel better," she said as he rose from the table. "It'll do us both good."

The rock star and the model ate their breakfasts quickly, and they were almost finished with their meal by the time Susan's sulky waitress thumped breakfast and Bloody Mary in front of her. The eggs were cold and the toast was rubbery. Her drink seemed to be lacking the one necessary ingredient. Susan imagined her plate sitting underneath an unplugged warming light while senior citizens and rock stars were served ahead of her. The model had taken the last sip of her coffee and the rock star was standing up, putting on a leather jacket over his tee shirt. They walked out, right by Susan's table, the rock star's hand resting lightly on, patting his wife's model backside, a gesture so intimate in its public honesty that she couldn't help but feel his fingers through her chair. She couldn't imagine why there weren't hordes of fans pestering the poor couple for their autographs and pictures. She never would have imagined their effect on her. When they walked by her table, Susan looked at her food, the wilted stalk of celery in her glass, but distinctly heard the rock star say, "Hey, lady." She was sure. By the time she looked up they were at the door talking with the hostess, their backs to her, casting their own light.

The old women at the booth were staring at her as if they were going to rate her performance, each of the women with her sagging arms crossed, forearm over forearm across their massive selves, the picture of lives lived in their observation of others. Susan watched them watch her. They were watching her chew, watching her sip her drink with distaste, their jaws moving in time to her own.

"Excuse me," Susan said.

She ran to the hostess's stand, but they were gone.

"Do you know who they are?" she practically shouted to the hostess.

"No." The hostess smiled. A pretty girl, she looked as though she enjoyed her job of saying hello to people. "They're not who you think," she said. "They just told me it happens a lot. People make mistakes all the time."

"But I'm sure," Susan began.

Then, the high school waitress grabbed Susan by the arm, holding her upper arm so hard that it hurt.

"You forgot to sign your ticket," the waitress hissed. S-s-s-ign. "Everyone on the tour has to sign a ticket. They told you that at the door, but you senile old biddies are the same. Boozers and crazies. You're the fourth one who's tried to stiff me."

"I'm not on the tour," Susan whispered.

"Then you gotta pay," the waitress screamed.

"My husband and I have room 421, and the breakfast is included." After such a terrible night, this couldn't be happening. *Jesus, preserve me from the wicked and the vile.* "I'll pay the drink with the room."

"Then I gotta see your key," the waitress said.

"It's our anniversary," Susan said, "and my husband's in the room."

"Your key," said the waitress.

"But," Susan began, "I—"

The light outside the windows seemed to blur, the buildings across the street wavered and rippled. Why, again, was she here?

"There, there," the hostess said, "there's no need to cry."

Susan put her hands to her head, finding the scarf and her greasy hair, and she thought that she had never felt quite so old or lost or forsaken before.

"Can't you see," the hostess said. She was addressing the hollow-chested girl, who worked her gum viciously. "Can't you see what you've done?"

[v]

Equivocation

(Joshua Bowen, 1996 / 1998)

HIS PARENTS HAD BEEN MISSIONARIES in central Thailand
since the early 1980s, and although he had been born
in Oakland, Joshua Bowen knew the river plains of central
Thailand better than he knew any part of the geography of
the United States. His grandparents lived in Wisconsin, and
when he was ten, he had stayed with them on their farm outside Madison while his parents took their first study leave in
southern California, but he didn't remember anything except
rolling green hills and cows, slabs of roast beef and pitchers of
milk. Little League baseball that he alternately dreaded and
loved. He was ten; what did he know? The ball hurt when he
was hit by it, the humiliation of a strike out was profound, and
the dream of success never abated. But, when the year was
over, he was gone again; home was something entirely other.
Then in his sophomore year of high school, his parents needed

to take another leave. He could have gotten a learner's permit and license that year and become a true-to-life American male, but by this time his grandparents had sold the farm and moved into an assisted living high-rise, so Joshua lived with his aunt and uncle and his cousin, Henry, in Portland, Oregon; Henry's family made do with bicycles, their monthly passes on Tri-Met, and a thirty-year-old Datsun that rarely ran; they weren't about to upgrade just so he could get a license when there was no money for insurance anyway. Meanwhile his parents went from church to church and from fellowship hall to Sunday School classroom, up and down I-5, in order to share their church-building experiences among the Thai. They had nine months with which to rebuild the funding base they needed for the expenses of their missionary service; their only currency was the story they had to tell and their ability to make others feel as though they were part of the mission and the work, since without the pledges of congregations and individual parishioners, they could not stay out in the field.

Joshua often fantasized about what that would be like, to live somewhere in the United States while his parents went to work doing normal jobs. Permanently, rather than a year here, a year there. His father had once been a hydraulics engineer, his mother an elementary school teacher. They could do those jobs again, rather than lobbying for charity every few years, but they were more interested in church planting strategies in southeast Asia and the introduction of water treatment facilities in remote villages than they were interested in a paycheck with federal withholding and Medicare deduction, a pension plan and a wise investment strategy. They had never gotten the message, that if greed wasn't good, a little self-interest had its place.

His mother had been his teacher until that last leave in Portland, when he went to Grant High School with Henry. The academic work at Grant was easy and repetitive, material that he had covered with his mother some time ago, but his year was difficult: he did not make friends easily, his clothes were all wrong, and while everyone spoke English, it seemed to be a language of shared references, few of which he understood. Jokes were either inscrutable or about him. Due to the vagaries of district boundaries, the student body consisted of a minority underclass and an affluent white upper class, and he fit into neither. And while Joshua had hoped that Henry might be a kind of older brother, he didn't make anything easier. A year older and a basketball player with his own set of teammates and friends and friends-of-friends, he tolerated his younger cousin with a resignation that bordered on condescension if not outright hostility. He had no desire to include his socially inexperienced cousin in any of his activities, no matter how often his parents encouraged it. But one Friday night, while Joshua's aunt and uncle were attending a neighborhood meeting of *Earth First!*, Henry took him to a party at Mt. Tabor. Henry's teammates were there, and Joshua drank red cup after red cup of beer and shots of vodka as they were offered and smoked each joint as it was passed, thinking that, at last, he was enjoying something of normal, everyday American life. He didn't remember the end of the party, but he did see the Polaroids that his cousin showed him the next morning, of him naked with his eyes closed, with his underwear (*tightie-whities!*) on his head like a do-rag. A red-headed girl that Joshua did not remember being at the party was sitting next to him and holding his limp, unimpressive cock in one hand. She was smiling for the camera, as though she and her left hand were unacquainted with each other. In one picture, she was looking cross-eyed; in another she had her red hair over her face. In a third, she had removed her own top, revealing small pink-tipped breasts. In all four pictures, she was holding his dick in such a way that it looked like one of those translucent sea creatures that lives only in the deepest water, never to see the refraction of daylight.

"Don't ever say I don't take you anywhere, that you don't meet anyone," Henry said, and pocketed the photographs. "And don't ever say anything about anything."

Joshua understood without needing to be told. The Polaroids would remain locked away in Henry's drawer, so long as Joshua kept himself to himself; he would not ask to be included in anything Henry did, and he wouldn't say a word about the party, the pictures, the alcohol, or the weed. Or, the girl he'd never met. As if he would say anything: he was more afraid of his parents finding out about the party than he was about anyone else seeing the pictures. His parents would be disappointed. They would have to have a talk, and the talk would take hours. Were his actions pleasing to the Lord? Did he consider a life of waste and excess, dissipation and prurience consistent with a life of purity? His parents had never spanked him as a child, but he often thought a beating might be preferable to the logical, step-by-step argument of his father's lectures or the emotional knife of his mother's disappointed sighs.

He survived his year in Portland by learning to become anonymous at school. He memorized the bus schedule and lived in the Hawthorne Powell's during his after-school hours. He drank coffee, wore only the clothes in his suitcase that were black, and affected an enigmatic and aloof persona; after all, he had looked into the middle-class life which his Evangelical parents adopted even if they didn't have the cash or credentials, and he had seen the emptiness and the contradictions contained therein. He read the novels least likely to garner his parents' approval if they had known. *A Sport and a Pastime. Couples. The Unbearable Lightness of Being. Sabbath's Theater.* He met a girl at Powell's who wore overalls and plaid shirts. She was on independent study and smoked clove cigarettes and read books by French authors, and one afternoon in her parents' basement, when she was supposed to be doing her math homework, they kissed and let their tongues slide around each other like eels inside each other's mouth. She let him unhook her straps and unbutton her Pendleton, but refused further access, even as she pressed the heel of her hand against his groin until he could hold out no longer, gasping with relief and embarrassment.

"What are you, a sadist?" Joshua said, panting a little in the aftermath. "A cock-tease?"

"It's my body," Chloe said, "and I'll do what I want with it. I don't want complications, and I don't need you telling me what to do."

"We could use something," Joshua said, to which Chloe clicked her tongue, *tsk!*, and refused to say anything further.

They made it an unspoken habit to meet one another on Tuesday and Thursday afternoons and retreat to her basement, where they grappled in tongue-locked silence, and Joshua learned to carry something absorbent that he could keep inside his underwear to minimize the amount of laundry he would have to do later in secret.

Toward the end of May, when the school year was nearly over and Joshua and his parents would be returning to Thailand, he told Chloe that he loved her, he would miss her, and that he would write her long letters each day until he could find a way to return, and in response, she laughed so loudly that he could see the silver fillings in her molars.

"You're such a poser," she said. "I knew you were going to be leaving. Why do you think I invited you down here? You think I want to do this forever? With you?"

"Of course not," he said. "I was kidding, I wanted to see how you would react. It's not like we're married or anything."

He managed to convince her, or at least she pretended to believe him for the sake of harmony and further kissing. They resumed their usual wrestling, above the waist for him, below for her, and ended with the ritual of his inevitable embarrassment because that seemed to be the thing that brought her the most pleasure, her control over him while keeping her distance. Being the cause of his humiliation with his jeans as a barrier. But later, as he walked home with his soiled handkerchief now in his back pocket, he touched the silver ring in his front pocket and thought with no small measure of relief, that waiting had been the right thing to do after all.

He spent the next two years in Manila at an all-boys junior high and high school. The school was operated by the missionary society in the belief that adolescent males were possessed of poor or no judgment, which could only become a distraction to their church-planting parents, and thus they needed to be in the care of trained and objective professionals.

Before Joshua left Portland, Henry had pulled him aside and handed him three of the four Polaroids.

"Keep 'em as souvenirs," he said. "Mementos from your year in the States. Good times had by all..." He let his voice trail off. "I'd give you all four, but you know. I'm keeping this one," he said, showing him the one in which the girl was topless. "You never know when you're going to need a little leverage."

He couldn't help but stare at the snapshots. The girl and the picture of her detachment from him, even while touching him in such an intimate way.

Manila was predictably awful but easier than Portland to navigate, especially if he could forget those moments of stateside humiliation. The Polaroids at the bottom of his footlocker, the memory of those furtive moments doing his clandestine laundry, the ring that he kept in the pencil drawer of his desk as a reminder better left forgotten. Each of the other eighty-five boys was a missionary kid, whose parents were somewhere in Asia, and no one had a monopoly on experience, with the possible exception of those boys, like Joshua, who had spent some time in the States unsupervised in secular surroundings.

Anthony Soderstrom recounted in graphic and luridly fictitious detail his numerous bouts of intercourse with the young women of Houston: who liked what, when, and where, for how long and how many times, and Wilt Comstock shared his stories of sex and drugs and hip-hop in Philadelphia. Joshua limited his participation to nodding sagely while saying nothing of the party at Mt. Tabor, the Polaroids, or Chloe's basement lair.

In the middle of his senior year, Joshua's mother sent him the Liberty Christian application form, which had already been filled out. All he had to do was sign it and put it in the mail. The application also included an essay in response to the question, "What experience has been your most important inspiration for faith?" He had, apparently, written about his love for the Christian church in Thailand, the importance of the first translation into Thai of the New Testament in 1843, and his experience of handing out Thai Bibles on a street corner in Lopburi when he was twelve. He had not realized how knowledgeable, fervent, or pedantic he could sound. Or like his mother. It was a revelation to know that the afternoons in question had been such a glorious success and that he had been so bathed in the warm waters of faith and spiritual vindication. He couldn't remember a specific day, there were so many of them when he and his mother had stood on street corners with their stacks of Bibles that no one wanted. What he remembered in general was the heat and humidity, and the way his shirt stuck to his back and armpits, as well as his own emotional discomfort, given the lack of interest shown by most of the Thai who ignored the Bibles on offer and waved their hands dismissively as they walked by. Their look of distaste.

He signed the application, but he inserted his own essay instead, one about *The Power and the Glory*, a novel which he had begun but never finished. In his essay he copied whole sections of the jacket copy and the analysis section of the Cliffs Notes. At the end, he wrote, "I have learned through reading Greene's novel that, although belief in an omnipotent and omniscient God is the core of most Christians' faith, the recognition and understanding of one's humanity, flawed though it may be, is the first step toward honesty and an authentic self." He waited for the inevitable discovery. Surely someone would take offense at his conclusion, and if not, then someone would certainly, surely, spot the plagiarism. He waited. And waited. But no negative consequences were forthcoming.

He was admitted without condition as a member of the class of 2002 and welcomed to the Patriot family. Glory be to God in the Highest.

WHEN HE WAS EIGHT YEARS OLD, Joshua was baptized by his father in the reservoir near the Pasak Chonlasit Dam. His mother had instructed him in how to pinch his nose with one hand and hold his father's arm with the other.

"Don't worry," she had said. "He will cradle your head, and then his other hand will cover your hand holding your nose and push your head into the water. That's the wrist you grab."

She demonstrated how his father would hold him. "Don't worry," she said again, a repetition which suggested that worry might really be worth considering. "It will only be for a moment, and then you'll come up from the water and into the light and you will be born again in Jesus."

She had spoken so softly and with such earnestness that Joshua could only believe that he would not recognize himself once he rose from the water. That he would be so entirely different. Would he have new powers granted to him by faith? Would he hear God's voice in the way that his parents did? They spent hours in prayer, with their eyes closed and their palms open, waiting for the Lord to speak and grant them direction, and they never failed to hear His words.

He would become a prayer warrior like his parents, and he would become a missionary, and he would bring Jesus to those who lived out their lives in ignorance and superstition. But then, when the time came, he was led by his mother and father and seven other new disciples, each in a crisp white robe worn specially over bathing suits for this occasion, and he watched as his father immersed the others into the waters of rebirth, and then it was his turn, and his father pushed him down and down and down, into the murky water of the reservoir, and despite his mother's assurances, he *was* afraid that this moment was lasting much too long, that his father was pushing him down in order to drown him for real and not just symbolically, and in that moment, he thought that maybe, like Isaac, he was being sacrificed for the benefit of God's work, a terrible cost, but one his parents would be all too willing to bear in order to be obedient, and maybe, just maybe, this time God would intervene a second too late if He intervened at all. But, no. He came up, the water parted from his eyes, he spluttered and coughed and blew water from his nose, while his parents and his fellow believers laughed and clapped their hands, and he waited for his special powers to become evident.

The sky was blue, the water brownish green. His parents were smiling and well-meaning. His fellow believers received him with hugs and well-wishes in Thai and in English. And then they ate a potluck meal together, and one after another, the new believers, Joshua included, offered up spontaneous prayers for the health and well-being of the Thai church. But that night when he went to bed, his special powers were not yet evident, and nothing had changed except he had gotten wet, frightened, and then relieved.

Two years later, he had been resettled in Wisconsin for his parents' sabbatical, and he spoke with them once a week by phone. He played baseball while his parents prayed and studied and raised money for their continued work in the vineyard of the Lord. While playing baseball, he learned that God seemed indifferent to his failures and humiliations at the plate or in the field. If God was a jealous God, He was also selfish and only willing to address His own concerns. Joshua could pray about the best way to spread the gospel—among the Thai or among his teammates—but strikeouts were not on His agenda. There, at the plate and facing a pitcher who cared nothing about you except that you were an obstacle to be dispatched, you were on your own, even if you wanted so much to be good. Maybe *because* you wanted so much to be good. You could want something overmuch, and in that desire was the root of sin, and so God in His benevolence kept success at bay. And then, he was back in Thailand with his parents, playing the dutiful son and helping his mother distribute New Testaments and claiming victory for Christ, no matter what the empirical evidence said to the contrary. You could see what you wanted to see, and you could make of God what you wanted, but that didn't mean He had to take notice. Or you of Him.

HE DID NOT GET A DRIVER'S LICENSE before moving to the dorms at LCC, but he did lose his virginity. Following his graduation from the academy in Manila, he returned to Thailand for a month and lived with his parents in Bangkok where they had relocated. His father was now the executive director for the mission society's church planting efforts in the whole of the country. Between their commute and work schedule, his parents were gone sixteen hours a day, and he had little with which to keep himself busy. He roamed his parents' apartment feeling singularly out of place, since he no longer had his own room with a door and, instead, slept on a futon in the living room. At night, he heard his parents in those infrequent moments when they had sex, five minutes of mattress-bouncing, headboard-rocking activity, followed by his father's satisfied grunt and one of his mother's expressive sighs, which—Joshua knew all too well—could mean any number of things, from "You have disappointed me severely," to "Job well done." The secret, as in the Thai language itself, lay in parsing the tones.

During the day, he looked through closets, finding only a few mementos of his childhood. The move from Lopburi to Bangkok had meant sacrificing much of what they had accumulated over the previous years, but his mother had kept two thin scrapbooks, one of their wedding in 1974 and his baby book, which his mother had started in the months just before and following his birth. His parents had been married at his grandparents' farm in one of the cow pastures, and in the wedding album they looked impossibly young, impossibly slim, and nothing like themselves. His father, so stocky and bespectacled now, wore a leather vest and his hair in a ponytail while his mother looked like a child bride from the pioneer West. There were six pages of snapshots, the colors yellowing in their corner frames, documenting his parents from processional to recessional and every step in between, followed by pictures of the reception in which cows figured prominently. On the other hand, his baby book was furnished with an ultrasound photo of himself in utero, so standard now, but such a novelty item then, that his mother had noted the date and findings with no small amount of self-importance. Then, there was the requisite thumbnail photo of him just after birth, red-faced, his eyes screwed up into something like frustration and outrage, his head and hands covered by some volunteer's clumsy handiwork. In the following pages, there were only a few photos from those years when they were first in Thailand, when photo processing and album-keeping would have been low on his mother's to-do list. After several blank pages, there was a triumphant announcement made with a black felt marker in all capital letters. POTTY TRAINED! And that, apparently, was the end of that, the end of his childhood record.

Other searches in closets brought little else to his attention. Not until he began to rifle through his parents' bedside tables did the real treasures come to light. His baby book notwithstanding, his parents were compulsive keepers of journals, and Joshua knew that stacks of composition books would most likely be found in the storage facility in Oakland, where they stored the bric-a-brac of the last twenty years, the detritus that could not be thrown away. His mother's most current journal rested next to her New Testament and a tube of K-Y jelly. Only a few entries listed events or activities; instead, they described her prayer concerns, Joshua foremost among them. *Dear Jesus,* she had written in December 1997 when he would have been home from Manila, *let our son see You in all your glory. Make him the man You have destined him to be.* Reading this, he wondered where his mother stood on the predestination-free will debate and what purpose such a prayer could possibly serve either way. Or this, written just that morning in July 1998: *Dear Jesus, how am I to love these people, who seem so innocent and yet are so perverse in their ways? I shall never understand how to love those whom I have grown to hate at the core of my being.* Something had happened, but she had refused to give language to the event or events that had triggered the reaction.

Sitting next to a mug of loose change, a box of Trojans, and an old address book, his father's journal was much more business-like in its record of who, what, where, when, and why. *Reverend Nhiako Lor on Pradipat Road, Wednesday at 1300 for discussion of church planting deficiencies and causes of same; he fears he is failing in his ministry.* It was like the solution to a game of Clue, over and over again. His father, it seemed, was not prone to self-reflection, at least not in the context of his journals, which revealed only the tasks in front of him. His address book was similarly minimal, but the inside back cover contained a pocket with business cards: colleagues in the mission society, several Thai military officers and civilian government officials, the phone numbers of tradesmen—plumbers, electricians, and the like—and then, at the very back of the stack, three cards which contained the names, addresses, and phone numbers of massage spas within walking distance of their apartment. On the back of the one for Red Cherry Happy Ending Soap Massage, the name Sunny was written in his father's engineering school printing. It had all the sophistication of a punch card for a sandwich shop: your tenth visit free.

He had walked past that particular storefront every day, occasionally in the company of his parents, but they had betrayed no sign of recognition. Back and forth he had passed, in daylight and by night, while Sunny and her kind plied their trade, and how had that business card not burned up his father's address book? The thought of going inside, of introducing himself to Sunny—*I think you know my father*—excited and sickened him simultaneously.

In August, Joshua asked his parents if it would be possible for him to leave for college a week early, to visit Portland, to see his aunt and uncle, as a way of reacclimating himself to a life in the United States. His parents seemed puzzled by the request, but given their long hours at work and their absence from the apartment, this much was obvious: they were not altogether unhappy to see their only child go.

His aunt and uncle were similarly puzzled but welcoming enough. Henry was gone; he had enlisted in the Air Force immediately after high school, and was now stationed in Germany at Spangdahlem; they were glad to have someone else in the house, even if only for a week and even if only to sleep. They gave him a house key and told him to make himself at home. He dropped his duffel bag in Henry's room, and then the next morning, after his aunt and uncle had left for work, he walked the fourteen blocks to Chloe's house. The exterior door to her basement had been repainted in the intervening two years, but the doorbell still worked, and he listened as the bell tolled the melody that she had chosen: "The Hall of the Mountain King."

But, when the door opened, Chloe was not the one waiting just inside. Instead, there was an old woman in a horrible, plum-colored wig, standing on the threshold in shorts and crêpey legs. Her purple lipstick had all but disappeared in the lines around her mouth.

"What?" she barked. "I don't got all day."

He managed to blurt out that he was looking for Chloe, that they were friends from some years earlier.

"They don't live here no more," the woman said. "They moved out a couple a years ago. Must of been just after you left."

"Do you know where they moved?"

"What do I look like? The Post Office?"

And with that, the woman closed the door in his face. Rather than returning to his aunt and uncle's house, he walked to Powell's, hoping against hope, but the only thing of interest was a used hardback copy of *Goodbye, Columbus.*

He was standing at one of the registers sorting through his wallet for cash when he heard her voice: "Well, if it isn't the missionary kid."

The girl in the Polaroid stood behind one of the other registers. He recognized the smile, even if she had cut her red hair nearly to her skull and now had three silver rings looping through one nostril and a silver band around the rim of her left ear. A little heavier, maybe, than she was in the pictures. She wore a tee shirt that said, Get Normal, a shirt that didn't try to hide the extra weight at her belly and hips. "Over here." She waved at him by holding up one hand and opening and closing it, as though her hand were blinking, Tralfamadorian-style, as if to say, "Remember this?"

"You should buy me a coffee," she said. "Given what we've been through together. I'm done in half an hour."

"Okay," he said. "Sure."

He stood awkwardly by the remaindered books table, while he waited for her, leafing through novels that no one had wanted then, and were a bargain that no one wanted now. Populated by made-up characters, who did things, talked, and exercised their flimsy right to exist in a reader's imagination, and yet somehow never established themselves the way that the characters in real literature always did. So much print, he thought, and for what? Whose eyes? Someone had typed all of this, someone had hoped...

"Magda," she said, holding out her hand. "Mary, actually, but I go by Magda."

"Joshua," he said.

"Henry is a piece of shit, by the way" she said. "I want you to know that." And then she added as a rider: "And an asshole."

"He's in the Air Force," he said, as though that explained something.

"Good," she said. "Maybe he'll crash. I can forgive him now, but I confess: I wouldn't mind hearing about a tragedy with his name included. You know what I mean?"

She had come to the party at Mt. Tabor with two friends, but they had ended up meeting their boyfriends, and they hadn't stayed together for long. She drank too much, she admitted it, an antidote to being alone in a crowd. She had suffered from anxiety disorder back then. And maybe a touch of OCD. Panic attacks were never that far away. And then there was Henry, whom she liked, she had to admit that, too. As much as it pained her now to say it. Henry said he needed her to do something, and this was when he could have asked her just about anything. That's when she saw Joshua for the first time: while Henry and his crew stripped Joshua of his pants and shirt and underwear and stuck his briefs onto his head like a crown.

He's all yours, Henry had said. Give it a good squeeze. Give it a squeeze while we record this for posterity.

Eww, she thought. Not that there was anything repugnant about Joshua. She assured him of that.

"I mean you seemed nice enough," she said, "just unconscious. And we didn't know each other."

"No," he said. "I saw the pictures the next day, and I didn't even know who you were."

She spread her arms wide. "This is me," she said. "Who needs pictures?"

"Speaking of pictures," he said. He explained about the three Polaroids in his footlocker, which was in the process of being shipped to his dorm room at college, and the fourth that Henry had kept, the one picture in which her breasts were exposed.

"Oh, god," she said. "Of course, he did."

The irony, she said, was that after it was all over, Henry and his buddies just laughed and laughed and laughed, and then they were done, and Magda was no longer necessary. Henry told her to go home. She knew, if she were honest with herself, which was a priority now, being honest, that if Henry had said the word, she would have gone with him, done with him anything he might have asked and everything she had fantasized about.

"I'm not proud of that," she said, "and if I could get my hands on him or those pictures, I'd tear them up into little bits."

He could guess where he kept it. He knew the drawer where the magazines were buried and the secrets kept.

"Although," she said, "come to think of it, here's another irony. If Henry hadn't blown me off, I would have been absolutely ruined, and there would have been no turning back. I wouldn't have gone to church and gotten saved. You have to hit your low point before you can begin to rise. You know what I mean?"

He didn't know exactly, but he was willing to act agreeable.

She walked with him back to his aunt and uncle's house, hooking her arm in his, and she told him the rest of her story while he opened the front door and they walked up the stairs to Henry's room: how a friend had taken her—*as a joke, really!*—to the Immaculate Warrior of Truth Tabernacle, this converted barn way out in the boonies of Clackamas County. Sophie, her friend, had told her about the preacher there,

Brother Carl, who was like a caricature of an Old Testament prophet.

"She said, You gotta see him to believe it. So, I said, Okay, let's get a gander at this guy. And, she was right, Brother Carl was a white-haired, white-bearded old-school fire-and-brimstone kind of preacher, who's been doing it forever. He loved Jesus so much, he hated everything else, practically speaking. I kept waiting for him to point a finger at me and say There's a sinner, I can spot a sinner at twelve-hundred yards, and she's definitely one of the worst."

She hadn't been transformed by her experience in the barn so much as stunned.

"I thought, 'I can do better than this,'" she said. "I mean, isn't Jesus supposed to be about love and forgiveness and compassion? Brother Carl was just condemnation this and fires of hell that. When he met me, he said my name was just an abbreviation of Mary Magdalene, who was a whore and a fallen woman and a scourge of men. As if I didn't know. So what? Judgment, judgment, judgment. Screw that. I mean, really."

While she yammered on, Joshua began rifling through Henry's chest of drawers and desk. Much of it had been thoroughly cleaned since his departure, so the socks and underwear that Joshua had been expecting were nowhere to be found. Even the bottom side drawer of his desk, which had been the catch-all, only held a few postcards and letters. But there was a false bottom, and the items below the plywood insert remained untouched: a few old *Playboys* and *Penthouses* as well as some postcards of women in various unnatural poses and the fourth Polaroid.

"See," he said, holding it up for her inspection. Now that he had it, and now that he saw his younger self, unconscious, with her younger and topless version holding him, he realized he was loath to give it up.

"What a piece of shit," she said, holding it by its edges, turning it this way and that. "I looked okay, I guess. But what a piece of shit," she said again and slowly, methodically tore the picture in half and then quarters and then into eighths, a deliberate gesture that felt to Joshua like a physical injury. "Love is love," she said, "and it can be expressed in so many ways, but that's not what that was."

SHE TALKED AND TALKED ABOUT JESUS and love and how, if the Prime Directive of non-interference was the one overarching rule of *Star Trek*, then love was the prime directive for Christianity. Everything else fell apart in the face of love. She encouraged him to talk as well, and he told her about his parents and his experience in Thailand and Wisconsin and the hell of two years before when they met without knowing one another. He told her about meeting Chloe at Powell's and their not-quite sexual relationship, how that's what he had been doing there, looking for Chloe.

147

"And you found me, instead," she said brightly.

"Yes."

"Good thing, too," Magda said, "since Chloe is now living in Astoria at a lesbian commune. I think she knew it all along, but she was willing to try being straight, at least up to a point."

"Up to a point," he said. "At least with me."

They sat on Henry's bed with the pieces of the Polaroid between them.

"I bet if I left this behind, you'd Scotch tape it back together again, wouldn't you?"

"Probably."

"Boys," she shook her head. "You are so predictable."

"I guess."

She stood up from the bed. "Take off your clothes."

"What? Why?"

"Come on. You love Jesus, I know you do, and we can share that love with each other. We'll wipe out Henry and all his nastiness."

He unlaced his shoes and unbuttoned his jeans while she pulled Get Normal over her head and unhooked her bra. If he didn't love Jesus in quite the way she thought he did, this might be the moment to try.

I had no idea, he thought, but he couldn't have said what that idea was or could be.

"Oh, honey," she said, nuzzling his neck and holding him in a way that felt remembered. "God is good."

"Yes," he said. "Yes, He is."

"Would you happen to have Mr. Rubber handy?"

"No," he said, the realization sinking like a rock in his stomach and groin. "I didn't know I'd need one."

"At least, no one can say you were calculating," she said. "But if love is love, pregnancy is something else."

She squeezed him hard, and he thought she might tear him out at the root.

"Don't you worry," she said. "Next time." And with that she dropped to her knees and took him into her mouth, and in less than a minute, he was groaning with relief and embarrassment, and she was spitting into her tee shirt, and then pushing him toward the bathroom and the shower where soap and hot water were liberally applied and she placed his hand and fingers where she wanted and directed him in how she wanted to be touched until she was able to yell Hallelujah and vows were made that tomorrow, maybe even later today, supplies would be obtained and they would meet again and again and again.

"We are such stuff as love has made of us," she said, her eyes closed to the steam. "We love and we share, and we know that we are essentially alone except in moments like these. Because God is good and love is love."

"God is good," he echoed in response. His voice broke. "Really, really good."

His week went by quickly, and when he left, Magda took him to the bus station, kissing him goodbye and deliberately reminding him that they might not see one another again but that they would always know one another through Jesus.

"Remember," she said, "in heaven there is no giving and taking in marriage, there is no selfishness, only the moment of love. Moments that pass."

And, in return, he gave her the silver ring that he had once intended to be an iron-clad promise and an anchor, but which now he told Magda was only a reminder of a memory and the ephemera of time and love past.

That's how he lost his virginity. And that's how he became a Christian. Of a kind that neither his parents nor he would have recognized. In that dream of his experience, he had no real insight into its meaning and had nothing by which to measure it. First, he had to attend college.

[vi]

A Vocation for the Next Millennium

(Felton Richards, 2001)

THE YOUNG WOMAN ENTERED HIS office in the basement of the chapel a few minutes before noon, closely followed by his assistant.

"I'm sorry," Linda said. "She doesn't have an appointment, and you're already late to go to lunch." She looked at the young woman, clearly hoping for the penny to drop. "We could schedule another time."

"I need to speak to you," the young woman said. She had a nimbus of frizzy black hair wildly out of control, a broad face, and darting dark eyes. She was carrying so many items that she gave the impression of a pack mule. "I don't think I can wait."

"Fine," he said. He nodded to Linda, waiting for the older woman to leave and for this young woman to unload her various burdens: an art portfolio, a tennis racquet, the bulging backpack from her shoulders.

"I'm sorry," she said, "I'm sorry. I have so much stuff." The pile grew around her chair.

"That's a metaphor for our time," he said.

"What?" she said.

"Nothing," he said. "Just an observation. That's all."

"Oh. I see. It's just that my schedule is ridiculous."

He looked at her from across his desk. "That's not really something I can help you with."

"What?" Again, the darting eyes. "No. No, that's not what I meant. I was just trying to explain why I have all of this. I have classes back-to-back, and I have to carry everything. I don't have time to go back to my room."

"That explains it," he said. He adopted the tone he hoped would sound as authentically kind as possible. His counselor's tone of Tuesdays through Fridays, as opposed to the ministerial tone of Sunday morning. "What can I help you with?" Where should the emphasis go, he thought, on the "can" or the "I"? What *can* I help you with? What can *I* help you with? Did it matter?

"Have you ever," she said, stuttering a bit, "have you ever had a moral failure?"

Have I ever had a moral failure?

Emphasis definitely on the "I."

Which was when she burst into tears.

HER NAME WAS LEAH GREEN, and she had come to Liberty Christian from Yonkers for no other reason than a less-than-fabulous high school GPA and LCC's generous and accommodating admissions requirements. Then, as a bonus, there was distance: the three thousand miles she could put between herself and her family and her faith. As a college chaplain, the Reverend Dr. Felton Richards was not unfamiliar with such stories; he'd heard them for more than thirty years: bright, articulate eighteen- to twenty-two-year-olds, who alternately felt enormous grief and equally great relief for putting such mileage between themselves and their parents or guardians. That distance could be measured in miles, or it could be measured in meaning, as in the change of viewpoint that education provides. The eighteen-year-old who left home in thrall to her parents' opinions and biases all too often returned at Thanksgiving ready to take up arms for an alternate and adversarial and alien perspective.

"But that's not my problem," she insisted. "Not really."

They were sitting at one of the tables in O'Malley's while the ancient black-and-white television in the corner silently played and replayed the planes hitting Towers One and Two. The stocky, forty-something bartender smacked a bar towel against the side of one leg and watched without interruption, as though by staring the outcome might change.

Against his better, more professional judgment, Dr. Richards had carried the art portfolio and the tennis racquet and walked Leah and her backpack past Linda and her disapproving look to his car and then halfway down the mountains past the big cat animal sanctuary to the bar and its gravel parking lot, its scarred booths and gossiping eavesdroppers, the lousy television and the trance of current events. Since his separation from Desiree, he had chosen the seventeen-mile drive to O'Malley's and anonymity over the two-minute walk to the faculty dining room, where he would have to endure his colleagues' sympathy and their veiled reproach, and he saw no reason to disrupt what had become his routine. Not until this moment anyway, when he remembered the bras hanging from the rafters and heard those two senior-citizen numb-nuts at the corner table, asking the woman who worked the tables if she had ever considered a Wonderbra.

"You could be a little more forward-thinking," one said. "That's what we are."

"You're forward, I'll give you that," the woman sighed.

"We only want you to make use of your gifts," said the other.

"The thing is," Leah was saying to him, "I'm from New York, not the city itself, but close enough, and here I am. We were attacked, and I'm on the other side of the country."

Count your lucky stars.

"Boys," the woman said, "I don't have the time or the energy." She gestured toward the television and its images of replayed devastation. "Don't you have anything better to do? Drink your beer, then go home and make dinner for your wives."

Me, too, he wanted to say. No time or energy, dinner or wife.

"I shouldn't be here," Leah said.

"No," he said. "None of us are ever where we're supposed to be."

One of the men lifted their now-empty pitcher. "Morty, we have time for at least one more."

"The two of you," the woman said, "are going to be the death of me. If I don't kill you first."

Morty?

Leah rapped the table with her knuckles to regain his undivided attention.

"'None of us are ever where we're supposed to be?' Wow. That's so wise." Her eyes, no longer darting this way and that, had now zeroed in on him in an expression that signaled distrust and anger, as well as an anxious optimism. An optimism that she seemingly now understood to be as misplaced as it was mistaken. "You get that from a bumper sticker?"

"Doesn't make it any less true," Dr. Richards said. "Take me, for example."

He would be leaving soon enough, he thought, a sojourner and a stranger in a strange land.

"As your chaplain, as anybody's chaplain," he said, "I'm a fish out of water, the lamest of lame ducks."

THE FIRST TIME he was forced to reconsider his vocation, Dr. Felton Richards was twenty-nine, five years removed from his degree at Starr King but still enthused about his role as

155

a mentor to the students at Sierra Presbyterian College, the forerunner of Liberty Christian. The college as it was in the 1970s reflected its denominational origins: private, cerebral, committed to social engagement but in the most orderly way possible. The college's denominational founders had been as certain of their doctrine as they were their election; debate was neither necessary or seemly, and political discussion considered crass. But, when he was hired in 1969, student protests occupied the mountain campus as often as midterms or finals, and Sunday morning chapel services were more often about rally recruitment and staging as they were spiritual reflection. For as dark and malevolent as the politics and policies of the late 1960s might have been, Dr. Richards enjoyed the energy of that time. The strategizing, the signs, the chants, the speakers, the parties with students only a few years younger than himself, even his two arrests at sit-ins in front of the courthouse in Fresno. But if he was honest with himself, he knew that he became bored all too easily, and when the rhetoric turned cooler and events of the day less pressing, he was finding himself less than fully engaged. He considered community organizing. Becoming a stock broker or a late-night jazz DJ. Something else, something different.

Such was the moment in 1974, two weeks before Christmas when the chapel's midnight holiday service was punctuated by an event so gruesome that more than twenty-five years later, he could not unsee it. Two men, cousins, neither of whom had any attachment to the college, voluntarily burned to death on crosses erected on the ridge overlooking the chapel. He had been inside, reciting the benediction and feeling a rare moment of quiet euphoria, very much in tune with the season, when he heard the *whump* of gasoline igniting and then the crackling of flames. Then, there was a rush to the doors and the screams and tears of his student parishioners whose most recent calls and responses had been all innocence: in praise of new life and new beginnings. *Silent night, holy night...* They had put away, for the briefest of moments, their protests of unjust and distant wars and their outrage over a corrupt administration and the evils they knew only in the abstract. But any joy they might have felt singing those old carols was immediately transferred to this most visceral of tragedies: the cousins' bodies curled and fused with the crosses like drumsticks while a third cross between them burned to a crooked black pillar.

In the days that followed, he had found himself entirely inadequate to address the emotional turmoil that such a sight had engendered. He had answers for why such things happened, one could always provide an explanation, explanations were all too easy, but he could not provide consolation for a horror that remained horrible, no matter how much one talked about the incident. In fact, talking about the two cousins only seemed to make the image of their blackened bodies that much more indelible. On the other hand, was it any wonder why a dark studio at three in the morning and dropping a needle down on twenty minutes of "Death and the Flower" had become more and more appealing?

"THAT'S AWFUL," Leah said, her voice flat, "but that was, what, almost thirty years ago?"

"It was a long time ago," he said. "You're absolutely right. And I've committed the unforgiveable sin."

"You have?"

"I've been boring you with my own story."

Dr. Richards lowered his voice and gestured with one shoulder toward the two older men at the corner table who were keeping their server captive if not quite entertained. "Here we have a pat example: old geezers who never know when to shut up. I don't mean to be like that. An old fart who can't listen to another human being."

He exhaled slowly.

"I've been boring you with my own story when you have your own story to tell. Let's start over. You came to see me because you wanted to talk about what's happened recently. You were, obviously, here at school when the planes flew into the Towers. You couldn't have known and you couldn't have done anything, you're grateful that you didn't have to live through the experience, and yet you can't quite get past that sense of guilt that you weren't there for the smoke and dust. The horror of it all. Is that how it begins?"

She shook her head although her misery was palpable. "I wasn't bored, and I know I couldn't have done anything. That's not it at all." Her hands went into the tangled thatch of her hair, and she pulled as if to straighten what could never be uncurled. "I'm just so awful."

In front of them a plate of nachos had appeared. Gluey with microwaved and virulent-looking queso. Dotted with jalapeños and olives. Direct from can and jar and processing plant. He could blame the recent routine of this lunch for fifteen extra pounds. His freshman fifteen, forty years after the fact. He raised his hand toward the woman. "Napkins, Morty?" he said. "And two of your cheapest, most watery beers."

"Another comedian," she said, "and my name is Elisa, no matter what these jokers say."

"I can't drink that," Leah whispered. "I'm only nineteen."

What nineteen-year-old turns down a free beer? For that matter, what nineteen-year-old admits to being nineteen?

"I agree it's undrinkable," he said, "but that's up to you."

The bartender carried one glass to their table. "Look," he said. "Dr. Richards. You don't remember me, but I was a student of yours back in the day. Way back in the day. Michael Wayte. I was in your seminar on American religious utopias of the nineteenth century, and I was on the chapel worship committee."

He set the glass of beer in front of Dr. Richards and looked at the table as though he were trying to read meaning into the faux grain of the laminate. "I was in the same year as your wife."

Above the bar, the Towers fell one after the other inside the rectangle of the television.

"You know I can't serve minors," he said, "especially ones from the college. The way it is now. I shouldn't even serve you unless you're trying to piss on our little piece of Gilead."

"I told him," Leah said. "I think he was being a smart-aleck. He didn't mean it."

"No worries," Dr. Richards said. "You don't have to worry about me." He pulled out the letter that had been riding in his wallet since the day he had received it, a letter that ironically enough had been dated September 11. The letterhead bore the cartoon Patriot mascot of Liberty Christian College, but the message was plain enough: his appointment was being terminated at the end of the academic year for reasons related to Article 5 of his faculty contract. "They can't fire me twice," he said. "They can only fire me sooner."

"Fired," Michael said. "Terminated. I thought they were all talk and bluster, this new Board. I didn't know they'd do it for real."

"They can and they do. Right there in black and white. But that makes me wonder: when did pink slips stop being pink?"

HE HAD NEVER INTENDED to become a minister, it was a decision made under the press of circumstance, and now

160

thirty-two years after the fact, his career was ending at the hands of others. In 1965, his local draft board informed Felton Richards that, given his imminent graduation from Berkeley, the United States government would be pleased as punch for him to join them in a Southeast Asian adventure. *His chance to see the world! How lucky for him!* Ah, but he wished to decline such a significant opportunity, and he needed an alternative in short order. His Bachelor's degree in history had provided a student deferment, but that exemption was running out. He was not married with a child. He had demonstrated no prior qualms—either religious or philosophical—about participating in the institutional violence of the military. His parents were alive and well, his younger brother was still in high school, and no one was counting on him as a sole means of support. Service in the National Guard or Reserves held as little attraction as the Army or Navy. His lone option was enrollment in seminary and following his studies, immediate employment in a ministerial role. Draft status gold. Starr King and the Graduate Theological Union opened their doors to him, he found that the classes, while not overly taxing, were interesting, Barth and Tillich and Kierkegaard in particular, and if he placed the question of belief to the side, he could view his vocation as one of counseling, support, and encouragement. God was not particularly necessary, the concept only a shorthand for describing higher human aspiration as distinct from baser impulses.

He fully intended to look for a position at a church or parish upon graduation, but then he saw a job announcement for the chaplaincy at Sierra Presbyterian. It meant one class a semester and direction of the students' religious life. And, if the pay was even less than an associate pastor's position at an urban church, there was also no more threat from selective service. He responded to the advertisement, and he got the job; he was young, handsome in a rawboned and gangly way, and since he viewed the position as an academic exercise rather than an evangelistic pursuit, he filled the Board's unwritten expectations. He taught his class each semester, and he kept the doors to the chapel open. He presided over worship each Sunday morning for those yawning and hungover students who, due to belief or conditioning, felt obligated to attend; he responded to suicide attempts, interpersonal dorm disputes, and hospital admissions. He admired the constantly rotating carousel of young women, who sought the attentions of an older, more experienced man. He fell in love a little each time. But, after nearly thirty years on the job, the changes that had been simmering for the previous several years, finally came to a full boil: the composition of the Board changed in a radically more conservative way, politically as well as religiously, and he knew that his time was drawing to a close; now that Sierra Presbyterian had become Liberty Christian, the landscape had shifted: the faculty union had been decertified, tenure was being negotiated away, and all faculty, staff, and administrators were being asked to sign faith statements with a morals clause attached. Beyond the usual felonies and the newer strictures regarding relationships with students, the various offenses included: ingestion of alcohol or drugs; sexual relationships outside of marriage; sexual relationships with another of the same sex; divorce for reasons of moral turpitude; having or assisting another in obtaining an abortion procedure; non-attendance at worship services of a recognized denomination; attendance at worship services of a prohibited denomination or group; inappropriate or provocative or controversial language. On and on. The list grew longer and more complex for each one-year contract. In short, he fulfilled his accidental vocation until he couldn't help but receive the deliberate call for his termination.

FOLLOWING THEIR MARRIAGE in 1976, Desiree had seemingly made it a habit of leaving him once a decade. She left in 1984 because he was distant and unavailable to anyone other than the students in his care, which was a fair assessment, and then again in 1993 because he was controlling and dismissive of her talents and abilities, which was not fair at all because she had no talents or abilities as far as he could see other than her appearance, which left him breathless and had not changed since the day they'd met. She left him for the third time in the late spring of this cataclysmic year when everything else was falling apart, just after finals and graduation. Unlike her previous departures when she had packed a suitcase and a book bag for a hasty and loud retreat, this time, she had organized a van and a pair of football players as muscle in order to take the living room furniture and the television, the dinette set and the coffee maker, the bed frame and mattress and dresser, leaving no record of her reasons. He had been out of town, attending a conference for college mental health interventionists, and when he returned, he found empty spaces and marks on the floor where the furniture had been. After twenty-five years, he was forced to accept such signs as fact that this might be a more permanent arrangement.

She had been his student in the Rites and Sacraments class he taught each fall. A sophomore from the state of Washington, she was notable for the gumboots she wore regardless of the weather, her height, a fraction shy of six feet tall, a cascade of straight blonde hair that fell to her waist, and an impressive bust out of keeping with her otherwise slender build. Talents and abilities? She had modelled for local department stores, but when in her senior year she auditioned to be a weather announcer for the local ABC affiliate, she had stuttered and could not read from the teleprompter without moving her head to follow the text. Her twenty-two-year-old vanity had precluded the glasses that would have corrected the astigmatism from which she had suffered since the sixth grade, and her contacts made her appear hypertrophic. Since he was the college chaplain, he had seen his role as one of support and encouragement in whatever form it might take, especially for a young woman so attractively made. He had volunteered to drive her from the mountains of academe to the valley of her ambition; then, in the wreckage of that ambition, without leaving the Delta 88 inherited from his parents and while still in the parking lot of Channel 47, he had consoled her in her desolation, and he had been the beneficiary of her immediate gratitude, her constitutional tendency toward unhappiness, and the years of her future loathing. The radio played "If You Leave Me Now" by Chicago while she hiked her dress above her hips, and he blessed all favors large and small. They married two months later, and for the next twenty-five years they danced the on-again-off-again tune of her leaving him.

She was not the first student he had slept with, nor was she the last, but she was the only one he had married, and in the wake of Desiree's departure, he had clearly been working on borrowed time. Three days after the divorce was finalized the termination letter had been written and signed, and he might have been tempted to think that a righteous and jealous God was simply trying to get his attention.

"WELL, FOR FUCK'S SAKE," Michael said. "Excuse my French. Your lunch is on the house. Not that it's such a gift."

"I think I violated just about every one of their tick boxes. It was clearly time to go. There have been rumblings for the past five years, ever since the name change; they just did me the favor of making a decision."

"Okay," Michael said. "There's that."

"In the meantime, this young woman has been trying to tell me what's on her mind, and all I can do is whine about losing a job I lost a long time ago."

"Maybe a soda? Iced tea?" Michael offered. "Since I can't bring you a beer. And then I'll leave you two to talk."

"What? We're not—" Leah began. "Tea, I guess."

"Good idea," Dr. Richards said. "She'll have an iced tea."

"We don't, I mean, we can have our lunch, and then you can take me back to campus."

"Good idea," Dr. Richards said again.

"It's just that I came at a bad time," Leah said to Michael's back.

Which was when they heard the tigers roar from the animal sanctuary half-a-mile away. The roar and then what seemed like its echo after the fact.

Leah shuddered at the sound. By this time, she had picked two chips that hadn't been covered in its radioactive cheese, eaten them slowly, and then pushed the plate of nachos toward him.

"They do that," Dr. Richards explained, "the tigers. They wake up for a moment and decide whether or not they're hungry, they roar, and then they pace or go back to sleep. You should see them. Beautiful creatures. A reminder of the

natural world. How it goes on in spite of our petty problems."
He glanced at the television and the tape-loop of tragedy.
"Even our not-so-petty problems. I could take you there if
you'd like."

"Maybe," she said. "I don't know."

She sipped her iced tea with a straw, stirred the lemon and
the ice cubes, then pushed the glass away as well.

"Elisa," she called to the woman, who was reading a magazine at the bar. Michael polished glasses next to her. Elisa's
senior citizen admirers were playing pinball and, save for the
electronic banging and clanging, dinging and pinging, were
quiet for the moment. "Elisa, how do you stand it?"

But in the end, they did not go to the Cat Haven, nor did they
go back to campus again. Instead, they drove past the animal
sanctuary and the campus with its river stone gate and telltale
archway sign ("I AM the Truth and the Truth Freedom") and
ascended the winding highway to Kings Canyon before dropping down again into the car park for Grant Grove.

"Now," he said, "we'll walk among the trees, and then
you'll tell me what you need to tell me, and I'll listen the way
I should have done two hours ago. Maybe these trees will offer
some perspective."

He opened his door. The air was different, cooler, the
sound hushed by the breeze and the rocking of the sequoias'
upper branches. Three buses were already in the lot, and

tourists were spilling from their doors, with their babble of languages, some of which he recognized—Spanish, German, French, Japanese—and others he did not. Maybe the language of the divine, as mad a thought if ever there was one.

Leah sat still in the passenger seat, clutching her armrest. "This isn't what I thought I'd be doing today," she said, "but okay."

They circled General Grant amongst the camera-snapping tourists and an extended family of Americans, who had three grandparents in walkers and wheelchairs and four toddlers on leashes that tangled together like kite strings.

"'The Nation's Christmas Tree,'" Leah read, "like that matters to me." She looked up, only to stagger backwards.

Dr. Richards caught her and, without knowing quite how it happened, held her hand the rest of the way around the trail.

"I'm sorry," she said. "That's been happening a lot whenever I look up. Losing my balance."

"The General makes everyone lose their equilibrium a little bit," he said. "You look up, but you never really see the top."

"I suppose."

"And then you see the fire damage and the fact that these trees continue to survive beyond us. Remarkable resilience. Something for us to consider."

"I get it," she said. "Another metaphor."

They walked through the tunnel of the Fallen Monarch, considering its life before its fall and the paradox of sound in isolation, considering the lives that had once used it as shelter and the generations walking through ever since. Generations coming and going, taking their pictures within this relic of prehistory, recording their moments in fading snapshots, before they themselves passed into the forgotten past.

"I suppose you come here, like, once a week," Leah said.

"Not really. I should. But I don't." Over the course of more than thirty years, he could probably count his visits on one hand. "It's too close to be interesting except when someone has never been here before."

"Doesn't matter," she said, taking a deep breath. "Everything in the world might be different, but my life is the same mistake over and over again."

THREE NIGHTS BEFORE SEPTEMBER 11, she had gone with two of her suite-mates to a party in Fresno. Dottie and Claire were sweet young Baptists, who had grown up together, gone to the same mega-church in their north Fresno neighborhood, and responded to the same altar call at the age of twelve. They sang hymns with their eyes closed and lifted their hands in the air when they prayed. But they also had what Leah thought of as a naughty streak. They stashed condoms and bottles of Southern Comfort in a locked steamer trunk, safe from the custodial staff, who were known to be the Dorm Director's eyes and ears, and who were unafraid to open closets and drawers for signs of illicit behavior among the residents. Their boyfriends were hosting the party at their apartment in

Bulldog Village, and they had promised Leah that she'd have a good time, meet some interesting people, and have the opportunity to live a little, away from the limitations imposed by the Liberty Christian Code of Student Conduct.

"Jesus never said not to have fun," Dottie said. "It's not a sin to have a good time."

Claire peered into the mirror in their shared bathroom as she applied mascara to lashes that seemed doe-like. "It's only a sin if you think it's a sin."

"Come with us," Dottie said. "We have a pass, and you need to get out of this room."

Leah didn't have much to say about what Jesus did or did not consider a sin, but she didn't consider herself a prude. She had lost her virginity her sophomore year of high school after a production of *The Hobbit* led to a cast party, a trash can of jungle juice, and a dark corner with her crush of the moment, Isaac Bauer. Isaac had played Gandalf and still wore peeling remnants of his gray beard and the spirit gum adhesive when they began to kiss and tear at each other's clothes. And if picking flecks of each from her teeth two hours after the fact weren't enough punishment for a moment of adult behavior, the yeast infection was. Not to mention the conversation with her mother and her mother's doctor two days later.

Since then, she had had several other boyfriends, some of whom she'd slept with and some she hadn't but wanted to, and not all of the former transactions had been conducted as safely and responsibly as they should have been. Passion has its place—*doesn't it?*—and reason doesn't always prevail. Until that moment in late January of her senior year when her period didn't begin and didn't begin and didn't begin, and instead, she felt heavy and leaden and one-and-a-half times her usual size. There had been another party and another longed-for crush during the winter break, and unlike those who lived with the foreboding of the new millennium and all of the Y2K anxieties of system-collapse, she had been feeling especially relaxed and carefree and happy that she was wanted and loved. Until she wasn't relaxed, carefree, or happy anymore, love being the trap that it is. She had not been brought up around prayer particularly—her parents came from families who were socialists and atheists, teachers and union organizers, and they believed in progress as the result of human effort and ingenuity rather than divine intervention—but she began to pray with a fervency that would have surprised her if she hadn't been so frantic for some relief. Which came one morning with horrible cramps, a gush of thick, red clots, and the irony of a sadness that surpassed the relief, a sadness that did not leave her despite the embarrassment of yet another conversation with her mother and her mother's doctor, both of whom chided her for her carelessness and moral inattention.

So, she had come to Liberty Christian not only because her grades were unremarkable and not only for the distance, but because she had some vague notion that she needed to go someplace barricaded and safe against the errors of human desire, and what safer place could there be than the mountain fortress of the Evangelicals with their purity rings and codes of conduct and insistence upon abstinence-only? Her parents were skeptical but accommodating. She packed her bags, flew across the continent, and she spent her freshman year going to classes, doing homework, even attending chapel for a faith not her own, doing nothing to dispel her own illusions. But, now in her sophomore year, her suite-mates were doing everything they could to reveal that the college was but an outline of safety and the suggestion of certainty, rather than the rock-solid fortress of rectitude it presented itself to be.

She went to the party with Dottie and Claire, and she met their off-campus friends, only to find out that they were no more interesting than the friends that she had left behind in New York. The Singapore Slings she drank were not that different from the jungle juice of four years earlier, the music was just as loud and just as unintelligible, and if Claire's boyfriend's roommate, Trevor, happened to be *goy*, well, that might be the only difference, and after her fifth drink she was really beyond making fine distinctions.

At four in the morning, Claire and Dottie scooped her up, helped her reassemble her clothing and belongings, and took her to a plastic booth in a Jack-in-the-Box on Kings Canyon Road. They stuck her head in the bathroom sink, made her brush her wild and wiry hair, and then ordered coffee and onion rings and French fries, and ate and drank and flicked catsup at one another until they had all sobered up under the effects of caffeine and grease and carbohydrates while the first flush of dawn appeared over the Sierra, home of their mountain idyll.

"That's it," Leah said. "We went back to our suite Sunday morning, and we made it back in time for chapel even though I had a headache that lasted until I woke up on Tuesday. Another stupid encounter with a stupid guy who forgot me as soon as we left, whose name I won't remember in a week. All Monday, I thought, 'how will I be punished this time?' Because in my world it seems like there's always punishment, I don't care if Jesus never said not to have a good time. You talked about the death of Stephen, by the way, and I thought, *There's always a cost when you're right as well as when you're wrong.*"

Oh, these young girls, he thought. These beautiful young things. Amoral as a tick or as sensitive as a seismograph. There didn't seem to be much middle ground. What had happened to a healthy enjoyment of the body coupled with reverence for the human connection?

"But you weren't punished, were you?"

"I wasn't? My aunt's brother-in-law worked at Cantor Fitzgerald. I have friends who lost friends and family members in those towers."

"You were punished because other people lost their lives after you went to a party? Do you realize how that sounds?"

They were sitting on the deck of the restaurant in Grant Grove. She hadn't eaten anything to speak of at O'Malley's, and she had mentioned the onset of a headache, so he had bought sandwiches and potato chips and water, and they watched the families that came and went from the tables and the gift shop, carrying packaged food and key rings, snow globes, and over-sized sweatshirts with Sequoia and Bear Republic designs. The wind blew scattered napkins along the deck, and she pulled the collar of her plaid shirt around her neck.

"Stupid," she sighed. "It sounds stupid. I know it sounds stupid."

"Don't be too hard on yourself." She had acted in a way that she had vowed not to, and so she was taking a punishment that was not a punishment at all, but the confluence of evil and the innocent. She was claiming causality when there was not even a correlation. Coincidence, in this case, the coincidence of time was the only factor. Her sense of guilt, however, was leading her to a conclusion that leapfrogged all common sense. Jewish guilt meeting the guilt of Evangelicals, who when they felt guilt at all were nigh unto frantic and sui-cidal. "Don't be so hard on yourself," he said again.

"Why not?"

"You can't control your feelings. And you can't always control your thoughts. But you can train them. In the same way that you can decide how to behave in the future. You can act differently. You can be deliberate. 'Assume a virtue if you have it not,' as Hamlet says. You can pretend. You can imagine yourself the way you want to be, and you can practice. You don't have to replay and repeat what you don't want."

"Wouldn't that be nice?"

A Golden Retriever walked across the deck, trailing an unaccompanied leash.

"Don't let your Self be an accident," he said. "Trust me, I speak from experience."

THE FACT WAS that he wasn't fired because Desiree had left him and divorced him. At least not that alone. While his divorce could have been cause, in this case it was merely coincidence. And he wasn't fired because as recently as five years before there had been a freshman girl from Rhode Island, like so many young women through the years, who seemed to think that Reverend Richards could provide the assurances that she needed and the trip to Planned Parenthood when that was required. He was fired for controversial language in a class he'd taught the previous spring, that season when Desiree was preparing her final exit. Of all the things he could have said in his lecture on Pilate and the trial of Jesus before the Sanhedrin, he didn't have to speak about the Florida recount, did he? The way that partisanship and belief and political expediency had driven decisions, rather than the fiction of legal objectivity. Even at the level of the highest court in the land.

"We need to be careful," he said, "in the way we twist our decisions to conform to our desires. Individually as well as collectively. If we accept a particular standard—ethical, legal, or moral—then that should be our guiding principle, rather than the beliefs that we cling to regardless of evidence to the contrary. We need to be careful that we don't start with a desired outcome and then figure out how to justify that end in language that we dress up like angels."

His students gazed at him as though he had sprouted a second head. He was hardly a model of probity or conscience, he knew that and they knew that, and he realized how his own words could be used against him. He talked and he talked, and there was a general shifting in seats, a nervousness he did not truly understand until sometime later.

What he didn't understand was their own particular perspective that, while God's Chosen One might have been a failed businessman with a drinking problem and Oedipal issues a mile wide, the Holy One works in mysterious and confounding ways, that He makes use of the humblest of His humble servants, and can use the darkest of back room maneuvering for His greater glory. He also didn't imagine that anything he ad-libbed in a class on a Tuesday at 3:30 in the afternoon would ever make its way back to the Admin building and the President's Office. In other words, he didn't understand his audience.

They were Young Republicans, after all.

O'MALLEY'S WAS EMPTY just before eleven o'clock on the Wednesday before Thanksgiving. Michael was gone and so, too, Elisa. In their place behind the bar, leafing through that morning's *Fresno Bee* was the football coach, rumored to be on the chopping block and waiting for the pages of the calendar to blow away into a new year. The college's benighted team had started strong and then, following a key injury, had fallen apart in spectacular fashion, and the Board was no longer interested in supporting any effort, athletic or academic, that reflected poorly on the Lord of Lords. Apparently, like anyone else, Jesus loves a winner.

"Coach Bonaventura," Dr. Richards said, "pulling a second shift?"

"Nope." He smoothed the front page on the bar, next to a glass of an orange-tinted red wine. "No, Father Felton, I am not. I'm officially off the clock: here, there, and everywhere. Did you know," he said, looking over his glasses, "that the median price for a single-family home in California is over 250,000 dollars and that the average annual price increase has been about nine per cent? And Fresno's median price is much, much lower while its increase just that much higher?"

"Thinking about real estate?"

"Thinking. Not doing. These realtors are so full of bullshit. The stock market has bubbles, the tech sector has bubbles, but they claim that housing has no bubbles. Just climb, climb, climb."

He took a long drink from his wineglass, followed by a wince. "This is terrible stuff. I don't know why Michael carries it."

"Or why you drink it."

"I drink it," he said, "because, when the time comes, it'll be easy to give up."

The Budweiser clock behind the bar buzzed, and when the hour hand had clunked into place underneath the XI, the mechanism went silent once again.

"So," Dr. Richards began, "I hear you're getting fired."

"The same could be said about you."

"True. I have until May to pretend otherwise. Maybe I'll get my real estate license. You?"

"My bags are packed. One more game this weekend, and then I expect to get the news. Happy Thanksgiving, you're fired. Then I'm gone. Back to selling insurance to the cocktail waitresses in Vegas. This place," he said, shaking his head, "lousy sons-of-bitches. Forgive me, padre, but they are the worst group of fucking Christians I ever did see. The cross is so tight up their assholes, they fart every time they say Amen."

"No apologies necessary. You're preaching to the choir. So to speak."

"They'll kill the program until they're ready to bring it back with some major coin. They'll buy some players who can play. They'll fix the stadium and the locker rooms, and hire some air-brushed, razor-cut coach who looks good on television. After I'm gone, of course."

Coach B pushed a towel around the bar, as though he had some intention of cleaning.

"Look, it's just us," he said, throwing the towel on the floor behind the bar. "Michael is down the hill yelling at one of his suppliers, and Elisa is taking the afternoon off. She needs a break from adult daycare. I expect Thing 1 and Thing 2 any minute now. What can I get you, my fellow outcast and reprobate?"

Dr. Richards pointed to the bottle in front of the coach. "I'll have what you're having."

The coach grimaced as though in pain. "Don't say I didn't warn you."

The coach unscrewed the top of the bottle and poured a glass full. Sure enough, it tasted as awful as it looked. Like grapes from a terroir of pesticide and sandpaper.

"You're right," he said. "This would be all too easy to give up."

[vii]

Weddings

(Michael, 1976 / 1994 / 2004)

DON'T GET ME WRONG, I had some opportunities over the years to get married, but nothing quite worked out. Things happened. There was a girl in college I was crazy about for a time, but she decided that Jesus was a better bet. Then she died in Honduras a few years later doing God's work, so you tell me if she made the right choice. Maybe I was just that awful.

My plan was to become a minister, but then I bought a bar, and that may have limited my opportunities somewhat, given the fact that most of the regulars at the bar were retired men in their sixties and seventies, old codgers who came in to drink watery beer and tell bitter stories about their wives and exes. A few women did come in, but they were either with a man already, or with a group of other women who were talking about their shithead husbands and boyfriends, or were looking to get hammered, again because of some male shithead. So, then, if they looked at me at all, I was in the role of minister, and getting lucky also meant taking unfair advantage. That happened once or twice in the early eighties, the unfair advantage, that is, and my stomach wasn't right for days afterward—it was too much like fucking a needy parishioner—so I made a vow that the bar was the bar and not a dating site. Ironic, right? Where else do most people go to find mates? Churches and bars, and both, it seemed, were closed to me.

In the meantime, friends and family members were getting married right and left and I was in wedding after wedding and the butt of every joke about being the groomsman who was unmarriageable. Nothing like paying airfare and renting a tux, only to be needled about one's single status and the uses to which socks can be put in the dead of night. *Thanks, friends.* Insult added to insult—although I will admit that women in a similar position have it worse, given the state of bridesmaids' dresses. That alone, in my book—all those ruffles and awful pastels without any regard for body type—is worth one free drink if not two.

I was best man for my best friend and teammate in college, Derrick Williams, and I felt the pressure of organizing the bachelor party and doing the toast at the reception, but then as it turned out, Derrick's cousin, Sammy, had the party pretty well wired—he had connections in the adult entertainment industry—and the toast was not hard to put together since I'd known Derrick for the four years of college and then three years after that, so it kind of wrote itself.

Derrick is the kind of guy...

Derrick always said that he didn't like football, but he liked it as a way of meeting girls...

When Derrick first met Tania...

Plenty of laughs and innuendo with the mock threat of saying something truly embarrassing. Derrick stayed on the edge of his seat, but he should have known there was nothing to fear. His secrets and the identities of his former girlfriends were safe with me. His wife, Tania, was a lovely girl, five years younger than we were, and her even younger sister, Lisa, was the maid of honor. There was some feeble effort put forward on my behalf, but it was clear soon enough that Lisa wasn't that interested or available. She called me Gramps and offered to help me down the aisle during the processional. She was kidding, I think, because she got married in Chile the following year to a petroleum engineer who was twice her age and filthy rich from the government graft that was thrown his way. That's what it seems to take these days.

I danced with Lisa at the reception, but afterwards I saw her smoking a cigarette in the parking lot with her Bluebeard boyfriend. She had his jacket over her shoulders, he had one of those brick-sized walkie-talkies that passed for a car phone in those days, and they each had an ear to it and were laughing at some private joke with whoever was on the other end, and it was a moment that made clear to me that sense of being excluded, an outsider at an event to which I had been invited.

My response to this was to go back into the reception and down drink after drink, as fast as the bartenders could make them. This was at a time when our faith did not call for abstinence or abstemiousness only moderation in all things, and even that was a recommendation rather than a rule. I chatted with the parents of both bride and groom. I helped the waitstaff clear dirty dishes and glasses. I danced with each of the bridesmaids, but I don't (or can't or won't) remember that since my attempts at dancing are the source of embarrassment rather than pleasure in memory; I can feel the rhythm and the beat, but my body doesn't know how to respond, and I have been told that my movements on the dance floor appear to be spasms rather than choices. I am told that I had a wonderful time, but all of my activity, frenetic as it was, only served to accentuate that sense of exclusion, rather than ameliorate it.

Which was the way I often felt in those years after college. I had the bar, but even there, I was presiding over other people's parties, and they looked at me as merely a substitute for Big Dick, the former owner, who had dropped dead one day and whose grandkids couldn't get rid of the place fast enough. I guess you could say I was lonely. I had graduated from Sierra Presbyterian, and rather than moving all the way back to Fresno and the San Joaquin Valley, I stopped halfway down the mountain and the For-Sale sign at O'Malley's and never made another move. That's not to say, I never went anywhere, I'm speaking metaphorically, but metaphorically, my feet were stuck in quicksand, and the more I fought against my fate, the more firmly fast I felt held. Although they were too kind to say so out loud, my parents thought it was a waste of a good education, and I can't say that I disagreed with them, but that's the way self-punishment works.

After college, most everyone scattered, since there wasn't much in the way of employment opportunities available at such a remote location, so friends of the previous four years were in short supply. But now and again, I drove the seventeen miles to the higher elevation of the college. I walked around until I became aware of how sad it must look to those current students and professors: an alum still living in the past, who hadn't yet learned how to move on.

Once, that first fall after graduation, I dropped into the Humanities office. The secretary, Susan Morrison was also an alum, although three or four years older than I was, and I took note of her for the first time. When I was a student, coming and going, she was merely part of the adult furniture. She was small, with sharp features, and there was a line above her nose as if she had been suspicious all her life, but here, I thought, was a kindred soul, someone who had not gotten very far away.

She was answering the telephone, opening and closing file drawers and typing letters on a typewriter, one of those electric IBMs of a time before computers or those early word processors, and the office was filled with the *ring-wham-crash* racket of an industrious nature. I asked her if she would like to go to coffee or dinner, and she looked at me with her apprehensive squint.

"Why?"

"I thought maybe you'd like to get off the hill for a little while."

She put one elbow on top of her typewriter. "You want to go to dinner," she said. "You want to take me to dinner."

"Let's blow this pop stand," I said. "One graduate to another."

"Sure. I guess so."

She didn't seem terribly keen, but we set a date for the following week, and I made a reservation at Nicola's because it was the best place for the money that I knew from my days living with my parents in Fresno. But then, when I knocked on the door to Susan's upstairs studio that Friday night, she opened it an inch behind her door chain and said she was sorry but she couldn't go, she was sick with a fever, and she was alternately shivering with chills or burning up. I thought maybe she had just changed her mind and had cooked up an excuse, but when I returned an hour later with aspirin and flowers and a pot of chicken soup from the Minkler Cash Store, she did indeed look like a wreck: her eyes were red, and her skin had gone from pale to pasty and clammy, and although she had on a bulky quilted bathrobe that looked like Sherpa attire, her teeth were chattering.

"I'm sorry," she said the first time I arrived. "I would have called, but I didn't have any way of reaching you."

And then the second time I showed up, she said, "Oh, my god, why are you here again? I couldn't look or feel any worse. Don't you know any better?"

So, we had the makings of a meet-cute, but it didn't turn out that way. She swallowed a handful of aspirin and ate three spoonfuls of soup and she arranged the flowers, but she kept dabbing at her nose with an embroidered handkerchief as though she had some sort of tic, and I could tell that we really weren't suited to one another. The handkerchief, for one thing, which she kept tucked into her sleeve the way my grandmother used to do. And her one-room apartment was fussy with ceramic and glass figurines on every flat surface, ballerinas and kittens and little boys with trays, and she had neither television nor stereo, so I couldn't figure out what she did with her time at night.

But the worst was when she began to talk about Jesus, about how He had rescued her from a destructive homelife and childhood, and how He had destined her for great things, and if she was the Dean's secretary now, well, that would change because He had promised her. That she would do great things because he had destined her to do so. *Rinse and repeat.* Meanwhile I was having flashbacks to Emily, the girl who dumped me for Jesus. Which was ironic since I was a believer myself back then and still was. Really, I was, but I was getting tired of being treated like so much second-rate material.

But, back to Susan: her eyes were bright and shining as she told me all about His big plans for her, and I wondered whether her fever might have returned, so I put my hand on her forehead. "I thought you were a business major," I said. "I never knew a business major who was so aspirational, who dealt in anything but numbers and profit-and-loss statements."

"I'm different," she yawned. "Practical, but for His purpose."

Before I could leave, she asked if I would mind sitting with her until she fell asleep? And would I mind holding her hand while she did so?

There are no answers to such questions any better than a hangman's noose, so what was I to say?

She lay down on her broken-down couch, and I covered her with one of those godawful grannie afghans made of clashing primary colors. When her breathing became regular, I disengaged and dried my hand, tip-toed out the door and down her rickety stairs, and then push-started the car as quietly as possible with all the tension and relief of a felon at a prison break.

So, here's my confession: I didn't call later to see how she was or to schedule another date, and I made it a point to avoid the Humanities office when I found myself on campus, although to be honest, I was finding it harder and harder to go back without feeling a little pathetic anyway. I felt rotten about the whole thing, but I knew I'd feel even worse if I gave in to the demands of civility and called her again, because it was already clear that she was one of those people who can make a career out of manipulating others on the basis of weakness; once you give in, your goose is cooked for real and true, and it takes all kinds of machinations to get free again.

I was relieved, then, to find out that she had gotten married. It was ten years after our one non-date, I'll give you that, but she was married and I was not. She got married to an English prof, who came to campus long after my time; I was relieved, but I was also a bit jealous, and I couldn't help wondering what was wrong with me.

So IT WENT, year after year, and what was I to do? Given the hours that the bar was open, I didn't have much in the way of free time. I tried going to different churches in Fresno since Sunday morning was the one time I could stay closed without explanation. But most every church I tried was populated by the aged and infirm, and anyone there who was my age was already married, and if the couple had children that's all they could talk about.

The only churches that were different were the megachurches in the white north end of town, churches that met in buildings that looked like hotels and conference centers; there were brochures and pamphlets in the foyers and classrooms and office spaces around the perimeter of the worship halls. Blond wood was everywhere and the carpets were as thick as mattresses. There were midweek groups for every niche into which one might fit: age, marital status, family size, intergenerational composition, trauma experience, addiction recovery, criminal enterprise, faith search. You name it, they had it. I went to one of the twenty-something singles groups, and the only things missing were the bar, the alcohol, the disco ball, and the overloud music. Otherwise, I might as well have gone to a nightclub, such was the level of anticipation and counterfeit eagerness. The desperation in the room was palpable. I wondered if the thirty-something singles group was equally strained, or if the members of that group had given up, given in, and settled for friendships.

When I entered the room where the twenty-somethings met, a skinny, red-headed girl with less than perfect skin, handed me a nametag and a Sharpie, so that everyone would know who I was.

"You're new," she said, "and we'd like to get to know you."

"Thank you," I said, "but why is it that I want to throw up?"

She laughed and put her hand on my arm with an optimism that was as strained as it was electric. "Don't worry," she said, pointing to her name tag decorated with hearts and smiley faces. "I'm Mindy, and we all feel like that. In the beginning, that is."

So I was the new blood for a week or two, and there was a certain level of interest, but when it became clear that I was not a doctor or lawyer, engineer or teacher but the owner of a bar in the foothills instead, interest waned. If I had been preternaturally handsome or naturally popular that wouldn't have mattered, but I wasn't, so it did. If you can't make young women go weak in the knees, then you better bring something substantive to either bank book or reputation and preferably both. Soon enough, I was just one among the many Michael and Mindy wallflowers. We were all that unfortunate, lacking in looks and personality, money and prestige. I could have moved on to other churches and groups of their kind, but one experience was enough, and I took to reading trashy detective stories behind the bar on Sunday mornings and keeping the place open for the truly unfortunate. Think me shallow? Me, too; I know I am, but shallow is as shallow does.

Elisa showed up sometime in the early nineties, she and her teenaged son and her full back tattoo, long after I had given up hope. Her son Gil had been accepted on a full scholarship to Sierra Presbyterian, my alma mater, and she was looking for a place to land while he hit the books and lived in the dorms. She had bar experience from her time in Oregon, so it seemed like a natural fit, even if I really couldn't afford to pay another person to do the job that was only keeping me about three-quarters employed. She also needed a place to live, so

I made her a deal, a full-time job with part-time pay and no benefits except the use of an outbuilding that was fifty yards away from the bar. At one time, long before, it had been a guest house for Big Dick's unhappy relatives, so it had a moldy bathroom and a tiny kitchen with a two-burner stove. And, since it hadn't been used in about thirty years, it was filled with a lifetime's worth of accumulated newspapers and roadside trash that Big Dick couldn't let go. She was welcome to it, I said, the guest house and all that was contained therein, if she was willing to clean the place and make it her own.

"Right," she said, surveying the mess. "Shangri-La, it's not. But it's everything that I was hoping for."

Which meant she had no hopes at all, a lack of expectation that I found simpatico, and if she was willing to roll up her sleeves and clean a place that I couldn't even look at, well, she was welcome to it, for as long as it would serve her needs.

She had a history, that much was clear, starting with the back tattoo with its story of Adam and Eve, the Garden and the Serpent. And then there was the son who must have been born when she was twelve, but I didn't learn much more than that during that first year that she worked for me. Gil's scholarship had come out of the blue, she said, and it had come at just the right time for her; she had felt her life drifting in paths she didn't like, so although her O'Malley's cottage wasn't exactly Shangri-La, as she said, it was better than the dripping rain forest of Estacada and being surrounded by drunken sawmill workers.

"Not exactly a trade up, then," I said. "More of a lateral move with extra heat and dust."

"You could say that," she said.

But she almost immediately developed a following. If the patrons of O'Malley's had missed Big Dick and his vulgar abuse, they had seen me only as a bland and uninteresting replacement. Elisa, on the other hand, was like an exotic bird to our regulars, who couldn't keep their eyes off her prominent bust, tight tee shirts, or her good figure, and when she bent over to pick up something from the floor, they prayed for her shirt to rise and reveal a little more of the tattoo, which seemed to go on forever, south as well as north.

"First good thing you've done," Joe Dwyer said to me, which was something considering that I'd owned the bar for nearly twenty years by that point. "About time you started to innovate."

"Anything for your custom," I said. "You know that. Keep paying regularly, and I might even serve you a beer that's beer, instead of the horse piss you usually swallow."

If she was a gale force of fresh air to people like Joe Dwyer, she was like a siren for me. I mean that. Would it be so surprising or unusual if I said that I fell in love with her from the first moment? I tried not to let it show, but I don't think I was very successful. I was just as bad as Joe Dwyer and Abel Ramirez and the rest of the knuckleheads that called O'Malley's home. Looking but not looking. Hoping to make her laugh, just a little. Striking up a conversation with Gil in those rare times when he slouched through the door.

I didn't do anything more than that, though, for reasons I can't even begin to fathom. Fear, maybe, even at the age of forty. Maybe because I was forty. I'd had greater ease around the female of the species at the age of seventeen. Suffice it to say that I watched closely enough any time someone near to us in age came sniffing around. She went out on dates now and then, but nothing seemed to stick, no better than my few social forays had worked out.

One Thursday night she stayed at the bar until closing; I usually let her make an exit half an hour or an hour before we closed, but this one time she stayed seated at one of the high bar stools, like a regular rather than an employee. She drank beer after beer and then switched to some off-brand bourbon because, as she said, she didn't want to waste anything that might taste good on the mood that she was carrying.

"It's a shit storm, Mikey," she kept saying.

And, "You could pour a little more in here, you know. All the way to the tippity-top. Come on… Bippity-boppity-boo."

I kept track of her tab for a while, but then tucked it in the back of the cash register like a memento, a souvenir program from an event not likely to be repeated.

Some of the real regulars were impressed—Joe Dwyer, for one, had phoned Abel Ramirez, and Abel had come back after cleaning up the dinner dishes for his wife—and I finally had to push them out the door at two in the morning when Elisa's head went down and onto the bar, and she began to hum fragments of "Que Sera, Sera" nowhere near on-key. So off-key that she could have been humming "God Save the Queen" and I wouldn't have known the difference.

I finished cleaning up while Elisa snored and drooled on herself at the bar. She was quite a sight. And then, just as I was putting the last glass away, she woke with a start, wiped her mouth with the back of one hand, and said, "Why haven't we ever?"

And I said, "I don't know," because I didn't, no matter how much I may have wanted to know or do.

"Huh," she said, then let out a long, wet belch. "Funny."

"I guess so."

We stumbled through the darkness back to her cottage, and she let me help her. And she let me help her pull back the covers of her refugee-from-a-garage-sale twin bed. But when I was about to turn off her lights and leave her to the hangover that she was sure to experience, she said, "No, no, no, no."

"What?" I said.

"Turn off the lights."

"That's what I was doing."

"But you stay." She sat up in bed. "And let's do this right."

I HAVE ANOTHER CONFESSION to make: I'm a sucker for Rom-Coms. I always have been, and I blame my parents for that.

They were older when they got married—World War II got in the way of any number of relationships—and then they were older again when they had me, their only child, so rather than paying for a babysitter they took me with them when they saw a movie; I got the backseat and a bassinet at the drive-in, and my parents made sure to sit in the back row with an aisle seat for indoor showings. I imbibed Hepburn and Tracy, Gable and Colbert, Doris Day and Rock Hudson as mother's milk, and I can't help myself for viewing the world through that particular lens. Of couples coming together, then breaking apart, and then coming together again. And how often the role of deception is both obstacle and vehicle for said romance. Deception of identity, deception of attitude, deception of motive. Lies in the name of love. Means giving way to ends. And maybe my only-child status is also partly to blame for this: this belief that to be alone is to be human, but to be coupled is to be complete, and completion is the product—on some level—of deceit.

So, when Elisa sat up in bed and began to lift her tee shirt over her head, I had some calculations to make. I could accede and join in the joyful fun, knowing that once Elisa woke up and was sober once again, an accounting would be made, and I would, in all likelihood be seen in a less than flattering light. Or, I could convince her to lie back down in bed again, let her sleep the sleep of the inebriated and irresponsible, and go chastely, if regretfully, on my way, knowing that I hadn't taken undue advantage. Knowing that a Yes, in some cases, is not the affirmation that it seems. It came down to the question of long-term versus short-term gains and losses, sure things and bets on the future, and I'm not too proud to say it: my chips went all in on the short-term and sure thing of the present moment: the back tattoo and the tee shirt and jeans thrown against the wall.

WE WOKE UP SKIN TO SKIN, crushed against one another in the confines of her narrow bed. My breath was bad, and hers was worse. My right arm had fallen asleep underneath her shoulders, and when I felt her stir, I tried to re-position myself, but I still couldn't feel my fingers.

"Shit," she said. She sat up and the sheet dropped to her waist, and while the light was dim for the hour was early, the sight was everything I could have ever wanted, even as I could see that my opportunity to be in such proximity was about to end.

And I thought, *Well, that was bound to happen.*

"Shit, shit, shit, shit, shit, shit, shit," she said, holding her head. "I knew it. Goddammit, I knew it."

"Sorry," I said. "I know I'm no prize. But last night, you—"

"No," she said. "This has nothing to do with you. Or me."

"No?" I said, not knowing whether to be grateful or offended.

"No. Here." She leaned over me and the edge of the bed and then handed me a piece of paper with the Marine Corps logo at the top. "He left yesterday afternoon."

She was speaking of her son, who, as far as I knew, was still a student at Sierra Presbyterian, but now, according to Elisa, was on a Greyhound to San Diego and boot camp with the Marines. He might have gotten there already.

"He hated it here," she said, answering my unasked questions. "At the college. Too much God, too much happy talk. And I was hoping it was just a bad dream."

"And I was the nightmare to replace it?"

She smiled at me. Rueful, I guess her expression was. "Don't be so maudlin. You're not twelve. It's not like we both don't have some experience."

"Right," I said. "No feelings here."

"Nope."

I got up, shuffling through the clothes on the floor, trying to locate my underwear, careful not to look her in the face.

"Don't get weird on me," she said. "Or sappy. Please?"

"No," I said. "We're good. It happened. It was one night, and you had your reasons even though you probably don't remember what they were. But if you have your reasons again, I'll be more than happy to be available and oblige. On the other hand, I don't suppose I should hold my breath."

"No. I don't think so. Maybe not. But it's not what you're thinking."

"Sure."

So finally, she told me the whole story and it took most of an early morning hour. How she and her older brother Carl had been hell raisers in their drippy hometown of Estacada, Oregon until she had had enough when she was sixteen and lit out for more exciting parts. Her odyssey to Haight-Ashbury and the folks she knew there, folks who knew other folks, who had names on record albums and in *Time* magazine. How she got the start of her back tattoo and its story of Original Sin from Lyle Tuttle in his studio on Seventh Street one night after an all-day and all-night party at the house in which Janis Joplin once lived. How she finally grew tired of that make-shift life and came back to Estacada, only to be convinced by her born-again-in-a-big-way brother to become a Christian of a particularly narrow and holy roller stripe and then to get married to their much older former social studies teacher. How she got pregnant just before he died, and then the whole fiasco with her second husband, Ric "Ricky Boy" Rabinek, that numbskull, who was so bad at being bad that his name was often cited on the radio in those thirty-second bits about dumb criminals. You know, using his real driver's license to rent the car that was used in a robbery, calling the police when someone stole his stolen living room's worth of electronics, etc., etc., etc. Out of all of that, Gil had been her one good thing, the fruit of a God-imposed, third-world-style union, and now, because he couldn't stand the whole God-thing, he was on a bus to the rest of his life, a life to be lived in camo and salutes and squared-away order, entirely alien to anything she knew.

"So, don't take it personally," she said. "Like I said, it's nothing to do with you."

"If you say so."

"I let things happen, and I don't do anything to stop them, even when they're all wrong."

I didn't say that I would have been thrilled if she continued to let our thing happen, no matter how wrong it might be, but I knew enough to keep it zipped, only to say that she was welcome to take the day off, go to Fresno, see a movie or wander the zoo or visit the big trees farther up the mountain. To take her mind off those things she couldn't do anything about. As for me, I was something she could do something about, and I knew that a decision had already been made and that easily enough.

I CAN'T SAY I didn't hold out hope, but I knew that my chances with Elisa were worse than slim to none. Call it none and less than none, our one night together notwithstanding. I stumbled back from Elisa's cottage to the bar and climbed the back stairs to my apartment as though I were both Sisyphus and the rock he was pushing. It might have been nine o'clock in the morning, but as luck would have it, there was Joe Dwyer, standing outside and pounding at the front door.

"What?" I said after trudging down the interior stairs. "What the hell do you want? You were here until two, and now you're back? You know we don't open for another hour. At least."

"Just checking in," he said. "Elisa seemed a little worse for wear."

"You're concerned about Elisa."

"Sure."

"Sure you are, you spy. You're here, looking for juicy tidbits." I rubbed my face with my hands. "Go start the coffee. Sweep the floor. Make yourself useful. Get a life. I need a shower."

And with that I left him to it.

DID I MENTION that about this time I noticed a change in weddings? Maybe I was just that oblivious, but it seemed like something of a pattern: the friends who got married in the seventies and early-eighties seemed bound and determined to reinvent the genre. Weddings in meadows and on top of mountains or next to lakes and streams. Gowns and brides-maids' dresses that were made from home spun fabrics, and groomsmen who wore leather vests and open collars. And the sentiments were surprisingly vague: love and roses and Khalil Gibran. But by the mid-nineties such ceremonies had turned somewhat sour. Maybe it was because these weddings were meant to celebrate the union of those who had tried once before and who now knew the risks. They couldn't quite manage the same level of blasé sunshine, only a grim commit-ment to making right what had gone horribly wrong the first time. Jesus was going to be the center of the relationship, and they were going to out-detail the devil. The receptions went from booze-filled catered affairs to punch and cookies and a tired cake, and both bride and groom appeared more relieved than exuberant, which was understandable since the photographer was often in the position of wrangling a wedding party that included children from different families.

Derek Williams, for one. He and Tania lasted twelve years and had three daughters, but then Tania got involved with a corporate lawyer from Fresno, and Derrick, who never made partner at his accounting firm, didn't stand a chance. Tania and her lawyer met at church, but Derrick seemed to be the one who had the religious rebirth. He doubled-down on Jesus even as his soon-to-be ex-wife flew away to Reno, a ski vacation, and a quickie divorce and remarriage. He and his girls fumbled their way through three years together, and when they walked together to church, they looked like that picture of the lost tribe. So, when Derrick and his three girls met Dorothy and her two boys at a church party for single parents and their children, their mutual needs clicked together like gears meshing for the first time. I had nothing against Dorothy, but I admit that she frightened me. She had wide-set gray eyes and a compact, no-nonsense frame, and she wore sensible shoes instead of anything attractive and uncomfortable. She spoke in a quiet voice, with the assumption that everyone else saw angels and demons in the same way that she did. She was a great believer in her own spiritual life, but I had heard stories from some mean-spirited others how hard it could be to live with someone so upright and otherworldly. How much pressure that created. That her first husband had died after he rolled his car off Belmont and into the Kings River, and if he hadn't done that, he would have drunk himself to death because he couldn't match his wife's righteousness, good work for good work. As I said, though, everything I heard was hearsay and as envious as it was unkind. But, when I met Dorothy and her sons, I had my own suspicions. Her boys were eight and ten years old, and they were already trying to turn mud into frogs, if you know what I mean, such was their mother's influence.

"You've met your match," I said to Derrick, "and then some."

"I know," he said. He had come up to see me at the bar, to explain why I hadn't been part of his second wedding, I hadn't even been invited to attend, and even though Dorothy was back in Fresno at their house in Old Fig, he looked guilty as he drank the watered-down beer that I poured for him. Dorothy's brother had been his best man, and he told me that had only been partly his choice.

"Don't get me wrong," he said. "Allan is a nice guy, but I don't even know him, not that well, but Dorothy thought we needed a fresh start. A clean slate. So I said okay."

"She'd make a good coach," I said, thinking back to our football days, when we would remind each other not to take what the coaches said too seriously; otherwise, they'd control your mind.

"Yeah," he said. "Maybe."

He seemed to doubt what I'd said, but I wasn't surprised when months went by and I didn't hear from him. Before the wedding, he'd come up the hill once a month or more, have a light beer and a pickled egg and chew over old times and old brine. But now? Crickets. I only heard about him through mutual friends, the same ones who expressed their doubts about Dorothy, so they may not have been the most reliable of informants. Still, the fact that he, in effect, had disappeared may have been the most telling bit of evidence.

I was thinking about this, and I was thinking about Elisa, who had had her own share of marriages, when I came downstairs an hour later to find that Joe had put the place in haphazard order so that he and Abel could get started on their first pitcher.

"Here he is," Joe said. "Mr. October. Rounding the base paths."

"Charlie Hustle," Abel said. "That's who you are."

"So, Mr. October, did you get yourself home?"

"Mikey and Elisa sitting in a tree, K-I-S-S-I-N-G," Abel sang.

"What are you," I said, "twelve? The two of you?"

And then Joe started making kissing noises, which out of his liver-spotted lips sounded more like wet farts.

"Don't make me pour beer over your heads," I said, which was the sort of thing that Elisa could do and not just talk about, and when she did it not that long before, they deserved it, and when she did it, I wished I had been the one holding the pitcher over their heads.

"Mikey, Mikey, Mikey," Joe said. "You know we love you."

"I know that," I said. "God help me."

ELISA AND I WORKED OUT OUR ARRANGEMENTS, and if it meant that we didn't get together but once a month or so, I was okay with that. Or, maybe I should say, what choice did I have? She wanted nothing more to do with weddings and marriages and relationships legally binding in the state of California, but she wanted to keep friendship intact, so if that meant a sexual life that was conducted only occasionally, at least we each had our privacy and our moments of connection with another person. Would I have liked more? Of course. Yes, yes, and yes. But that option wasn't on the table, and I let her dictate the times and places.

In the meantime, I heard all about Gil's exploits, his success and graduation from boot camp and then his deployment to Bosnia. She let me read his letters, which were laconic in the extreme and did not say very much about his experiences except the place names of Sarajevo and the Sava River, the cold, and the anger that seemed to have no object or center.

He came home in late 1996, visited with his mother for a week, and then was gone again, back to a peace-keeping mission intended to last for only a year, but which lasted for several years more, with more place names like Srebrenica and Kosovo, and had little to do with the making of peace through peaceful means. Then came 9/11, and he was gone once again, this time to Afghanistan. He was promoted to sergeant, but he refused commissioning as an officer. And, then, just as suddenly as he had left college, he had an opportunity to separate from the Marines and he took it; he came home to his mother's cottage, stockier than when he had left and with even less explanation.

"I was done," he shrugged. "And my scholarship is still good, plus my bennies. I checked it all out."

"No kidding," I said. "After all this time. You know they changed the name, right? And a few other things. Not always to the good. But this is what you've been defending."

A year or two after he left, Sierra Presbyterian had become Liberty Christian, and the Prospectors into the Patriots, and if he thought the place was too much God before he left, he would have a surprise coming upon his return. If Sierra Pres had once prepared ministers and teachers, LCC was in the business of preparing televangelists and fundraisers, conservative politicians and anti-abortion crusaders. The college president was a toady and the Board members were loons, and I wouldn't have been surprised to learn that their meetings were conducted in robes and hoods.

"I'm aware," he said, "and I know the score. I need a degree and a teaching credential. That's it. If I wear my dog tags and fatigue bottoms, I won't need arguments."

"You'd be surprised," I said.

He was sitting at the bar, and Elisa was fussing over him, making a BLT and drawing one of our few decent beers, playing Mom. When Joe Dwyer and Abel Ramirez came in, they took one look, snapped to attention, and gave his back a salute, which he could see in the mirror.

"Cut the crap, you two," Elisa said.

"At ease, gentlemen," Gil said. "I was a sergeant, and now I'm not. I'm doubly unqualified."

The two older men moved forward and enveloped him in a two-on-one hug. Joe's face might have been damp. My eyes were certainly misty.

"Oh. My. God," Elisa said. "I'm surrounded by babies and children."

She pretended outrage better than anyone I ever knew.

ON THE OTHER HAND, I can't pretend to imagine what Gil had seen or endured. I am not that gifted. And, since the closest I came to serving in the military was a lousy lottery number in 1973, I have only dodged bullets, never faced them, and I don't know what I would have done if the jungles of Vietnam had truly been in my future. Canada? Maybe, since flight is generally my first response, as I am a master of avoidance.

When I met Gil the first time, he was an eighteen-year-old swimmer for a mediocre college team, long and loose-limbed and wide-shouldered. Now, he was ten years older, filled out

206

and a brick monument to personal development. He had lost count of his tours, but he remembered firefights and ambushes and IEDs the way I remembered football games, though he was much more loathe to talk about them, whereas I could blab for hours about trick plays and unlikely touchdowns. The other difference, of course, is that I didn't wake up screaming from bad plays and turnovers, of which there were more than a few, but still, how trivial was I by comparison? Elisa had told me that there were some nights in the cottage when sleep was hard to come by, and while neither one of us wanted to jump to stereotypical conclusions, we were alert to what he might need.

"Counseling?" he said. "I've had counseling. To here and back, and I'll probably get more." He shook a pill bottle in front of his mother. "Along with the Prozac and whatever else the doctors are dishing up. I'm not dumb."

"No one's saying you're dumb," Elisa said. "Not by any stretch."

But later that night, I heard the creak of my outdoor staircase, and there she was tapping on my door, which I had assumed I wouldn't see or hear for some time if ever again.

"I'm worried," she said when I brought her inside, selfishly hoping against hope.

"You're his mother. You're supposed to be."

"No." She shook her head. "That's not what this is. He's got a head full of it still. Eight years of being at attention. Eight years of listening. Eight years of watching. He has nightmares, which you know. Last night he was drinking bourbon and cutting himself with an X-acto blade. Up here." She motioned to her bicep. "So it won't show. Deadening and refreshing, that's what he called it. It's not like he doesn't have plenty of other scars inside and out. I don't know what else to do."

Neither did I, nothing beyond watch and wait, nothing that promised an immediate or guaranteed solution. And that's what we were left with, the promise of uncertainty in the long term and the guarantee of no guarantee, the essence of life in a nutshell, which, given my own anxious nature is something that I hate. Only this felt potentially more explosive than life-as-normal.

And, then, wouldn't you know it? Life-as-uncertainty gave us yet another turn.

THE INVITATION ARRIVED in a blue envelope. My young friend DDP was getting married. DDP! Of all people! Dalvin-Demarius Philipi Jenkins, who had once single-handedly brought hope to the Liberty Christian football program in the fall of 2001 only to be cut down by a knee injury two weeks after 9/11. The injury was significant and he was in a cast for months after his initial surgery, and while his doctors had held out hope for a full recovery, a later surgeon eventually amputated his leg six inches above the knee, a consequence of the severity of the injury and a vicious staph infection that could have cost him his life as well as his leg.

But now he was getting married to a young woman he'd met in his brief time at LCC, Virginia Newland, and she was none other than the college president's daughter. The daughter of Dr. Cheryl Newland, college president and onetime Flannery O'Connor scholar. Virginia had been a senior the year that DDP had been on campus, and she had been there, done that, and seen it all.

"Can you believe it?" I said. "How ironic is that?"

"That's something," Elisa said, but she didn't seem to be terribly impressed by the weirdness that life can bring.

"I mean, here's this young man, who does more in two weeks to bring attention to the college, and then when he gets hurt, they disown him and try to deny the bill."

As awful as the injury was, the real horror was the way the college treated him when all was said and done. His scholarship had been rescinded, and the Board had attempted to remove themselves from all responsibility for his medical bills. He was poor, he was black, and he had been a juvenile offender, tried and sentenced as an adult. And while Jesus had changed him, and he had been paroled, and all of that had happened before he came on campus, that hadn't been good enough for the current administration. They had brought him to the mountain to play football and advertise the college, but his body had been broken, and they had tried to wash their hands of him. DDP was getting the last laugh, though, by marrying the president's daughter and doing so in the college chapel.

"Hah," I said. "I love it. I can't begin to tell you how much I love it. You'll go with me, right?"

I said this to Elisa, but she only stiffened and then said something to the effect that she'd prefer to gouge her eyes out with a spoon.

"Trust me," she said. "Weddings are bad enough, but I will never, ever step foot on that fucking campus. Never again. Why would they hold their wedding there? The place where they were so mean to him? Take Gil. He could do with a reality check."

She blamed the college for her son's military career, and I can't say that I disagreed with her logic, although I thought that, given his return and given his newly resolved educational plans, her grudge was no longer warranted.

"Give him some time among the looneys," she said. "You can play tour guide and show him the sights and remind him of all he's missed."

Which is what we did. The week before, I pulled a jacket and tie out of the mothballs, and after arguing with his mother, Gil went to Fresno to buy a basic suit. She had advocated for him wearing his dress blues.

"You could give them an eyeful," she had said. "Medals and all. Remind them of all they've never done."

And then, when he returned from the mall, she clucked her tongue. "You look like an undertaker," she said, wiping her eyes. "Beautiful though you are."

Before we left, Elisa gave me one last warning. "If Virginia Newland is only marrying Dee as a way of getting back at her mother, then the fuck-ups are just going to get distributed from bad to worse, worse to worst and back again." She smoothed down the lapels of my jacket, which I admit could have done with a pressing. "That would be the awfullest thing."

"I'm sure that's not the case," I said, but privately I had worried that as well.

I saw no indication of that, however, when we entered the darkness of the chapel, this building that I knew only too well from my time here almost thirty years before, and began to read the order of service.

"Look," I said to Gil, pointing to the back page.

> *We welcome beloved family and friends as we celebrate the union of our daughter, Virginia, to the love of her life, Dalvin-Demarius Philipi Jenkins: two beautiful souls destined by the Lord to be His hands and feet in the world, one flesh together until the end of their days.*
>
> *Blessings,*
> *Mr. Robert and Dr. Cheryl Newland*

"They're at least trying to seem happy about it," I said, although catching sight of Dr. Newland and her tight smile, I wondered about the sincerity of their sentiments. "That's her," I said, gesturing toward the small woman wearing a black sheath dress and pearls, who was shaking hands and chatting up guests as if this were a campaign rally. "She came just after you left. She knows how to play the game the way the trustees want it played. Her and Bobby Thornton." I almost added "that putz," but I let it go since this was a day meant for celebration, rather than a settling of old scores or a bearing of old grudges.

And then there was Dee walking with only the smallest, least-noticeable hitch from his prosthesis. Walking up the center aisle in order to shake my hand and then give me a long, hard hug, from which my chest felt compressed. He could have lifted me overhead, he was that strong still, and still very much the athlete even missing two-thirds of one leg. "Mr. Michael," he said. "I'm some kind of happy you're here."

"I wouldn't have missed this for the world," I said, and then I pulled Gil to his feet. "Dee, this is Elisa's son, Gil. He's back from the wars. Literally, I mean that: he might as well be back from the dead, it's been so long since we've had him with us."

The two young men looked at one another as though they recognized something of themselves.

"You need to know each other since neither one of you lasted long in this place, I'm sorry to say."

"Okay," Gil said, "but I'm coming back."

"And, I guess I am, too," Dee said with a laugh, "whether they want me or not."

And, then there was the service: the processional and the bride walking down the aisle and hymns and readings and a homily and all the corny attempts to be significant about the meaning of marriage, the rings and candles and—well, you know the drill. Virginia was a lovely, lovely young woman, as poised as her mother, but without the shellac and varnish of the public figure. I could see Dee melt as she processed and then reached for him at the end of the aisle. And, then we were off, ticking the boxes in the order of service, one after the other, but I was lost in this moment that was made up of so many other moments and people from the past and in this space meant for silence and reflection: Dee, of course, but Gil and his mother, whether she was physically with us or not, Dr. Newland and the Reverend Dr. Felton Richards, who had been disgraced in some way and thereby fired after thirty-five years of service to the college, but who was the officiant for the ceremony nonetheless—one more thumb in the institution's eye, I thought—and even Dee's best man, Coach Bonaventura, who had brought Dee to the college in the first place, but like Dr. Richards had been fired two months after Dee's injury, not because Dee was hurt, but because he couldn't win a game without him, and because he wasn't airbrushed enough in the upper-middle class white Christian way.

"It's like old home week," I whispered to Gil. "All these people I thought never to see again."

He shrugged as though he were sitting next to an old fart

who can't keep chattering about himself in a moment meant for solemnity, and I guess he wasn't wrong.

Just before the recessional, we were asked to stand and sing Newton's "Amazing Grace," the original verses as well as a few extras that had been added for good measure. We looked to be in full throat for a while. "Amazing Grace" might seem like an odd choice for a wedding service, but then, I thought, what did a marriage need more than grace? Love and devotion will get you so far, but a little luck and divine favor can't hurt. We were singing Stowe's last apocryphal verse about "ten thousand years" when Gil nudged me. Tears were pouring down his cheeks like rivers and he didn't bother to wipe the water away.

"Look," he whispered, putting his arm over my shoulders, so he could whisper in my ear. "Why are you waiting? Why haven't you married my mother?"

[viii]

The Love Song of Little Walter Book
(Walter Book, 1987 / 1998 / 2004)

THEY WOULD GO THEN—"you and I"—he suggested, to a quaint little bistro that he knew in the Tower District of Fresno. Not a deserted street at all and not overly chichi, no false pretensions, but pleasant and accommodating nonetheless. Not one of those commercial places that were thrown together in the north end of town with prefabricated and artificially antique parts, by designers who tried too hard with dim lighting and ferns, brass railings and leather banquettes and the drone of one awful piano track after another, each one a variation of "Is That All There Is?" and the false mourning of nostalgia. Your head wouldn't be swiveling to find Peggy Lee. No, it was quiet and clean and the food was fresh, the chef an artist of understatement and simplicity. The waitstaff knew him and always looked forward to another opportunity to serve Dr. Walter Book, Ph.D., and Dr. Book's guest.

"I would like you to be that guest," he said. "You see? We could stroll the galleries and look at art. Go to the used bookstores and find a first edition."

Susan looked up at him from the platen of her typewriter. The cross made of nails that she wore around her neck clanked against the Selectric keyboard and made the typeball jump, ruining yet another form. Petition for Removal from Academic Probation. Three students were waiting in a line in order to get signatures from her boss, the dean, who was at that moment in a telephone conference with his pregnant wife, whose raised voice could be heard from beyond his closed door, but at this moment the students, rather than being impatient, rocking back and forth on their heels, seemed content to wait and hear what she would have to say to this most modest of proposals. Her face was pale and nearly translucent. Her eyes darted. Left, right. A vein was visible at her left temple, and he imagined the feel of it pulsing just below her skin.

"You're asking me to dinner?" she said.

"Yes," he said. "Yes, that is precisely what I'm asking you. It's God's will, you know," he said. "He told me so. He pointed you out and said, 'She's the one.'" He winked, in his best ironic manner. Which was when he handed her the cone of yellow roses he'd been holding behind his back, so suddenly that she sat up, startled, as though he had thrust forward a petrified snake or an unseemly body part.

216

"They're b-b-beautiful," she stuttered. And then she began to cry. Crying and hiccupping to the point that she lost her breath. The students clapped in approval. Walter bowed. God smiled. He, Dr. Walter Book, was sure of that.

THIS IS THE STORY he told himself. And told himself again, whenever the reality of married life became less than the expectations created by the repetitions and replays of his fantasies. How, as a young, newly-hired instructor at Sierra Presbyterian College, he found in his department a secretary—I'm sorry, forgive me, how careless and unthinking, I should have, I meant to say, *administrative assistant*—the woman who would be the love of his life. Jesus had heard his prayers and had sent to him, Walter Book, his soulmate, intellectual partner, and emotional confidante, and he, Walter Book, had brought her back to his tiny college gatehouse where they had each other to themselves and did not have to worry about the perspectives of others.

In the mornings, they would pray for the day ahead, that they would both be His hands and feet, voicing His thoughts and words in speech as well as on paper.

"Let us pray," he imagined himself as saying at the dinner hour. This, after a long day in classrooms and offices and faculty meetings. "Bless us, oh, Lord, and these thy gifts..."

And she would say, "Amen," and then bring an unending series of ceramic serving bowls to the table. And while they ate, they could talk about the course of their day: his classes, her household tasks (which no longer included secretarial duties, thank you very much; Dr. Book had no need of a wife who worked), and their mutual assessments of the students that he had seen in class and the students she had seen as she crossed the campus grounds. He could provide her with an abridged version of his lectures and what he had said in the department meeting regarding certain students' inferior preparation in reading and writing. Wouldn't she like that? Of course, she would. She still remembered the drudgery of those meetings and the impossibility of taking the minutes, who said what and when and why, and while she was not unhappy to miss them, she could still feign an interest. They might share poems like Barrett and Browning. And they would pray again, this time for the young men and women, who had so much to read and digest and learn, about themselves, the world, and their Lord and Savior.

At night, they would slip between ironed sheets, she in a crisp linen nightgown, he in silk pajamas. They would kiss for luck, and they would kiss to say good night before they put their respective pairs of glasses on their respective end tables. *Let me not to the marriage of true minds…* And they would sleep in chaste companionability. Good night! Sleep tight! Don't let the bed bugs…

Thank you, Lord. Thank you, Jesus. Amen.

WHEN WALTER'S FATHER DIED, Walter was fourteen, with a face full of acne and worry, and the corners of his eyes were crusty from the tears he had shed, out of obligation as well as fear and sorrow. He was pudgy and soft in a place, Estacada, which did not treat the pudgy and soft and bereaved with much kindness. Which was when his social studies teacher had grudgingly let him use his classroom as a refuge and an escape from the cruelties of the lunchroom and the playing fields of the middle school. He sat at a desk at the back of the room and wrote little stories of heroes who saved children from fires and bandits, the horrors of the nuclear age or the rubble of earthquakes while Eivar Mortenson graded tests and papers. After rescuing the children, the heroes would create small paradises out of the chaos from which the children had been saved. Mr. Mortenson never said a word, and he never, ever read a word of Walter's stories. Didn't even glance at them. He remembered Walter from the year before when he had been in his class, a class that Walter remembered with no great fondness or interest, for he had not liked the taciturn Mr. Mortenson then. But whenever Walter knocked during the lunch hour, Mr. Mortenson opened the door and then motioned for him to take a seat with no questions asked, no excuse needed, no discussion required. Mr. Mortenson didn't like the playing fields much either, and Walter suspected that his presence was as much a favor to his teacher as it was an imposition.

A deacon in the local Presbyterian church, Mr. Mortenson never spoke of his spiritual life or religious practice, but Walter knew of his teacher's affiliation if not his faith. He and his mother, on the other hand, attended services at a Bible church in Upper Highland, a holdover practice from his mother's family. The minister's message was clear: believe and be saved from the fires of hell; turn away and be damned to the flames. His father had refused to go, saying that such idiocy was the province of the superstitious and uneducated and those who needed to shave their foreheads, so close was hairline and eyebrows, but then he had died, so what did he know? After his father passed, he and his mother rejoined his mother's family in the weekly fright-session-as-sermon, and Walter dreamed dreams that often ended with red fire and the fear that the judgment of the Lord was his likely end. Walter pondered his father's fate as well as his own every Sunday morning. And while he sat in Mr. Mortenson's classroom every weekday at noon, he watched the older man in his domain, surrounded as he was by student bulletin board displays of the three branches of American government on the north wall and the European devastation of the Black Death to the east. His eighth-graders had taken special delight in drawing pictures of serfs with pus-laden tumors in their necks. He marked his students' tests with his suit jacket removed, his collar unbuttoned, tie askew, and his shirt sleeves rolled back to his elbow, and Walter felt a prickle of excitement on the back of his neck. *Jesus save me from the judgment to come*, Walter thought, and eventually the hero of his stories became the good Lord Himself, and the image of Jesus that he carried in mind became confused with Mr. Mortenson's bare forearms and the place at the base of his jaw where he had nicked himself shaving that morning. And he wondered what a Sunday morning might look like with a Jesus of love and the offertory plates in Mr. Mortenson's hands.

THE JESUS THAT LOOKED LIKE MR. MORTENSON had promised Walter that He would never leave and never forsake him, and that promise had been enough to get him through high school and college, but it seemingly had not extended to dissertation writing, which Walter began in 1982. At that point, the Jesus of Upper Highland had taken over, forcing Walter to the flames. Looking over his shoulder, Walter had proposed an analysis of the literature of trauma from the 1920s, using a Christian lens through which to view the wreckage. He would use Septimus Smith and Clarissa Dalloway as templates of characters functioning for better and for worse in the aftermath of global war and illness and in the throes of a loss of an institutionalized faith. His committee was unenthusiastic and disorganized and the last members of the English department to be assigned, and Walter understood that this was a sign of the esteem with which he was held. One professor was going simultaneously through a divorce from his wife, an affair with a grad student poet, and a harassment lawsuit, and none of these issues were related. Another committee member was ill, which Walter understood as a euphemism for rehab. While the chair of his committee, an Anglophile, Dickens scholar and recorder enthusiast named Welch, rejected his initial proposal and only signed off on the revision with Walter's promise not to include in his discussion any works written by Germans. Narrative or theological.

"We've had enough of that kind of thing, don't you think?" Welch had said. "Brrr," he made a noise as if he were freezing. "All that Teutonic blather."

"By all means," Walter said, and he waved one hand above his head. "Up to here."

Of what kind of thing he had in mind, Walter was unsure, but he agreed nonetheless. Whole-heartedly, even. No Germans. Done.

The next directive would be to incorporate materials from Professor Welch's little-known and underappreciated former mentor, Dr. Robert Helsinke, from Indianapolis, whose work in the Studies of Sacred Text as Literary Code, Welch thought that Walter would appreciate, given his spiritual leanings.

"An individualist, I will not live to see his like again," Dr. Welch said of Helsinke, who had died while paragliding at the age of seventy-six. He sailed over a ridge in Pacifica and was dead by the time he came down an hour later. "He was a man who was so far ahead of his time that he was periodically mocked for his positions. When he was noticed at all, that is, but at some point, I have no doubt he will be considered in the vanguard of a new school of criticism." He had several unpublished articles that he thought Walter might find useful. "And invaluable. Invaluable," his professor declaimed, enunciating each syllable with brimstone-like clarity.

"Yes, sir," Walter said, understanding in that moment that Welch thought his mentor a crank and Walter equally flawed, his dissertation in all likelihood never to be finished or reviewed. "I'm sure they will prove to be useful."

"Invaluable. His monograph on Captain Ahab as archetypal extremist will illuminate your thinking."

"Yes, professor. Invaluable."

"No one else," Welch said, "is doing this kind of work."

"LET'S HAVE WINE WITH DINNER," she too-often said. It had become a habit and a pattern for their evenings. "Don't you think that would be nice?" And tonight, she was already opening a Riesling that he despised for its sugary-sweetness, without even the pretense of discussion. Dinner, with Susan picking at his thrown-together tuna-noodle casserole and its cement-like white sauce. He ate everything she didn't. She drank the wine and then sat in front of the television, replenishing her wine glass from the beginning of a second bottle for three hours afterward. By ten o'clock the back of her head had rocked back onto the back of the couch, her mouth hanging open. This, after a day in which, he had received a phone call from the campus police chief.

"Michael Wayte found her," Lieutenant Perez said. "The O'Malley's guy. She was walking on the shoulder of the highway."

There wasn't much room for uphill and downhill traffic as it was.

"That's dangerous," the lieutenant said, "what with all the trucks. He had to make two u-turns just to pick her up and bring her back."

"Of course," Walter said. "Extremely dangerous. I don't know what she was thinking. And I don't know how he had the presence of mind."

"She told Michael she was on her way to see the tigers."

"The tigers," Walter said. "Oh." An image of his wife instantly flashed into view: Susan, intent on walking the pathways of the Cat Haven, tottering along the scree of the highway in a dress and pantyhose and her good dress pumps. Her purse swinging from her forearm. "But that's miles away."

"Sixteen-point-two miles," the lieutenant said. "She managed two. I have to give her credit." Two miles downhill was not nothing with log trucks and RVs blasting around the curves. "He brought her to the office, and I brought her back home and made her some coffee, and I'll stay with her until you get here, but she doesn't seem too happy."

Walter thanked the police chief and hurried across campus to the refuge of their gatehouse.

The evenings had been a cause for worry for some time. The alcohol, of course. Her periodic eruptions and outbursts. Her grievances and anger, real and imagined, came pouring out like lava. But she had always been something of a surprise to him, her reactions and obsessions hard for him to predict. Their anniversary at the Shakespeare Festival some years earlier, for example, when she became fixated on a younger couple that she had noticed in the lobby of their hotel. But now the days were likewise becoming marked by Susan's increasingly erratic behavior. She had wandered before, her eyes seemingly focused on another reality, but she had never before left the borders of campus; he found her a couple of times each week in the chapel, listening to those students practicing for recitals on the organ. At other times, she might have been in the bookstore in the Commons, where she was known by the clerks to shoplift items that were pocket-size: magnets with the campus logo, erasers, batteries; they knew to call Dr. Book the next day to make up the difference in the register. At home, he might catch her staring at the stove, perhaps, as if the arrangement of the knobs and burners needed to be translated and interpreted. It was not uncommon for her to read the same article in one of her women's magazines ten times or more, and each time it was new and its information so startling that she would be forced to tell him about the secret life of Cher yet again.

He came home and relieved the police chief of his babysitting duties, and then he made their execrable dinner while Susan drank until she passed out. When he came home, he had found her sitting on the couch, staring at the blank television screen, her jaw clenched.

"Maybe we should pray," Walter said, when the police chief had closed their front door. Because this, too, was a pattern, if only in fantasy and nothing they had ever truly shared. "Dear Lord," he said, with his eyes only half-closed just in case she bolted and reached for the kitchen knives. "Dear Lord, please be with my wife and my helpmate. My best friend. Help us to address these concerns with reason and with love, compassion and wisdom. Please, dear Jesus. Amen."

Who plans for such things? A wife who has gone off the rails. Let me ask You that, Jesus. Let me ask You that.

"Oh, please," she said, staring holes in his forehead. Her eyes had never closed. "All I want is a little dignity. A little love. Passion. Or a car. Is that too much to ask? I'm trapped here, and I'm treated like a child while you're interviewing replacements, Betty or Bob. Replacements for me. I'm the kept child of the exalted Dr. Walter Book, Ph.D." She turned her head to look at him. "As if. As if such a thing could be possible."

Her head hit the back of the couch some hours later, and the next morning, after canceling his classes, he began making certain difficult phone calls.

AMONG THE PAPERS in the box that Dr. Welch had given him was an article on *Mrs. Dalloway* as Gateway Sacrament for Nonbelievers that Helsinke had intended for *Renascence* but had neither submitted to the journal nor published elsewhere. With his dissertation clock ticking, Walter found himself relying more and more on the thirty-year-old badly typed manuscript, filled as it was with the hash-marks of cross-outs and the faint pencil scratches of emendations. Balloons littered the margins with text and arrows. Phrases and clauses became notes. Notes became text. He typed, praying for the soul of the dearly departed Dr. Robert Helsinke of Indianapolis and offering thanksgiving, if not citations, for ideas no one else had seen or heard in decades much less read. "No other eyes but mine," he breathed even as Jesus saw. When he was done, he paid one of the university typists to make the fair copy, the final draft submitted a month before his clock was due to expire. Only then did he put the lid back on the box and the box inside the oil drum behind his mother's house; he doused the contents with gasoline, lit the match, and watched the sparks of judgment fly upward to the tops of the dark and forbidding trees.

What was it like to die while drifting to the earth? Did he know that he was dead even as his ideas would have new life?

He wrote Dr. Welch a note with the submission of his last chapters. "As you may be able to see, I am heavily indebted to Dr. Helsinke's work," he wrote, hoping his confession would be understood for what it was, "and I hope I have not mis-characterized his ideas." But by this time, his committee was in shambles, decimated by lawsuit, hospitalization, and sickness—even Welch pleaded illness, a lingering case of strep throat, so he said—and his defense was conducted via telephone; it lasted no more than a desultory twenty minutes. His doctoral regalia—gown, hood, and tam—arrived by FedEx three months later in a box filled with Styrofoam peanuts and tissue paper. As it turned out, though, he skipped graduation in order to interview at Sierra Presbyterian, the only institution to respond to his application.

Praise the Lord and pass the host!

Mr. Mortenson-as-Jesus had come through, after all.

THE BOARD-AND-CARE HOME recommended by Susan's neurologist was thirty-five miles away in Sanger, a four-bedroom, three-bath ranch in a neighborhood of similar size and style homes. The Bermuda grass was cut so near to the ground that dirt showed through. The shrubbery was trimmed into boxes, orbs, and cubes. Theodora, the woman who owned the home, was a former hospice nurse who looked like a farm wife from the prairies of the 1930s; she wore print aprons, brooked no nonsense, and was not afraid of using restraints for those patients who became restless or abusive. She made Walter nervous at their first meeting when she straightened his bowtie and picked a piece of lint from his blazer. Her husband,

Lloyd, who did the yardwork, maintenance, and other unspecified heavy lifting, watched without saying a word.

"Your wife will be fine here," she said, "and you are not to worry."

"I should warn you: she'll be extremely agitated."

Theodora shrugged her practical shoulders. "Who wouldn't be? It's a prison sentence without a trial, a betrayal of the highest order. If it were me, I'd be pissed and throwing bricks. *If* I understood what was going on. Which none of them ever do, not entirely. But they always understand abandonment." And here she shrugged again, "What else are families to do? What else would *you* be able to do long term?"

That night, when Susan made her evening invitation to a bottle of wine, Walter waved her away and pulled out a full bottle of Hendrick's and the vermouth that he'd been hiding from himself as well as from her.

"Martinis?" he said, holding up the bottle of gin.

"Willy, you old sharpie, you," she said, clicking her tongue against her top teeth. Her glasses reflected back the light from their tiny pocket kitchen. "You're intending to get me drunk, aren't you?"

"Yes, my dear, I am." He considered it an ironic kindness, in this case, to be truthful. "So drunk, you won't know what hit you."

"You'll get me drunk and then have your way with me. I know you. You, beast, you."

She passed out at her standard time, and when she woke the next morning, he fixed a Bloody Mary for her, a Virgin Mary for himself, both with their telltale stalks of celery and drops of Worcestershire and horseradish. She propped her head in her hands and groaned, but she ate the toast that he fixed and the drink he had prepared, saying nothing. She was dozing by the time he bundled her into the car for the drive to Sanger, and she was only partially awake when he helped her from the car and into the wheelchair that Theodora and her husband had brought from the inside of the house.

The odor of gin and the heat of vodka hovered in the morning air.

"A little anesthesia," she said. "That's fine. A hangover and ordinary confusion. I'll take it from here. Better leave now before the recriminations begin."

He nodded, aware of his own cowardice, aware of what this woman and her silent husband must really think of him, of Susan, but grateful to be granted the permission to escape. To flee into his next, new life.

"Don't you worry about a thing," the woman said. "Another day or two, you'll be a stranger, and she won't know that anything's different."

WHEN HE BEGAN his career at Sierra Presbyterian, he became aware of time passing in a way that beggared memory. He threw himself into teaching and committee work and scholarship, not that there was anyone who necessarily cared what Assistant Professor Walter Book was or was not doing as the case might be. He showed up, he taught his classes, he was not responsible for scandal. That was good enough for another year and another contract. But then there was his marriage, which, unlike his career, began to unravel almost as quickly as it had begun. Susan chafed at the lack of anything meaningful for her to do, even though it was she, who had tendered her resignation the day after their engagement. It was true that he'd had questions about the appropriateness of her continuing to work in the same department after their marriage, but to quit outright, without anything else to do? It was a recipe for ennui, her living in the gatehouse without any other employment. She chafed at her own idleness, and she chafed at how busy her husband had become. How important within this little universe he was apart from her.

Still, the years went on; he taught, he published an article here and there among the Evangelical intelligentsia (and, yes, he knew that there are some in the academic world who would argue that this is an oxymoron), he began to play a larger and larger role within the department; meanwhile, Susan drank. She drank during the day, and she fomented her theories about his use of her; she drank at night, her paranoia bloomed, and she named other women as potential competitors. On occasion she threw a glass at the closed study door once he had moved more or less permanently into the coat-closet room that became a bedroom in fact if not by choice. After drinking a bottle of her sweet white wine, she had been known to yell, "I hate you!" in that tired and cliched way of any estranged secular couple, and now and again members of campus security make their periodic visit to ask that they turn down the volume of their marital bliss. A student cadet, wearing an orange vest, will arrive in a golf cart, knock on the gatehouse door, and ask politely that the Books lower their voices. *Please.* They are embarrassed, but calls have come in; concerns have been raised by students walking from the library and past the gatehouse. They plead for restraint. To keep private matters private. Walter will answer the knock at the door and suggest with a knowing smile that they have been interrupted in a conjugal act, one that requires a certain degree of role playing and theater and the danger of public discovery; the cadet will blush, apologize, and leave, with stories to tell among the cadet staff. Walter will not correct or amend the impression, and only the police chief, Lieutenant Perez, will most nearly decipher that which lies behind the closed door.

Ten years after Walter's hiring, Bobby Thornton, the Chairman of Chronos Athletic, was elevated to the Board of Trustees of Sierra Presbyterian, and the staid institution began to show new life, moving away from their mainline denominational roots and toward a more vigorous, assertive statement of Christian faith and conviction as befitting Liberty Christian College, the school's new name and identity. No greater evidence for this conviction was the rebuilding of Golgotha, the three-cross memorial site, where two cousins burned themselves to death in 1974 in protest of the school's apathy and apostasy. The wooden crosses that burned were replaced by steel crosses, a bronze plaque was affixed to a granite boulder, and a rose garden was planted surrounding the site, which became a destination spot for Easter Sunday sunrise services. Throughout the year, morning, noon, or night, the occasional visitor might be observed sitting on the bench in silent contemplation or prayer.

When Dr. Cheryl Newland was selected to be the President of Liberty Christian, a circle of sorts was completed, since the oldest buildings that comprised the college dated back to Prohibition and that time when it was home to an order of aging nuns who were oblivious to the fact that the cellars of their cloister were being used as a storage facility by enterprising bootleggers. It is, Walter liked to think, a reminder that housed within us all are the seeds of our self-deceptions and our worst behaviors. Cheryl Newland was a polished presence, but beneath that veneer lay a fear and sense of inferiority that Walter recognized instantly and intuitively. So familiar did it seem that at a reception for her as the new president, he was unable to stop snickering as the trays of canapes circulated through the faculty dining room. The high-pitched titter was uncontrollable and as mortifying to himself as well as those around him. His laughter was so overwhelming that tears started from his eyes. Bobby Thornton looked at him with an expression of open and undisguised disgust. Even well-lacquered, well-defended Cheryl Newland seemed taken aback by this faculty member who had seemingly lost his mind. Nothing helped. He was so far gone, he could have made an appearance on one of those mental health commercials. The mutual embarrassment grew until Reverend Richards, the college chaplain, put one angular arm around Walter's pudgy shoulders and ushered him from the room.

"Maybe a little water?" he said, guiding him toward the student dining hall and the soft drink dispensers. "Swallowing might break the cycle."

Walter nodded, choking back the last of his unfunny hysteria. He took a breath, then gulped water as fast as he could, hoping not to inhale while he was mid-swallow.

"It's like hiccups," the minister said. "Once you start, it's hard to stop."

"Yes," Walter said; he was panting but finally able to control his own breath and voice. "I don't know," he said. "It felt like I could look at anything, and it struck me as hilarious. The little tassels on Bobby Thornton's shoes. The students with their serving trays. Cheryl Newland's hair. All of it, hilarious. And then I couldn't help myself."

"Well," the minister said. "You're better now. That's the main thing."

"I am."

"Good." The minister squinted at him. "You don't think much of our new president, I take it."

Walter shook his head, resisting the temptation to honesty. "I have no opinion one way or another. She had nothing whatsoever to do with it. The laughter, I mean."

This was at least partially true. He had had one of those moments of clarity when it seemed that all was visible. He had lived his entire life in fear of being mocked and exposed: for what he lacked in physical stature and social grace, for everything that he didn't and would never know about men, women, and himself. For the dubious nature of his degree and credentials. But he was not alone. Not just the new president, but each person in the room had appeared naked before him as they would to God, and they had all been revealed without disguise or camouflage: an assemblage of lesser intellects and greater egos, frightened to death of being discovered for the collection of quivering flaws that they were. Could there be anything funnier than that? Could there be anything more tragic?

LEAVING SUSAN AT THE BOARD-AND-CARE HOME was one of the hardest things he had ever done. Just as hard would have been not to have taken her at all. To have continued in the same way, day after aggrieved day. Nearly as hard was following Theodora's order to stay away for at least the next week in order for Susan to "settle in" as the former nurse had put it. Guilt times guilt equals a crushing burden. Settling in. As though Susan were sailing for Bora Bora and parts unknown on a cruise ship, rather than a single level ranch house in Sanger. Her room in the board-and-care was Spartan and compact, so—in that way, at least—her environment was not unlike a ship's cabin even if the scenery wasn't quite so exotic or changeable. Rather than sailing from one port of call to another, she was traveling backwards into the absence of memory.

Without Susan at home and prohibited from visiting her at the board-and-care, his evenings were empty, a luxury of time.

"I will revisit my dissertation," he said to the ticking sideboard clock.

"I will write a new article on 'Death in Venice,'" he said to the figurines on the end table.

"I will read a novel that is slated to become part of our literature," he said to the empty wine bottles in the recycling bin.

In the end, however, rather than do anything productive and rather than drink the terrible wine that Susan had ordered by the case or take electronic IQ tests for reassurance, he drove down the mountain to Fresno and the galleries scattered throughout the Tower District. It was a Thursday night and the ArtHop crowds were shuffling from one exhibit to another with stops for drinks along the way. After a dispiriting tour of black-and-white photographs and another walk past display walls of hotel-room-style landscapes and romanticized Native Americans, he retreated back to his car and the highway, aware of how far from his first date fantasy his reality had diverged. Rather than return home to the gatehouse, however, he turned into the gravel driveway and parking lot of O'Malley's, that eyesore among the pines. He had come here a time or two through the years, but this was nothing like a stopping place of habit. He was no regular. Even so, he knew Elisa, whose son had gone to the college for a time; she was now jawing with two of the old geezers at one of the back tables, and he recognized Michael, the one who had come to Susan's rescue not so long ago, who was an alum of the college from its Sierra Presbyterian days, long before Walter had arrived. He settled onto a bar stool and tore a cocktail napkin to shreds while waiting for a gin and tonic, the only drink he could think to name. A squat monument of a man wearing a voluminous Hawaiian shirt sat on the stool to his right, drinking a shot and a beer without any great fondness for either the whiskey, the beer, or the bartender. Or so it seemed.

"Since when did you become the Pillsbury Doughboy?" the man said to Michael.

Michael shrugged, unperturbed. "I was fat the day I was born." He set another shot and pint on the bar. "I like to think of myself as consistent and reliable."

"Man, you let yourself go. I'm big, but you are one pudgy motherfucker. I bet if I stuck my finger in your belly-button it would come out butter."

"Dr. Book," Michael said, directing his attentions back to Walter, "pay no attention to this reprobate. Telofa was my roommate a million years ago, and he thinks there is no greater joy than making me feel bad about myself."

"Got that right," the Hawaiian shirt agreed. "Kick him when he's down."

"Dr. Book teaches at what's left of our alma mater."

"Oh, yeah? What do you teach?"

"Literature," Walter said, though for reasons he couldn't identify, he felt reluctant about such an admission, as though the information would be held against him at a later date.

"Oh, yeah? Literature?" The monument tottered on his stool. "'And what rough beast, its hour come round at last, / Slouches towards Bethlehem to be born?'" He slammed the shot glass on the bar. "You teach that kinda shit to the little Republicans?"

"Something like that," Walter said. "Yeats' eschatology makes them panic a bit. But to be fair, they get nervous no matter what they read. When they find out that Tolkien was Catholic, it makes them worried about reading *The Lord of the Rings*. Some of them haven't been allowed to read Harry Potter. The sign of the stigmata is a Satanic ritual, and *Song of Songs* is Jewish pornography. I feel like I'm introducing them to the things they've been sheltered from their whole lives."

"Poor darlings," Michael said.

"The dealer of their education, that's me. They leave class thinking themselves rebels, or they go back to their dorms and write letters home."

"Huh," Telofa said. "That's a shame."

"If we've been successful, they go home at Christmas break and they hate their parents." Walter looked at himself in the back mirror of the bar while he drank the G&T. He had allowed his excitement to take hold of him. His forehead was shiny and red, and the thinning hair at his temples was damp. In his blazer and bow-tie, he didn't look like anyone who belonged. Not here, not there, not anywhere. "Of course, ten years later, they've become their parents. By and large, the majority of them are sweet kids, but they're either scared of just about everything, or they want to make money."

"Telofa, here, if you can believe it, was a surgeon, him and his fat fingers, but now he's an *artiste*."

So, now it was his turn: "Is that right?"

Telofa, it turned out, had made a pile as a result of an orthopedic limb positioning system, a timely patent, and an even more timely surge in knee and hip replacements. The pile had bought him early-early retirement from his surgical practice and a place in the mountains where he now carved totems, welded steel plinths, and cemented rocks into giant cairns.

"There's a market for that," Walter said. "Who knew?"

"There is. Anything phallic," he said, his laugh much higher-pitched than one would have thought for a man his size. "We are what we are."

"You ought to see it," Michael said, "his art yard. No shortage of erections."

Telofa turned on his barstool so that he was facing Walter directly. Put a meaty hand on Walter's knee to give it a squeeze. "Yeah, you ought to come over," he said.

WALTER AND SUSAN WERE MARRIED in the college chapel on a late Friday afternoon after classes had concluded for the week. They had originally hoped that the ceremony could be held on Saturday morning, but the chapel had been booked for an organ festival and competition, and as it was, their wedding flowers were dwarfed by the festival banners already decorating the otherwise austere and dimly lit interior. Dr. Richards officiated; Dr. Richards' much-too beautiful wife, Desiree, and Dean Reilly, their mutual boss, signed the license as witnesses.

"Go forth in love and peace," Dr. Richards pronounced to their gathering of five. "Go forth as husband and wife, in equality and solidarity amidst the chaos of the world."

And so, they did go forth into the world, stepping outside and squinting into the radiance of an angry late-spring sun.

Their reservations for a hotel in San Francisco had been booked for Saturday evening when they had thought their wedding would be that same day, so following their Friday ceremony, they walked back to the gatehouse, carrying the three vases of wedding flowers to what was now their joint residence.

"That was lovely," Susan said, sniffing a little, in preparation, he thought, for a happy, little cry. "I n-n-n-ever thought, that—"

She didn't complete the sentence, but she did fall into his arms.

"There, there," he murmured. "Nothing need be done. Not right now." He stroked her hair and kissed the top of her head. "Everything will be just fine."

Her arms grew tighter around him, and he closed his eyes.

"Oh, Jesus," he said, "help us to be good to one another. Help us to love when love is not easy."

Susan relaxed her grip. "No," she said. She held his face in her hands. "Don't do that."

"What?"

"Be a person, please," she said. "I've been with Jesus all my life, but now I have you."

Since they had come to the chapel directly from work, Susan wore her office outfit, a white blouse with a bow and a black skirt and jacket, while Walter wore his classroom blue blazer, silk shirt, and bow-tie. But now, she began pulling at the bow and unbuttoning her blouse. She unzipped her skirt and let it fall. "Save it," she said. "For once, let's say grace after the meal."

"You're a little tiger, you are," Walter said.

And she made a sound in the back of her throat that

sounded like a growl.

"Really, but we—" he said, patting her now bare shoulder. "Don't you think that our first time should be special? Tomorrow night in the hotel for our honeymoon as we'd planned?"

"Undo my bra, Walter," she said. She had taken her glasses off, and her eyes, although a bit crossed, were focused on a spot somewhere behind his head. "Now, please, the bra. We can talk later."

He reached around her to fumble with the hook-and-eye of the clasp, careful of the clasp's mechanics, careful to touch as little as possible the skin of her back. "I never know," he said. Freed, her small breasts bobbed in front of him, and he felt a contraction within his groin. "I never know how— Oh, you are something, aren't you?"

"Now pull my panties down."

Yes, dear.

While he obeyed, she was stripping him of blazer and suspenders and tie. Silk shirt flung to the wall, dress pants in a puddle at his feet. Conscious of his white, unshapen lumpiness, his unformed, unforgiven unloveliness.

One arm went around his neck, she rubbed herself against him, and he smelled the human odor of two bodies near the end of a long and stressful day.

"I want you to take me, Walter," she breathed. "Take me. I want you to crush me. To love me."

He put his lips on hers and reluctantly tasted the sourness of another soul. He would have to be a husband. To the best of his abilities, and not to be suspected otherwise. He would have to go through with this. If only to be polite.

[ix]

Used

(Leah Green, 2002 / 2014)

S HE MET HIM ONE FRIDAY night in February in the parking lot by their dorm when Claire's car wouldn't start.
Claire and Dottie, her suitemates, had gone to Fresno to visit
their indistinguishable boyfriends, and as they left, Claire
had tossed Leah the keys to der Führer, her father's charcoal
gray Bonneville. "Just in case," she said, "you need to visit
the whorehouse." By which she meant a need to escape the
Liberty Christian campus with its Student Code of Conduct
and Stadler Hall with its matronly Resident Director, the
redoubtable Mrs. Hazel Grimes, and her rules and strictures,
however erratically enforced.

She hadn't planned on going anywhere, but after reading
seventy pages of Muscatine, most of which she had highlighted and little of which she had understood, she thought
that a drive down the hill in the dark with the radio on might

clear her mind of what was now a muddle of the medieval ages. But when she turned the key in the ignition, the only sound she heard was the telltale click and fizz of a battery no longer able to perform its function. Her choices were simple: go for a walk around the arid hillscape of the campus, a walk she'd made dozens if not hundreds of times in the last two years; hope that someone on her floor was ordering a pizza; plead her cause to someone else with a car; or call campus security for a battery and jumper cables. She locked the car, returned to her room and dialed 7-711 and waited for someone to answer. When the answering machine turned on and encouraged her to dial 911 if this were a real emergency, she hung up the phone, pulled on her peacoat, and walked to the security shack on that road between the gatehouses and the Administration building. Sodium vapor lamps illuminating the quad turned the overcast sky orange, while in the security office, the blue light of a television glowed, a suburban neighborhood of one.

A student cadet sat at the desk with the small portable set turned to "America's Funniest Home Videos"; children were apparently getting buckets stuck on their heads and running into walls at the direction of their parents, accompanied by the soundtrack of adult laughter on tape and in the studio audience.

"I called," she said.

"Oh?" He turned the volume down, but the television remained on. "Did you leave a message?"

"No. My car won't start."

"Okay."

"You have a battery cart, don't you? I've seen it."

He tipped back in the desk chair. "You could have left a message, you know."

"Sorry to interrupt your show."

"No big deal," he said, waving it away. "It's stupid."

He looked her up and down, assessing what, she couldn't tell.

"So, can you get the battery cart?"

"I would if I could," he said. "The cart was stolen last week."

"From the security office? The battery cart was stolen from the Liberty Christian security office?" She shook her head. "Do you see a problem with that?"

A shrug and a yawn. "People are people. And around here they're more like people than usual."

The phone began to ring, but rather than answer it, he let it ring until the answering machine clicked on, and Leah heard the murmur of the outgoing message. The electronic tone sounded and then the machine clicked off again into silence.

"Must not have been that important," he said.

"Or it was a real emergency," she said.

"Either way," he said, "where would you like to go?"

YEARS LATER, LEAH WOULD TELL and retell this story to various individuals and groups, rarely satisfied that she had gotten it right. The details were not confusing, but what they added up to was a sum unrelated to its parts.

Joshua—Joshua Bowen, according to the nameplate he wore above his left shirt pocket—took a set of keys from the pegboard on the wall and a walkie-talkie from the desk, then placed the Closed sign in the window and locked the office door behind them. Outside, he opened the passenger door to the Jeep, which the police lieutenant used during the day. At night, the cadets used a golf cart to make the rounds of the dorms, checking that the outer doors were locked and using the searchlight to scan the bushes for potential intruders or illicit student behavior; they used the golf cart, Joshua said, because it was quiet and they were students and even a college with an endowment had limits to their liability insurance.

"You won't get in trouble?"

"Let's see about your car," he said.

They drove to the nearly empty parking lot where the Bonneville sprawled across two spaces.

"It's my suitemate's actually. She calls it der Führer," Leah said. "I don't know why. Her father gave it to her, but it's not a German car or anything. He might have had a Mercedes before this. I don't know. It's gray."

"Okay, that's interesting," he said, although it clearly wasn't.

In the Jeep's headlights she could see how slender and small he was and how oversized his uniform shirt and trousers fit him. Then he opened the hood and he was hidden as he affixed the jumper cables from the Jeep to the Bonneville.

"Maybe," he said, now only a voice, "it's the kind of car Hitler would have driven if he were alive and wearing Bermuda shorts at Sunshine Village."

"Maybe."

"Try starting it," he said, and the Bonneville sprang to life immediately when she got in and turned the key in the ignition. "Let it run for a bit," he said and unhooked the cables.

"Maybe I just need to meet her father," Leah said when he had slid into the passenger seat next to her.

"Maybe," he said. "Or maybe because der Führer is just that dead." He tapped the battery gauge in front of her. "I think the alternator is gone. You might get somewhere, but you won't get back."

She turned the key to Off, and der Führer was still. She turned the key back again, and they heard the click-click-pause-click-pause, and then nothing-nothing-nothing.

"Maybe," she said, realization blooming like a time-lapse nature video, "maybe she only calls it that around me. Since I'm Jewish. Maybe she thinks she's being funny. Or not."

"Either way," he said again, "where would you like to go?"

HERE'S WHAT SHE LEARNED ABOUT HIM: he was a senior with one of those made-up majors (The Church: Communities, Communes, and Collectives). Since he had no idea what he would do with himself once May arrived, he planned to continue working at the security shack during the summer, monitoring all the little snot-nosed church campers and sports campers and hacker campers who would be crowding into the dorms while the real, older brats were gone. He would cross from one side of the platform to the other, shake Dr. Newland's hand, accept the empty leatherette diploma-holder, and then when everyone else had packed up, moved out, and abandoned the campus, he would come back to the night shift for the next three months as though nothing had changed in the slightest. His parents were missionaries in Thailand, and he had no interest in returning to Bangkok. There really wasn't room for him in their tiny apartment anyway; when they moved from their larger house in Lopburi so that his father could take the director's position, they weren't expecting him to return. Maybe not in so many words, but their assumptions were clear.

"After August, who knows," he said. The walkie-talkie garbled and squawked, but he pushed it away.

"That's awful," she said. They were sitting in O'Malley's because it was the only place nearby she could think to go. A band of PG&E workers was playing terrible country-western music through overwrought amps and singing with even more terrible voices, and she was nearly shouting to make herself be heard. "Two years from now, I'll have to beat my parents away with a stick if I don't want to be kidnapped and taken home."

He shrugged and held up his hand to order a second beer while she stared down into her Diet Coke, which was better than staring at the stage, the band, or the size 52EEE-sized bra that hung limply from the rafter above them.

"It's okay," he said. "It's not like they turned my bedroom into a sewing room or a craft room while I was gone. They moved. But I don't have a room, and when I go there, I sleep on a mat in the living room. I don't want to go back."

"Still," she said, "your parents. You don't think they want to see you?"

The band broke into a bad, up-tempo version of "Ring of Fire" and hoped that volume and speed would make up for their multitude of sins.

"The walls are so crappy I hear them fucking in the next room. Like it means something to them, like they know what love is. What do you think of that?"

Which was when the woman from the bar came with Joshua's second Bud Light and offered Leah her most sympathetic glance, as if to say, "I don't know what you're doing here." But instead, she said, "I'll come back with more Coke," and touched Leah on one shoulder.

Wasn't her name Elisa?

"I think," Leah said, considering. "I think that everything makes noise, and there's not much we can do about it."

"Except not be around to hear it," Joshua said.

HE DRANK TWO MORE BEERS while the band made their noise, joyful or otherwise. She drank more soda, used the

Port-a-Potty outside, and then stood in the parking lot to look at the sky which was still overcast and as dark as dark could be. Elisa stood near the door smoking a cigarette, the tip of which made an angry pinprick of orange light. Hearing the band from outside was only slightly less painful than hearing them from ten feet away.

"Been with Buddy-boy long?" she said.

"I'm not 'with-him' with him," she said. "We're just hanging out for the evening."

Elisa peered around the doorframe and into the wall of sound. "Goddammit, they're still here. I hate band night when it's the locals. Every prick with a guitar and an electrical cord thinks he's Eric Clapton or Hank Williams."

"My roommate's car wouldn't start, so Joshua—"

"Joshua Bowen. That's his name." Elisa stepped on what was left of the cigarette. "He's been coming here ever since he could fake an ID. He's only drinking now because he's finally legal and his ID is real. But you may want to be the one to drive home."

"Sure." She looked through the doorway and into the bar. Joshua was sitting in their booth, drinking his beer and listening to the awful music with a look on his face that said he appreciated what the band was trying to do even if they were terrible. His applause didn't appear to be ironic, unless she was too insensitive to register it, and she thought, He really is kind of cute, him with his narrow face and too-big uniform and his eyes that appeared to be too easily hurt.

"Honey," Elisa said. "Honey, are you listening to me."

THIS IS WHEN the story became more difficult to tell. And more confusing. When Leah told Joshua what Elisa said, he laughed and laughed, but he did not give her the keys; he told her that there was nothing to worry about, that he was fine, Elisa's concern notwithstanding. And, honestly, his driving didn't seem any different from three hours earlier except that when they passed the turnoff for the Cat Haven he began to sing "O God, our help in ages past" in what might have been his best impression of an operatic tenor or "Willy the Whale" before moving on to "Blessed Assurance" in which he out-Gaithered Gaither, which was already a parody, and seemed to be something of his point.

When they returned to the security shack, Joshua hung up the keys to the Jeep, replaced the walkie-talkie on its base, and listened for messages, of which there were none, although there were three more telltale clicks. Real emergencies or calls of not much importance. He kept the Closed sign in the window and said she should stay, the evening was young, although it was already morning, and since she really had no desire to go back to what was likely an empty suite, she stayed, which was when he showed her the tiny room at the back of the office, a closet, really, where they kept a fold-out metal-frame bed and a mattress covered in one of those itchy Army blankets so that those on the night shift could catch a few hours of sleep if they needed to. They sat on either end of the bed with their backs against the wall and talked and talked, as though they were playing Truth or Dare if the dare was contained in the depth of the truth they told. He told her about Thailand and growing up there with his parents whose lives were consumed by their outreach to the Thai people, among the most unchurched people in the world, to the near-total exclusion of their son. Even during that one year when he had been stateside while his parents were on sabbatical, he had been alone, and for the last two years of high school he had been sent to Manila, a precursor of the separations to come. "Read Orwell about boarding school," he said. "Read Dickens about being an orphan. Every Missionary Kid could tell you about that." And she told him about growing up in a secular, socialist Jewish household in Yonkers, where the ground was still rock hard and frozen, unlike here where blossoms from the fruitless pear had been falling for a week or more along with every other kind of pollen known to God and man, making everyone sneeze rather than shiver; her family didn't know what to make of her for going so far away and for surrounding herself with the *goy* of the privileged upper classes. She could have done that for so much cheaper so much closer to home. A private Christian college—nearly everything antithetical to her parents' ethos, except their tolerance and their desire to accommodate her. It had to hurt them. "But I knew I had to get away," she said. "I was making too many mistakes with my life." In turn, he told her about discovering that his father was not above using an endless number of Thai prostitutes and spa girls in addition to his mother. Which was when she told him about the time when she nearly had an abortion, not that one can almost have an abortion any more than one can be almost pregnant, except that she miscarried before she could make the appointment. "That's when I knew," she said, touching the corners of her eyes. "That's why I'm here. I needed to have some sense of certainty. Right and wrong."

Joshua reached across the bed to hold her hand and said, "I don't know how much of this will mean anything to you, but no matter what the bozos here might say, the central tenet of our religion is love. Love first, love last, and love always. God is love. Jesus is love. Love is eternal innocence. If doctrine becomes more complicated than that, then it's just a tool for evil and division." He had made a study of it, he said, in his work on communities, and while some communities were inspired by lunatics and their fringe ideas, some of those ideas had merit no matter who the crackpot might have been to first espouse them, they were more relevant than ever, and he couldn't understand how love and true communion between believers could exist so far down the list for most of the Evangelical world, assigning all the dos to the bottom and the don'ts to the top. Why should we restrict ourselves to ancient prohibitions when those prohibitions have scarred us for millennia? Why be bound by tired orthodoxies when airplanes fly into towers and the world as we know it is being destroyed? "The Kingdom of Heaven is in you," he said. "You are perfect in love and perfected in Jesus."

"Well," she said. "Okay, now that's the thing you need to realize."

And that's when it became confusing because the first word that came to mind was *meshuganeh*, and nothing could have been further from her mind, but then they were staring into one another's eyes so intently that she could no longer see his orphan's face and she could no longer think of objections, and then they started kissing, their hands exploring each other's hills and valleys, and he was taking off his baggy uniform shirt with its name tag, and she was unbuttoning her Pendleton and unzipping her jeans, and when she heard the clank of his belt buckle hitting the cement floor, she asked him if he had any protection, but he said there was no need, that they could connect with one another skin-to-skin, and from practice he had enough control and the discipline that he could help her to come without needing to as well. Her pleasure was his pleasure, and he was not so greedy to require reciprocity. She doubted that this was so but was already so far beyond argument that she could not say *No* or *Wait* or *Let's have a think about this because I've done my time of remorse and regret* or *There are more issues than pregnancy, you know*. But she didn't because he was whispering, "You are love, you are love, Jesus brought you here to me," which feathered in her ear until he had her positioned just so, and she was gasping and crying that Yes, she was love and so was he and all the world and everything in it, this was love, too, and there was other gibberish of this kind—to the point that she wondered if this was what those speakers of tongues felt like to lose such control over one's utterances and if that was the case, then count her among the Holy Rollers. *Hallelujah! Praise Jesus* (no matter how wrong that might be)*! Amen.*

SHE CAME TWICE or maybe three times depending on how she counted that last long interlude, and he was as good as his word, withdrawing before any potential damage was done, and he left her panting underneath that scratchy wool blanket as though she were already wearing a hair shirt, but one that wasn't necessary after all, since she had never felt this guilt-free before. Not a vestige, a scrap, of second thought. Rather, the blanket served as a kind of bonus penance, a redundancy or a precaution against the next time of feeling bad. At five-thirty, he woke her up, with a cup of tarry black coffee and an upturned flashlight next to the bed.

"My relief will be here soon," he said.

She blew her hair out of her face. "Okay," she said. "I just need, I need to get—" She felt as though someone had lowered her into the bowels of the earth and was shoveling dirt on top of her, she was that discombobulated.

"Shh." He put his finger against her lips. "You have a little time."

"I feel …buried. Dead and gone."

"You're funny," he said. "But you're alive. Trust me."

"I'm going to sleep for days," she said, "thanks to you, mister."

She reassembled herself as best as she could although nothing felt quite right under her peacoat, as though every button to her name was in the wrong hole, and then she walked across campus in the dark and back to her dorm and the silence of her empty suite, Dottie and Claire evidently having decided to stay over in Fresno with Boyfriend A and Boyfriend B. By the light of her study lamp, she undressed and discovered that she had indeed buttoned her shirt the way a six-year-old might under duress, and in their bathroom, she took stock. She was, after all, attractive, she decided, and that was from an objective standpoint since she did not usually feel so detached. She could say such things to herself and not think herself delusional. Some might even call her cute and, in certain lights and in certain moments, the word beautiful might even be appropriate, an assessment seemingly affirmed just a few hours earlier. Maybe not in the classic blonde, blue-eyed, California Girl, Beach Boys' sense of the word, but her body had its own drama and its own story to tell, one that was a little more exotic than most of these white bread Evangelicals knew what to do with, Joshua being the clear exception. On the other hand, there were times when she could hardly get out of the way of her own body, her breasts and hips feeling like so much extra packaging. And yet, on that metal, fold-out bed, she had felt as athletic and lithe as one of those fourteen-year-old Romanian gymnasts who spin in the air with what seem to be wild abandon and yet land on target with nary a bobble or twitch.

When she left the security office, she had thrown her arms around Joshua and kissed him one last time, and he had said that they would have to do this again, that they were just beginning to know one another, and she had thought, *Well, duh. Why wouldn't we?* Which was when she had floated back to her suite, thinking how different an encounter this had been from her last date, just before 9/11, when she had gone to Fresno with Dottie and Claire, gotten drunk and gone to bed with one of their boyfriends' friends, call him Boyfriend C, because his name she now couldn't remember, an episode that had left her feeling as though her insides were made of ash. In the aftermath, she had actually gone to see the chaplain, Dr. Richards, seeking counsel because that hadn't been the first time she'd betrayed some interior rule of the Self she didn't understand. The whole world was under attack, and she couldn't shake the idea that it had been her fault somehow. As though her behavior could be the cause for global catastrophe. *Stupid, stupid girl.* For what she had done as well as for how she had conflated the personal with so much larger, more important concerns. And while Dr. Richards hadn't exactly been helpful, he had distracted her by taking her to O'Malley's for lunch and the big trees at Kings Canyon for perspective. He had cheered her up despite his own troubles, such as his divorce from his wife of nearly thirty years and his getting fired from the college for reasons that were vague but no doubt embarrassing or criminal or both, given his reluctance to provide details. What was truly ironic was that he had cheered her up and helped her forgive herself, even if he hadn't really been able to dispel her sense of guilt (she had, in fact, felt guilty for taking his time when he clearly had so many other things on his mind) whereas two hours with Joshua in the romper room activity of sex that he had called *communion* had left her feeling as though she had a right to such pleasures of the body. Their encounter had proceeded from love, true intercourse, rather than two bodies merely slamming against each other. If that wasn't different, she didn't know what was. She might as well have been born again, even if that wasn't what the Evangelicals intended by the term. Unless it was, in which case she had been a fool all along.

But, Leah decided, there was nothing so obviously different that anyone else would notice. She saw the same person in the mirror, wide-cheeked and wild-haired, prone to anxiety and over-examination, but now she could look at herself with a kinder, more compassionate eye. And guilt, as Joshua had said, was just a concept used by institutional authority to maintain a vestige of control. She didn't feel guilty, so why invite its arrival? And when Claire and Dottie asked her how her weekend had been, she said Okay and left it at that, other than explaining to Claire that her car was obviously in need of a little work and would need a jump start to get to whatever garage she or her father used. For their part, Claire and Dottie were full of intimate details regarding their boyfriends and themselves—hot tubs and first martinis and a hotel room with pay-per-view channels, none of which their parents would likely approve if they ever knew—and while it seemed like much too much information, Leah smiled and said Yes, it sounded like they had had a good time all right. But she couldn't quite let the evening go either, to the point that she said in as casual a way as possible: "Do either of you know Joshua Bowen? He was the one who helped me get the car started and told me it was probably the alternator." Which was when Claire and Dottie looked at one another in a way that would have been called overly dramatic if they had done so on stage, a glance that might as well have been a smoke signal or a flare.

"He's an odd duck," Dottie said.

"But he's not unattractive," Claire added.

"No, not unattractive at all," Dottie said. "In fact, I think you could say that he's very attractive. To a fault, for a small man."

Dottie had an older friend from school and church who had gone out with Joshua during the fall semester of their sophomore year. Joshua seemed nice and respectful if a little socially awkward, easily enough explained by his being an MK and living in several different out-of-the-way and exotic places without much American socialization. On the other hand, Marielle was innocent and kind, the sort of person who prayed before every meal but without making any kind of show of it. She was kind and open-eyed, a sweet, sweet, *sweet* girl, Dottie said, making "sweet" sound like the most pejorative kind of synonym for "stupid," and after two months of going out with Joshua, Marielle had made an appointment with the school psychologist and then, a month after that, left school altogether. Dottie never did get the whole story, other than the fact that Marielle was now attending an alternative Great Books school somewhere in the desert southwest and had declined all requests for her current e-mail address or phone number. Something had happened. What that might be was anybody's guess, and whether Joshua had any part to play in Marielle's new residence among the Gila monsters and armadillos, it was impossible to say but open for rampant speculation.

"Be careful," Dottie said.

"And don't be stupid," Claire and Dottie said together.

This from these girls, each of whom wore a purity ring on a finger and kept condoms in her purse. What was one to make of these Baptists, Church of God-ers, and Pentecostalists, Leah wondered. As Dr. Richards once told her, they were as righteous as a temperance crusade and as knowing and cynical as the vice squad. But, according to Claire's mother, there's the Ideal and the Real, and you damn well better know the difference; to be in the choir, it's your job to make sure the polyester of your robe is flame-retardant.

"Innocence is nice," Claire said, repeating her mother's advice, "it's all well and good, but naïveté is stupid. And stupid is as stupid does."

So much for the WYSIWYG of Evangelical rectitude.

So, THEY SETTLED into something of a routine. Joshua worked on Monday, Wednesday, Friday, and alternate Sunday nights in the security shack, but Friday night belonged to her, Joshua said, and when she walked through the darkened campus after ten o'clock, she found him as before in front of the portable television while the phone rang and the answering machine picked up. They watched whatever inanity was on for half an hour, and then put the Closed sign in the window while they retired to the closet and the metal bed frame at the back of the office where they talked and talked in anticipation of what they both knew was the point of being together.

Joshua had certain theories about Christianity and faith, which were distinctly at odds with those taught in the Liberty Christian religious seminars. "Most of the people around here are Christians in the sense that they go to church and it creates their calendar," he said. "Christmas, Easter, you know, but it doesn't really do anything to affect their personal lives except give them a reason to shop, and they don't really believe anything except in the most abstract way. You wouldn't know that they're Christians any more than you'd know they're Rotarians. And then there are those Christians who believe what they believe and live what they live and one has nothing to do with the other."

She couldn't help but think of Dottie and Claire and Claire's mother and all that steely concentration required in order to have two separate and sequestered lives.

"There are those," Joshua said, "who see their faith as a tool for controlling their own lives and the lives of others, keeping a lid on everything that God has given us, as though we're boiling pots about to explode. They're extremists, no better or worse than the Taliban, and you might as well wear a *burqa*. Then, there are some who see their faith as not only controlling behavior but also political direction, all that 700 Club, Pat Robertson, Praise Jesus, Jerry Falwell, hold your hands in the air bullshit. The Bakkers, Jim and Tammy Faye. They just want money for themselves, even though they claim it's for the benefit of 'ministry'; they want power even though they call it something else. Christian values, maybe. One nation under God is just their code for a Christian theocracy and for everyone else to get out. And 9/11 is just the proof of their case."

"Oh," Leah said.

"Love is surrender, love is sacrifice, love is everything," Joshua said. "Jesus lived, Jesus died, and Jesus lived again to love us all."

You do know, Leah wanted to say, that I'm Jewish.

"That's who the true believers are, those who are willing to love and sacrifice and care, without ego or jealousy or fear."

He told her about a time when he was much younger, before he had been shipped off to boarding school, when he still lived with his parents. He went out into the streets on a near daily basis with his mother, distributing tracts and Thai translations of the New Testament, most of which were refused. They wandered the streets and the markets through the heat and humidity, only to have their offers rebuffed with waving hands and the rapid-fire tones of dismissal.

"There are those who seek persecution," he said, "as a sign that by being persecuted, they are among God's elect. But it never occurred to me, how much my mother disliked the Thai people and their culture, and yet there we were, speaking about love. *Phra yesū rak khun*, we said, Jesus loves you, in our American-accented Thai. I think she was happy when they rejected us and threw Bibles back in our faces because it validated her hatred."

Another time he was talking about what he might do after his days as a student were over and he could no longer work in the security shack. "Maybe," he said apropos of his interest in communities, "I'll buy a place in Dunlap and start a communal farm. Artisanal products. Honey. Olive oil, that kind of thing. Arts and crafts. Work the fairs and Saturday markets. I'd need investors and others of like mind, who would be willing to work together and live together and share every-thing of their lives. Be a true family."

"That sounds nice," Leah said, playing with one of the buttons of his uniform shirt, which she was now wearing. "I like the sound of that," she said, because his romanticism seemed so laudable, even if he had no answer for the questions of money, friends, or expertise.

In her Chaucer seminar, they were reading the first of the *Canterbury Tales*, and she couldn't help herself from secretly enjoying the sentiment, if not the ironic tragedy, of "The Knight's Tale" more so than the ribaldry of "The Miller's Tale" or the sour taste of "The Reeve's Tale," both of which seemed crueler than absolutely necessary, but she wondered which story—if any—most truthfully represented the world. And don't tell me, she argued, within her own internal dialogue, that it's *The Merchant of Venice*. That would be much too easy.

"Maybe," she said, hoping to stop such thought, "we could share a little more."

Unlike most Liberty Christian students, Joshua did not live on campus. He had moved from the dorms after his freshman year and rented a studio in a falling-down building across the highway from campus on the southern downhill slope. The two-story, cinder-block building looked oddly out of place, overrun as it was by oak and pine and the fire-haz-ard of untended chaparral. Built in the 1920s when the

265

Administration building of the college was once a convent, Villa Bona had housed those visitors, usually family members, who had made the journey up the winding mountain roads and the traveling priests who administered the sacraments to the nuns. The villa now housed an eclectic collection of residents: a few junior faculty so new to the campus and the area that they had found nowhere else to live, a few married students, older upperclassmen, some itinerant PG&E and Cal Fire workers, and Joshua. Following his night duty in the security shack, he walked across the highway from campus as the sun rose behind the mountains, and once, in late April, after a Friday night shift, he invited Leah for Saturday morning breakfast.

They walked in the false blue light of dawn, holding hands, which given their earlier exertions felt both oddly domestic and somehow even more sensual. The campus was quiet but for a pair of raised voices in one of the twin gatehouses at the college's main entrance.

Joshua cocked his head in the direction of the gatehouse. "Dr. Book lives there," he said in a low voice. "His wife has issues. Problems."

"Oh."

"I don't think they get along very well. The lieutenant has had to intervene a time or two."

"No kidding?"

They walked past the gatehouse as though they were spies evading detection, and then ran across the two-lane highway

266

laughing like fools. His studio was on the bottom floor, on the downhill side of the building and faced a steep slope and a gully and the tops of trees. He had one door and one window, and the studio was dark even at noon and furnished with only the barest of necessities: a twin bed, a table and chair, a two-burner gas stove and a dormitory refrigerator, a sink, and a commode behind a screen. Nothing was new, but everything was in order. Not clean exactly but not dirty either, just old and without frills. Institutional drapes, the color of mold, covered the window. It was something like an artist's garret if the garret were a basement and the artist a sexy Puritan. She could imagine herself staying here with him and making a nest of it. Until a telescope of years brought her back to *meshuganeh* and the sense that she shouldn't give in to fantasy.

"I can make eggs," he said, "or eggs. Your choice."

"Pancakes and bacon, please."

He gave her a look of mild annoyance.

"I'll have eggs," she said, "if that's okay with you."

"You can imagine what happened next," Leah says more than a decade later to the three girlfriends in the living room of her tract home. Once again, back home among the *goy*, back in the dust and heat of the San Joaquin Valley. It can make the head spin. Eight-and-a-half months pregnant, she waddles to the refrigerator for more wine for them and more fizzy water for herself. Crackers, eight varieties of stinky cheese that make her want to puke, hummus, vegetables arranged on a plate. "Or, maybe you can't," she says. "Extra pours for those who can predict the future of my past."

They have gathered in her home for a girls' afternoon and impromptu baby shower (by un-invitation only) since her husband is out of town on business. He is often out of town on business. Once a police officer for Buffalo, New York, her husband has parlayed that experience into an agent's position with the Secret Service: he works with the currency division of the Treasury Department, shaves his head to hide his male pattern baldness, wears a striped tie each morning to the office, and goes by his boyhood nickname, Chip. He lifts weights in the garage on the weekends and trains Flotsam, their remarkably stupid Labrador to bark at old women, shred the newspaper, hump a guest's leg. Who marries into the Secret Service? Who marries a man named Chip? The answer, apparently, is Leah, but that is nothing she ever would have predicted, even though for this group it is now common knowledge.

Less commonly known is this: after her sophomore year at Liberty Christian, she transferred to SUNY-Binghamton to be closer to home, only to find out that, although she had completed her first two years of college, she was nearly starting over as a second-semester freshmen. Most of her units did not make the trip with her, all those required Bible-as-x courses. Bible as literature, Bible as history, Bible as social theory, even (shudder to think of it now) Bible as science. It turned out that the joke was on her, after all. She hadn't needed to travel so far away from her family to create that necessary distance nor did the Evangelicals give her the guarantee of safety that she had envisioned and hoped for. So, it took her four more years at Binghamton, six in total, in order to get a four-year degree. A slow learner, she often said in her own defense. But that's where she met Chip, so her life couldn't have worked out better if she'd planned it. Chip, Malcolm Brown, Jr. on his driver's license and to his family (more *goy*! yet another earth color!), a chip off the old block, who's chipper in the morning as he shaves his shining skull, the best and only husband she ever intends to have. Does that make him the Chippest? It's enough to keep her from thinking about the alien who currently owns her body and soul, who will undoubtedly become the Chipperiest if such a thing be possible.

How ironic is it, that Chip's first posting after getting the Secret Service gig would be the Fresno office? They shuffled off from Buffalo and landed in Fresno. She had run away to find herself only to discover that her departure and destination were one and the same. She had blanched when he told her. "You know what it's like," he said, "everything you could ever want is three hours away." While nothing is always right at hand, she thought.

The women who are with her now are *her* friends, rather than the wives of her husband's fellow-agents, women she has met at lectures and concerts and art galleries, other women, like herself, who explore what there is to see in this agricultural metropolis (she wants to say wasteland, but that wouldn't be fair, not entirely). They explore without their husbands because otherwise they'd never leave the house, except for work or play group or the grocery store.

"You found him in bed with another girl," Samantha said, the recent transplant from Alabama, who wears fake pearls on a nearly daily basis and never carries the same designer bag twice. "They were doing the two-backed monster with his shining white butt in the air. One of your roommates, maybe, underneath him. Or you showed up at his apartment unexpectedly and found him canoodling with a little sixteen-year-old tramp, and you threw the walkie-talkie at his head."

"*Bzzzzz.*" Leah makes the sound of a game show buzzer. "Incorrect. Excellent guess, a predictable assumption, but totally untrue as it turns out."

She is not being entirely honest, though. There were those days when she sensed that she was crossing the paths of others, like herself, going to or leaving from the security shack or Joshua's studio. She had Friday nights, but who knew what was transpiring on the other nights and days of the week or weekend? She could guess but was not tempted to find out.

"You're right about one thing," she said. "I wasn't the first, last, or only." Joshua had intimated as much.

What *is* untrue is Samantha's prediction of Leah's reaction; what Samantha and the others don't know is that Joshua had

270

never been devious, had never disguised the fact that he had other liaisons, that there were others with whom he had communion. Jealousy had been forbidden, a condition from the very beginning. Promising to hold all things in common, Joshua had said, included people as well as things. She was free to do as she wanted or needed, and so was he. And love was love, so long as it was an expression of Christ's care for the church. Which was when Leah tried to say, "About that…," but the conversation never quite moved past *non sequiturs* and a resumption of some new sexual activity. And while she knew that at some point the conversation would have to be finished, she was willing to wait, to let sleeping dogs lie and fanatics do their slow burn.

But she turned out all right. *Everything turned out all right in the end.* Really. That's what she wants her girlfriends in the living room to know. Not all at once, but then that's what happens to slow learners.

HERE'S WHAT ELSE SHE LEARNED about him: he claimed not to have a driver's license, a bit of information not made clear until that Saturday morning when there was a knock at Joshua's door, and two girls, neither of whom Leah knew, stood waiting in bikinis and sandals and gauzy coverups.

Janice, like Joshua, was a senior, and Liv, a junior, and they greeted Leah as though they were long lost sisters. There were hugs all around and the chatter of introductions. They had heard so much about her, they said, and so they had come to kidnap them both for a day by the Kings River. She could get a swimsuit from her dorm room, and then they'd go.

"I don't know," she said, "I have so much to read." The final pages of Muscatine and "The Parson's Tale," penitence and redemption, awaited her. "I'm way behind."

"We won't," Janice said, "take no for an answer. Bring your books. The day is lovely."

Janice and Liv were lovely, she wanted to say. Two blue-eyed, Norwegian-style blondes, both of whom looked as though they had sprung from the same mold that had produced Claire and Dottie. What was she doing in their company?

Janice used a remote to beep open a newish Acura. "Come on," she said.

It was a direction not to be refused.

They drove nearly to the valley floor before turning off onto a minor road, so unassuming that Leah would have missed it on her own, and then up and down and through Wonder Valley and then suddenly the river opened up as though it had been in front of them all along, which, she supposed, it had been. Leah sat in the backseat with Liv while Janice drove and teased Joshua about his lack of a license. "J's in front, L's behind," Liv said, "how's that for symmetry?"

"I got a license," Joshua said, "when I got hired, but I never carry it, and it has the wrong address, anyway. It hasn't stopped me from driving."

"It should," Janice said.

"I haven't registered to vote, either," Joshua said. "I'll never have to serve jury duty."

"And you're proud of that."

Liv told Leah that she and Janice were both art majors focusing on the revival of folk arts and crafts, and they hoped to produce enough paintings and baskets and wall-hangings to sell at crafts fairs. That they would have to live plainly and do without, which wouldn't be a hardship but would be good training for their spiritual life as well as for the art that they hoped to produce. Do that for a year or two before applying to art schools unless they were so content with their lives that they couldn't imagine doing anything else. Janice and Joshua were graduating this year, and Liv was planning to join them in whatever housing they were able to find. Leah would be welcome, too. The more, the merrier.

"God is so good," Liv said, "don't you think?"

"Oh," Leah said. "Sure. That's good you have a plan."

At Winton Park, they spread blankets on the stones by the river and wedged water bottles into the water to keep them cold and set out their bags of crackers and cheese, a loaf of unsliced bread and a bottle of red wine. Leah set her backpack down on the blanket and eyed the water which rushed by at a velocity that seemed angry and felt much too cold for a dip, even from a distance.

Janice closed her eyes, tipped her face to the sun, then spread her arms out and breathed deeply. "We're so glad you

273

have joined us," she said to Leah, wrapped her in an embrace, and kissed her cheek. "So glad."

"I'm glad to be here, too," Leah said. "It's a beautiful day."

"A beautiful day that the Lord has made," Liv sang.

"It's time," Joshua said.

The four of them held hands as they stepped into the river, cold at their ankles and freezing at their knees and thighs. The water pulled against their legs while Joshua prayed: "Heavenly Father, we thank You for Your love and blessings that you have presented to us in each other. Give us the strength and courage and will to live what we believe. Help us to complete each other. In the name of Jesus. Amen"

"Amen," Janice and Liv echoed.

"Hmm," Leah murmured.

"It's time," Joshua said, turning to Leah, "for you to be baptized into our family of love and into the love of Jesus Christ."

"Like I said," Leah began, "about that, the Jesus part."

"The best part of us," Liv said.

"What?" Leah said.

"He is the best part of us. He's what allows us to love."

Janice pulled her into her arms. "Give yourself up to love."

Liv embraced them both while Joshua stood apart.

"Be a part of our whole," he said, "or stay apart and live with the holes in your life. You are the one who must choose."

"Maybe," Leah said, "I'll just sit on the blanket, after all. The water's pretty cold."

"Jesus loves you," Liv said, "and without Him we are nothing."

"What the fuck," Leah said, looking into the shock and hurt of Liv's eyes. "You know that I'm Jewish, right?" She looked at her legs, pale in the spring sunshine. "I'm as nothing as nothing can be."

THE REST OF THE AFTERNOON was something of a blur. Leah went back to the blanket and her backpack and her books, aware that Joshua had turned his back to her. The three of them remained in the river, performing some kind of ritual, Joshua dunking the two girls in turn, and then allowing them to tip him backwards underneath the water. But then, that moment accomplished and in the past, they proceeded to play, jumping on one another and attempting to push each other into the cold water, the girls ganging up on Joshua while at other moments, he formed an alliance with one or the other of them. While they were thus occupied, Liv shrieking and on top of Joshua's shoulders, Leah gathered herself, pulled her jeans and top over her damp legs and swimsuit, and walked back toward Janice's car without any thought of what she might do. Her phone was useless out here by the river, the signal hidden by the foothills.

In the parking area, a family of four was packing up a van, a caricature of the family vacation gone wrong: a boy and girl, whining for junk food, their legs gray with dirt, the father irritated and issuing directives that no one followed, the mother trying to satisfy three others' demands by doing the right things that no one wanted.

"Could I," Leah began. "I just realized I need to get back to school for a study group. My friends are going to be a while yet. Would it be possible for me to get a ride with you?"

They were going home to Fresno, the father said, and while that was not in the direction of campus, they could take her to Minkler, and maybe she could call from there for someone to pick her up.

"Fine," she said. "That's good. Thank you so much."

She climbed into the rear bench seat, while first the boy and then the girl were strapped into chairs that looked like space capsules. And then, she watched the hills give way to the white fences of the horse farms and ranch houses along Piedra as the children fell asleep in their car seats and their parents stared through the windshield without speaking. At the Minkler General Store, she snaked her way between the children's seats, and then out the sliding passenger-side door.

"Thank you," she said again to the children's mother.

"Just let this be a lesson to you," the mother said, waving her hand toward the back of the van. "Wait a long, long time."

Leah slammed the side door closed, and while their limbs shifted in their respective car seats, neither child awoke.

"You're sure you can get hold of someone?" the mother said.

"Thank you," Leah said one last time. "I'll be fine."

And, in fact, she did not even need to make a call, for there at the register, buying a carton of Newports was Elisa, that long-suffering saint of O'Malley's.

"You," Elisa said. "You're a bad penny, you are."

[x]

It's Not Ambivalence If You Don't Know How You Feel

(Michael, 2009)

ELISA DIDN'T SAY YES, BUT she didn't say no, and then she did say no, and then after another month she said yes, and then the economy collapsed, and the world was falling apart, and we both had other things to worry about. Maybe you can follow that, and if you can, you're a more adaptable human than I.

Her son, Gil, wanted us married, and he wanted us married before he left for Afghanistan. Again. He'd been there before, he knew what could happen, and he didn't want his mother to be alone. That was his reasoning, but we both told him in so many words that saying "I do" wasn't magic, and it wasn't a solution to someone else's problem.

"Tell him, Michael," Elisa said.

"It's not magic," I said.

"Tell me something new," Gil said.

It's not like Elisa hadn't been married before. Her first husband, Gil's father, had died about the time that Gil was born. Her second husband was shiftless and lazy and even his criminal activities were marked by a lack of effort. She never knew what happened to him after their divorce and her move from Oregon to California, but she was waiting for that day when he'd show up, needing money and a place to hide.

"Okay," Elisa said, "here's something new: you could not re-up, you could not go back to a warzone, you could get a job with your fancy degree, find a girl, and raise a family. You could do all these things and quit worrying about me."

"That's not new," Gil sighed. "And I told you: it's not a military assignment."

"But it's a lousy neighborhood," I said.

He had gone back to school at Liberty Christian, he had gotten a degree in computer science, but rather than go out and find a job with a company with medical and dental, a parking space and a retirement plan, he was going back to the Middle East as a civilian contractor. He'd be working with computers, but he'd be doing so in trailers decorated with sandbags, and the programs had something to do with guidance systems rather than game design, which was all the rage among his fellow graduates, all of whom were ten years younger. Why would he do such a thing? I didn't know, and he seemed disinclined to tell me or his mother.

"It's something I need to do," he said. "And you need to make it official."

It's not like we hadn't talked about getting married. We'd talked, or rather, I had talked, and then Elisa told me to shut up, she had better things to do than pick out china patterns, which was her way of saying that the whole topic was ridiculous. Couldn't I be happy with the way things were? This is the way things were: I lived upstairs from the bar, she lived in her tiny storeroom house fifty yards away, and every now and again one of us would visit the other and stay the night. Sure, I could be happy with that, but I also could foresee a day when she wouldn't be happy with that, and I'd never see her again, especially with Gil on the other side of the world. Don't we all want a body on the other side of the bed at night, and don't we want that for the foreseeable future? I did, but I wasn't sure that she did, and while it made me feel like a rest stop rather than a destination, I also knew that arguing about it would do me less than good.

The thing is, I wasn't doing all that well, and I can't blame Elisa for not wanting to be weighed down with another's grief. She had Gil to worry about as it was. Maybe I shouldn't have been watching the news. She was with me one night when I sat up in bed and couldn't catch my breath. Like those times in football games when I'd had the wind knocked out of me. My mouth was open, but nothing was going in or coming out.

She rubbed my back and murmured her reassurances, but I just knew this was going into the logbook for future reference and rebuttal.

It's not like I had money in the stock market or real estate, but I saw my regulars, most of whom were on retirement income, at the bar less and less frequently. During the boom years, they bought each other pitcher after pitcher of low-calorie beer and insulted each other's manhood, but now? They must have been buying generics at Costco and socializing with their televisions rather than each other. I'm sure they missed their reciprocal and brotherly abuse since low testosterone goes a long way. Meanwhile, I was having alternating dreams of padlocking the door to O'Malley's and being led away in handcuffs by IRS agents. My daytime waking life was invading my nights, and there was little to no relief. Three o'clock in the morning is always three o'clock in the morning, and your soul can take it from there and create its own nightmares.

About this time, I started to pray again, only my prayers bore little resemblance to the elevated language of the Book of Common Prayer as remembered from my youth. Instead, my words went something like this: Oh, God. Oh, God. Oh, God. And, as pointless as this may seem, the repetition and the direction made me feel some better, a little less frantic anyway. It's not like I suddenly found a renewed interest in church or became devout in any disciplined way, I just felt better for a moment, and a better moment was fine with me.

One night while Elisa was with me, I woke with my usual anxieties. My breathing was shallow, but I still had some air in my lungs, and my mind was spinning and turning loops about all the ways I was leaking money: on my bank balance (next to nothing) and the bills that would be coming due (property tax, suppliers, etc.) and the likelihood of more custom (not very). I got up, went to the cupboard above the sink and poured a generous amount of cheap bourbon (even I had been reduced to warehouse generics), and then stared into the darkness. "Oh, God. Oh, God. Oh, God," started up in my mind, and I must have been saying it out loud as well because Elisa said "Asked and answered," before she snapped on the too-bright overhead light that made the kitchenette look as blue as an interrogation room.

"Look, buddy," she said, "you need some help, either financially or psychologically or maybe both. You're wearing out the floor and your stomach and it's not good to be stressed morning, noon, and night."

"I'm aware," I said.

She sat across the table from me in one of my fat man tee shirts, her only nod to the fact that I'd turned off the heat two hours before we'd locked the doors on the bar. Her hair was all over the place, and seeing her in my shirt and at my table was nearly enough to drive out what Holly Golightly might have called the mean reds.

"I know," I said. "I know."

"The hell you know," she said. "If you know, then maybe you need to do something about it. Lift weights, see a shrink, join a choir. If you must. Something more productive than drinking their stock."

"Good suggestions," I said, "even if none of them will take care of the immediate problem."

"Then what will?"

"Oh," I sighed. "You know that saying about two wrongs not making a right? It's something like that."

MY PARENTS HAD MOVED into Twilight Retreat ten years earlier, a name they had disparaged at the time, but now that they were in the mid-eighties, they didn't see the humor in it anymore. They were as healthy as two people in their mid-eighties can be, but they knew enough to know that this was no retreat, more like a rout with cease fires along the way. My father had stopped teaching when he was in his early sixties, claiming burnout and a lack of sympathy for his students, but while he built bookshelves in their garage and drank coffee with his other retiree teacher friends, my mother worked at an insurance agency examining claim forms and investigating suspected fraud. She was one of those people who write the piss-off letters, and rather than making her bitter or cynical, her denials seemed to keep her in good spirits. Don't ever underestimate other people's balls, she was fond of saying, they're not afraid to lie through their teeth even when all the evidence is in black-and-white.

What I'm saying is this: they worked hard, made their money, paid their bills, and took care of their obligations. They took seriously their membership in the Greatest Generation, and they weren't shy about it since they'd made do without in the Depression of the thirties and lived their best lives through a war in the forties. And, when they didn't feel quite so strong anymore, they didn't live in denial: they sold the house, moved to the Retreat, and didn't make a word of complaint.

As a Boomer who didn't go to Vietnam, I didn't have the same credentials of overcoming a global catastrophe. And seemingly, as a result, I didn't have the same tenacity or pluck. On their dime, they put me through college at Sierra Presbyterian, and when I told them that I no longer saw myself as a member of the clergy, they didn't bat an eye. I think they were a little relieved, frankly, since they had never been quite so enamored of church as I had been. And, when I told them about O'Malley's, they might have blinked, given my newfound and wildly different vocational direction, but they didn't go to pieces, only said that the decision seemed rash and flawed in any number of ways. Which, of course, it was.

Don't get me wrong, my parents were neither stingy nor mean, but they did have some expectations for their adult son. And one of those expectations—maybe the primary expectation—was self-sufficiency. They stayed out of my private life, and in return they asked for me to be a grown-up, but here I was, hat in hand, so to speak, hoping for a bail-out.

"How much?" my father said.

"You didn't get into all that house-flipping," my mother said, "did you? Because that was a disaster waiting to happen. Did you get stuck with one of those balloon mortgages?"

"No," I said. "You know me. I don't have that kind of energy, emotional or otherwise. To be a flipper. And, twenty thousand would clean things up, I think, taxes and bills and what have you, but I appreciate whatever you can do. I could apply for a loan," I said, "but given the times we live in, the ultimate answer to that seems like a foregone conclusion."

My father whistled. "Okay. Twenty. I know it's been a rough patch."

"Stupid bankers," my mother said. "Assholes, excuse my French. Someone should throw the book at them. But you won't see any of them going to jail," she added, a prediction that turned out to be all too correct.

In the end, my mother wrote a check out of a money market account for twenty-five thousand because they could tell that I'd underestimated what I truly needed, and as my father said, this was merely an advance against probate. They were beyond generous even as they reserved their judgments in the silence of their own thoughts: over my own fitness as a manager of finances and as a member of a generation too soft and pampered for its own good. And, as I took the elevator down to the lobby I felt as elated as I felt sick to my stomach. Fifty-four years old, and here I was, accepting money from my parents like a teenager on a Friday date night. And a whole lot more of it.

Thank God they had it. Oh, God. Oh, God. Indeed.

I THOUGHT ABOUT telling Elisa that I'd gotten the money from a loan shark, I was that embarrassed. Embarrassed about having gone to my parents, embarrassed about having such an option available, but I decided in the end that the truth was a better bet, even if it did make me look and feel like an utter failure. But since that's what I was, I needed to face facts without hiding behind a closed door.

And, as expected, she didn't cut me much slack. "Boo-hoo, you. Poor, poor you. At least you have parents," she said. "Parents who are kind enough and with means enough to make it happen. You're lucky in that regard."

"Very lucky," I said. "I know it. I know I am."

"Poor little rich boy," she said. "A safety net a mile wide. So, what's with the moaning and groaning?"

"Not that rich," I said. "Not that rich, relatively speaking. I didn't want to take advantage. I didn't want to presume."

"Get out of here. They were probably thrilled that you asked."

"I wouldn't be so sure about that."

Elisa went on and on, about how parents—if they were any kind of parents at all—would turn somersaults in the mud for their children, no matter how old the children might be.

Drunks and reprobates and neglect had run in her family, so she knew the truth by the negative, and in her view, the highest compliment one person could give to another was that they had taken care of their own.

"Look at Joe and Abel," she said.

"Yes," I said, "just look at them. And what a fine time they're having."

Our two most regular regulars were in their seventies, and both had their own health issues: prostates and leaky pipes, for starters, but then Abel was diagnosed with a tumor in one lung, and Joe came to the bar with the top of his head swathed in bandages like a figure out of that Revolutionary War painting, the one with fifes and drums and flags, if grapeshot were replaced by melanoma. So, they were both feeling beat up and sorry for themselves, when Abel's wife came back from a checkup with a referral for an oncologist specializing in the worst stages of breast cancer, and Joe's wife started putting her car keys in the freezer and couldn't remember the way the faucets worked. There were days when she couldn't remember Joe's name without a hint. Joe and Abel had their hands full, and that's a fact, and we went whole weeks without seeing them, when before their health and their wives' health all went south, you could have set your watch by their appearances and their back-and-forth abuse with Elisa. Now, when they did come to the bar, their time was mostly spent in a recitation of the latest bureaucratic fiasco and medical expense and how they were stockpiling their most recent prescriptions of opioids and sedatives.

"I'm telling you, it's a shitty, shitty thing," Joe said.

"Shitty ain't the half of it," Abel said.

"Don't get old," Joe said.

"Don't get sick," Abel said. "Pick a date and die in your sleep."

Why wouldn't we give them the free pitcher now and again?

Elisa received her own test of family responsibilities, not only due to Gil's absence, but then with an unexpected visitor.

We were sweeping the floor and washing the windows and knocking down the spider webs in the rafters because there was no one inside the bar we needed to serve, only a back-packer who was sitting in the sun at one of the out-door picnic tables; it was early spring and the idiot hikers were beginning to come out in singles and pairs and herds. This one was eating a brick of freeze-dried dog turd, and she had asked for a cup of water when a tall, jack-knife of a man stood in the doorway. He had white flyaway hair and a gray beard that touched the second button on his grimy Pendleton, a look that said he was either homeless or a member of ZZ Top. His eyes were yellow and wolf-like.

"I am here," he said, his voice more croak than bellow.

"Fabulous," I said. "Couldn't be happier unless you're here to buy a drink, and if that's the case, I'm ecstatic."

"Satan, get thee behind me," he said. "I haven't had a drink in thirty-four years."

"Bullshit," Elisa said. "And I know your bullshit better than anyone."

And that's how I met her brother Carl, the trailer park prophet from Clackamas County, Oregon, the brother who masterminded the cross burning when I was a student at Sierra Presbyterian, an event that cost two cousins their lives.

Elisa stood in front of her brother with her hands on her hips. "You've been drinking your own Kool-Aid, ever since you gave up beer," she said. "And I'll bet you've had an occasional whiskey or two, just to help you swallow the poison you've been spouting over the years. Don't tell me you haven't."

Carl's white hair went side to side, but he didn't say no.

"I regret that," he said, slumping into one of the booths. "I regret a lot of things."

"I should hope so."

Something about the way he was sitting, with his yellow eyes boring holes into the wood grain of the table made me say: "You're sick, aren't you?"

He nodded slowly. "Soul sick, for sure, but now the container is wearing out as well."

"We've had our share of that around here, and the look is hard to hide."

It turned out that after years of ignoring on-and-off abdominal pain and eating Maalox tablets by the bucket load, he had finally gone to the doctor, who had given him the bad news: stomach cancer and three months, tops.

"So, I'm sorry," he said to Elisa. "I wanted to be the one to tell you and to ask your forgiveness."

"Oh, fuck," Elisa said, sliding into the bench opposite him, "is this your make-amends tour?"

"Something like that. I shouldn't have made you marry Eivar. That was wrong of me."

"No, you shouldn't have," Elisa said, "but as it turns out, that was the best thing you could've done." And I could tell that she was thinking of Gil and the last thirty years of motherhood and worry and pride because without one she wouldn't have had the other. "Now, if you had made me marry Ricky Boy, that would be another story, but I have only myself to blame for that. On the other hand, you could have been a little nicer. A little kinder. Sending everyone to hell isn't exactly the New Testament way, is it?"

"Well," he grumped, "it works for some." He paused and then put his hand over hers. "It worked for me."

He'd been punishing others for the last thirty-plus years because what he needed was to punish himself. Stomach cancer, on the other hand, had made such efforts unnecessary.

"What a load of crap," Elisa said, but she didn't say it unkindly.

"Yes." He unfolded himself from his side of the booth with all the ease of an unbalanced washing machine. "I suppose it is."

"And now you're just going to go like that?" Elisa said. "You show up after thirty-odd years, tell me you're dying and ask for your bullshit forgiveness, and then split?"

"No," he panted from the exertion of standing up. "I want you to meet someone."

An ancient VW van sat in the gravel parking lot, and a woman sat in a lawn chair next to the passenger side door with an enormous hound of indeterminate breed at her feet. I was going to stay inside and keep polishing the bar as a nod to family and family complexity except Elisa stopped me.

"Oh, no you don't," she said *sotto voce*. "You're not getting off that easy.

When we emerged from the relative darkness of the bar into the sunlight of the parking lot, the dog lifted its massive gray head and bayed as though there were a full moon until the woman yanked on the rope leader tied to the arm of the chair.

"Shut up," she said, a fierce woman in a peasant blouse with hair that matched Carl's beard. "Fucking cunt of a fucking dog."

"This is Sister Brenda," Carl said, coughing into the crook of his elbow. "My wife as of three weeks ago. And our puppy, Magda."

"Oh," Elisa said. "Congratulations?"

"Who knows," the woman said. "Excuse my language, but has your cancer-ridden husband ever brought home a dog without warning? On our *honeymoon*, no less. Especially one like this, one who needs two area codes?"

"I'm not married," Elisa said. "Not now, and maybe not ever again."

"Thanks," I said, "for the warning."

"And then he leaves me with this stupid, stupid dog with the stupid, stupid name while he goes off doing God knows what."

"The Lord's work, my sweet. And, I didn't want you to be alone."

"Uh, huh. Tell me another one."

She glared at her husband. And then they both started to laugh, she loudly and from her belly while he gripped his and said, "Heh, heh, ha," as though it hurt too much to let his humor go.

"The Lord's work," she said. "That's a good one."

So, THEY STAYED, Carl and Brenda, that night and for the next several weeks. They parked their van behind the bar, and after Elisa looked inside at the cramped quarters, she offered the use of her storeroom house to them.

"What could I do?" she said. "They might as well be homeless."

That was fine by me since I knew where Elisa would be sleeping and keeping herself for the duration.

"Do we know how long they're staying?" I said.

"No," she said, "does it matter?"

"Not on my end."

That first afternoon, I asked if they'd eaten anything recently because they both looked like they'd been surviving on jerky and Ding-Dongs or anything else wrapped in cellophane and purchased in a gas station, and I offered them a meal, anything off our menu of toaster oven or barbecue burned specialties.

"We're a bar, not a restaurant," I said, hoping to mitigate O'Malley's shortcomings. Meanwhile, their dog—a puppy (as it turned out, Carl wasn't speaking hyperbolically) since she was only eight months old but already ninety pounds—their dog continued to howl in periodic dismay, which, as the afternoon wore on, woke up the tigers at the Big Cat Haven, who then proceeded to growl and chuff with greater volume than normal.

"What is that?" Brenda said.

"Tigers," I said. "The lions are too lazy."

"What?" she said. "No bears?"

"Probably a few at the higher elevations, but I haven't seen one in some time. If the drought goes on any longer, though, they'll be in our trashcans like raccoons."

Carl drank glass after glass of low-calorie, no-taste beer, licking his lips after each drink. He ate next to nothing, saying his stomach couldn't take much these days beyond liquids. "But this," he said, holding his glass, "is ambrosia, just what the doctor ordered."

"Only if his name is Kevorkian," Brenda said. "But you do you. Until you can't."

"Just so you know," Carl said, directing this information to his sister, "Ricky Boy is dead. You don't have to worry about any more uninvited ghosts from your past. We're it."

"Yeah?" Elisa said. "When did that happen? He fall off somebody's roof while stealing copper wire and someone's out of date satellite dish? Loan sharks get him?"

"Nope. Run over by a log truck on 224. He was walking the ditch bank and must have strayed on the other side of the line."

"Eww," Elisa said. "Even I wouldn't have wished that on him."

"They had to pick him up in about six pieces," Brenda said. "Ricky Boy mash."

"Nobody deserves that," Elisa said, "no matter how much of an asshole and idiot he was."

"'I said in mine heart,'" Carl recited, "'God shall judge the righteous and the wicked: for there is a time there for every purpose and for every work.'"

"He was drunk on light beer, your Ricky Boy," Brenda said. "Let that be a lesson to you about time and purpose and work."

THEIR STORIES CAME out in fits and starts, thirty years' worth of Carl preaching his fire and brimstone gospel to the believers for whom such a fierce and uncompromising religion is attractive. They picketed abortion clinics and bombed at least two. They led protest demonstrations during Pride Week because Carl had declared that the Westboro Baptist folks shouldn't be the only outliers yelling at fags. He stood on a packing crate in Pioneer Courthouse Square in Portland and the parking lot outside Clackamas Town Center and preached his

294

turn-or-burn message to all who would listen, which admittedly were not many. Most just wanted to buy lunch.

Brenda, it turned out, was Brenda-come-lately, and while she listened and thought his version of Jesus was interesting and strange and as exotic as jack fruit—among others, she also used the term "absurd"—she was intrigued by the man even if she wasn't about to fall under the sway of his version of Holy vengeance.

"We argued for six months," she said, "and I yelled and screamed at him until he wised up. I knew there had to be a real person in there somewhere instead of all that bluster and guff and condemnation. He'd been living with that version of himself for so long, he didn't even know who he was, and when he let that part of himself go, he cried and cried. Maybe it was the meds he was on, or maybe he truly felt bad. I don't know, and I don't think he did either. And then he asked me to marry him since he was going to die soon anyway, and maybe that was the meds as well because they tend to make a person weak and dependent. I said yes, knowing what I was in for, but," she tapped his glass of beer which he had taken to drinking morning, noon, and night, "I had no idea he was going to so single-mindedly accelerate the process."

Meanwhile, Magda was making herself at home. For such a large, ungainly, and graceless creature, she had a habit of showing up when she was least expected and with a stealth that bordered on the metaphysical. Open the refrigerator, and she was there, her fur the color of smoke, waiting for a hand-out. Take a shower, and a snout would appear underneath the curtain, her nose snuffling at the drain so she could drink the runoff, with or without soap. She had figured out how to turn doorknobs with her dinner plate paws, and closed doors were not an impediment. Locking a door worked, but then she clawed and howled with a persistence that would have been admirable if it weren't so awful to hear. So, we left the doors unlocked and more than one early morning was marked by the sound of her paws on the stairs, the door creaking open, and then the shifting of the mattress when she landed between us, her breath and tongue hot against our ears.

"She likes you," Carl said, "which means you're good people. It took her a while to warm up to me, and even now she's still reserving judgment, which is all that I deserve."

"I might be okay with being a little less likeable," I said, "especially at four in the morning."

I wasn't the only one in Magda's field of affection, of course. She put her paws on Elisa's chest as often as she was allowed, and the one time that Joe and Abel came into the bar, Magda immediately buried her nose in their crotches as though she had the right. Within a day after Carl and Brenda had arrived, Magda had occupied a position as something of O'Malley's mascot and guard dog, and she served something of that dual purpose when first-time visitors arrived; for some she was all slobber while others elicited only erect fur and a low growl.

One afternoon, while Elisa and Brenda were letting Magda run in the hills, Carl asked if I might take him to see the college.

"Walk the grounds, see the sights," he said. "You know."

"You mean see where the crosses were?" I said. "Sure."

So, I locked the doors with a note for Elisa, and we drove the seventeen miles in my rattletrap Datsun, past the Cat Haven and the tigers and lions, to the campus that I had once known as Sierra Presbyterian. Carl peered out his window to the downslope of the mountain.

"Long way down," he said. "And not much of a guardrail."

"It does make you keep your focus," I said. "Especially at night."

But then we were driving between the gatehouses and in front of the administration building, where there were a few open parking stalls for visitors. The pine trees were rocking in the breeze, and students crossed the quad carrying books and backpacks from the student union and commons to the classrooms and laboratories and library. They looked well-fed and white and satisfied with themselves, but that might have just my own guilt ratcheting inside my head.

"Nice," Carl said. "Nice place."

"It is. For those who can afford it and whose parents want the shelter for their impressionable innocents. My parents could afford it, back in the day. They still can, I guess, but now they'd worry more about the narrowness of the experience."

We walked down to the cone of the chapel.

"I spent a lot of time here," I said. "Back when I thought I'd be in a different line of work."

"You, too?" he said. "I always wanted to be a minister. Even when I was a hellraiser, I wanted to have a group of people I could call my own."

We stood outside the chapel, taking in the teepee-shaped roofline and the cross at the very top.

"There's not much to see inside," I said. "It's dark, and there's an organ, but not much else. That," I said, pointing to the ridge opposite. "That's what you came here to see."

We hiked across the bridge spanning the dry creek bed and took the steps to the Golgotha memorial: three crosses, now made of steel, a granite stone with its bronze plaque citing Romans 12.1, and the rose garden bordering it all.

"It didn't look like this in the seventies," I said, "when the crosses were wood, and it was a lot more rustic."

"No. I don't suppose it did."

He told me then, in a rush, how, as leader of the Immaculate Warrior of Truth Tabernacle, he'd been contacted by a similar group in Fresno. There was a very informal network of such radical believers, and Carl had been very much a part of it. They had two volunteers, he was told, who wanted to make a statement about the lukewarm nature of the college, how the college had become flaccid in the eyes of the Lord, as secular as any public institution, and they wanted to make a public display.

"It wasn't supposed to happen like it did," he said. "It was supposed to be a wake-up call. A call to arms. Spiritually."

His brother-in-law was supposed to meet Gilbert and Victor, and then they would light the wood crosses on fire, set off the fireworks, and leave. Simple. Only Gilbert and Victor didn't stop there. Fire and fireworks, check. But then they climbed onto the two outer crosses and allowed themselves to be roasted alive like chickens on a spit while poor Eivar made his frantic getaway, forever traumatized by the sight and made guilty by his escape.

"'Living sacrifice,'" Carl read. "What would they know?"

"Beats me," I said. "I was there that night, and I didn't see any. Living sacrifices, I mean. Just two guys going out in a blaze of glory, if you'll forgive the cliché."

"That's my point," he said, "the whole thing was a cliché from start to finish. And two people died. For what?" He shook his woolly head. "I don't know."

I was a junior in college, and it was the last chapel service of the fall semester in mid-December. The night was dark and sleety and cold, and the chapel was illuminated only by candlelight. We had run through the usual Christmas songbook: "Angels We Have Heard on High," "Oh Come, Oh Come Emmanuel," "Silent Night," and all the rest, ending in darkness and peace, a sentiment that was only relieved when we came outside into the starlight and began to chatter amongst ourselves, ready for the term to be over and the holiday season to begin, but then the crosses above us exploded in fire and light, and fireworks erupted one after another, and then before the action could register with any of us, the two cousins, Gilbert and Victor Martinez, had joined the crosses in their deadly embrace, leaving us to stare, slack-mouthed in wonder and horror. We had no idea what the point was supposed to be, and we didn't until some days later when a letter that the cousins had written was printed in *The Fresno Bee*, even if by that time the news had already moved on to other things. The aftermath of Watergate and Nixon's helicopter departure, the availability of gasoline, where *The Exorcist* was playing. None of us had been the wiser, such was the effect of the cousins' irrevocable decision.

Carl and I sat on one of the benches among the roses and watched the students come and go from our perch as dusk fell and lights began to glow in the commons.

"Well," he said, standing again with some effort after maybe half an hour had passed. "I did what I came here to do. I remembered what I was supposed to remember."

"And that is?"

"That the world is a shitty place, and it is human beings that make it so. Like me, shitty as shitty can be, thirty-plus years ago."

WOULD YOU BELIEVE ME if I said that, as we were making our way back to the car, a Liberty Christian police officer stopped us? It's true, and I can't say I blame him, for we did make an unsightly pair, Carl in his grimy Pendleton and trash picker beard and me in a moth-eaten and paint-spattered Sierra Presbyterian sweat shirt. We did look like the ne'er-do-wells we somewhat were, and I can understand if there was some question as to our fitness or right to stroll the garden that was the campus. We were looking at a map underneath one of the emergency lights, Carl and I, when he asked to see our identification. He might have been twelve, this cop, with the downiest of fuzz above his upper lip, a pistol in a holster bigger than his leg, and a nametag that read Bowen. Which was when I recognized him as someone who came into the bar from time to time; he tended to drive Elisa batshit with the way he drank alone and stared into space if he wasn't picking up some young thing. In that regard, he actually shared some characteristics with Carl.

"Really?" I said. "You know me. Michael Wayte from O'Malley's. I know we don't look like much, but I am an alum of this place, even if that predates the Liberty Christian name. See," I said, pointing to my sweatshirt.

"I have to check," he said. "Anyone who's not a student. It's my job. Even if it seems a little stupid. Please."

"It does seem stupid," I said, but I got out my wallet and my driver's license because I know the world is filled with foolish humans and their equally foolish requirements and you can waste any amount of time kicking against the pricks. That is, if you'll forgive the phrase taken out of context.

On the other hand, Carl said, "Fuck this," and began to walk toward the car.

"Excuse me," the cop said and was just about to reach out to stop him.

"Hold it," I said, stepping between them. "Officer Bowen. Trust me, we're leaving. You'll never see us again unless you come back to the bar. I think my friend is having a nineteen-sixties moment besides dying from cancer, and I'd hate for this to become something more than it is. We don't want stupid to beget stupid."

He sighed and handed me back my license. "Fine. If you're leaving."

"You can watch us get in the car and pull away. I won't mind."

Carl wrenched open the passenger side door while I shook the officer's hand.

"Thank you," I said, "for understanding."

"I don't, but that's not unusual."

He stood underneath the emergency light, writing down my plate numbers, and as we were pulling away, a group of girls surrounded him as though they were asking for his autograph. A fan club of freshmen girls, flitting like moths to a flame.

"Fucking cops," Carl said, for he had had his share of encounters both before and after his conversion, I knew that much from what Elisa had told me.

"That could have been worse," I said. "And it almost was."

He exhaled slowly and gripped his belly. "Thank you," he said. "There might be some outstanding warrants. There probably are some warrants. I don't have time to deal with all that."

"Okay," I said. "I get it."

The road was dark as we traveled down the mountain, but the lights of Fresno glittered beyond the ridges and the bends of the highway.

"I'm sorry," Carl said at last. "I'm sorry, I'm sorry, I'm sorry. I've been an asshole all my life, now as well as then and before. I know it, and I guess that's what I came here to say. I guess that's why I'm here."

We woke to Magda whimpering and running in her sleep between us, which wasn't that unusual after Carl and Brenda had arrived, but the whimpering and the running started around four in the morning and didn't end until we got up at seven, and that was longer than her worst episodes.

Elisa went downstairs and Magda went with her, and then they came back, both looking puzzled and afraid of what they knew without knowing.

"The van's gone," she said.

"Maybe they went for breakfast," I said. "They wouldn't have left the dog otherwise. Would they?"

"Maybe," she said. "I don't know."

We waited an hour or more. When they hadn't returned, we opened the door to Elisa's storeroom house and found a magnum of Cook's on the table and a card with a message in Brenda's handwriting:

This may not be what you were wanting to hear, but we're leaving this morning, Carl's afraid that we might have stayed too long. Wearing out our welcome with you, calling too much atten-tion to ourselves up at the college. He's paranoid and nuts, but what can you do? I told him that no one cares, not around here, but he's convinced that the feds want him for stuff from twenty years ago. Anyway, we're gone, who knows where to next? We are like the breeze in that regard. Ha, ha. Please accept the champagne. Drink it at your wedding, which you need to have because you need a little celebration after putting up with us. And the dog. By the way, we're leaving Magda in your care. She likes it here with you. Better than with us and our dirty van.

Below that Carl had scrawled, "I named the dog for some-one who told me I was a boil on the ass of humanity. I will try to be kinder in the time I have left. Jesus be praised, hallelujah! Amen."

So we had a dog, two sizes larger than any dog should be, a dog which we had neither wanted nor asked for but who loved us nonetheless, and we had a bottle of cheap champagne, which is something of a white elephant gift for the owner of a bar, and my suspicions were confirmed when I saw that it was the bottle I kept on hand for someone's surprise special occasion. The dust circle on the shelf in the cupboard where it had recently been stored was still intact. But we also had the exhortation, yet again, from a member of the family, so I said to Elisa, "What do you think? First Gil, now Carl."

And she said, "We might as well get the monkey off our backs and then we can buy a new bottle and store it on a higher shelf. Fucking light-fingered brother."

"Oh, God, Oh, God. Oh, God," I said, but I'm sure I was grinning like a maniac, too pleased with His beneficence and my own good fortune, for some prayers are meant to be ones of thanksgiving.

"Fucking dirtbag Carl!" she said.

[xi]

The Band Sets up to Play

(Elisa, 2014)

A FRIDAY NIGHT IN AUGUST, ninety degrees and dry as a sauna, and the gravel parking lot of O'Malley's is beginning to fill with its usual assortment of pickup trucks, motorcycles, and dust-caked SUVs. Here and there sits a gleaming Lexus or a rustbucket Volkswagen of another era, each looking as misplaced as the other. The heat from the valley below has risen to meet them, but a breeze is beginning to whisk the worst of it away and the shadow from the ridge to the west is taking some of the sting from the sunlight. Soon enough, the sky will relent, from white to pale blue to navy to that deep, deep shade that seems made of iron. Stars will burn bright, and an ivory moon will rise above the merrymakers.

The vehicles in the parking lot and the band members hauling their various pieces of overworked and battered equipment all speak to what could have been a busy weekend night ahead: of beer and wine, alcohol in shots and alcohol mixed into any number of abominations, of ones and fives and tens, rolls of quarters and dimes and nickels in the drawer, of the credit card scanner and slips for running tabs. That, however, is not their audience tonight, and Michael (*goddammit!*) is not present to witness this evening or the night giving way to morning, on what should be the highlight of his business week, a night that he has voluntarily screwed up ahead of time. A night that also has been screwed up beyond his control. His mother has fallen in the hallway of Twilight Retreat, and while she's not broken a hip, thank God, she's sore and shaken; "nonplussed by her own frailty" is Michael's assessment—as stunned in spirit as she is bruised in body—and his father has given way to his increasing anxiety about their own inevitable mortality. In response, Michael has gone to Fresno to be the dutiful son, pat their backs, say There, there, and put a face to some feeling of comfort and security and reassurance. For today, at least.

But that's Michael, who's gone, who's left everything else for Elisa to do: although she would like to put a sign on the door and tell the Stepford people from the college to go away, go home, get fucked, because of who and what they are, although she would like to do that, Elisa dons an apron instead and begins to prepare for the hours that lie ahead. Glasses are washed, towels laundered, the cupboard with its gigantic industrial size bags of tortilla chips and 10-pound jars of salsa is stocked. She has enlisted the help of two sensible young women who work the cafeteria at Liberty Christian during the week and at O'Malley's when needed on Friday and Saturday nights and the "help" of Joe Dwyer and Abel Ramirez, her seventy-year-old devotees, Thing One and Thing Two, who worship her through their two-on-one litany of adoration masquerading as insults. *Elisa*, one or the other of them will call, *are you lonesome tonight?* She can do this. She knows the drill. She can set aside her feelings about the crowd she is about to face. And, she can get through it, no matter if she wants to or not.

As SHE MOVES BACK AND FORTH behind the bar, she steps over Magda, the Wonder Dog, that oversized hound gifted to her and Michael by her brother five years earlier, and every time she steps over this dog, this generator of hair and shit, drool and noise, she is reminded of how many things changed in conjunction with their dog ownership. There was her reconciliation with her hellfire and brimstone preacher brother whom she hadn't seen in nearly thirty years and who had decided to come out of the woodwork just to tell her that he was a changed, more reasonable man and that maybe that newfound reasonableness was due to the fact that he was dying. And then he disappeared, one step ahead of any law enforcement agency that might have heard of his brief reemergence, and in leaving, he also left her the dog and a bottle of champagne that he stole from the O'Malley's cupboard. Before his departure, Carl had encouraged her—exhorted, might be the more appropriate word, since he didn't entirely leave his bombast behind—to marry Michael and make it official. Michael had been yammering about it for years for reasons unclear to her. And Gil, her son, halfway around the world in Afghanistan, had been after her as well, just before he left. What is it with men and marriage? It's usually the woman who wants to know her position in the world and her place in relationship to a man. Not her. Fuck that. Carl, with his pretense of transformation and his stomach cancer, had been the tipping point, though, and she had said Yes, in a moment of weakness, but then he left and she had dithered once again. Six more months went by, Magda grew and grew and became an ever-present feature of her life with Michael, whose eyes were becoming more like Magda's every day. Magda wore her down with projections of her own reproach, and Michael wore her down for good with silence on the matter. His refusal to speak of it further. He could be such a stubborn son of a bitch, just by being nice.

"Okay, goddammit," she said. "Okay. We'll get married. You're such an old lady."

"Fine," he said. "If that's what you want. It's not like I'm pressuring you."

Hah. He could be so exasperating.

So, they went to the county clerk's office, paid for the license, then paid for some starchy woman with shellacked hair to read out the Do you take this, blah, blah, lawfully, blah, blah. *Take this?* But it was done and she had yet another new last name, only this time it wasn't her husband's. Enough of that. Not Burkhardt, her birth name. Not Mortenson, her first husband's name or Rabinek, the name of the second. And not Wayte, Michael's last name with all its homophonic connotations of mass or importance, sorrow or gravitas. Of delay, neglect, or anticipation. Not going to happen, none of that. She'll use a thesaurus of her own and on her own behalf, if you don't mind. Just Elisa BMRW, thank you very much. Her own life and the history of her relationships in an abbreviated nutshell. One she owns. If Prince could have an unpronounceable symbol for a name, then she can have her own glyph, and if it's hell to write on checks or convey to someone over the phone, so be it. Even if Thing One and Thing Two call her ElBuMRaW behind her back in voices that they think are whispers, even if they apply a name to her that sounds like she's become a witch, she will be herself, a fifty-eight-year-old woman, married once again, yes, for the third time, who can do what she wants. *Take that.*

MICHAEL BOOKED THE BAND several weeks ago without telling her. They came by several times, carrying cards and demo discs, even—*of all things!*—a mission statement which made sense rather than being merely bizarre once it became clear that the four musicians are loyalty-oath, faith-statement employees of

Liberty Christian College, that redoubt of Evangelical supe-
riority seventeen miles away and two thousand feet higher in
elevation. And since they come from that particular community, they bring their own audience and ethos, an attitude, a
point of view that the bar doesn't usually countenance and
one she doesn't find simpatico in any way, shape, or form.
They must have presumed upon his generally accommodating
nature; they must have worn him down. That's why Michael
never said boo until just before he left when he gave her the
BTW. That coward, he knew what her reaction would be.
He knows what she thinks of the college and the Christians
and the holier-than-thou, classist bullshit they represent. If
she had known who was coming and when, she would have
booked passage for Aruba or hopped a bus for Visalia. But
then, Michael's mother fell, and damn it, she likes Michael's
mother; for that matter, she likes Michael's father as well, so
she is screwed, screwed, screwed beyond all measure. She can't
be a bitch; she can't just disappear and leave the bar to Joe
and Abel. There wouldn't be a bar to come home to, much less
the upstairs apartment. So much for her expectations of the
band and the crowd and the evening ahead. It's a recipe for
unleashed and festering anger. Anger that has nowhere to go
except in Michael's direction, if and when he chooses to say
goodnight to his parents and come home.

Here's where it gets worse, what's worming its way under
her skin. The band's name is Lazarus Rising, which is so much

donkey squat as far as she is concerned. She knows the Lazarus story, and in her mind, that's one more mark against them. One more reason for her to be pissed off. Lazarus came from the sepulcher, stinking of his death and trailing his days-old rags and his well-meaning, tear-stained shroud. That's all well and good, but here's her question: wasn't his resurrection just a vehicle, a gag, one that gave Jesus an opportunity to be a little weary of women, exasperated and put-upon? Just to show how much control He really had? *Woman, leave me alone, I'll get there when I get there, and if I get there after your dear brother is dead and gone, well, what does it matter? I make the rules.* A woman, yet again, made to wait and do the housework and the grieving and then made to feel bad for a moment of impatience while a man gets to dictate the terms, the time and place, the when, why, and how. Well, each to his own; she will steer a wide berth of the band and what she can only presume will be their false optimism, good cheer, and clean looks. None of that for her. She can only hope that after they set up, no one will come to hear them play.

But, lo and behold, as amps and instruments are plugged in and wires are strung like tenement clotheslines, the grow-ing electronic hum merges with the hum of the numbers beginning to fill O'Malley's. More people at seven o'clock than she's seen in several years. The whole college has turned out, it seems. Some customers have even spilled out onto the picnic tables outside. Her helpers, Amy and Miranda, who know this crowd better than she does (and with greater sympathy, it should be noted), are steadily taking drink orders—pitcher after pitcher of soft drinks with a few discreet glasses of beer and wine among the more adventurous—while her "helpers," the Demented Twins, are threatening to burn the place down via nachos and toaster oven. The acrid smell of burning queso and singed tortilla chips fills the room, and simultaneously a smoke detector begins to wail, a nail of sound puncturing the various resonances and hums. She grabs a towel and whirls it above her head like a whip, fanning the smoke and the stink away while standing on a chair above the happy, humming, oblivious throng.

Wonder Woman has nothing on her.

"Joe!" she calls. "Abel! You're killing me!"

THEN AGAIN, WHAT IS DEATH REALLY? Or rather, what does it mean for those left behind?

This is not a joke but a real question for Elisa. One that's been nagging at her for some time. Joe and Abel are a case in point. Each man's wife died within days of each other six months previously. Breast cancer and complications from Alzheimer's. Long-suffering sisters-in-arms, Theresa and Maria might just as well have made a date with each other for the long goodbye, their declines were that inevitable and precipitous. Once vibrant, hard-headed women, who were more than a match for their idiot husbands, they were, in the

313

end, betrayed by their bodies, and they left like dinner guests excusing themselves from the table, never to be seen again. All of which is to say that the Demented Twins were left behind, with their memories and the bills. As a result, O'Malley's now might as well rebrand itself as Adult Day Care for the true service that she and Michael provide. Elisa brings Joe and Abel their pitchers of light beer, but Michael treats them like the family that they have become over time, uncles on their uneven march to join their better halves; even so, their heads rarely rise above their shoulders, and their insults are rote and pro forma as they look in the middle distance for that which is no longer. She has also noticed that among the regulars, Joe and Abel have become segregated. Outcasts of an unacknowledged sort. They have always been a duo, but now they are two alone in the midst of all the other swillers of beer, as though the others of their age and kind are afraid of catching what they've got. The Widower Flu Survivor Virus. No matter how clear it might be that they will all eventually catch what they've got, no chances are being taken.

Given all that, she now and again catches herself looking at Michael and wondering which of them will go first and who will be left to pick up the pieces. Her behavior in her twenties wasn't exactly exemplary, but her best guess for first out the door is Michael, who doesn't do a thing to take care of himself. No exercise to speak of and a diet that has a distinctly brown palette. He will be the one to go first, of that she's sure.

He might have been an athlete once upon a time, but you'd hardly have an inkling of that now, as soft as he's become and as reluctant as he is to visit a doctor for anything other than the resetting of a bone. So Michael will drop dead of a heart attack or a stroke, and then she'll be left on Survivor Island, and the thought of that, of being abandoned (*snap your fingers!*) just like that, makes her mad, as though she needed any other reasons for the anger that seems to live just below the surface of her skin.

And now, here you have this band, with its cheeky reference to a man who supposedly died twice, as though once wasn't enough for his grieving sisters to endure, and what do they play? They're all over the map, music-wise, a mash-up of styles and sensibilities with no rhyme or reason that she can see other than audience calculation. Honky-tonk and blues and country-rock to begin, yes, but then as the evening wears on, a standard or two from the American Songbook mixed in with the requisite gospel numbers and hymns because (apparently) you have to know your audience and realize who and what you are. The secular numbers give the crowd the sense that they're taking a risk, by looking into the darker and seamier sides of life, while the gospel tracks and the hymns put the audience on their feet and their hands in the air, waving back and forth like a field of so much brainless grain, to which she has only this reaction: *Really?* One more re-orchestrated and harmonized verse of "How Great Thou Art" or "Amazing Grace" and she'll start chugging the Basil Hayden as anesthesia. Too much is too much, but if she's honest with herself this is the way most music hits her, no matter the genre or content. Even in her teens and twenties when she was hobnobbing with musicians in the Haight in the early seventies, it all seemed like a put-on and a con job. So much of it merely an excuse for self-delusion. She has no affinity for those who treat popular music like it's a doorway to another dimension, and so-called Christian rock meant to compete with its secular equivalent doesn't even deserve consideration. Concerts and altar calls both presume a certain level of brainwashing that she wants no part of; hands and arms waving in the air, cigarette lighters making stars in a dark arena, it's all just Kool-Aid to her.

To her mind, Lazarus Rising is one more copy of an imitation of a forgery in the form of a quartet: a vocalist, a guitar, a bass, and a drummer, and each seems to have adopted a glossy, sanitized version of the secular persona that he or she has elected to play. The possible exception might be the drummer, a doe-eyed blonde who doesn't look a day over sixteen and hasn't pretended to any sort of musician stereotype. Given her rock-hard belief in nothing being what it seems, she wonders what wild child lurks beneath such a demure exterior. No one could possibly be that innocent.

But, midway through their second set, Little Miss Deer Eyes stands up from behind her drum set and begins to sing "This World Is Not My Home" without accompaniment.

The vocalist and guitars step to the side and let her have the moment. She does not possess a trained voice, but it has its own purity, and she resists the song's usual tempo and over-embellishment; by the third verse, the others have come in behind her, not harmonizing exactly, merely filling in the corners of her own clear notes and welcoming everyone in the bar to join as well, which they do while respecting the delicacy of this rendition of an otherwise clumsy song, which is when Elisa finds that her eyes have begun to water, from tears or allergy, impossible to tell.

The angels beckon me from heaven's open door
And I can't feel at home in this world anymore.

There have been moments during the twenty-some years that she has worked and lived at O'Malley's when some emotional disturbance has made it imperative that she leave her duties in the bar and remove herself to the privy out in the parking lot. Since she and Michael have been married, she's just gone upstairs when the need arose, but tonight she makes her way outside like old times, through the Christians at the picnic tables, Magda padding behind her, so she can then wait her turn. Hating herself. To open and close the plastic door and turn the plastic lock in front of Magda's anguished eyes, before she allows herself to give in, to pull down her jeans and grab her ankles, her forehead on her knees, while Magda bays at the moon in tune with the sound from inside the bar.

The band will finish their set. They may end in prayer or,

317

god knows, an altar call or both. Who cares? She knows how to keep her distance from such things. Miranda and Amy will take care of the Christians and their nachos and soft drinks, and while Joe and Abel are always a danger to themselves and others, she is willing to take the chance that the bar won't blow up in her absence.

After their five-minute wedding, she and Michael had called Gil's work number, to let him know the good news: that they've heeded his instructions, after all, that his mother was once again a married woman, but he did not pick up the call. Not that surprising given the twelve-and-a-half-hour time difference and his work and a thousand other reasons. So, she left voice mails, and she sent texts and e-mails but received no response. She left messages with the contractor for whom Gil was working, and a week went by before they heard anything: and that was a nothing, only that Gil was missing, but with only the vaguest of details. Nothing about who or why or how. No one had claimed responsibility for kidnapping an American. No body was found and no video of torture or mayhem went viral. Disappeared. Just gone. She called her idiot Congressman, and even that dickweed Republican came up empty. Yet another erstwhile Christian, so glued-in to the intelligence community for reasons having nothing to do with intelligence, at least not his own. Gil left his work trailer in the middle of the afternoon, for reasons only he knew, and five years later what has happened since remains a mystery.

318

What isn't mysterious is how much blame there is to go around. She can't put it all on the pinhead asswipe who represents her district, nor can she entirely criticize Gil's employer, those vultures who look to make a fortune out of a warzone. They are what they are. And, when she's honest with herself, she can't even blame those Christians up the hill from the bar, who first repelled him with their sanctimoniousness and sent him off as a soldier because he couldn't tolerate their bullshit, and then after his return, sent him off again because they provided him a degree and the expertise that might be useful in prosecuting yet another American military blunder. No, they're not entirely to blame, those self-righteous war hawks who somehow never seem to serve. She blames herself, first and foremost, for not protesting enough, for not saying No to Gil, for not preventing his departure, for not hating him sufficiently for being so foolish as to court the danger that he's found.

What also isn't mysterious is how a coincidence has turned a decision made out of her own ambivalence into a cause-and-effect punishment. Against her better judgment, she got married for the third time, no charm apparently for the woman who had vowed never to do that again, and Gil disappeared. She is still married, and Gil is still gone. What is she to make of that? Is this how God operates? She has a whole-back tattoo that illustrates what happens when God and humans are at odds, so why should she or her son be spared?

And, of course, she can't help but lump Michael into the same blame that she assigns herself since this—marriage, like any suburban, conventional couple—is what he wanted, and he kept pushing and pushing in his nicer than nice way. Him with his past ties to the Christians and his pastoral approach to bartending. Now look. This world is not my home. Indeed. Why isn't she just passing through? She'd like to pass the past. For one day, she'd like to refrain from taking it out on Michael, stop punishing him for the coincidence of unrelated events and her own superstitions.

What did Lazarus ever do to deserve a second bite of the apple? She'd be happy enough to receive a little holy sarcasm if that's what it takes... *Go ahead, Jesus, abuse me.*

Against the heels of her hands, her eyes feel like swollen jellies. She could bathe in the water of her own making if she allowed herself to give in completely to everything she is feeling in this moment. Which is when there is a tap-tap-tap on the plastic door of the privy, followed by Joe's tentative voice, that alpha dog of the Twins: "Elisa? Elisa? Are you okay in there? Elisa?" Meanwhile, Magda, her dog of sorrow and her brother's conscience, wails.

Okay? How could she be? *Let me count the un-ways...*

MICHAEL WHISTLES AS HE RUMMAGES through the drawer of the cash register.

"What?" he says, holding up the thick sheaf of credit

320

card receipts. "You did this much? You did have a good night."

"I told you," she insists. "Your Christians came through."

He has come back at midnight, two hours before their official closing. He has spent time with his parents and chatted with their friends and fellow residents, he has consulted with his mother's doctor, he has talked with the director of their assisted living facility, and he has spoken genially with the facility's staff. They like him, and they will do as he asks, and now after the hourlong drive in the dark, he is at his usual station behind the bar, stepping back and forth over the sleeping Magda, fat dancer that he is, getting a sense of what he's missed.

"They weren't drinking, were they?"

"Sugar water, mostly. A little beer, a little wine, not so anyone would notice."

It is a running joke between them that so many of the LCC folks they have known are horrified by alcohol or pot or dancing but completely at home with the fellowship of sugar, fat, and obesity, they are that hypocritical regarding right and wrong and the behavior of others.

"So, they sat, listened to the music, and ate chips and cheese."

"And beans and burger and guacamole. That's about it." She sips her bourbon, which at the moment doesn't taste like anything at all and is doing less than nothing for the mood she'd like to achieve. "They sang when they knew the words.

No drunks, no fights. No telling about tips, but I can't imagine them stiffing the girls. They see them every other day of the week, and no matter how cheap they might be otherwise, they're going to have to look them in the eye."

The band played from eight until eleven with a twenty-minute break at nine-thirty, and when the band left the stage for the second time, the crowd mostly went with them. About the time she emerged from the privy, her jeans buttoned and her eyes dried, a scant few of the regulars, chased out by the crowd and the music and the too-earnest earnestness, drifted back in while the band disassembled their equipment. They slouched in their chairs and they drank in a particularly sullen, dispirited way, and they exuded the kind of edginess that preceded a stormfront or a fight. Michael rang the bell for closing twenty minutes after he arrived. No point in prolonging what had already been a busy and successful evening. No point in having the night go south for the sake of two more shots of Jim Beam for which the drinker might not even be able to pay. Amy and Miranda said their goodbyes and collected their shares of the tip jar while the Demented Twins seemingly vanished. To no one's sorrow, Elisa thinks.

"Thank you," Michael says. "I know you didn't want to do this. You didn't want to be around these people."

"You've got that right."

"But it seems like it went okay." He looks at her over the

glasses that he has recently begun wearing all day long and not just for reading. "You seem okay."

"Do I? I wouldn't be too sure."

The dark clouds that rolled in during the band's second set, that wave which sent her to the plastic pit toilet in the parking lot, might have dissipated slightly, but she's still aware of the anger and anxiety simmering within her, waiting for an opportunity to erupt, to spew over Michael as the nearest and dearest recipient.

"Maybe," he says, "maybe we need to take a day. Go to the beach. Or a decent restaurant. Something different."

"My reward, I guess," she says, "for not killing anyone."

"Something like that."

"No, thanks."

"No?"

"You heard me."

She won't be bought or placated that easily. *Tell your brother Jesus to bring my son back.* That might do the trick.

On the landing at the top of the stairs leading to their apartment, Joe and Abel materialize like Tweedledee and Tweedledum. Joe holds the railing, calling down, while Abel holds a plumber's helper. Demented Gothic.

"Mikey," Joe says, "there's been a little problem."

Abel chimes in: "The lock on the privy got jammed or something, so we had to let folks use your bathroom."

"What are you talking about?" Michael says.

"It's a mess," Joe says. "I'm not going to lie."

"Who knew that Christian people could make such a stink," Abel adds.

"Water, water everywhere," Joe says. "And other stuff."

"Don't worry," Abel says. "We'll clean it up."

"ElBuMRaW," Elisa says. "ElBuMRaW's to blame."

"What?" Michael says.

"I had a meltdown," she says. "I had a meltdown, and I kept the toilet occupied."

For there would have to be no more bourbon left in the world if she's going to let Thing One and Thing Two cover her ass.

[xii]

Weather or Not, She Was Good

(Cheryl Newland, 2016)

THE RAINS THAT BEGAN THAT October—that same fall which saw the Great White Evangelical Hope elected—were followed by a series of so-called Pineapple Express storms the following spring. The rainfall totals, up and down the state, relieved the depletions of the previous seven years and encouraged many to believe that the worst of the drought had passed. Everywhere in Born Again America, gratitude and relief were palpable.

At Liberty Christian College, for example, special services of thanksgiving were held in the chapel on Wednesday evenings on what was becoming a nearly regular occurrence: in late November for the results of the election and in conjunction with the traditional holiday; in mid-December for Christmas, of course, but also the rain which had fallen and the projections of more to come; in January for the Inauguration and the installation of God's man at long last and the end of the national nightmare of liberal smugness and secular human-ism; in February for the rain and the rain and the rain; in March for the wildflower blooms made possible from so much precipitation; in April for the end of the governor's drought declaration; in May for all the signs of new life: of the green grasses of the spring and the promise of the summer and the years of blessing to come. May the agenda of God Almighty have sway in the world. In Jesus' name for ever and ever. Amen.

It so rarely rained, and temperatures so rarely fell below freezing that Dr. Cheryl Newland might have been for-given a moment of superstitious anxiety when the skies grew increasingly dark after Thanksgiving. A native of the Midwest, though, she was not unused to violent and change-able weather; she was hard-headed and a realist, and she kept it as a point of faith that however good the world might seem, it was only a flawed counterfeit of the world to come and, as such, was bound to disappoint. And yet, over the course of nineteen years, she had grown accustomed to the unremitting, unvarying shade of blue overhead and the temperate climate of the college's mountain remove; they were above the fog but below the snowline. This paradise, ordained by God, was it not the best of all possible worlds? How easy it was to believe that nothing could ever change that, no matter how dark one's convictions might be.

326

"If I wanted to shovel snow or wear rain gear, I'd go back to Cleveland," she said to her husband one morning that December. "Or Bloomington. Or Tulsa." She poured her second cup of coffee for the day. "No," she considered, "not Tulsa. No tornado sirens for me, thank you very much."

His response was a vacant look behind his thinner-by-the-day copy of *The Fresno Bee*. She envied his track suit and his unshaven face and his weight which hadn't fluctuated by more than a pound since their wedding thirty-seven years earlier. She envied his general obliviousness to anything that didn't directly involve him. He worked from home, and because they did not budget for his erratic income, that work rarely caused a ripple in his blood pressure. He chewed a bagel, turned to the local news from the front page, and resumed reading.

Last night the rain had fallen, the wind had blown, and water had crashed against their windows most of the night. Her husband snored, the result of his untreated sleep apnea, something else to which he was oblivious, and after midnight, she had moved to their small living room and the love seat too short for sleep, her cold, uncovered feet dangling from the end and her mind too aware of the noise outside and in, too full of the events to come.

Their daughter and son-in-law and the twins would be coming from Sacramento in another two weeks for Christmas and while she would be happy—overjoyed, *yes, really, she was*—to see them, the timing couldn't have been much worse.

327

Or the arrangements. As president of the college, she and her husband and daughter had lived in the President's Mansion, an oddity of organic architecture on a ridge half-a-mile away from campus, a house officially named Manlever Hall for one of the college's past presidents, but which the locals referred to as Tits Up for its twin domes, unfortunate chimneys, and the silhouette they created at sunrise. The roof leaked, the windows were poorly sealed, and in high winds the house played a series of discordant notes, but its great advantage was space, enough for three families' worth of children if one had them. But then their one child, Virginia, married and moved away, and after twelve years of rattling around by themselves in that drafty barn of architectural curiosity, she and Robert had decided to downsize: they moved from Tits Up to one of the campus gatehouses, the one to the south of the main driveway, vacated most recently by that bilious English professor, Walter Book, and his sad and demented wife, Susan. The gatehouse was room enough for Robert and herself, but add two more adults and two ten-year-old boys? Chaos could only be worse if Chihuahuas were included.

As if that weren't enough, her performance review was scheduled the week before Virginia's arrival, and rumors were afloat that the Board of Trustees had someone else in mind for her position: that this performance review, scheduled more than a year ago for the end of this fall semester, was simply a pretext in order to bring in their own man, emphasis on the male aspect of that equation. The all-male Board had nothing against her particularly, or so the rumors had it, except that she had been president for nineteen years, a lifetime in academic administration, and she was, well... a she and wasn't this an Evangelical God-fearing college, after all? Come to your own conclusions. The time was long overdue to set things to rights. God knew, she should have seen it coming with Bobby Thornton, that crusty, liver-spotted toad of a man and current President of the Board, who, even at the age of seventy-six, got his way through shouting louder than anyone else in the room. Even when invoking the name of Jesus. When she tried to pray for him and for her relationship with him, she couldn't keep the dream images from her mind: a man waving a big dick, a bazooka of a dick, intimidation for all to see. For all to cower before. For nineteen years she had kept Bobby Thornton and that big dick mollified and charmed. She had kept him believing that he was the one person without whom the college would surely fail; for nineteen years she had put a hand on his arm, laughed at his crude jokes and *tut-tut-ed* at his innuendoes, and played the flirt, *the little lady*, played the role she knew he wanted her to play. She had kept Bobby Thornton at bay, but to what end? At the age of sixty-three, her time was up and her charms losing their hold. So it seemed. They didn't call it the patriarchy for nothing.

And now, as she walked under her umbrella from her refuge of the gatehouse to the slate-roofed Administration building, on a campus with few students present given the Christmas holiday, it was raining once again, the skies nearly as dark as night, the walkway lamps still illuminated even at ten o'clock in the morning, on a day when she had more obligations than time. She could recite her day-planner from memory:

10:00-11:00: President's Cabinet

11:00-11:30: Meet with enrollment management committee—trends and projected targets; data for performance review

11:30-12:00: Drive to Fresno

12:00-1:30: Luncheon (Rotary? Elks? Kiwanis? Check with Linda) and keynote address (the role of the spiritual in contemporary higher education; use the story about the minister, the educator, and the mayor)

1:30-2:00: Drive back to campus

2:00-2:30:Review academic dismissals/expulsions with Provost MacMillan

2:30-3:30: Preview architectural renderings for football stadium expansion with Coach Santos

3:30-4:00: Meet with basketball teams/coaches/AD for pictures and pep talk

4:00-5:00: Informal Q&A with Dean of Students Gregory and residence hall directors regarding enforcement of co-ed policies and open hours

5:00-6:00: Dinner in faculty commons with Faculty Senate President Book

6:00-9:00: Reception for regional choirs, followed by adjudicated concert

9:00-10:00: Review of self-evaluation-in-progress

Her drives on either end of the luncheon would be the highlight of her day if it weren't for the phone calls she was expected to make while driving: so-called "retention and reconnection" calls to various alums, donors, and friends of the college, calls that might result in increased donations and renewed pledges or result in complaints, criticisms, and axes to grind.

In the portico of the Admin building, she shook the rain from her umbrella. Linda, her administrative aide, was already waiting with phone messages and an updated daily schedule. One of the phone messages was from Bobby Thornton, regarding a potential donor. Nothing surprising there; when he wasn't a tsunami, he was a leaky faucet, wearing one down, drip by drip. She pitied the would-be donor. Another was from her son-in-law for a return call, which was as surprising as the message from Bobby Thornton wasn't. Dr. Book, that pompous asshole, was requesting additional time beyond their dinner hour. Not a chance in heaven or hell, earth, sea, or sky. A dinner with that man was an inducement to anorexia. You might think you had an appetite until he began to talk about himself, his faith, how blessed he was. Blah, blah, blah. No matter the subject, it always circled back to himself. He talked while spit and food particles collected in the corners of his mouth. He talked and talked, and then he talked about himself some more. Who did he think he was? Her time in the car had become worse by half.

Umbrage and whining, cloying gratitude, emotional manipulation, and self-serving flattery. That's what she would be facing, hour after hour, all day long. Shoot me now, she thought, if that's what it takes. Shoot me now, Jesus, if that's what it takes to be good. Being shown the door might not be the worst thing, after all.

She blamed Robert. And God. Robert and God. Her husband was the instrument of God's will, the reason that they had come to the mountains and California and Liberty Christian in the first place. She had been happy enough serving in a full-time role as part-time dean and part-time literature professor at New Harmony Union, and while the pay was appalling, the job was fulfilling, and she considered her life satisfying. Satisfying enough. Most of the time. Some of the time. At least that. The students were sweet and polite and grateful, and if they weren't the most incisive or well-read or *studious*, she found the aforementioned qualities of subordination and civility enough. Most of them were attending through a combination of church scholarships and government grants, and they knew where the bread was to be buttered and the degree to which courtesy could paper over deeper flaws.

For his part, Robert had become less and less enchanted with his work in a Raymond James office and was eager to try his hand at day-trading, using funds from a grandfather's estate, but to do that, without the pressure of gambling, they both knew that her income would need to improve, and they both knew that this was unlikely to happen in Indiana or at New Harmony. Ever.

So began an eighteen-month tour of job applications and headhunter interviews, mission statements and vision statements and personal philosophies, trying to make her round-peg self fit into the square holes of community college positions, trade school jobs, and four-year public university openings. Finally, Robert handed her the job posting for the President's position at Liberty Christian College, recently rebranded from its historical name of Sierra Presbyterian.

"This is made for you," he had said. His glasses, which had thickened over the years, reflected back at her, hiding his eyes.

"It's a President's job. I've never been a full-time Dean, much less a Vice-President."

"The job is made for you," he repeated.

"Fine," she had said. What was one more application? By now, she was used to the tedium of trying to stretch herself to match another institution's expectations. Especially for a job for which she was clearly unqualified on the sole virtue of her résumé.

But, she had to admit that the process went so smoothly as to seem divinely ordained. Interviews with the search agency, interviews with the hiring committee, presentations in public forums, lunch-time chats with selected groups of students. Nothing created the least problem or caused a moment of anxiety or doubt. Even a one-on-one meeting with Bobby Thornton, himself new to the Board at that time and one of the driving forces for the name change and the new, more aggressive Evangelical stance that the college was adopting. Those dour, cheerless, mainline Presbyterians were making their low-energy exit and a new cohort was stepping forward into their place. Believers with a more robust, more vital faith, a faith that took control of scholarship, rather than the other way around. Believers who believed that they had a right to public visibility, public leadership. Onward, Christian soldiers... Indeed.

"Time to dust off the cobwebs," he had said. "Shine her up, make her new."

She couldn't tell if he was referring to the college or her. Because, if she were honest with herself, she needed a little refurbishing of her own. As comfortable as she had become at New Harmony, that was the same degree to which she had begun to go through the motions: in her classes as well as her administrative duties. When was the last time she had reread one of the books she had taught? Or, the last time she examined, really examined the paperwork that her administrative aide brought her to sign? It was all such day-to-day stuff, and there was nothing about which to get excited or passionate. She had found herself longing for a scandal or a tragedy—a drug bust in the science wing, an orgy in the dormitory, a death following some ill-begotten horseplay or a momentary lapse of judgment—if only to break up the monotony. Was that an indication of her own moral and intellectual deficiencies?

If New Harmony had become a rut of her own making, then Liberty Christian would be something of a high dive into a basin half-full of water. And, she knew from the very beginning that Bobby Thornton and his allies on the Board were not hiring her for her leadership qualities or her vision as much as they were hiring her as someone to manipulate and use to their own advantage while they remade the college in their own image.

"We're going to make changes, you and I, and the county—maybe the country—will never know what hit it," Bobby Thornton had said, but it was clear that he needed no suggestions from her regarding the changes he had in mind. This understanding was made absolutely clear during a tour of the campus on one of her first visits. As they walked toward the conical, teepee-shaped chapel, Bobby Thornton had pointed to the knoll overlooking them to the north.

"Look," he said, pointing to a spot that, to her, looked to be no more than a mound of rocks and dirt. "There used to be three wooden crosses up there. You can't see anything now except the stones that used to be at the base of each one. Twenty-some years ago, two cousins climbed up the two outer crosses, lit all three crosses on fire and burned themselves alive. According to the letter they had sent to the police and the campus administration, they died to protest the lukewarm nature of faith that the college represented. They were a sacrifice, a warning to the college that its leaders did not heed, not then at any rate, but we will not make that same mistake now."

She looked in the direction that he had pointed, but try as she might, she could not see any evidence of that moment, not even in her imagination. What could have impelled two human beings to give up their lives in a gesture that most would consider as out of proportion as it was futile?

Twenty years ago, Bobby Thornton had said, they had bulldozed the site and raked the ashes and pretended that nothing untoward had happened. But now, to commemorate the name change and all of the other changes in store for the college, the Board—meaning Bobby Thornton himself—had authorized a new Golgotha: three steel crosses set on a concrete pad as a reminder of what the true mission of the college was to be.

"'I appeal to you therefore, brothers,'" Bobby Thornton recited, "'by the mercies of God, to present your bodies as a living sacrifice, holy and acceptable to God, which is your spiritual worship.' We are going to put that on a plaque, and we are going to be committed to making their sacrifice mean something. We are going to worship with our whole hearts or go out in a blaze of fire and fury. So help me, God."

When she was offered the job, she took it, with her eyes wide open, knowing that she was joining ranks with the fanatical and the extreme and the nakedly, politically ambitious. All for the sake of a title and a paycheck, for the benefit of her husband and daughter. And maybe, a little bit, for herself as well. And it was just possible, she thought, that she might be able to soften the edges. Just a bit. She watched the steel crosses being erected and the granite-and-bronze marker installed while she held her tongue. She could maintain civility and decorum and lobby for a rose garden to border the site. She could accommodate the Board's excesses, even as she remained true to the moderate nature of her faith.

"Remember," Bobby Thornton said, on that day when he called her with the news. "You and me. We're changing the world, or at least this part of the mountain."

IT TOOK SOME TIME TO ACCLIMATE to California and all of that unnatural heat and sun, but she and Robert and Virginia had managed, and if they received Christmas cards from the friends they left behind, cards with pictures depicting two feet of snow and ice, well, then, they coped by embracing their feelings of shame and moral inferiority, just as they had coped with celebrating Thanksgiving in shorts and tee shirts. Not that there weren't some challenging moments of their own: those infrequent days in January when she had meetings in Fresno, and the tule fog was like so much cotton wool, an opaque curtain of mist and oblivion. Then she drove with one eye on the center line and the other on the taillights that were sure to materialize out of nothing. Other drivers flew past her, like so many Furies, with their horns blaring, their headlights flashing their presence. How they saw anything in front of them, *if* they saw anything in front of them, she had no clue. They were racing blindly into the void with no instrumentation available.

The summers, on the other hand, seemed to arrive in the valley as a blaze of dry, super-heated air, gusts of which periodically rose through the ridges of the mountains. Stands of pine trees, casting shade normally no warmer than eighty degrees, sagged in ninety-five-degree heat, while the valley below sweltered at more than one-hundred-and-five and the air thickened, further trapping the heat with a dome of dust and ozone.

Albeit with some hovering sense of subconscious misgiving made tangible by the weather, she had settled into their new home, an alien region that, she was reminded all too often, bore a great deal of resemblance to the Holy Land in its climate, its crops, and its pent-up hostilities. Every morning, it seemed, the *Bee* carried the latest story of a drive-by shooting, a husband-wife murder-suicide, a convenience store robbery gone wrong, or a prostitution sting involving a member of the city council. The seething resentments of class and ethnicity, pronouncements of morality and the practices of human behavior. They were spared confronting such anxieties in their mountain aerie, perhaps, but the reality of the world was only twenty-five miles away.

She had to admit it, though: she had thrown herself into her new home, her new life and new role in those early years; she hadn't noticed that her workdays were lasting sixteen or more hours, and despite her absence (or was it *because* of her absence?), Robert and Virginia had thrived. Robert had succeeded beyond her wildest expectations while day-trading in the wild and woolly late-nineties, and Virginia, after finishing her high school work via correspondence, had enrolled at LCC like the good daughter she mostly was. As the president of Central California's preeminent Christian college, which was how Bobby Thornton insisted the school be branded, she needed a good daughter, and the sullen and passive-aggressive teenager with problematic skin had suddenly blossomed into a poised, thoughtful young woman. When and how had that happened? She knew the definition of grace, but she couldn't help feeling that God had blessed them too easily and might just as easily change His mind.

The only strain occurred during Virginia's senior year, long after her mother had lost that nagging sense that the ease in their relationship was too good to be true. And, of all things, the strain involved the events of 9/11, a football player/juvenile offender, Bobby Thornton, and medical insurance.

It was something of a cliché, wasn't it, the moment of 9/11 and its aftermath. Where were you when you heard or saw? The nation stood still that day and in the days that followed, and yet she couldn't quite rid herself of the sensation that everything that had happened had happened far, far away to people she did not know, and no matter how much she knew she should grieve, her feelings were strangely detached, as though she was carrying them in a bag by her side rather than within her chest. To make matters worse, there was the game of football, the football team, and the football program, all of which Bobby Thornton claimed to be of utmost importance for the name recognition of Liberty Christian and its role within the wider, secular world.

"You don't have a football team, you might as well knit," Bobby Thornton had said. "Waterloo was won on the playing fields of Eton, and American military might is football. First, last, and always."

The football team had been only recently reestablished after a twenty-year hiatus, its won-loss record was a dismal 5-31 after three years, and she had to wonder what that said about American military might. But then, Coach Bonaventura found a young man, Dalvin-Demarius Philipi Jenkins, who single-handedly reversed the team's fortunes and outlook. That the young man in question was a juvenile offender who was given an adult sentence was—in football terms—beside the point. As were questions about his academic preparation or his willingness to abide by the LCC statement of faith. As it turned out, he believed more thoroughly and more honestly than most, and if his preparation was spotty, he was curious and bright intellectually, dogged and tenacious, but no one cared. Not really. Could he play, could he contribute to a team that was so sadly lacking? Those were the relevant concerns. He could play, as it turned out, so well that he raised hope previously missing for Liberty Christian boosters.

They won, but then, like a curse descending, the planes of 9/11 hit the Towers and the Pentagon and that field in Pennsylvania, and in the first game played afterwards, DDP had been injured, so severely that a year after the fact, his leg was amputated six inches above the knee. Some said the injury was caused by Coach B using DDP on both offense and defense, that he had been overworked and exhausted. Others maintained that the prayer group DDP had established following 9/11 had played a role, that he had been fasting in conjunction with his two-hour prayer sessions, all of which had depleted his stamina and resilience, thus making the injury that much more likely. And still others, Bobby Thornton among them, said that, given DDP's past behavior and criminal record, his injury was merely a sign from God of his unworthiness to carry the LCC banner forward; Bobby Thornton said all this as loudly as possible, but much more quietly he had made an aggressive move to deny responsibility on the part of the college for Dee's medical bills. That she had finally dissuaded

Bobby Thornton from pursuing such a course had helped, but news had leaked, and no less an emissary than Virginia had been the one to barge into her office.

"You can't do it, Mom," Virginia had said. "I can't believe you'd even consider it. He's better than any of us, and you'd turn your back on him?"

She had held up her hands in an attempt to slow, if not stop, the runaway train of her daughter's tirade. "That's not going to happen. Mr. Jenkins is a Liberty Christian student, and he was injured participating in a sanctioned Liberty Christian activity. We will honor our responsibilities. Regardless of what you might have thought or heard or thought you heard."

"Then why is everybody talking about it in the dorms and the cafeteria?"

"Rumors," she had said, "just rumors. People talk even when they don't know what they're talking about." Although she knew that, in this case, the rumors had been at least partially true. At least if Bobby Thornton had had his way, which he usually did, even if he hadn't in this case.

Getting *her* way had involved a certain *quid pro quo*, though: for one, firing the football coach, who had been on staff for four years and (since he drank in public and smoked in private) had made his moral failings known on more than one occasion. That much was easy, and, two, firing the chaplain, which was not. He had been on staff for more than thirty years, but he had pissed off Bobby Thornton in some way, and he became a bargaining chip. Everything with Bobby Thornton was a negotiation, a bluff, and a double-down, and she wasn't proud about her part in that particular hand. The problem was that it continued, year after year, as Bobby Thornton exerted a greater and greater role in the hiring of faculty and staff and administration. Climate deniers. Creationists. Historical revisionists. She knew all this, and she had seen it coming, and somehow, she had managed to find a silver lining. What she hadn't known then was the end-around that Bobby Thornton would pull, without her knowledge or consent, voiding DDP's scholarship while he was still in the hospital, while the doctors were still trying to save the leg he would eventually lose.

What she also hadn't known was the degree to which Virginia's heart had been struck by DDP's plight, a young black man so different from herself, nurtured in youth homes and prison, but overcome by a vision of Jesus, no less stunning than Saul's on the Road to Damascus and a conversion no less complete. Virginia's Christianity had been cultivated through Sunday School and youth camps and felt boards, verse memorization and a profession of faith in an eddy of the Wabash River, whereas DDP had been struck down in his jail cell by a profane Jesus who had told him that now was the time to get his shit right. Just do it, or reap the consequences. In retrospect, she wondered, how could Virginia not have been intrigued?

Liberty Christian was not a big place, and it would have been a statistical anomaly if they hadn't met, and yet five years after Dee's injury she had been surprised—blind-sided, in fact—when Virginia had announced that they were engaged. After making sure that Dee's medical bills didn't hit the evening news and accepting Bobby Thornton's *fait accompli* of the scholarship revocation, she hadn't kept track. She hadn't known that he had enrolled at Fresno City College, and had gone on to get a degree in Human Resources or had been hired by the governor's office to craft policy statements regarding urban youth programs. She certainly hadn't been aware that they had kept in touch or were dating. What would she have done if she had known? But when they were married, she made sure that the college was front and center: the chapel was the venue, the fired chaplain was the officiant, and the fired coach the best man. Sometimes, she knew, the best defense against embarrassment is a whole-hearted embrace of one's defeats. She stood with her husband, and she smiled as though she were running for office. *Shoot me now,* she had thought as they welcomed each invited guest, *shoot me this instant while I am still civil.*

Shoot me now had become her mantra and her index finger against her temple her personal sign of the cross, and she had been thinking and doing so, deliberately and by reflex, since their move to California. Shoot me now: termination, her sure-fire method of goodness. All thanks to Robert. And God, of course, and yet she often wondered whether she had misinterpreted His will, for the sake of her husband, their collective finances, and her own sense of self.

They had met in their senior year of high school, and she had to admit it: she couldn't tell if they had ever really known one another. They were eighteen and hormonal but constrained by the dictates of their church and faith. Would they have been just as happy if their consciences had allowed a quick fuck? She didn't honestly know. What she did know was that she had enjoyed being the spouse on the fast track: college and graduate school and then a full-time job with benefits, a captive audience, and at least some small measure of prestige. Unlike Robert, whose life was measured by the anonymity of a cubicle and the degree to which he could maintain his solitude. But, after a short period of gratitude, her years at New Harmony had constituted something of a stall, a plateau, and in the end, she had been grateful for the push that Robert had supplied, all too willing to see the arc of her career as divinely ordained when it was all too possibly a product of her own ego. Could leadership become merely an attention-getting device?

As a girl she had been fond of those stories of women, who gave themselves for their faith and families. Where had that selfless girl gone? Or, had that merely been a conceit, that her little girl dream of selflessness was only another form of narcissism before she had the language to define it? She had started with Joan of Arc at her stake only to end with the

Grandmother and the Misfit and the promise of a bloody trade-off for salvation.

"So there was a mid-sized town in the Midwest—I won't name names—a town that was losing its manufacturing and industrial base and as a result homelessness was becoming a growing problem. Encampment villages were growing underneath the overpasses and alongside the freeway. When the police ordered them to move their sleeping bags and lean-tos, they simply picked up their belongings and moved to another location. The tax-paying, property-owning residents were getting nervous, frightened, and angry.

"To consider this matter, the mayor met with two of his closest friends and advisors, an educator from the local community college, and the pastor from the church that he attended. No, no," she said, "this is not a joke, and they did not walk into a bar. Although that might have been the easiest solution."

She shifted her feet behind the podium and waited for the expected titter to die away.

"He asked them to do the impossible: to write down their one-sentence assessment of how to fix this complex and complicated problem in the long-term.

"The mayor wrote on his slip of paper, We have to transform the economic context by reaching out to businesses that have a future, offering tax incentives and developing partnerships.

346

"The educator wrote, We have to revolutionize our way of thinking about education and retraining and the changes that are taking place within the world of work.

"And the minister wrote, We have to convert our hearts, build greater empathy and compassion among those that have for those that haven't."

She was conscious of the broad rear ends shifting in their wool suits and polyester-blend skirts and the metal protest of their folding chairs, but she forged on nonetheless.

"As many of you know, I come originally from the Midwest, and I come from people who are nothing if not practical. Do you have the votes or not? Do you have the money or not? These are certainly political virtues and practical realities, but there is the virtue of knowledge, of what is right, even if it flies in the face of the immediate answer, and then there is the even greater virtue of wisdom found within the spirit, that causes us to go beyond what we know empirically and ethically. All of which is to say that pragmatism that is not leavened with a knowledge that goes beyond the superficial and a deep knowledge that is devoid of wisdom will avail us nothing, even as wisdom that does not recognize the practical will not have a leg upon which to stand.

"We need one another, and we need to recognize the balance and interaction between the practical, the intellectual, and the spiritual, in order to solve the intractable problems of our time and community. At Liberty Christian, we are striving, as a constituent within this community, to be part of such multi-faceted solutions, and as an educational institution, we are striving to encourage and create leaders for tomorrow, young men and women who will find the answers that have escaped us today."

At the end, the applause was polite but tepid, as was fitting for such regurgitated pablum, her audience finally released to finish their slabs of Chocolate Decadence and their scoops of melting Cherry Garcia. Spoons clinked against bowls. Jaws moved. A laugh here and a titter there echoed in the hall. When she finished, feeling a little nauseated as well as exhausted, she sat down in her seat near the poinsettia-festooned podium while the Grand Poobah of whatever group this was stood up in his too-tight maroon blazer to encourage the faltering applause.

"Well, that was fine, just fine," he said, his hands coming together like twin hams. His neck bulged red against his collar and the redder red of his jacket. "Such fine words. My mama told me to go to college, and there are days, especially when I'm elbow deep in someone's commode pulling out the seven-year-old's GI Joe... Then, I wish I'd listened. Again, our thanks to Dr. Newfoundland and our friends at Liberty Christian College. Please give her another round of applause."

Newland, she wanted to say, *is that so hard?*

"Oh, Lord," Mr. Grand Poobah said as he collapsed into the seat next to her. "My wife says I look like a stroke waiting to happen wearing this thing." He wrenched at his tie and popped the top button of his shirt, releasing the pressure on his neck. "Better."

He sighed, then drank from the glass of water at his place. "You know," he said, "that Bobby Thornton, he and I, we go way back. You tell him hi for me, won't you, darling?"

"Of course," she said, mustering the smile she did not feel. She pressed one finger to the side of her head. "Of course, I will."

CELL SIGNALS IN THE MOUNTAINS near the college were notoriously unreliable. Calls dropped without warning and there you were: one more yammering idiot speaking into the void, only to realize that no one was left to listen, and like the tree in the forest, you hadn't been making a sound after all. She had learned, when driving from campus to Fresno, to wait, to make her retention calls when she was far enough down the mountain. But there were times, on the return trip, when a call went long only to be dropped, the victim of a granite outcropping, a stand of pines, the rare rain squall, or another line-of-sight obstacle. And then there were the inevitable apologies, via text or e-mail, that would need to be sent. More time to be expended in the name of saving the same.

And that's what happened while speaking with her son-in-law, Dee. He was clearly upset, but between his agitation, the rain and her windshield wipers, and the signal cutting in and out, she was hearing only every fourth word.

"Dee," she said, beginning to shout, as though that might help their connection, "I'm going to pull over. Let me call you back." Which was when the signal vanished anyway, so who knew how much he might have heard or what he might have said.

She was halfway up the mountain when O'Malley's, that falling down, eyesore of a roadhouse, hove into view on the left side of the highway. Rain was pelting the tin roof of the bar and the gravel parking lot and the three other cars that looked as though they had been abandoned years ago. Her Highlander slurved through standing water and next to a pickup that was more rust than paint, and when she got out, she made sure to lock her doors before dashing inside.

The woman behind the bar was reading a magazine and chewing gum, and when she looked up, her eyes widened.

"I know you," the woman said. "Don't think I don't."

"What?"

"Michael!" the woman yelled as she stood up and put her magazine underneath the bar. "This one's yours. You'll have to excuse me," she said, addressing Dr. Newland. "I'm sorry."

She went out the front door without looking back, in spite of the rain and in spite of the fact she had neither coat, hood, nor umbrella.

"Dr. Newland." A stocky man, wearing an ancient Sierra Presbyterian sweat shirt, stood in front of her. "What can I do for you?"

She held out her cell phone. "I need to make a call."

"We're between cells, between mountains, and thirty years behind the times," he said.

"Why did she—?"

"Elisa?" He shrugged. "Her son went to Liberty Christian. Off and on." He shrugged again. "She doesn't hold warm feelings."

"I see," she said. "I'm sorry to hear it."

"Use this." He set a black Bakelite telephone on the bar. "It's a museum piece. Every year, someone tells me to get rid of it, and every year someone needs to use it." He dropped a phone book dated 1999 on the bar next to the phone. "I even keep this. For old times' sake."

"The telephone will be fine. Thank you."

"Sure."

He moved away for a semblance of privacy although the two eighty-year-olds at the table by the woodstove were clearly straining to hear what she might have to say and to whom she might be saying it.

"Joe," he said. "Abel. I need you to give me a hand."

"There are some things you need to do yourself," one of the old men said. "And I ain't going there."

"Don't be crude. Or I'll sic Elisa on you."

The three shambled into the rain, sharing a plastic poncho above their heads, while she put a shaking finger into the rotary dial.

"Dee," she said at last. "It's me."

When Virginia was born, Robert had been at an agents' conference in Florida. Her obstetrician had assured them that first babies were rarely on time, usually late, and almost never early. So, of course, in her thirty-eighth week, her water broke at two in the morning, and she had to call a neighbor for the ten-minute drive to the hospital. Four hours and one C-section later, she was sitting in a hospital room with a red-faced, angry infant, who already seemed to have made up her mind that she had been promised something else entirely, and while Virginia fussed and clenched her tiny fists inside her tiny mittens, Cheryl realized that she was also crying. Like daughter, like mother. Why? She didn't know. The neighbor had called Robert, who was booking his ticket home, but he wouldn't arrive until the next day. Her mother lived by herself in Baltimore with three cats and a growing sense of paranoia, and she had told Cheryl months before that she wouldn't make the trip until the baby was a little older and a little less germy. So, although balloons and baskets of flowers from colleagues at New Harmony had already begun to arrive, she wept. Nurses came and went, but the tears refused to slow. A woman from housekeeping emptied the trash, and she wailed.

"It's you and me, baby girl," she choked. "You and me."

And, given Robert's habitual silence, his general reserve, it had been the two of them from day one until the day of Virginia's wedding. For good and bad, better and worse.

Through the sullen days and the repentant nights. And now, over this ancient telephone, her son-in-law was telling her that Virginia had suffered an aneurysm in the back yard while she and Dee were playing with the boys. She had thrown a baseball to one of the twins, put one hand against her forehead, vomited, and then fell to the ground in a heap, and only the fact that Dee had been required to take a first-aid class the previous month, a class in which strokes and aneurysms had been covered, meant the difference between Virginia being rushed to the hospital with a fighting chance for some measure of recovery or being slowly driven to the morgue, her face frozen in its rictus of pain.

"I don't understand," Cheryl said again and again. "I just don't get it. What happened?"

"Mom," Dee said, a term he hardly ever used for her, so she knew now just how serious this was and might yet be, "she's going to be okay. But I'm no doctor, obviously. *I think* she's going to be okay. She's alive. But maybe you ought to come."

"Yes," she said. "Yes. Right away. I'll be there as soon as I can."

She set the phone back in its cradle and cradled her own head in her arms on top of the bar and began to sob as though she were suffering post-partum once again. Her daughter, her baby. She could look ahead as though backwards through a telescope, through a narrow tunnel of time, seeing the months of pain and frustration ahead that Virginia would endure. She was alive but might need to relearn so much—walking, talking, actions that hadn't required thought since early childhood—and while her mother would be there to help, she wouldn't be able to take any of that burden away… She sobbed. *Jesus, be with my girl.* For time, for loss, for helplessness.

Crying hadn't felt this good for years. Crying with abandon, without self-consciousness or shame, no Bobby Thornton to witness what might be perceived as weakness or sentiment. Crying solely for another.

"I'm sorry," the woman from behind the bar said. Dr. Newland had not been aware of her return, only the sound of her son-in-law's voice, how difficult it had been to parse the meaning of his words and the hard news they had signified. The woman's hair and shirt were drenched, and water dripped onto the bar when she touched Dr. Newland's shoulder. "I'm so sorry," she said. "Let me get you something. A drink or a cup of coffee. You're going to have a long day ahead of you."

[xiii]

SOB Is Just Another Way to Spell Sob

(Bobby Thornton, 2017)

BY HIS OWN ADMISSION, BOBBY Thornton was an asshole and a son of a bitch, and he had no intention of making apology for the state of his disposition. He had one wife, two exes, four children, one business with five subsidiaries, two plastic-and-alloy knees, and a bad hip that one of his golfing buddies was going to fix with some sort of space age ceramic sometime in the near future. He was the CEO of Chronos Athletic and Chairman of the Board of Liberty Christian College, and he was worth a few million bucks to the bankers and investors when they had extra money to loan. What's a few? On a good day, he could go eight digits. On a good day. When the market was inflated. Don't ask about the not-so-good days. Most folks thought he ought to be happy with what he had, but most folks could eat it because one day out of seven, he'd open up a newspaper (when he could find one), find the sports page, and see the name Phil Knight, and he'd be reminded that he hadn't achieved half of what he wanted. Phil Fucking Knight, him and Nike and his swoosh and his all-star athletic endorsement team. What celebrities Nike didn't gobble up, Adidas and Under Armor and Asics did. So where did that leave Chronos? In the dumper, that's where; he had to be creative, resurrect some broken down has-been or come up with some off-the-wall marketing and advertising strategy if he wanted to keep Chronos breathing in market share. But all of that played hell with his blood pressure, currently tripping along at 185 over 96, and that was even after Dr. Popapill upped the Clonodine.

Then, there was Gloria. He couldn't look at her without thinking Wife Number Three and all the wasted energy if not alimony that implied, and he looked at her every morning as she lay flat on her back, her mouth hanging open like a cave of fillings and crowns and veneers, the acerbic and sour aftertaste of the night before, the dental bills and the therapy bills all his. Not that he was anything so great himself, no matter the time of day or night. When they met, she was twenty-seven, a pharmaceutical rep, and in full possession of her divorcee's charms—the too-tight tops and a Malibu tan—while he was forty-three and, without knowing it at the time, looking for what turned out to be his last conquest, the last hurrah while he still had a little juice left. Since then, Gloria had taken on the role (unasked for, by the way) of his backup conscience;

and, while he might see that role as redundant, she thought his conscience was lazy and too forgiving and, therefore, needed a bit of a boost: he could be better than this, if she had anything to say about it. After all, he had accepted Jesus Christ as his personal Savior and Lord thirty-two years ago while they were sneaking around on Patrice, Wife Number Two, and wasn't that supposed to make a difference in one's behavior? *Voila!* Magic! Make him a new being and a different sort of person! Even though in becoming a new person, he had to act as he had always acted. He hadn't thought much of it at the time—since taking the pledge was just a way to get under Gloria's choir robe and, in his own experience, nothing worked faster on a girl than the pretense of vulnerability. Let his face go limp. Use his coon dog eyes. Layer on the sensitivity and spirituality with a trowel. But a little righteousness, even of the pretend variety, has a way of sneaking up on a man—*God, help me*—you know it does, and he has been looking over his shoulder ever since. *My words fly up...* For Gloria's sake he had been willing at the time to go through the motions: heed the altar call, get dunked in the fish tank at the front of the sanctuary, but he reserved his right to doubt the ability of people to change in any radical, significant way, shape, or form. What was he supposed to do, turn into Francis of Assisi, let birds roost on his shoulders, *make me a channel of thy peace*, and all that glorified fucking bullshit? That was never going to happen. He had tried for a little while and he could

357

manufacture it when required, he could put on that impassive, untouchable affect and let his voice go quiet, but in the end, that wasn't his personality and never would be, no matter how long he pretended otherwise.

Today, for instance, on a day of blue skies in April in the year of our Lord 2017, he had a list as long as his arm of shitty things he had to do, most of which involved telling people they no longer had jobs or telling people to tell *other* people that they no longer had jobs. Losers and the luckless. A dean on temporary appointment, who couldn't be bothered to get his desk cleared by the end of the day. Probationary faculty whose classes were chaotic and confused. A longtime security guard who, surprise, surprise, has been *shtupping* the freshmen girls for years. And no one had known, not even their own campus police force? But he would start with the president of Liberty Christian, Dr. Cheryl Newland, and for that he would do the dirty work himself. Not that little Miss Cherry, her sixty-five-year-old ankles uneasily balanced over her Jimmy Choos and her own last gasp of sexual appeal, didn't already know the boom was lowered and coming toward her at break-neck speed. He had hired her, he had groomed her and worked with her, flirted with her and manipulated her for more than twenty years, and every year, he had thought that this was it, this would be the year when he would have to tell her, Time to go, Betty Boop. Don't let the door knob hit you, blah, blah, blah. Turned out, though, that it was always easier to keep things the same in order to do his work under the cloak of darkness, rather than deal with the fallout in the clear light of day. The work that needed to be done. But this was the year. She was too old, she was a woman, and he had a new puppet ready to go, this one a man who looked good for the cameras, airbrushed, razor cut, and manicured, who ticked all the Evangelical boxes of appearance. The best indicator of godliness. Better yet, he had worked at LCC once upon a time, and Bobby knew how to work his levers and gears.

Oh, these goddamn square head Baptists and Methodists and Pentecostals, they could drive a body nuts with their yammering about this, that, and the other thing, starting with the Trinity of Evangelical irritation: creationism, abortion, women in leadership. But the list never stopped there, not really. There was always something more. For twenty years, he had given them the college that they felt entitled to have.

Evolution is a theory, the world is young, and scientists should check their assumptions.

The Bible is the inerrant Word of God: yesterday, today, and tomorrow.

Life begins at conception.

Promiscuity and homosexuality are abominations of equal gravity.

The man is the head of the household, and marriage is one man and one woman.

Climate change is a hoax.

The media is a tool of the secular, hearts-and-flowers, liberal elite. Cry me a river.

The culture wars are the visible manifestation of that great spiritual battle between Satan and the agents of righteousness.

Jesus could return at any moment, probably when you least expect it, and then, don't you know, there will be sorrow to equal the joy.

He had intervened in the hiring of faculty, made sure they were teaching the right things, saying the right things. The football team was winning championships, spreading the message of a muscular Christianity far and wide, attracting media attention and donors like flies to shit. And, on top of all that, he was about to give them a mister, rather than a sister, as president, but even then, he was sure to hear some new grievance, some new complaint about how he had failed them and fucked over the Lord God Almighty Himself. As if he had told Jesus to bend over. Every decision he makes has less to do with the right thing and more to do with what will keep them at bay. According to Orwell, he's murdering elephants, only to look good.

Goddamn them to hell!

HERE'S ONE MORE GRUDGE: it's 1970, he's twenty-eight years old and working his way up the Sport Chalet food chain. He's with Wife Number One, Brenda, former cocktail waitress at Trader Vic's and possessor of a prodigious set of knockers.

Coconuts got nothing on her. She comes off as a bit dim, but Bobby knows there is more lurking behind her layers of Maybelline than meets the eye. He comes home from a late night at the office—he's taken a set of identical shoe representatives from Japan to dinner, trying to work a favorable deal on their crappy line of lightweight running shoes—only to find his wife curled up in the fetal position on the couch. *What's wrong, honey?* His immediate suspicion is that he's once again done something to foul the nest when she explains that she went to church. Oh, church, he says. That's nice, thinking that this is one way of adding a layer of respectability to their marriage, which has become the stuff of office mythology— behind his back and to his face—given said knockers. But church should not leave one curled up in the pre-birth position, now should it?

Turns out she's gone with a girlfriend to hear a guest preacher, who turns out to be none other than Hal Lindsey, who has been getting everyone all worked up, convinced that the Rapture is at hand and the world as we know it is not long for this—well, world. You know the guy. *The Late Great Planet Earth.* Gog and Magog. Four horsemen and the grapes of wrath. And you thought those duck-and-cover drills of the fifties and sixties were scary. She and her girlfriend drove home on the San Diego Freeway out of their fucking minds. How Brenda got the Camaro home, he doesn't know. She might as well have driven with her eyes closed. He doesn't mind the church thing; he's had his own dose of Catholicism as a kid, but he'll be damned if his wife is going to go off the deep end over some hellfire-and-brimstone, end-of-the-world bullshit eschatology. Yeah, yeah, he knows the big words. Premillennial, dispensational—there you go. Turns out, though, the joke is on him. Without him knowing anything about it, Brenda gets all fired up and goes whole hog: the next day, after she's recovered from her fetal-position nap long enough to get up off the couch, she heads off to Orange County and Melody Land Church, where she falls in with the charismatic lunatic fringe, starts speaking in tongues, and with a few other like-minded souls drives out to Palm Desert to wait for the Rapture and the Lord's promised hallelujah return.

Would you believe that he makes both drives, Disneyland and the desert, over the course of the next six months? Bobby Thornton, gung-ho Sport Chalet regional director of marketing at the tender age of twenty-eight, heading out to no-man's land to fetch back his Trader Vic's bride, only to return empty handed, his entreaties met with stone cold resistance. Jesus is coming back, she says. She will be flying to meet Him in the clear desert air, and there is no longer any point to their marriage.

The paperwork of the divorce was handled entirely through the post office over the course of the next six months, and the last Bobby heard, maybe a year ago now, she and her knockers and Jack, her tongue-speaking, some-time plumber, full-time survivalist and husband, were responsible for eight biological children and fifteen others who found their way to Brenda's door as if by magician's spell. As for the imminence of the Rapture, the 1980s had come and gone, and she was still waiting. Earthbound like everyone else, more than thirty years after the fact. So much for the fear-mongering and the prison house of the end times or any hope of a quick release.

Nothing had changed, after all, but, God, how he hated to lose those knockers…

"…Look Cheryl, you've had a good run," he said, "and you'll be treated fairly, you'll get a severance, but the Board's decision has been made. It's out of my hands." *A lie, of course, since the Board makes no decisions without him making their minds up for them. She knows that as well as he does.* "I feel awful about Virginia," *which is the way he feels, but that, too, contains the germ of another untruth,* "but maybe this is a blessing in disguise. You'll be able to spend more time with her and the rest of your family," *because isn't family time just a euphemism for You've been canned?*

He knew that her daughter, Virginia, a Liberty Christian alum, recently had had some sort of catastrophic health issue. What the hell was it, again? A stroke, aneurysm, heart attack—one of those things to which people in their thirties ought to be immune. Jesus, he ought to be better at remembering shit like this, but details, other people's details, if they didn't affect him directly, tended to fly out of his mind as quickly as they entered. What did that say about him? Nothing good, he was sure.

As Chairman of the Board of Trustees, he had bullied his way into office space in the Administration Building because on the periodic visits he made to campus he found that it was easier to deliver bad news to someone when he was behind his own desk rather than facing the desk of the poor sap getting the axe. He kept his office chair raised, and he had deliberately ordered visitors' chairs that were soft and three inches lower than expected. He might as well have been a judge in his own courtroom. The staging helped, and he wasn't above using it to his advantage.

Surprisingly though, little Miss Cherry wasn't playing along. She refused to sit down and remained standing in her school-color-coordinated blue suit and red blouse, she resisted the usual Evangelical hug in favor of a brisk handshake, and she began talking almost immediately about her vision for the next academic year, a year that unbeknownst to her was not going to include her. He had had to interrupt, in order to bring the hammer down, and tell her the bad news flat out.

"So, who?" she said. "Who are you bringing in? Walter?"

"Walter Book? God, no." The thought of that fat, pompous ass, Walter Book, as President of Liberty Christian College made him want to scream profanities in clear violation of the Liberty Christian Code of Conduct, but he could not have a conversation with that puffed-up Eddie Haskell dipshit without needing a shower afterward; having to work with him would be a disaster compounding a catastrophe. Although, come to think of it, how ironic would it be to get rid of Cheryl, only to replace her with a man so gay and so unaware of his own proclivities that his closet might as well be a billboard? Let the square heads chew on that.

"We have someone from the outside," he said. "Well, he's been gone a few years, but we're bringing him back."

"Who?"

"Lyle Schubert," he admitted.

"I see." She crossed her arms over her chest. "You're bringing back a former Dean of Student Life who wouldn't say boo to a goose, much less to you. Not as insufferable or as flammable as Walter, but a total lightweight."

"I remember someone else who didn't have many credentials to her name," he said. "Not at the beginning anyway."

She remained, frozen in place in front of him, and because he couldn't look her in the eye, he focused on her LCC lapel pin with its ridiculous cartoon eagle logo, aware that this meant from her perspective he was staring at her suit-jacketed breasts. Ogling, leering, in this day and age. He raised his gaze to settle on her chin but could go no farther, even as he beat back the usual interior refrain, a fantasy that reminded him of his sixteen-year-old self and all that yearning: we could have done something, you and I, if only we had let ourselves do it.

"It worked out okay," he said, at last, "but now we're moving on."

"You're moving on," she said. "I'll be moving out."

"You won't have to rush," he said. "There's no hurry. Lyle and his family are going to use Manlever."

"Good for him. Tits Up could use a willing occupant." A joke wrapped inside a farce.

Neither spoke for a moment, letting the image of the erstwhile President's Mansion play in their heads and the image of empty-headed, no-offense Lyle Schubert, his cosmetics-counter wife and their eight evil children laying waste to the place. She and Robert and Virginia had lived in it for several years, but it was drafty and over-large, neither comfortable nor artistically distinguished, and once Virginia was gone and off on her own, Cheryl and Robert had moved to one of the college's microscopic gatehouses.

"You better pay for housekeeping and maintenance," she said, "if you don't want your architectural gem falling into disrepair."

"I called it that, didn't I?" he said.

"You did. Once upon a time."

"I couldn't stop this, you know."

"No, of course not. When has Bobby Thornton ever bucked the will of the Board?"

He shook his head. "Not the Board. The Board is nothing. I'm talking about our fellow travelers in Christ. The whole aggregate of boosters and donors. All the good people in the pews with their entrenched way of seeing the world, a point of view cemented by every small-minded sermon they've heard and every idiot Sunday School class they've attended. They've been foaming at the mouth for the last twenty years, so I'm throwing them a bone, which happens to be you. You were never part of their game plan. They're now just getting their way, whether I like it or not."

"We do what we do," she said, "and one way or another, we do what we want, don't we? No matter how much we claim otherwise."

His mouth always hurt after doing something disagreeable, and after Cheryl left the office without even the grace of a parting handshake, much less a hug, the throbbing started in earnest. His goddamn dentist had bungled a dental implant sixteen years earlier, and the nerves in his jaw and gums and tongue worked together sending up a symphony of jangled and discordant pain, and when his mouth wasn't on fire, his tongue felt like it was twice its normal size, a rubbery, swollen piece of slimy beef fat. There were moments when he was afraid that a listener in his office or on the phone might suspect that he'd been drinking, especially if he had been, his tongue seemed that unwieldy and uncooperative. All because that fat fucking bartender from that falling-down roadhouse down the highway decided to take issue with a joke, punching him in the mouth without warning while they were watching a football game. The first football game after 9/11, no less. One moment, and sixteen years later, the pain was still with him. From the locked drawer in his desk, he took a slug from the bottle of Maker's Mark and swallowed four Advil, hoping to dull the cacophony within.

It was a joke. Good joke, bad joke, tasteless remark. What does it matter? Why couldn't anyone ever take a fucking joke anymore?

HE'D ONLY BEEN ON THE BOARD for a few years at that point. He'd hired Cheryl Newland, and he'd pushed for the renaming of the college from Sierra Presbyterian to Liberty Christian. They were going to jazz things up, move the college from its poky 1940s Frozen Chosen beginnings to something more fitting for the demands of a new millennium. He was trying to upgrade the athletic program since nothing rebrands an institution more quickly than a winning football team, and nothing deodorizes like success. He'd hired a coach, a has-been from Las Vegas so down on his luck he had fallen back to selling insurance to the cocktail waitresses on the Strip. Like Cheryl, he was meant to be a stop-gap, someone he could use for a couple of years before they spent some serious funds and made the big splash. After a couple of mediocre seasons, though, Coach Bonaventura brought a black kid out of prison, an out-and-out felon with a conversion story, no less, who played like a sledge hammer, and their fortunes were turned upside down, and he thought he might be stuck with Coach B at least as long as this kid was making touchdowns and tackles and leading cheers on the sideline. He was living inside the script for *Bad News Bears* or *The Mighty Ducks*, and Bobby had nightmares about the role he might be assigned. Then 9/11 happened, and then in the first game back from the dead, the black kid, whose name is nothing but initials, gets hurt. He gets hurt, and fucking hell, football players get hurt all the time, don't they? You know they do... That's when he made a joke, just to lighten the mood, and that's when that fucking roadhouse moron popped him in the face to the tune of one dangling incisor and a lifetime of reminder. Every time he does something unpleasant now, he gets a jolt, and you'd think it would make him more cautious, more cognizant of how his behavior affects others, but no. How was he to know that the kid would eventually lose his fucking leg? For Chrissake...

And, really, he had to go back further than that. To Gloria. He could blame Gloria for all of it. When he thought of it, his involvement with the college and the board, his church membership, the way he'd ditched Patrice, all of that began with Gloria, and the more he thought of it, the more he thought that the Arabs had the right idea, about keeping their women locked up, covered up, unseen and unheard. If there was any truth to the cliché about a good woman being behind a man's success, then it was also true that one little whisper in a man's ear could bring it all crashing down. Thank you, Lady Macbeth. Keep your big ideas to yourself. Screw you. And you, you unlucky-lucky Thane, forget your courage, much less the sticking place, and make the best of your life today and today and today. Be happy with ESPN and a three-bed, two-bath in a thirty-year-old subdivision with the gutters falling from the eaves.

After Brenda and her knockers decamped for the desert, he was lost for a time, there was no other way to put it. He started drinking, and then he started drinking more, and the next few years unraveled predictably: Sport Chalet downsized and reorganized and he lost his job because he was expendable and he didn't always smell appropriate at ten in the morning. He drank some more, or at least others told him that he did until he stumbled into an AA meeting at a Unitarian church in the San Fernando Valley, which is where he met Patrice, who had had her own ups and downs, not the least of which was the fact that she was a poet who wasn't very good. He couldn't make head or tails of it, anyway, but what did a shoe salesman know? She had a row of thin journals on her shelf, all of which tended to shout the certainty of their artistic ethos at the expense of anyone else. He had read a few of her poems, in which she had written about past lovers, impossible sexual positions, her C-section scar and her irregular menstrual cycle, lost weekends and projectile vomiting and three-day hang-overs, vaginal yeast and breast hair, and he had thought, Better let this one go. She was crazy as a loon, and she wasn't that naturally attractive, anyway. Her face was a little lopsided, her right eye a little higher than the left, her lips pursed in a perpetual smirk while she raked her coarse auburn hair with her fingers. She was skinny to the point of anorexic, smoked constantly, and her apartment was littered with ashtrays overflowing with cigarette butts, the filters stained by her purple lipstick. She had little to no interest in sex, and their bedroom activities seemed more experimental than experiential, and he had thought, yet again, Stay away, better let this one go. But, he didn't, of course. How could he, given such a challenge? She had been married for a time, not long apparently, because when he asked, she waved her hand through the air and didn't respond further. She had a son, who lived with his father, and she had no plans to maintain contact. Her family was loaded, with money so old by LA standards that no one seemed to know where it had all come from any more. She could write her poems in silence and smoke her cigarettes in isolation, drink vodka shots morning, noon, and night, and poot out the odd unwanted baby, and every now and then she went into rehab for a little drying out time, followed by a new phase of confessional work at AA, embroidered by a new set of those godawful poems, which after a short while began to include him in less than flattering terms; he entered her range of attention somewhere after a celebration of pubic hair but before genital warts. She was everything he was not attracted to, but given his relatively fragile state—abandoned, unemployed, and an admitted alcoholic trapped somewhere between Steps Two and Three on the AA ladder of wellness— she was temptation personified, so of course they got married three weeks after meeting. He was the one pushing for the license; what does that tell you about the nature of love and irrational attraction and the vagaries of human behavior?

What it told him was that her family's money was available to be used, and once he was mostly sober again, he launched Chronos, ten years and several zeroes behind Phil Fucking Knight, a head start that PFK would never lose and over the years would only increase exponentially. He felt a twinge of guilt over taking Patrice's family's money. A twinge. He wasn't quite as calculating as all that, really, or at least he didn't think he was, and it was a twinge he found easy enough to tamp down, let fade, and rationalize away.

He was doing the family a service by delaying Patrice's next stint in rehab.

His business was the only one of the many, many family handouts that actually showed a positive return on investment.

He only took what was absolutely needed and only came back twice for more when the company was in its most delicate of start-up stages.

Still, living with Patrice as his golden goose was no picnic. Even after rehab and AA, they were both still drinking because Patrice was never going to change, not unless you locked her up in a windowless, doorless room somewhere, and even then, she'd probably find something to guzzle and something to smoke, so long as she could keep writing a poem about it afterwards. She was just that resourceful and willing to generate her own material. And he was still drinking because she was, but he was working on it, trying to curb the worst of his impulses, to keep them corralled to a manageable level. If he went to AA, which he did only when times were really and truly bad, he spoke little and confessed less and kept a finely calibrated sense of which step he was currently and actively avoiding. And this after seven years of marriage to a woman who drank with an intensity that was frightening to the same degree that she was indifferent to him.

Which was where and when he met Gloria, she of the too-tight tops and push-up bra, her own recent divorce and an over-fondness for full-bodied Zinfandels bordering on the monomaniacal. She, of that first whisper in his ear.

"You need to leave your wife," she said.

Which was exactly what he'd been thinking ever since he'd first heard Patrice read a poem in which he figured prominently to a room full of 1980s-vintage beatniks—the bartenders with their beard stubble and the baristas with their nose rings and butterfly tattoos on shoulders and ankles and in places implied rather than shown. They nodded their heads while she Plath-ed him as Daddy, a Nazi with running shoes and fitness apparel, and when she ended, they exhaled their soft affirmations. They might as well have snapped their fingers like Daddy-o's from the fifties, such was their collective agreement and loathing of the figure in the poem.

That will do, he thought. Enough is enough.

Gloria was a member of a Baptist church the size and design of a Costco warehouse, whose gospel message seemed to have sprung from the same credo of prosperity and abundance as measured by bulk and volume and comparative pricing. She had taken the lessons of AA and let them evolve into full-blown Fundamentalism and a spiritual materialism, and she wasn't above raising her hands in the air behind the pastor whenever he intoned the name of Jesus or prayed over the collection plates.

Gloria sang with the 11:00 AM choir, and thus they began their undisguised flirtation every Sunday at 12:30.

"You need to leave your wife," she had whispered in his ear, Sunday after Sunday, "and you need to do it now."

Finally, one hot Sunday in May, he had come to the choir room following the service, and he stood at awkward attention as she and the other sopranos relieved themselves of their polyester fire starters.

"Hold this, will you?" she had said, extending to him her purse. "Do you mind?"

He knew that Patrice wouldn't mind; she barely recognized him as it was, his comings and goings, his role as a person other than a bit player in one of her dreadful poems.

He supposed he hadn't minded then either, taking her purse without much thought, although he hadn't expected to be holding it thirty-two years later as well.

So, GLORIA WAS THE ONE. She got him back to church and wheedled him to attend more than one AA meeting a month, she got him connected to Liberty Christian, and she pushed him to take his position on the board, which is why he is where he is today, trying to placate and deflect the square heads with their incessant demands for moral hygiene and doctrinal purity, none of which any of them wanted applied to them specifically or personally, but they wanted him to be the sheriff nonetheless. It's no wonder that his mouth is a mess, zinging and throbbing, as though a hole has opened up in his jaw. Rather than stay in his LCC hiring-and-firing hideout, he takes one more bolt from the bourbon in his desk drawer, then cancels the rest of his appointments for the day. He says, "Where's Jerry?" to the secretary he shares with the Public Information Officer, a onetime local radio news announcer, who wanted a break from the early morning drive-time slot. They need to put out a press release, Dr. Cheryl Newland stepping down, etc., etc., Lyle Schubert named to replace, etc., etc. But Jerry's secretary only shrugs. They'll have to deal with it later. It's ten-thirty in the morning. She says something about a meeting in the library's computer lab with some of the tech people and a reporter from Channel 30. So, okay, he doesn't need to be sent back to radio at 5:30 in the morning yet. But goddammit, it's coming; he can feel it on the back of his neck and in his mouth. He'll have to make a shitload of phone calls later from home, the police lieutenant, for sure; otherwise, if they're not careful, they'll need a campus daycare, sooner rather than later. Not to mention the incensed grandparents-to-be, whose tuition payments and donations they'll never see again.

The house he shares with Gloria is not that different from Tits Up in one sense: it's just as overlarge and drafty, and like Tits Up, it has more design appeal than livability even if it's only five minutes away from campus. But, while Tits Up is all curves and slopes and embarrassing silhouettes from its domes and chimneys, the house that Gloria built is all steel and glass and straight lines. There's so much glass and so little furniture within, the house barely makes a shadow. She had wanted a showplace at a higher elevation than the college or Manlever Hall because in her mind it was only right that the Chairman of the Board of Trustees should have a show-piece in which to live, a home unrivaled by anyone connected with the school. The driveway snakes through blue oak and grassland that by April has already turned golden, and he's struck as always by the brittle hardness of the landscape: the baked grass, the thirsty trees, vegetation that has survived for hundreds if not thousands of years in its oven-like sunshine and heat. And then he's surprised, yet again, by this house, which rises suddenly at the end of his quarter-mile driveway and to see through windows front and rear, his wife, sixteen years his junior, lying on the chaise longue, pool side, her face tilted up to the sun, as though there is no such thing as skin cancer. The difference, he thinks and not for the first time, between the ages of fifty-nine and seventy-five is a chasm of epic proportions. What was once a conjunction of vitality and experience has become the joining of the sly and decrepit, and he wonders—not for the first time—if, on those days when he's in the Chronos office in Fresno, she has anyone else on the side.

He goes to the kitchen and takes another shot of bourbon, gargling it like mouthwash before swallowing and then rubbing more along his gums. Outside, Gloria's four Maltese puppies chase empty Gatorade bottles around the cement deck. Running and pouncing on the plastic bottles, the four mops look like windblown dandelion heads, and the bottles bounce and skitter as they make their high-pitched barks and bite one another and bat at the bottles until the bottles bounce into the pool, the water blinking back the sun, and the puppies can't move a step more, flopping in the shade beneath the chaise longue and their mistress, their tongues extending between their evil little teeth.

"What?" She pushes her sunglasses to the top of her head, squinting at him as he falls into a matching chaise. "You look like you've seen a murder or something."

"I fired Cheryl this morning."

"That explains it," she says. The sunglasses come back down, and she lies back and undoes her top, offering her fifty-nine-year-old re-engineered breasts to sun and sky and only incidentally to him. "You offed your girlfriend."

"My mouth hurts," he says.

"So, go to the dentist."

"I went to the dentist," he says. "Why do you think it hurts?"

She turns her head and stares at him over the tops of those props, her glasses: "It hurts because once upon a time you were an asshole and you got popped in the mouth."

Sympathy is clearly in limited supply unlike the sunshine which is now blistering the top of his uncovered scalp.

She barks a laugh and the puppies cower. "Never made it to Step Eight and Nine, did you?"

"I was too busy in the choir room as you'll recall. Refresh my memory."

"'Make a list of all persons you have harmed and become willing to make amends to them all. Make direct amends to such people wherever possible, except when to do so would injure them or others.' You might try James 5:16 as well. Confession may be good for the soul, but it's just as good for blood pressure, acid reflux, and nerve pain. You're on the pay as you go plan, buster."

"Good to know," he says and struggles to stand. He needs that new hip, and his legs have apparently been replaced by pipe cleaners.

"Where you going now?" she says.

"Phone calls, and then I got to see a guy."

"Okay," she says. "In case you're wondering, O'Malley's is the first right past the tigers."

"I know where fucking O'Malley's is." Once again, it amazes and irritates him how well she reads his intentions. Look, he knows he was a bit of a douche, but goddammit that was sixteen years ago. Is there no statute of limitations for a bad moment? A bit of unguarded talk, a little diarrhea of the mouth? He said something stupid, and he knows he can be an asshole. He gets it, he gets it. But goddammit to hell, here he is, like a fucking robot, getting behind the wheel of the Range Rover for the seventeen-mile drive down the hill to O'Malley's and then whatever it is he's supposed to do. Amends, apologies, whatever will make his mouth feel right. When he should be talking to Lieutenant Perez about his little ass-wipe officer and his late-night seraglio.

For some reason, against all the laws of physics, the drive downhill takes longer than the drive uphill, and he has half a mind to turn one stop too soon and take a walk around the big cats instead. But he doesn't take the chickenshit way out; he pulls into the gravel parking lot of O'Malley's, even as he thinks about the Range Rover's paint and the likelihood that a trip to the auto body shop will be one more piece of collateral damage that he is liable to suffer. He pulls in close to the door;

there's not another car in the lot as it's not quite noon, and he clearly has the place to himself.

Through the open door, he can see the bar and the fat toad who punched him. He's wiping down the bar and polishing glasses and talking animatedly to a woman sitting on one of the bar stools, reading a magazine, and ignoring everything the toad says. She might be nodding in agreement, but she is hearing nothing. She's paying more attention to the outsized hound that is fast asleep and curled around the legs of her stool. After three marriages, he can read the signs. He opens the Range Rover's door, and at the sound, the fat toad's head pops up along with the dog's, at which point the dog begins to howl and howl and carry on.

"Bobby Thornton," the toad says when he steps into the bar. "You must be lost."

"You ever think of paving your parking lot?" he says, keeping one eye on the dog, who, in looking in his direction, looks like she just spotted lunch.

The woman looks in his direction, and her face goes through a complex series of transformations. There's recognition but also anger and loathing. And maybe pity. Lately, he's gotten better at recognizing pity. She steps down from her bar stool, snaps her fingers at the hound, who immediately goes silent but watchful, and together they take their sweet luxurious time going upstairs to whatever rooms are above.

"Did I do something?" Bobby says.

"The dog could care less, really. She's just a smoke detector. But Elisa? She's not a fan. Of the college, of you. Take your pick."

"Of Jesus, Evangelicals, or one Evangelical in particular?"

"Him, she's got no beef with, personally. It's the rest of the posse she can do without, and you're part of that. Sorry."

He raises his hands in surrender. Seventy-five-year-old hands, he realizes with something like shock.

"I can't help who I am," he says, and then without thinking about it, he gets on that high horse of umbrage, the one leap he can still make easily. No need of a stepstool or an extra pair of hands. "And I'll be damned if I'll apologize for that."

"No one's asking you to."

"And I'm sorry if she doesn't care for our particular brand of Christianity, but I can't help it. That's on her."

"She's a big girl," the toad says. "She knows how to take responsibility."

"Do you?"

"Is that what this is about?" the toad says. "Responsibility?"

"I'm here—"

He takes a breath which is when the toad gets rolling first: "Okay, this isn't easy, but since you're here, and you seem to be asking for it. You said some stupid stuff years ago at a football game, and I hit you. I was angry, DDP was hurt in a bad way, and you were a jerk, but I shouldn't have done that. I can apologize for that." He sticks a fat hand in his direction. "I hope you can forgive me, and maybe, after all these years, we can put it behind us."

Ah, shit, he thinks. Because there is nothing worse than getting beat to the punch. In either a fight or an apology. "You son of a bitch," he says, swatting the other man's hand away even though his jaw is sending up the SOS. His mouth contains multitudes of warning with its flares and rockets of pain. Talk about seeing red; he specializes in anger *and* supplemental reminders. "My mouth hurts every minute of every hour of every day," he says. Fuck Steps Eight and Nine. Whatever. "You're not getting off that easy."

"Well," the toad sighs, his rejected hand remaining in the air, "at least we share some mutual feelings."

In the back of the bar, at a table by one of the windows, two geezers even older than himself are parked in chairs that might as well be a park bench, the way the popcorn misses their mouths and litters the floor.

"You are one sad, miserable fuck," one of them says, "and don't think we don't know it."

"And who the hell are you?" he says, not unreasonably to his mind.

"Your better angels," the other geezer says.

"Now, boys," the toad says, "no call to be ugly."

"Oh, please," the woman calls. She is now standing at the top of the stairs, dog at her side, looking down on them all. If she had a pot of boiling oil, they would all be in trouble. "Ugly is," she says, "as ugly does. And I'm looking at it."

The dog has begun to howl again as though he had stolen the moon.

"Amen," says one of the geezers.

"Amen, brother Ugly," says the other. The geezers are looking at him, Bobby Thornton, and throwing daggers, as if, after all this time, he should know.

[xiv]

When I Think of How I Love You

(Michael, 2018)

ISTORY IS A FUNNY THING. We don't always know what's significant. We hardly *ever* know what's significant. What was important then might not be so now; what's important now might not be later. Once upon a time I thought I loved God, but now I think that maybe I was just trying to keep my options open. You know, *In case of fire, break glass*, that sort of thing. There have been times when I've felt closer to the divine, all those moments filled with intimations of the numinous, signs and wonders amidst the natural world. A white bird atop an evergreen. A new blade of grass. The sound of a bell tolling for us all. And then there are those other times when I thought, Give me a break, what a lot of hooey. A cosmic joke that has been going on for millennia, meant to keep the rebellious and misbehaved in line.

On the other hand, I fell in love with Elisa the day she walked into O'Malley's, and even though it took her fifteen years before she would say yes and it's been another ten that we've officially been together, I haven't had a day when I thought, What was that all about? You can call me soppy and too smitten for my own good—I'll gladly own it—but if we didn't have love, what would be the point? Still I can't be so blind as to realize that there might well come a day when one of us decides the other is just a gasbag and not worth the trouble. You can guess who the gasbag is in that scenario, so I make the bed in the morning, do my share of dishes and laundry for our apartment as well as the bar, and I wipe down our plastic shower to keep the mildew at bay. I police myself because you never know what might come out of my mouth and what that might reveal. I don't take anything for granted because life is nothing if not filled with the unexpected.

When my parents died, one right after the other in the space of two weeks, I thought, Well, that's it, I'm an orphan now, but I didn't really believe it, the term didn't bring up any deep well of feeling, and I'm not sure that many others would find much sympathy for a sixty-four-year-old orphan. Still, I could only manufacture the kind of grief I thought I should be experiencing by dint of will and arbitrary decision. I thought then there was something deficient within me, call it empathy or sentiment or love, whatever, and while I think I may have been right, it may only indicate that waking up next to Elisa each morning made it hard for me to register the depths of grief. Mourning should not be a skill that needs to be taught or acquired, but like those high-functioning autistics who have a difficult time reading faces for emotional cues, I was having to decipher myself, and I don't think I ever got it quite right. How sad was I supposed to be?

More than thirty years earlier, my father had purchased a double-stacked plot out at the Clovis Cemetery, back when Herndon was a two-lane road in the country rather than the expressway that it is today, and he and my mother had picked out a granite marker and had it etched with their names and birth dates, so the only thing left to do was fill in the death dates and plant them in the ground when the time came. My parents knew how to organize their lives even to the point of morbidity, but I don't think they envisioned a time when their place of eternal rest would be deafened by the roar of semis thundering past or that the cedars would be trimmed to look like the ornaments of a Dr. Seuss village. So, some things may be better left to the moment when crisis comes.

But then at the beginning of August, my mother fell for the umpteenth time because she was too stubborn to use the walker that she needed, and she never did navigate their living room very well as she was always and forever running into the coffee table or my father's recliner or the hutch where all the half-read books were piled; she picked up bruises from these encounters like a piece of overripe fruit. She staggered and tottered, tottered and staggered, until she finally broke a hip and fell for good; she caught pneumonia and died all in the space of a month, and at the end her usual feistiness had been flattened by sedation and the ambience of a bed in the ICU. My father, whose temperament I seem to have inherited, was lost if she was so much as in another room, and when she died, he had so few reserves left, he joined her shortly thereafter. I found him one morning unresponsive in his bed when I came at the breakfast hour to help him downstairs. The cause of death was listed as "cardiomyopathy" but really that's just heartbreak by another name.

I hadn't had a chance to set the date for my mother's service before my father died, so like all of their plans, the funeral was efficient, but even though their friends and neighbors got a two-fer, their tiny Episcopal chapel echoed with the loneliness of *abstentia*, there were so few of their contemporaries alive and ambulatory. The minister was a newly minted young woman from a seminary back east, and she was visibly relieved when I told her that I wanted to deliver the eulogy and that even though there was no need of a sermon, she would still get her cut.

"I know how you depend upon such things," I said, "and we're already cheating you by having one service when there easily could have been two."

"Oh," she said, "no worries. Since I didn't really know them."

So, Reverend Apple (that was her name, I'm not making this up) led us through the service, and then when it came time for the eulogy I stood up in my once-a-decade suit and said my piece to the empty pews and hearing aids. I told the story about my mother's heroism the year of the Christmas tree fire, and I told about my father's avocation: the elegance and craftsmanship in the furniture he built, and the fact that the furniture was built more for beauty than it was for function. I went on and on.

My parents, among the other things I said, *didn't like being the center of attention. Neither one of them. So, the fact that they could go out together is helping to lighten the load, I'm sure. Aside from the fact that they neither one liked the spotlight, they were as different as different could be, albeit in complementary ways. My mother was fire while my father was balm, and I am sure to wake up some morning and think,* What do I do with myself now, now that my parents are gone? *And then I'll have a cry, I hope, and all that choked-up feeling won't be stuck inside me anymore. Because it is an awful congestion. My parents were good people, and they were fortunate enough to have had good and stable lives, but that only seems fair given the history they had to live through as children of the Depression and young adults in the midst of world war. And it only seems right that now they get a little peace, even if that means hard cheese for me and everyone else that knew them.*

"Amen," I said at last, and the few bewildered souls repeated it, although from their mottled lips it sounded more like a question than a refrain. Elisa even threw in a "Praise Jesus," though I don't know where that came from and neither did she, so embarrassed did she look afterwards. Some bit of conditioning, resident from her crazy brother, must have come unstuck. Reverend Apple made the announcement about the graveside service to be performed at the cemetery immediately after the funeral and then extended the invitation for a reception to be held at O'Malley's immediately following the interment. As I expected, there were fewer attendees at the cemetery given the scorching noontime heat of the valley in August, and only the minister and her twelve-year-old daughter managed the trip into the foothills by the time we were assembled at the bar.

Elisa had platters of hors d'oeuvres, and Joe and Abel did their best to arrange napkins and silverware. I had assembled a poster board with some of the pictures of my parents that meant the most to me, as well as my mother's favorite pearl necklace, her box of baking soda, and my father's set of chisels. I had a guestbook, but seeing page after blank page was embarrassing, so I put it away for another time, another reason.

I had been sure that some of my parents' old friends would make the drive, but I guess I had been thinking about them from twenty or thirty years ago, when they were still hale and hearty and full of spunk, but now they were afraid to get too far away from their oxygen tanks and televisions. I remembered them as doctors and lawyers, office managers, activists and teachers, but at the end they had turned frail and fretful and not a little bit selfish, and I struggled not to blame them for what age had done.

"This is very nice," Reverend Apple said, looking at the picture board. "I wish I had gotten to know them. They look like lovely people." And when Elisa offered the minister's daughter a plate with some salmon mousse and crackers, stuffed mushrooms and hummus, she said "Thank you," very politely, and took the napkin that Abel offered her, but later I saw her dispose of plate and napkin in the trash, with the salmon, mushrooms, and hummus uneaten and untouched because, after all, what would a twelve-year-old want with salmon mousse when there were taquitos in the freezer that we could have put in the toaster oven? Magda buried her head in the waste bin, and I knew she was having a field day. All of the food would have gone into the trash and then into Magda except that we ended up having a larger than usual cheap-beer crowd at four o'clock, and if they liked cheap beer, they loved free food, so we didn't have to worry about leftovers or waste. I even received my share of sympathy and condolences. One of the bonehead Cal Fire chainsaws said, "Tell your parents, thanks for sharing," as he stuffed salmon mousse into his mouth by the spoonful. So, then, I knew my grieving was done, for the time being at least, the one benefit of others' obliviousness.

Things weren't so easy for Elisa since every new event seemed to remind her of Gil. And deaths were a surefire method for making her blue, even though she had received a letter here and a postcard there from him in the years since he walked away from his contractor's job in Kabul. He wasn't dead, but we could no more imagine him alive because we had no context with which to surround him. He might as well have lived in a green screen Disneyland. The last postmark we had was Kuala Lumpur, and that was at least six months before. Each note to his mother was only a slight variation of the previous one: "I love you, I'm fine, just traveling and getting my head right. Be nice to Michael." This last part a particular favorite of mine, as you might well imagine. While it was good to know he had the value of a stamp, Elisa took only minor comfort from these periodic reminders that he was still present in the world. He could have written more deeply about the places he had been and the sights he had seen. He could have explored the reasons for his wanderlust more thoroughly. He could have come home. I half expected him to show up at any moment, so I wouldn't have been surprised to see him, and I often thought, Today will be the day, and I often prayed, Jesus, bring our boy home. But you wait and you wait and you wait, and after you've waited that long, your mind turns to other things, just because you have to, you know? I didn't forget Gil, none of us forgot him, and certainly not his mother, but we had lost the dailiness of his absence until another absence made itself known, and then we thought about Gil all the more. And in my case, it was one more reason for me to doubt the efficacy of prayer.

Which was on my mind a lot. Prayer, that is. Because it seemed no matter which way I turned there was some new human need that couldn't be eased very simply. Take Cheryl Newland, the former president of Liberty Christian. I have to admit that I hadn't had much use for her in the years that she was president of the college. She was Bobby Thornton's more attractive toady, and she kept the college veering to the right politically and socially, all at his instigation. She did what she was asked, but even as she did what she was told, she wasn't spared in the end. To make matters worse, her daughter, who had married DDP, had suffered an aneurysm a few months earlier and was in that long process of recovery and rehabilitation, so I could be sympathetic for someone who had suffered compound losses. She had come into the bar on a day when it was raining as though God's promise to Noah had ended, and that's when she had gotten the news about Virginia. Thank god for Elisa. It was her usual habit, whenever anyone from the college came into the bar, to turn her back and walk out, such was her instinctive reaction to anyone or anything associated with the appearance of piety or the Evangelical tradition. But she came back in time to see Cheryl get the news about her daughter, and the two women were able to embrace one another and comfort one another about the children they had birthed and raised and lived to worry about.

And since that day, the two women had been in the habit of meeting at O'Malley's maybe once a week or more to talk over coffee or cheap beer or (if the day had been particularly vexing) a poorly mixed martini from my heavy hand, with

392

extra olives on the side as an alcoholic's version of crudité. Dr. Newland became a regular fixture until even Joe and Abel, those old benighted goats, started to tease her about her shoes and bring her popcorn. To Cheryl's credit, she took their ribbing with good grace, and when Joe told her about how his wife had suffered from Alzheimer's and died, she broke down and cried and said she regretted how little she and the college had done to lend comfort to the community at large, so ingrown and self-absorbed had they become. Theresa, Joe's wife, had suffered her memory lapses with a sense of humor until it became too much for her; she stopped eating one day and nothing could be done to coax her mouth to open. To all appearances, she was healthy enough, but her brain had been hollowed out like the Halloween pumpkin, and then when she clamped her jaws shut, there was nothing to be done but watch her melt away to the nothing that was left.

So, these two very different women, who wouldn't have said boo to one another under other circumstances, became something like friends in the company of other friends, but the day that Bobby Thornton fired Cheryl, the oddest thing happened: Bobby Thornton came in at noon, the first time I'd ever seen him darken our door. It seemed that he had something he needed to say, but I couldn't get anything out of him except how bitter he was about the tooth I had broken when I had punched him so many years earlier and how his implant had given him pain ever since. And this was after I had apologized, something I wouldn't have thought I would ever do. It just popped out, unbidden, as though the very sight of him had made me confess, and then he seemed unhappy about that, as though he wanted to carry on the fight from sixteen years earlier, pissed-off old coot that I knew him to be. When Cheryl came in later that day to tell us about getting fired, we told her who had been here earlier.

"Really?" she said. "I didn't even know he knew this place existed."

"Neither did I," I said. "And then he showed up, mean and hateful, and spitting mad."

"Nothing different about that," she said. "He's only gotten worse with time."

"Nothing different but his presence. He kept bitching about his car and the gravel in the parking lot, Magda wouldn't stop barking, and he never did say what he wanted."

So, we let it go at that, and we nursed our separate griefs together, which is how a congregation ought to work after all.

I forgot one important detail, however, in all this. Did I mention that I was rich? I didn't think so. Rich. Richey-Rich rich. At least by my dismal standards, I was rolling in it. Rich as Croesus.

A month after my parents' BOGO funeral, their lawyer called.

"Look," he said, "you have some things to take care of. And, I don't know why it hasn't been done already."

"We had a service," I said, "and so few people showed, I guess I thought I was done."

"Michael," he sighed, "you're how old? Sixty-four? Be an adult for godsake."

The lawyer—Sydney Bercuse was his name—scheduled a time the following day for me to come in because he had his doubts about my follow-through if he left it to a phone conversation. He probably had a point. I was in no shape to take notes or be very proactive about anything. All I wanted to do was take a nap, which I was doing between two and four every afternoon. Elisa tended the bar with Joe and Abel in attendance and the rest of our bitter, under-employed or unemployed, afternoon patrons, and I fell asleep upstairs the moment I lay down, and when I woke, I might as well have been sleeping in mud, I was that disoriented and sluggish. And then at night, I'd close the bar at one or two, depending on the day and the crowd, and go to bed and lie next to Elisa and stare at the ceiling, trying to remember what my parents looked like and how their voices sounded. Just a few weeks after the fact, I found their senior citizen selves had already become blurry. What they were like in their prime was gone entirely unless I looked at photographs, the old black-and-whites, and the fading color snaps with serrated edges. The one thing that wasn't unclear was how disappointing I must have been to them. A college graduate with a degree in religious studies, who owned a bar that every day was closer and closer to falling down and burying me inside it. Not exactly bragging rights at the neighborhood barbecue. I have to say this, though: however much disappointment they might have felt, they kept it hidden from me, so it's possible I was just projecting my own disappointment and assigning it to them. Elisa would turn over, I'd sigh, and then she'd elbow me in the ribs. "Get over it," she would say in her half-sleep. As if that were possible.

My meeting with Sydney Bercuse, Esquire, took place in his office in the raw north end of Fresno where all the money, medical offices, and churches had been moving for the past thirty years. Being in his office was like being in one of the television shows about lawyers, all dark wood and plate glass windows, just a reminder of the career you might have chosen but didn't. Attorney Bercuse, as it turned out was maybe twenty years younger than myself, the son of the man who had originally handled my parents' estate. So, even though he was as bald as an egg, and he had dark rings underneath each eye, I was being told to be an adult by someone of another, younger generation entirely. He might have thought he was dealing with a lucky and undeserving ne'er-do-well, but he didn't betray any judgments other than his one reprimand on the phone.

In his office, he was all business. There were things that needed to be done. Death certificates. Banks. Insurance.

Contacting the financial planner that my parents had used, a Mr. Aldon Giddings.

"Good grief," I said. "I had no idea there were so many steps before one could die for good."

"You haven't done any of these things yourself?" His look was quizzical. "A will, DNR, power of attorney, advanced medical directive. A revocable trust."

I shook my head. "I own a bar. And in the best of times, it's month-to-month, and dying is the least of my concerns. In fact, dying might mean fewer headaches."

He pinched the bridge of his nose as though he had the headache. "I see," he said. "We have a few, no, a number of steps we need to walk through, and when it's all over, you'll want to talk with Aldon Giddings further. Rollovers, reinvestments, tax liabilities. That sort of thing."

"That sort of thing," I said. "Sure. Of course."

"Your parents didn't talk with you about this?"

"They might have," I said, "but I probably wasn't that good at listening. Not about this, anyway. I'm afraid I came when I needed their help, rather than the other way around."

"Look," he said, and here his voice became gentler and more understanding, "no one likes talking about this. Estate planners talk about money and property because that way they don't have to talk about what death is, only its material consequences. You can get your mind around the legalities and the filthy lucre much better than the feelings you have when

397

you can't pick up a phone and call your mother on Mother's Day. But that doesn't mean you can ignore these other issues. Because they're real."

"No," I said. "I've been remiss." Because I had been, and much of that was due to my desire to remain my parents' child rather than their adult son, so dependent I had to wonder if they could have claimed me all these years on their taxes. I could take care of the odd errand here and there: picking up a prescription, writing their bills, talking to their care providers. A child, that's who I had been, unwilling to face up to my responsibilities. So here I was at sixty-four, trying to make up for lost time in the adult development department. The long and the short of it, though, was this: my parents had been frugal and thrifty for the entirety of their long lifetimes, and after the expenses of assisted living and those last years of geriatric medical care, they had gifted me, their sole survivor, everything else that was leftover, and for two denizens of the middle-class, that was quite a lot. They had squirreled away much more than I had thought possible.

When I came back to the bar after my meetings with Messers Bercuse and Giddings, I must have looked stunned because Magda started to keen while Elisa said to me, "Oh, boy. Bad news, I can see it in your eyes. Your parents had debts, and they left you holding the bag. Am I right, or am I right?"

And I said, "No, you've got exactly the wrong end of the stick. We have been blessed beyond all imagining. I'll never know what it's like to be a success on my own terms because by dying they pre-disastered me. I'm insulated against all bad happenstance. And by extension, you, too."

WE LOOKED AROUND ourselves like cicadas coming out of our burrow after seventeen years in the ground, and nothing was the same. O'Malley's, never picturesque, looked particularly down at the heels. So, we made a list, and before we were through, we had a total of fifty-thousand dollars in projects, for Elisa had watched her share of HGTV and the Food Channel. New refrigerators and an honest-to-god oven. New paint, new floors, new plumbing and wiring, because the fact we hadn't started a fire was only by miraculous intervention. The previous year the drought had finally broken, and this year the spring was glorious with wildflowers and blossoms beyond measure, and we joked that even O'Malley's was set to bloom. At odd times and places, I would find myself murmuring, "Thank you, God, for the flowers of the field. Thank you, Mom and Dad, for my inheritance. Thank you, thank you. I do not deserve any of it, for I am as unworthy as I am willing to accept your largesse."

Even Elisa seemed moved by the changes and the transformation that we saw taking place around us daily, and more than once I caught her singing, although the songs were often from the back catalogue of Jefferson Airplane and Buffalo Springfield and other anthems from the sixties. And when that happened, when she saw me watching and listening to her, she was liable to turn a little bit sour. "So, if you die," she said, "what happens?"

I think she was joking. Really, I do.

So, HERE'S SOMETHING I did not know at the time, and that's how one tiny thing can set off a chain of events and turn history on its ear and what's not important becomes extremely important in the blink of an eye. I mentioned that Dr. Newland had been fired the previous year, and in response to that and Virginia's medical crisis, she and Elisa became fast friends and thick as thieves. What I neglected to mention was that Cheryl was just one of many Liberty Christian employees who had gotten the sack. Bobby Thornton had gone on a rampage, and firing became a blood sport to him. In addition to Cheryl, he had fired Harold Toomer, the dean in charge of the STEM departments; he had given a lecture to one of the college's sponsoring churches about Climate Change and how the President and his administration had failed to protect the nation's future. He might as well have said that the President was a grifter and a con man and stupid at that, all of which would have also been true and no less offensive to his audience. Dr. Toomer had been under scrutiny for some time since he had failed to demand his biology faculty give air time to Creationism over Darwin. How he had lasted at LCC for fourteen years had been a mystery. Almost as great a mystery is why he had stayed.

Walter Book was another casualty, which was a much greater surprise, but not for the reasons that you might think, even in this day and age. His sexual orientation was something of an open secret to everyone but himself, but he had built a stout defense nonetheless. He had been married until his unfortunate and demented wife died, but there had long been apocryphal stories of Dr. Book frequenting the gay bars in the Tower District of Fresno even while he had been married. I doubted such stories then because I didn't think he would have known how to *find* a gay bar much less conduct himself in such an environment. I practically had to play matchmaker one night when I introduced him to Telofa and then pushed him out the door and said Go. Go find your true self among the cairns of Telofa's art yard.

He had been tenured for thirty years and while his scholarly reputation was modest, it was more than most of the other LCC faculty whose reputations extended only as far as the Sunday School classes they taught in their respective churches. He had served as his department's chair, and he was the Academic Senate President, and even though most considered him a windbag and pompous and a pain in the ass, he had worked with both Cheryl and Bobby Thornton on numerous projects—because in academia as in church life, you don't always get to choose your fellow travelers. So, we all thought he was immune to the Fundamentalist axe until it turned out he wasn't. And when word got out, we came to find out that he was fired, not because he was gay but because he had plagiarized sections of his dissertation on *Mrs. Dalloway*. His dissertation was littered with passages from referenced and unreferenced sources from the most arcane journals and other unpublished articles. One of his scholarly antagonists had ferreted out the thirty-five-year-old theft, and when the facts became known, Bobby Thornton didn't have a choice but to do what he had wanted to do for years. Everyone had known he was gay no matter how closeted and married he might have been, but they had known that for so long it would have seemed embarrassing to do anything about it now. His plagiarism, though, was a new discovery of an old sin and very, very convenient since his termination would not cause a law suit on the basis of discrimination.

So, the firings happened to some of the most public and well-known figures in the life of the college. We heard that there were faculty members who had views at odds with the LCC Articles of Faith and others who had criticized Bobby Thornton at one time or another, and they were all walking around looking over their shoulders, whispering to one another in the faculty dining room about who might be the next to go.

One of the least well-known among the fired was an alum named Joshua Bowen, who had worked as a student security guard and then a police officer on campus for the last several years. He had been in the habit of coming to the bar and ordering beer, and I was in the habit of bringing him ginger ale until he was twenty-one and had a license if not the attitude to prove it, since I'd had my share of interactions with him. He was a little shit with a uniform, a badge, and a gun until the day he was fired, and when that happened, the news was buried. It didn't even make the Board minutes. One day he was sitting at the desk in the Security Shack or patrolling the grounds in the college Jeep, and the next day he wasn't on campus, with the Lieutenant pulling double shifts and telling those who asked that Joshua had left for personal reasons, a euphemism which raises a red flag for anyone with a mind even slightly tilted toward skepticism. His departure was something of a mystery, and since we never saw him again after his dismissal, not even at the bar, the rumors were rife, anything from selling opioids to embezzlement of department funds to attending the Unitarian church and supporting abortion rights. We heard any number of reasons since for the last few years more LCC employees had been coming to us at the bar as a place of some refuge, and they were eager for a place to talk and dish dirt on one another. One of the more unbelievable rumors we heard involved his relationships with the female students on-campus.

"He has a trailer in Dunlap, and he takes girls there and turns them into sex workers."

But this was a rumor brought to us by none other than our own Mercury, Joe Dwyer, who said he heard it from one of his post office friends, who heard it from one of the campus maintenance workers. In other words, an unimpeachable source, but then we heard something similar from Miranda, who worked in the LCC cafeteria and on Friday and Saturday nights did double-duty for us.

"Huh," I said, and then I said "Huh," again because none of that made any sense to me. "A campus cop and former alum, a missionary kid to boot, is running his own sex ring? That reminds me of Hillary Clinton's pizza parlor. I'm having a hard time wrapping my brain around it."

"What did I tell you about your repressed Fundamentalists?" Elisa said. "They're all crazy as loons and nowhere near as monogamous." Because as it turns out loons mate for life and the male does at least some of the housework. We looked it up, and Google wouldn't lie any more than our President.

Miranda said she didn't put much stock into any of the rumors. For one thing, Joshua's trailer was in Squaw Valley off Hopewell Road, not Dunlap, but as far as the girls were concerned, that had the ring of truth because even she had had her run-in with Joshua. "He's got some pretty bizarre ideas," she said, "and he picks on the girls who are vulnerable." She was a regular churchgoer, but it should be noted that she had never gone to college much less to LCC and her boyfriend was a plumber's apprentice who wore his MAGA hat even in his sleep, so what she deemed bizarre or vulnerable had its own inflection. "He invited me to the river," she said, "him and his Squaw Valley trailer park homies," and at this, she shivered, but she didn't fill in any more of the details. It was a curious story, and none of us was the wiser until later, and by that time we became aware of how important this one moment had been, even when we had no idea.

As I said, our drought of seven years running had finally broken the previous year, and our spring was glorious, but the summer turned still and dry and baking hot, just as we were coming to a frenzy in our renovations. Temperatures were often in the eighties before nine o'clock in the morning and hit their peak at well over one hundred after four in the afternoon. Even the dust in our parking lot was despondent. We sold watery beer by the tanker-load to our work crews and those from the community who needed a piece of shade to call their own.

So, it was no surprise when the fires started in earnest in June and July, and we held our collective breath each time we saw a column of smoke rising from a ridge either to the north or south of us. We saw more and more Cal Fire trucks on the highway, and at noon and five and eight their yellow hardhats came through our door. They needed water and beer and sandwiches and then some more water, so we learned to stock up on twice the number of flats we usually kept on hand. One of the hardhats belonged to my own college teammate and best friend, Derrick Williams, whom I hadn't seen since his marriage to his second wife and spiritual overseer, at which point he had been banned from the possible contamination of my influence.

He came into O'Malley's one evening around eight o'clock, looking a bit sheepish and lost. His face was streaked with soot and grime, like an advertisement for manly endeavors, but then again, his hair was streaked with the gray of our shared age, and his yellow jumpsuit sagged from his shoulders as though he had once been a much bigger man.

"Long time, no see, brother," I said. "What a surprise." Which it was since it had been a decade or more since the last time he had sneaked away from home for a visit, and then he had come in his accountant's suit and tie. "You look like a new man if exhausted."

"Something like that," he said. He sat on a stool while I set a beer in front of him and Magda the Wonder Dog put her paws on his leg and her muzzle in his crotch. "I'm grateful for the love," he said, "but I could use more than that. It doesn't have to be anything good." So, I pushed Magda away and put a shot of Jim Beam next to the beer glass, and he polished off both in short order and then motioned for a refill.

"You've clearly made some changes," I said, "but aren't you a little old for this?"

"I did, and I am," he said, "and I owe you an apology."

It turned out that he and Dorothy had parted ways several years earlier while his dissatisfaction with his accounting firm grew and grew. He had been passed over for partner on several occasions, and Dorothy would have had him quarantined for his own spiritual good, allowing him the freedom only to go to work, home, and church with her and their shared broods, the unhappiest of Brady Bunches. He finally had had enough when his girls were in high school, and Dorothy insisted on them adopting a dress style that bordered on the Amish in severity and simplicity and dowdiness.

"They would have hated me, and I already knew what their dislike could mean." He rubbed his eyes with the heels of his hands. "I already hated myself as much as possible. I didn't need anyone else in that role, and I shouldn't have stopped coming here for a visit now and then since I needed a lifeline."

"You were busy," I said, "and your life had taken a different direction. That was clear enough."

"The whole thing was wrong," he said, shaking his head, "from start to finish. I finally quit pencil-pushing other people's money when I told Dorothy we were through, and when I got the job at Cal Fire, I was originally just doing spread sheets for a different reason, and I had traded one cubicle for another. But when the girls were done with school, I took the pay cut to be in the lines. I'll keep at it until my legs go, which might be tomorrow."

I told him how obliged I'd be for him to keep his legs in shape and the fires as far away as possible. "We finally caught a break," I said, waving at the signs of our remodeling, and the projects half-done, "and I'd hate for it all to go up in smoke."

He looked around. "I see. This might not be the best time."

"Well," I said. "We had the money."

"Money talks," he said.

"But only if you listen and know the language," I said. "For me, it's like another country, and the best I can do is Esperanto."

"Look, Michael," he said, "keep your premiums up to date."

He had a dark mind, and after the unhappy endings of two marriages and given the job he had willingly taken as an antidote, I suppose he had a right to his outlook. But I had no interest in doom and gloom at that moment because I was too full of optimism fueled by a bank account that was flush for the first time in, well, ever. Still, I couldn't ignore the smoke that rose all around us and fouled the air everywhere, turning our skies brown and lowering our visibility to a couple hundred yards, and I couldn't ignore his warning.

I had the money; I paid my insurance.

Even so, when October turned to November, I thought we might have avoided all acts of man, God, or nature.

You know what's coming, don't you? I can hardly spoil a surprise that is no surprise at all. Two weeks later, O'Malley's burned to the ground, and since it was a pillar-and-post structure and made of little more than wood and its resident termites, who were singing Kumbaya with the rest of us, there wasn't even a slab to mark its absence. I had built my life on a foundation that was as rickety as could be, metaphorically and literally, and we were lucky enough to be dressed when we had to flee. We took nothing but the clothes we threw on, nothing else other than Magda, and she was little more than an accessory, like carry-on luggage that you remember only because it falls on your head from the overhead compartment.

We heard the pounding on the door at six in the morning, a time on the clock that hardly registers for either Elisa or me, but Magda bolted upright at the sound and began to yowl. Outside our front door, Derrick Williams stood in full gear, backlit by what seemed a blast furnace, and he didn't seem happy to be the bearer of bad tidings. "You have to go," he said, and I believed him.

"But you can't go down," he said. "Your only way is up," because the fire had started somewhere to the west of us at a lower elevation and was now straddling the highway and threatening to boil upwards at a million miles an hour. "Shelter at the college. You know where the athletic department is located. They're setting the gym up for you."

"Great," I said, thinking that they had never been that good at accepting community refugees even in my day, and now we were going to be housed in a place that smelled like the onions of sweat. "What happens when we're at the top and there's no more up?" And then I thought, Oh, God, oh, God… What about the tigers? Will they be coming, too?

THERE WAS SO MUCH we didn't know at the time, and even if

we had known it, I'm not sure we could have taken it all in, much less processed it, everything changed so fast. Besides, when you are running for your lives, the who, what, when, where, and why really don't enter into the equation. We jumped into our arthritic Datsun and prayed that it wouldn't give out on the uphill climb. With Elisa and myself in the front seat and Magda sprawled on top of us both, I had a hell of a time finding second and fourth on the gear box. Magda's ribcage kept getting in the way. The orange glow was in our rearview mirror, and now and again a tongue of flame shot up along the mast of a tree with all the enthusiasm of Pentecost, and if the Datsun had been a horse, I would have been whipping it the whole way.

Half a mile up the road, the sodium vapor lights were on at the Cat Haven, and as we passed, I caught a glimpse of one of the trainers hosing down the grounds with their high-pressure hoses. How long the water would last was a mystery, and what they would do with the animals if the enclosures were threatened, I didn't want to guess. Horror could go any number of ways.

The seventeen miles seemed to take forever, and I found myself muttering my usual refrain of petition, "Oh, God, oh, God, oh, God," while I watched the curves of the highway in front of me and the glow behind me. And then, a mile away from campus, we joined a line of taillights that stretched to the college gates.

Derrick had told us to shelter at the college, and we were not the only ones who had gotten the message. Among those milling around in the first light of dawn and the fiery nightlight were Joe and Abel, Amy and Miranda, and a whole host of our other regulars. I saw Cheryl Newland and her husband Robert handing out Styrofoam cups of coffee from the gatehouse where they were still living despite Cheryl's firing so many months earlier while the new president of the college, Lyle Schubert, was greeting the stream of community members as though this was the end of a church service, and he was thanking a new crowd of reprobates for our attendance and contribution to the offertory. Students walked around in the chill of the morning in their sweat pants and down jackets, bunny slippers on their feet and the ubiquitous crosses and fishes around their necks. Missing was Bobby Thornton and his wife, which we thought a little odd, but we figured they were hunkered down in bed in their glass and steel palace a few miles up the road. Why would they need a shelter when they already lived in a high-tech redoubt?

A Fresno County Sheriff's deputy was waving us toward the gymnasium although we weren't the most cooperative herd of sheep, given our distress. "Please, folks," he kept saying, "please." We had to walk a circuitous route as there were barriers and Sheriff's cars in front of the access road to the chapel. We could also see the portable floodlights illuminating Golgotha on the ridge above, and the flashbacks were immediate. I thought Oh, God, it's not Christmas, but it might as well be 1974 all over again.

"What is this?" I said. "What happened?"

But the Sheriff's deputy could only move us forward and told us nothing but to watch our step as we hurried our way down the hill.

In the gym, we found the floor covered in yoga mats with a gym towel folded on each one. The college wasn't really set up for disaster relief, but the athletic department had provided what it could, and there were a few feeble jokes about a Jazzercize session breaking out. No one sat down as we were all too wired from the early hour and the uncertainty of what we might be facing and for how long. Instead, we walked around and around the perimeter of the basketball court as though we were the slowest NASCAR race ever. Some even made a joke of passing others and changing lanes, using their arms as turn signals, but that was just a mask for our nervousness.

Hour after hour passed. We heard helicopters and fire tankers overhead; sirens were a constant. The campus police chief, Lieutenant Perez had welcomed us even if he didn't respond to our questions any more than anyone else in uniform, and then he left us on our best behavior. Amy and Miranda, who were on the clock anyway, wheeled in coffee urns and platters of pastries, but there is a limit to how much gooey sugar and lukewarm caffeine a person can ingest, and it didn't take very long before the gymnasium doors were thrown

412

open by the itchiest among us. By this time, even though we were supposed to stay where we were and away from the students going to and from their classes, most of us refugees were wandering the campus like sightseeing hoboes, drifting here and there through the smoke, and of course we were drawn to places that we knew to be off-limits. The barriers and floodlights might as well have been magnets. And, of course, we were no sooner stepping within the perimeter of the chapel, but another Sheriff's deputy was waving us away.

"Can't you say what happened?" I said. "Tell us something." Elisa was still in the gymnasium trying to calm Magda whose wailing could be heard at least as loudly as the sirens and on the same frequencies, and the least I could do would be to bring her some news. "Can't you give me a clue?" But that only elicited an eye roll that would have made a fourteen-year-old girl proud, and then he told me to mind my own business, that they had more important things to do besides fueling our already considerable capacity for sticking our noses where they didn't belong.

"Fine," I said, "but your charity is lacking."

He waved me away with both of his middle fingers extended. Not very professional, but I took his meaning for what it was and the fact that he had other more important things on his mind.

For some, this was their first time to step foot on campus, and I could have acted like a tour guide whereas they were treating it like field work among the Martians. In the bookstore, I ran into Joe and Abel, who were riffling the pages of a textbook for an abnormal psych class.

"Do you see a problem with this?" Joe said. "I mean, really?"

"Pots and kettles, man," Abel said. "Kettles and pots."

I shook my head and moved on. By this time Elisa was on the quad in the brown, unbreathable air, trying to keep Magda from terrorizing the students who were carrying backpacks and, to Magda's way of sensing the world, the lunch that must be inside each one.

"Get over here, you goddamn dog," Elisa called while heads whipped around in her direction.

In our hurry, we had neglected a leash, so I had gone into the bookstore to buy an extension cord, a much-too-expensive and less-than-satisfactory substitute, as it turned out.

"Jesus Christ," Elisa said, not caring if anyone was around to hear it. I had collared the dog and tried, without a great deal of success, to make her stop leaping at every backpack she saw. "Jesus Christ," she said again, although a little more quietly, "I can't tell you how much I hate it here."

"I know," I said. "But don't blame me. This is not my home anymore."

Sometime around the lunch hour, an irritated Lieutenant Perez began rounding us all up again as there had been complaints about the campus becoming unmanageable, what with all the undocumented and unscreened visitors. Students no longer felt safe. There was a limit to institutional charity if we didn't all remain compliant. Didn't we see that?

"Look," he said an hour later, after we had all been gathered again, "you can't be jackasses, alright?"

And, Pastor Butcher, who was serving as school chaplain offered to lead us in prayer as a means of stilling the troubled waters, but most everyone stared at the ceiling so as not to laugh or sigh once he began "Oh, Lord" this and "Dear Jesus" that and "bring us through these troubled times because You know we love You, etc., etc., etc." with a few Thees and Thous thrown in for good measure.

When the chaplain was through, Lieutenant Perez stationed half a dozen student cadets at the doors, but that was more symbolic than anything; they couldn't have stopped a ground ball much less a revolt of fifty or sixty nervous mountain folk and Pastor Butcher's praying hadn't exactly tamped down the collective anxiety in any meaningful way. Instead, since his prayer was predicated on a general level of shared belief and a knowledge of our election, it meant that most of us were outside the circle of efficacy. Even so, we stayed where we were, grudgingly confined to our yoga mats and half-eaten pastries.

In the meantime, since there was nothing else to do and we had all been on different parts of the campus and had talked to different people, we fell back on our chosen pastime. The rumors started circulating in abundance once again.

O'Malley's had been engulfed, and the Cat Haven's enclosures compromised. One soft-hearted trainer had opened the gates before beating a hasty retreat. Cal Fire was letting the hillside burn in response to funding that was lower than requested, and since none of the firefighters had signed up to be mauled by a freaked-out, fire-driven tiger, they weren't going out of their way to be heroes. Walter Book and Telofa had burned alive in their hillside *atelier* of debauchery rather than come back to campus for shelter and humiliation. Bobby Thornton was speaking to the Governor regarding a disaster declaration for the county, which if true would have been the stuff of comedy routines since the two men were known to loathe one another. The thought of them speaking on the phone with each other was a joke in itself.

We sat there and we sat there, and time passed in slow motion. They fed us dinner, and then we were given the run of the campus on our honor while the Commons served dinner to the students. We watched from the quad as they ate in that brightly lit space, talking with their mouths full and throwing napkins and croutons at each other like the juvenile campers they were in fact if not in age. Then the lieutenant and his cadets rounded us up again before darkness fell, and they wheeled in a television so we could watch the news, as though that would be of some comfort, given all the fires that were burning up and down the state. The Camp fire, Malibu, us. Although given the relative size of the fires, we barely rated a mention, even on the local stations. We tried to sleep since nothing passes time better than unconsciousness, but even that restorative was denied us, and so we started to replay the rumors that by this time had become embellished with our own speculations, stories that, repeated often enough, soon took on the incontrovertible nature of fact. As though we couldn't be depressed enough. And then it was dawn of the next day, and Derrick Williams was at the gymnasium door, looking more aged than he had twenty-four hours before, and he hadn't looked all that good then.

"I'm sorry," he said, "about the bar. We did the best we could, but resources were short, and we didn't get the worst of it. The town of Paradise is gone and who knows how many people. Here, we lost a bar and some new appliances all of which happened to be yours."

So, the news had been awful before it became horrible, but none of our rumors were true as it turned out, only that first bit about O'Malley's—the part that affected Elisa and myself the most—but it took a while before we knew for sure, and then as with so many things, the truth turned out to be much less interesting if more strange than the rumors.

I HAVE NO REASON to doubt what Derrick told us that day and the stories we heard in the weeks to come, but I'm not sure I believe it yet. *People!* We are such stuff as idiocy is made of, and we are all susceptible to various forms of madness, but it seems there is no limit to what some folks will do.

Derrick handed the keys to his Cal Fire truck to another of his yellow-hatted crew, and he squeezed into the Datsun's front seat along with Elisa and me while Magda was relegated to the bed and the shell, which she hated, and she wailed for the entirety of our journey, but what could we do? We picked our way down the highway, going all of twenty-five miles an hour and then waiting while Cal Fire equipment turned on or off the road. Through our side windows, we saw the burned-out swaths of our brittle vegetation, now char and ash, smoke rising from the black ground, embers here and there still glowing. Bulldozers and chippers were already at work cleaning up what was left under the pressure of the season.

"All we need now," Derrick said, "is a good rain and we'll have mudslides taking out the highway."

At the entrance to the Cat Haven, the gate was closed across the driveway, and the oaks and eucalyptus and dirt were stained red with fire retardant.

"I get it," I said. "The tigers rated a little higher than our beer taps."

"Don't be bitter," Derrick said. "It doesn't become you."

Which may have been good advice and the right way to look at it but didn't lessen the blow or my feelings of abandonment. O'Malley's was as promised. Gone. One burned-out car decorated our parking lot, no doubt a relic from someone's too-muchness of our last night as a place of business and the kindness of a designated driver. Even the gravel looked scarred. The only thing standing was our defunct chimney and fireplace and the twisted metal of the new stove and refrigerator we'd installed a month earlier. The bar was gone and the taps had melted. The outbuilding that Elisa had used as an apartment before we were married might never have existed for all the proof we could see.

"Oh, God, oh, God," I said. "No matter how much you said otherwise, I didn't think it would be so true."

"Insurance?" Derrick said. "Did you listen to me at all?"

"What are you? Tommy the Torch?" I said. "Yes, the first of each month. I may be a child, but I'm not stupid."

"Well," Elisa said, "don't congratulate yourself too much. You know I hate a braggart."

So out of seven-thousand acres, we were the only property damage, and although we were the smallest fire on this day, we were also the only one that did not originate in an accident or a trick of the weather.

Even earlier than our early morning evacuation, Joshua Bowen was the last of the family to leave their trailer encampment on Hopewell Road. He closed the door to the ancient Nomad in which he had lived for the past twelve years and looked through the opened window one last time. The squat pillar candle continued to burn inside the pie tin filled with kerosene. The inside of the Nomad had been littered with old newspapers and liberally doused with kerosene as well. So, too, the other four trailers parked in a semi-circle around their camp table and benches, and underneath the dry, needle-sharp branches of the pines.

Love is love, he had written in a statement to *The Fresno Bee* and posted the day before. *But the enemies of love are many, and the purity of love misunderstood and threatened by the forces of darkness.*

The trailers and trees would make a great light, and the world would take note. Unbelievers would be astonished, and believers struck to the heart.

He opened the door of Janice's rusting Acura, the legacy of her graduation some sixteen years earlier. The others had taken the equally aging Suburban and Odyssey just minutes before, headed for Bobby Thornton's glass-and-steel folly. The small candles made the windows of the trailers glow, and then quietly, one by one, the glow in each grew brighter and with the tint of anger.

Let the whole earth burn and with it, the wicked and the indifferent and the wolf who hides himself among the sheep. For to be among *the flock is not sufficient for salvation.*

Flames were just beginning to curl from the windows of the first of the trailers as he left, and he felt himself linger to the last possible moment in order to watch the successive bursts in his rearview mirror.

JOSHUA BOWEN HAD HIS OWN HISTORY, as it turned out. After graduation, he and Janice Stingley had pooled their considerable resources to establish the beginning of their family compound on the property on Hopewell Road. Her family was wealthy and indifferent, and if Joshua's was not, he did have keys to every building on campus and he knew the locations of all the surplus no one would miss. At first, they lived in a tent and then in their succession of trailers, he and Janice and then Liv Mason as well, the three graduating seniors beginning their adult lives in a *ménage à trois* that became *quatre* and *cinq* and then *ainsi de suite* as others from among their class and subsequent years were added to their number. They loved the Lord God with all their heart, and they loved one another with every other part; they shared what they had in common, which was mostly themselves, their trust funds, their arts and crafts, their handmade artisanal goods, and their minimal paychecks. Joshua was not the only male, but he certainly was the group's leader, no matter that he was among the group's shortest, male or female. He ruled by assumption and without challenge. Members were free to come and go as they liked, and if they didn't like, they could go, such was their lack of claim.

No one at Liberty Christian seemed to know that one of their former students and current employees had formed a family group based on complex marriage and mutual criticism, those nineteenth-century principles of John Humphrey Noyes and the Oneida Community. If they had partially dispensed with male continence in favor of condoms and IUDs and the Pill, what of it? Even Holy Scripture allowed for new dispensations. Officer Bowen (class of '02) showed up to work each day at one in the afternoon, and he made his rounds, filed his paperwork, and (on the face of it) interacted with students, faculty, and staff in accordance with departmental guidelines and expectations. The fact that he often had a bevy of freshman female admirers boogie-boarding in his wake did not send up any red flags. Not even the alumni office seemed to think it odd that over the course of sixteen years more than two dozen alums had used the same post office box in Squaw Valley for their mailing address. An inconvenient fact is a truth all the easier to ignore. Easier, that is, until a parent complains and threatens to go public. A parent with money, especially, and connections to other fat-walleted donors and their Evangelical congregations up and down the I-5 corridor.

So, at the direction of Bobby Thornton, Lieutenant Perez had given Joshua his termination notice for cause, which advised him that he was a disgrace to the institution, that his actions and his doctrine, and his lifestyle were in violation of the LCC Code of Conduct, and that Liberty Christian would have nothing further to do with him.

"Basically, you shit in your own nest," the lieutenant said, "and you've got no one else to blame."

"I have been perfected in Jesus," Joshua said, "and you can say nothing to me."

"Nothing in the contract about that, you know."

"You wouldn't understand," Joshua said.

"I don't," the lieutenant said, "and I don't want to. In my experience, one wife at a time is enough."

That wasn't the only thing or the worst thing, though. No, that occurred when two Fresno County deputies showed up at the doors of their trailers with eviction notices from the property owner, who under pressure from Bobby Thornton and the college had determined that it was time to have the dead and dying pines logged out, the trailers removed, the tract cleared: time for the squatters to go.

Janice had answered the deputy's knock in a camisole and panties. "But this is our home," she said, after reading the notice.

The deputy had shrugged, looking but not looking. "Just the messenger," he said. "You have a week."

That precipitated a family meeting of the eight faithful who remained: Joshua and Janice, and Carl Noblett, a computer tech from Cincinnati; Belle West, a photographer from Los Angeles; Syd Marsden, who worked the Menswear department at the Fresno Macy's; Krystal Gattis, a second-grade teacher from Sanger, whose parents had been told that she lived in an environmentalists' collective; Rochelle Salwasser, who worked in a boutique at a mall in Clovis during the week and at Sierra Vines pouring wine on the weekends; and, Amy Erskine from Eugene, who had not, as yet, found a vocational or artistic path, but whose conversation was as good as income.

There had been defections through the years, but two of the most recent had hurt the most deeply: Liv Mason, she of their original threesome, had departed two years earlier at the instigation of her family and an unspecified auto-immune disorder and Margot Wilkins, who had graduated only the previous year and whose father was the senior pastor of a church and multi-purpose convention center complex in Nevada; he demanded she come back to traditional piety and practice and their air-conditioned four-thousand square foot home in Las Vegas. He also was the source of Liberty Christian's inevitable, if tardy, investigation.

They of the remnant sat at their communal table and prayed through their grievances and petitions to determine the will of the Lord, prayers that ultimately became part of Joshua's *Fresno Bee* manifesto.

We are being persecuted for our beliefs and the life that those beliefs dictate.

Religious freedom is under attack, and attention must be paid.

We are a family of love, and yet the world offers only hate and spite.

Oh, Jesus, Jesus, Jesus, God of hosts and Son of Glory, we beseech Thee.

They decided that, like those enlightened communities of old, they would move, they would flee the evil of their persecutors, but in moving, they also decided that their concerns would be seen and heard.

Hence, the fires started in their trailers, now as disposable as beer cans.

Hence, Joshua's manifesto.

Hence, their journey at midnight to Bobby Thornton's house to sing their rebuke and exhortation.

Repent, ye wicked. Be struck to the heart. Be amazed by His love and compassion and care. Let the fires of righteousness purify what is impure and let the waters of justice roll down.

They would be moving on.

SINCE THE CONTESTED ELECTION OF 2000, because there was no telling what moral thresholds those disgruntled liberal atheists might be willing to cross, Bobby Thornton had been in the habit of sleeping with an unloaded Smith & Wesson .38 Bodyguard in his nightstand, and after the election of 2016, the revolver had been loaded even if it remained holstered, per Gloria's edict, as it had no mechanical safety. So, when the members of Joshua Bowen's family of believers began to sing "Love among the Angels" at one-thirty in the morning and their high untrained voices drifted through the windows opened to the cool night air, Bobby struggled, first with the drawer of the nightstand and then with the holster and then with the nighttime, allergy-induced phlegm in his throat so that he might shout his Stand Your Ground warning, "I've got a gun and I know how to use it," the latter claim of which was a lie that the croak of his own voice betrayed. The hymn singers were not so easily dissuaded, and they sang the Oneida poem as a chorus, as though their voices had been set on Repeat. They managed their favorite harmonies before the first bullet pierced the screen and whistled above their heads. The second bullet took off the little finger of Gloria's left hand as she reached out to stop her husband, and the third bullet crashed into the ceiling and brought down a blizzard of plaster particles that coated them head to toe and caked every orifice and wound in dust and insulation. Gloria's four Maltese puppies barked their incessant, unstoppable alert, using their terrible-to-the-human-ear frequency.

"You fucking idiot," Gloria said. "You fucking fucking fucking idiot."

The family scattered to their cars as Gloria grabbed a towel from the bathroom and wrapped her demolished hand while her silent and newly chastened husband struggled to think of the number for emergency.

"9-1-1, asshole," Gloria sighed.

His brain seemed momentarily disconnected from his hands and fingers. How to dial?

"Twinkle, twinkle little star," Gloria sang as her hand throbbed, "what the fuck is your par? Jesus Christ." At which point, she fell onto the floor in a heap, attended by the licking tongues of her yipping Maltese court.

Outside, on the apron of the Thornton driveway, Joshua leaned into the driver's side window of the Suburban.

"Deputies will be coming soon, the highway will be a mess," Joshua said to Janice, who was behind the wheel, her face shadowed by the blue dash light. "Take 198, and I'll meet you in Visalia. At the Fox."

"Okay," she lifted his hand and kissed his fingers. "Don't be long."

They had been together in various combinations of others for twenty years, and this had the feel of both an ending and a beginning.

"No. Not long." He had unfinished tasks, the details of which she didn't need to know. "I'll see you soon."

Janice backed the Suburban out of the driveway, followed by Syd and the Odyssey, and he watched their taillights as they followed the highway east and south.

He went in the opposite direction, back toward the college and in the direction of their trailers, the fire from which was glowing on the other side of the hills. Already, he could hear helicopters beating the air. As he slowed to turn into the entrance for the college, a Sheriff's car and ambulance raced past in the other direction, their lights flashing and sirens blaring. The urgency nearly comic in its extremity.

He took a left onto the rim road that dead-ended behind Golgotha. Below him the college slept in spite of the sirens and the chatter in the air, the only illumination the blue emergency lights on the quad and in front of the library and chapel. An elusive half-moon slipped behind a lacework of clouds. He parked, removed one last can of kerosene from the trunk, and began to douse the rose bushes. He lit the farthest corners of the rose garden to give himself a moment and then shimmied up the center cross and hooked his legs over the crossbar, one on either side of the post.

The roses and the grass, dry from the heat of summer and an arid fall, burned brightly around him. The student union was dark, the dormitories and classrooms quiet. The chapel's conical roof dominated the foreground, inside of which was an organ and dim, shaded spaces, a counterfeit of spirituality if not its substance. For four years, he had lived here and studied here, in the shadow of Golgotha and under the influence of the Martinez cousins, who had sacrificed themselves; he had studied that which had been congruent with his desires and rejected the rest. A community in spiritual, emotional, and physical unity was the only thing that mattered. And for the next sixteen years, he had worked here and built his haphazard family of like-minded believers and dreamers. A dream once realized but gone now, for persecution comes in many forms. From the unbelieving world, certainly, but the fiercest criticism comes from those who purport to know the truth but bastardize its message. Love is not love if it hates, and love is not love if it issues edicts and restrictions.

If the Martinez cousins could light the former Golgotha and themselves as a warning and a cautionary tale, then he would unleash the Lord's warnings through his own self-sacrifice. But that was when he heard the chop-chop-chop of the helicopters overhead, and that was when the air turned liquid and red with blood, when his death grip was torn from his cross of choice and slammed him to the gravel below. His head hit the granite memorial hard enough that the dawn and the fire and the smoke turned once again into night.

I SAID THAT HISTORY IS A FUNNY THING and its meaning elusive. At the time of the fire, I could only see the scorch marks in the parking lot and the burned-out sticks and ash of the bar and the fact that the upstairs apartment I'd called home for forty-some years had vanished into the air. Gone like that, gone in a day. I didn't know right then that the fire was no act of God, and it took some time before I could accept that it was the act of humans who were acting on God's behalf, or so they claimed. All I could see at the moment was that God, for some unknown and mysterious reason, had turned His back on me and us, or if the turning wasn't intentional and the tragedy was simply random, then He didn't care much at all. If there was a lesson in there somewhere, like Job, I was having a difficult time seeing it. Not that I wanted to.

"Goddamn it, Michael," Joe Dwyer said after he and Abel had pulled up behind us. "You know how to throw a party, but you never did know how to tell the guests to leave."

"Shut up, Joe," Elisa said. And then, "Fuck you, Abel," so he wouldn't feel excluded.

"Well, shit," I said while I kicked at the blackened stones. "This is what's left of a life."

"I know, buddy," Derrick Williams said. "It's gone."

"Up in smoke," Elisa said. "Your blaze of glory, or what's left of it."

"Please," I said. "Spare me." I knew she was giving me the business because she had never really believed that our lives could be any different or easier, and she had told me so and told me so. Meanwhile, I had held out hope that we had nothing but good things in store. She was claiming a victory, no matter how bitter.

Meanwhile Magda bayed and wailed underneath the cracked camper shell.

"Where to now?" Derrick said.

"Fresno, I guess," I said, "and the cheapest motel that will let us bring a dog of larger than normal size and no manners whatsoever."

"Or," Elisa said, "we could just go with her to a kennel. Alpo may be the best we can hope for."

IN RESPONSE TO Bobby Thornton's 911 call, a Fresno County Sheriff's deputy arrived at the Thornton domicile to find both Bobby and Gloria on the floor of their bedroom, passed out. He waited for the ambulance and paramedics to arrive and watched as both of them came to, groggy and unfocused. Gloria's first conscious act was to slug her husband with her

430

good right hand. The deputy bagged the revolver that was revealed after the EMT rolled Bobby Thornton over, and checked for the number of bullets remaining in the cylinder.

"My God in heaven, can you believe how stupid this man is?" Gloria said. She held up her left hand and her crusty rust-colored towel. "Is there no end to Mankind's stupidity?"

"No, ma'am," he said. "The bottom floor for that gets lower every day." Then, before he could begin his drive back down the mountain, threading his way around the Cal Fire trucks parked every which way on the shoulders of the highway, a drive he was already dreading, given what he had seen on the way up, before he could leave the Thornton's driveway even, he received a radio call about a fire at the college and an unconscious man. When he stopped at the gatehouse, he was met by Lieutenant Perez, who slid into the passenger seat and directed him to the rim road behind Golgotha. There they found a dazed Joshua Bowen, covered in the red goo of Phos-Chek, sitting next to the middle cross in the midst of the charred roses and blinking away the smoke and fire retardant while holding his head. The deputy pulled up next to him. He and Perez got out, and the deputy opened the back door of his Explorer. "I need you to come with me," he said.

"Idiot," the lieutenant said. "You are such an idiot."

"The truth is not always recognized," Joshua Bowen said, shaking his head, "and purity is only achieved through fire and redeemed by love."

"That's a nice thought," the deputy said. He had read his Scriptures as a boy. "But baptism by fire retardant is no guarantee of salvation."

As for Janice Stingley and Syd Marsden and the rest of their family—they were on the run for less than an hour when they were confronted at Hospital Rock Picnic Area in Sequoia by members of the Park Police. The Park officer who took them into custody took note of their manners and the way they disposed of their trash after they were charged with arson and trespassing. They had been eating bologna sandwiches and drinking lemonade from juice boxes, a Sunday School class of eight-year-old adults having a picnic.

JOE AND ABEL OFFERED THEIR HOMES to us as a temporary refuge, but I was in no mood for sociability and I could see Elisa's face twitch the moment that Joe made the offer, and I don't think either was too disappointed to be refused. I was not even in good enough shape to drive after seeing my life's work, such as it was, so entirely erased, so Elisa drove and Derrick sat up front with her while Magda and I tried to hold our positions in the back of the truck. I felt sick. Nauseous from the highway and the Datsun's faulty exhaust, the motion and the smoke, but mostly just sick at heart.

What would my parents think? They had been my life preserver in more ways than one, but now there was nothing to show for that either. I couldn't help it even though I knew they were beyond thought and judgment. Or maybe they weren't. What did I know? Maybe they were in the hereafter, despairing of their only son and the mess he'd made of his life and prospects in spite of all their earthly help. And, maybe they were in cahoots with the Almighty, giving with one hand while taking with the other. The thought made me wail with Magda until the first red light when Elisa turned in her seat and started banging on the back window with her elbow, and she had a look that was the sternest I had ever seen.

"What's the matter with you?" she said in the parking lot of one of the airport hotels. Magda and I were both staring at the asphalt, unable to look her in the eye. As if in punctuation, one of the fire tankers chose that moment to rumble down a runway and lurch into the air. In unison, our heads tilted, and we watched, willing it to rise above the rooftops.

"I'm done," I said. "We are outcasts and refugees. Where do we go from here?"

Elisa sighed. "We get a room, we take a shower, and we order clothes over the phone. We get some food for but-ter-brain. And we keep living one step at a time. Don't be such a baby."

"Okay," I said. "Okay. Maybe I'm overreacting, but you don't have to be such a Nazi."

"Maybe?" she said. "Maybe you're overreacting? We could have been asleep until the fire was licking our toes. We're alive, and we're together, and we got to spend a night at the alma of your mater. No reason for you to be a drama queen."

"Maybe," Derrick said, who, during all of this, had been standing to the side. "Maybe this is a good time for me to say my goodbyes."

ELISA WAS RIGHT, OF COURSE. When was she not? A shower did me any amount of good, and after toweling off, I saw the world a little differently, even if I had to put on three-day-old underwear. There were things to be done and phone calls to make. We sat down on one of our queen-sized beds while Magda lolled across the other, twitching and moaning in her sleep, and we made our list. I started first with Sydney Bercuse, who made the correct, sympathetic noises and had his own list of tasks for us, and then he said, "You could finally go to seminary, you know," which was a statement that stunned me into silence, maybe even wonder and reproach, as I didn't know how to answer such a ridiculous idea. But then I called our insurance agent, who said "Oh, dear" and "My goodness" every time I paused. "The way I see it," she said, "after the investigation is done, you'll have two choices. We'll be happy to help you with the restoration process or we'll cash you out." That was comment enough to make me think that everything would be all right. But, what she had said subsequent to that was something I wasn't ready to hear, and so I didn't.

"Just so you know, if you rebuild, your premiums will be higher, if I can write the policy at all," she had said.

I wasn't ready to take in any more bad news, though, and I might as well have had my fingers in my ears for all the warning I heard. All I could think was that we could make a new O'Malley's rather than a renovated one, and we would provide everything the community needed. I was full of such plans until Elisa stopped me.

"Slow down, buddy," she said. "This is not something we rush into."

"No, of course not," I said. "If we have to wait a week, or so, I'll understand."

At which she rolled her eyes and as much as said that there was no reasoning with me, no matter which phase I happened to be in.

It was my conversation with Aldon Giddings that finally slowed me down. Like Sydney Bercuse, my parents' financial planner had his office in the newer north end of Fresno, but unlike the lawyer, Aldon Giddings worked in a space not much bigger than a shoe closet—his was an office inside someone else's—and his furniture looked like the college leftovers that Goodwill had refused. This might have given another person some doubt about his abilities, but I found it comforting as though he knew what was truly important. While we talked, I could tell he was making coffee in one of those one-cup machines that create waste, even as they prevent over-consumption.

"Look," he said, "you could rebuild, but my guess is that your insurance bills will be higher than any income you're likely to produce. If you can even *get* insurance. More and more companies are getting out of the foothills market entirely. It's not like the climate's getting better. Fire season is year-round, and if it's not next summer, it'll be the summer after that. You'll be hosing down your new roof, praying for the wind to die down, and kicking yourself for a fool. Take the money. You couldn't have done better if you'd lit the match yourself. And this way, you don't face criminal prosecution."

"Oh," I said.

"And take a look at yourself," he said. "You're how old? Mid-sixties, right? You're not getting younger. Do you really want to start all over again? Take the money and buy a condo in town, live off the retirement money your parents didn't get around to spending and find something interesting to do."

"I'm being put out to pasture," I said. "Sydney Bercuse told me to go to seminary."

"An excellent idea!" he said. "Use your time to contemplate the mysteries of the divine and the confusions of man. Better than some old sot's glass of whiskey, don't you think?"

"Oh, come on," I said. "That makes me think that the last forty years have been one long mistake." I was Mr. Optimism once again although leavened with more than a whisper of doubt. "Having a bar is not so different from pastoring a church except that the winos are nicer than most of the ushers

I've known. More tractable anyway. Why would I want to make such a change this late in life? I have a wife that I love, a dog that I tolerate, and friends that I care about. We've taken our lightning strike, and it has done all the damage it can do. God has carried us this far, and you don't think He'd hit us with the same plague twice, do you?"

Acknowledgments

Writing is, in most cases, a solitary act. Days of staring into a white screen or an empty page, which is its own kind of perfection. Then, with the first word, we ruin the void, turn it into its own messy, flawed thing. Thank God for writer- and reader-friends, who were willing to serve as guinea pigs and first audience: James Coffey, Calvin Hoff, Deb and Greg Lapp, Don Noble, Nancy Spiller, Mark Wish, and Steve Yarbrough. That you have been friends and colleagues, in some cases, for more than thirty years is testimony to your patience as well as love. My gratitude is boundless.

As a book becomes reality, it needs guidance and (once again) patience, and I couldn't have found a better place for *The End of Good Intentions* than Fomite Press or better publishers and editors than Marc Estrin and Donna Bister. Thank you for your willingness to share this awkward and ungainly story of faith and doubt and the angers of certitude. And, I wouldn't have found Fomite, if it hadn't been for the intervention of Caitlin Hamilton Summie, whose own Fomite books are lovely and deeply imagined. Thank you.

Faith, likewise, begins as a solitary experience before it finds a community of likeminded souls, and as with the first word on the page, the moment that two or more come together is the moment that faith can either become exploration or rigidity. I have experienced one and been guilty of the other, not always in equal measure. For those in the fellowship group at Lewis & Clark College of nearly fifty years ago, please accept my regrets and my apologies; I ask for your forgiveness for the past as well as your continuing forbearance.

My own reading has certainly played a role in the making of this novel and my own thinking, but I'll mention two books in particular: Spencer Klaw's remarkable account of the Oneida Perfectionist community, *Without Sin*, was one of the first times I saw how groups can dictate individual behavior and religious thought; the character of Joshua Bowen would not have been possible without those Perfectionist notions and their peculiar mix of utopian idealism and masculine selfishness. The other book, Kristin Kobes Du Mez's *Jesus and John Wayne*, I discovered late; in fact, I didn't begin reading it until I was in the middle of proofing the pages of this book. (Thank you, Judy Urschel Straalsund for the nudge and the recommendation.) While Du Mez's history of the last seventy years of the Evangelical movement did not add anything to *The End of Good Intentions*, her careful and comprehensive scholarship validated much that was within my own imagination and memory. I owe a debt to each and recommend both highly.

Without the support and love of my family, the selfishness that is necessary to sit alone and turn sentences around would not have been possible. For nearly fifty years, my wife, Dr. Deb Everson Borofka, has travelled these pathways of faith and art with me; she has always been willing to be honest about who I am and what I produce, sometimes painfully so, but always from love. Our daughters, Katherine and Kristian and their respective families, have likewise encouraged me, and their pride in my work is possibly the biggest reason I can put my fingers on the keyboard each morning. Thank you, my beloveds.

Finally, this book is dedicated to the memory of Jim Zazzera—college friend, Presbyterian pastor, and inveterate traveler—who laughed when I said that my main goal every second of every day was not to be an asshole. Your greatest gift to me was the fact you didn't tell me I was wrong. Peace to you, my brother. I miss your joy, as well as your compassion.

About the Author

Photo credit: Deb Everson Borofka

David Borofka is the author of *Hints of His Mortality*, *The Island*, and *A Longing for Impossible Things*, and the winner of the Iowa Short Fiction Award, *Missouri Review*'s Editor's Prize, *Carolina Quarterly*'s Charles B. Wood Award, the Emerging Writers Network award, the *Prism Review* fiction prize, and *Jabberwock Review*'s Nancy D. Hargrove Editors' Prize. Since his retirement from Reedley College in 2019, he has embarked on various obsessions beyond fiction: anxiously viewing Alabama football and insisting to anyone who will listen that Gizmo is, in actuality, his wife's dog.

Fomite

Writing a review on social media sites for readers will help the progress of independent publishing. To submit a review, go to the book page on any of the sites and follow the links for reviews. Books from independent presses rely on reader-to-reader communications.

For more information or to order any of our books, visit:
http://www.fomitepress.com/our-books.html

More novels and novellas from Fomite...
Joshua Amses—*During This, Our Nadir*
Joshua Amses—*Ghats*
Joshua Amses—*Raven or Crow*
Joshua Amses—*The Moment Before an Injury*
Charles Bell—*The Married Land*
Charles Bell—*The Half Gods*
Jaysinh Birjepatel—*Nothing Beside Remains*
Jaysinh Birjepatel—*The Good Muslim of Jackson Heights*
David Brizer—*The Secret Doctrine of V. H. Rand*
David Brizer—*Victor Rand*
L. M Brown—*Hinterland*
Paula Closson Buck—*Summer on the Cold War Planet*
L.enny Cavallaro—*Paganini Agitato*
Dan Chodorkoff—*Loisaida*
Dan Chodorkoff—*Sugaring Down*
David Adams Cleveland—*Time's Betrayal*
Paul Cody— *Sphyxia*
Jaimee Wriston Colbert—*Vanishing Acts*
Roger Coleman—*Skywreck Afternoons*
Stephen Downes—*The Hands of Pianists*
Marc Estrin—*Hyde*
Marc Estrin—*Kafka's Roach*
Marc Estrin—*Proceedings of the Hebrew Free Burial Society*
Marc Estrin—*Speckled Vanities*
Marc Estrin—*The Annotated Nose*
Marc Estrin—*The Penseés of Alan Krieger*
Zdravka Evtimova—*Asylum for Men and Dogs*
Zdravka Evtimova—*In the Town of Joy and Peace*
Zdravka Evtimova—*Sinfonia Bulgarica*
Zdravka Evtimova—*You Can Smile on Wednesdays*
Daniel Forbes—*Derail This Train Wreck*

Fomite

Peter Fortunato—*Carnevale*
Greg Guma—*Dons of Time*
Ramsey Hanhan – *Fugitive Dreams*
Richard Hawley—*The Three Lives of Jonathan Force*
Lamar Herrin—*Father Figure*
Michael Horner—*Damage Control*
Ron Jacobs—*All the Sinners Saints*
Ron Jacobs—*Short Order Frame Up*
Ron Jacobs—*The Co-conspirator's Tale*
Scott Archer Jones—*A Rising Tide of People Swept Away*
Scott Archer Jones—*And Throw Away the Skins*
Julie Justicz—*Conch Pearl*
Julie Justicz—*Degrees of Difficulty*
Maggie Kast—*A Free Unsullied Land*
Darrell Kastin—*Shadowboxing with Bukowski*
Coleen Kearon—*#triggerwarning*
Coleen Kearon—*Feminist on Fire*
Jan English Leary—*Thicker Than Blood*
Jan English Leary—*Town and Gown*
Diane Lefer—*Confessions of a Carnivore*
Diane Lefer—*Out of Place*
Rob Lenihan—*Born Speaking Lies*
Cynthia Newberry Martin—*The Art of Her Life*
Colin McGinnis—*Roadman*
Douglas W. Milliken—*Our Shadows' Voice*
Ilan Mochari—*Zinsky the Obscure*
Peter Nash—*In the Place Where We Thought We Stood*
Peter Nash—*Parsimony*
Peter Nash—*The Least of It*
Peter Nash—*The Perfection of Things*
George Ovitt—*Stillpoint*
George Ovitt—*Tribunal*
Gregory Papadoyiannis—*The Baby Jazz*
Pelham—*The Walking Poor*
Christopher Peterson—*Madman*
Andy Potok—*My Father's Keeper*
Frederick Ramey—*Comes A Time*
Howard Rappaport—*Arnold and Igor*
Joseph Rathgeber—*Mixedbloods*
Kathryn Roberts—*Companion Plants*

Fomite

Robert Rosenberg—*Isles of the Blind*
Fred Russell—*Rafi's World*
Ron Savage—*Voyeur in Tangier*
David Schein—*The Adoption*
Charles Simpson—*Uncertain Harvest*
Lynn Sloan—*Midstream*
Lynn Sloan—*Principles of Navigation*
L.E. Smith—*The Consequence of Gesture*
L.E. Smith—*Travers' Inferno*
L.E. Smith—*Untimely RIPped*
Robert Sommer—*A Great Fullness*
Caitlin Hamilton Summie—*Geographies of the Heart*
Tom Walker—*A Day in the Life*
Susan V. Weiss —*My God, What Have We Done?*
Peter M. Wheelwright—*As It Is on Earth*
Peter M. Wheelwright—*The Door-Man*
Suzie Wizowaty—*The Return of Jason Green*

Made in the USA
Las Vegas, NV
27 December 2023

83567575R00267